By ADRIAN RANDALL

Countermind

Published by DSP PUBLICATIONS
www.dsppublications.com

COUNTERMIND

ADRIAN RANDALL

DSP PUBLICATIONS

Published by

DSP Publications

5032 Capital Circle SW, Suite 2, PMB# 279, Tallahassee, FL 32305-7886 USA
www.dsppublications.com

This is a work of fiction. Names, characters, places, and incidents either are the product of author imagination or are used fictitiously, and any resemblance to actual persons, living or dead, business establishments, events, or locales is entirely coincidental.

Countermind
© 2017 Adrian Randall.

Cover Art
© 2017 L.C. Chase.
http://www.lcchase.com
Cover content is for illustrative purposes only and any person depicted on the cover is a model.
Interior Art
© 2017 Neolexx (Own work) [CC BY-SA 3.0 (http://creativecommons.org/licenses/by-sa/3.0) or GFDL (http://www.gnu.org/copyleft/fdl.html)], via Wikimedia Commons

ISBN: 978-1-63533-268-1
Digital ISBN: 978-1-63533-269-8
Library of Congress Control Number: 2016915185
Published February 2017
v. 1.0

Printed in the United States of America
∞
This paper meets the requirements of
ANSI/NISO Z39.48-1992 (Permanence of Paper).

COUNTERMIND

ADRIAN
RANDALL

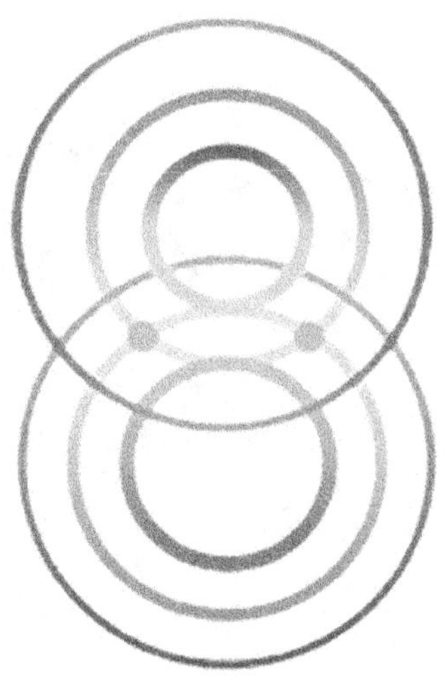

Prologue
The Future

"WHAT DO you think?" Siam asked, seeing the look on his boyfriend's face. "Be honest."

Years on the run had taught Jettrin how to school his features, but it was hard to conceal his skepticism at Siam's handiwork. The dented, scuffed, matte-black plastic casing of the alarm clock was gone. The only original remnants looked to be a circuit board, a digital display, and a disc-shaped speaker, all nested in a tangle of discarded wires fished out of the same garbage bin where they'd found the clock. That morning, near Khaosan Road, Jettrin had seen a tourist ride a scooter right over a rat, and the resulting mess somehow struck him as less gory than this Frankenclock Siam had assembled.

Jettrin took a deep breath. "Does it work?" he asked at last. Siam plugged it in, and the display lit up with a line of red zeroes. Both boys grinned.

"Set the alarm for 5:00 a.m.," Jettrin said.

"That's too early," Jai finally said as Siam set the time. He'd watched the entire operation from the corner of the squat, limbs folded resentfully around his body.

"Go to bed," Jettrin hissed.

"I'm not tired."

"I didn't ask. We're leaving before the sun's up whether you're rested or not. Go."

Jai cursed Jettrin under his breath but stalked off to the tiny bedroom and shut the door snugly behind him. At least he didn't slam it.

Siam finished setting the alarm, and both boys curled up on the makeshift bed of piled tattered blankets, gripping each other tight.

Jettrin dreamt again of the man from Countermind. Wherever they fled, wherever they hid, that phantom pursuer was there, always standing outside their window, gazing up from the sidewalk below with those cruel eyes and that dark smile.

The dream wasn't quite a nightmare this time, but it was enough to rouse Jettrin from slumber. Groggy, he pulled himself up out of bed, felt his way through the darkness to the bedroom door, and eased it open.

He could hear Jai whimpering. Jettrin sat on the bare mattress and gently jostled his little brother awake. Jai responded by burying his face in Jettrin's shoulder, crying for a few minutes, and then passing out again. Jettrin kissed him on the forehead, lowered him onto his back, and made his quiet way back to Siam.

Jettrin had never actually seen the man from Countermind. Only when Jai had this nightmare and, panicking in his sleep, reached out for his big brother telepathically, only to involuntarily share the dream with him. Drifting into unconsciousness again, Jettrin hoped the interruption wouldn't cause them to oversleep.

It wasn't why they overslept. When Siam had fixed the clock, they'd checked that the time worked but had never actually tested the alarm.

Jettrin woke first, rolled over, and looked at the alarm clock. The numbers glowed red within the jumble of wires. The time, per the dozenal numerals shining through the black glass of the display, was 10:A4.

Jettrin snapped instantly to full alert. He yelled at Siam, kicking him out of bed, and the two of them pulled on their jeans, socks, and tennis shoes, tottering precariously while dressing, with nothing to steady themselves against but filthy pockmarked concrete walls. Once clothed, Jettrin strode to the bedroom door, crossing the tiny squat in just two lanky steps.

The door opened from the other side before Jettrin reached it, and Jai stood there, scratching sleep from his eyes, still dressed in an oversized logoed T-shirt dangling past his knees.

"Did you sense me coming?" Jettrin demanded.

Jai was defensive. "No, I *heard* you. You're *loud*."

"Then why aren't you dressed? Put your damn clothes on."

Jai vanished back into the bedroom to change. Jettrin turned to the window to examine the noisy avenue in front of the apartment building, pressing his forehead against the rusting iron bars. The obstruction limited his field of view, and the traffic was too thick for him to easily pick out any threats. With the cacophony of shouts, ringing bicycle bells, and honking cars, he had to wonder whether the alarm would have done any good even if it had worked.

"Is the little bother ready?" Siam asked from the front door.

"Don't call me that," Jai said, reappearing in the bedroom door. Now fully dressed, his threadbare backpack in hand, he gave Siam a surly look. Jettrin shouldered his own backpack off the floor, took Jai's small wrist in hand, and led him to the apartment's entrance. But he stopped short of opening it onto the hallway, first pressing his ear against the door.

Sounds of domestic life spiraled into his cochlea: spouses arguing, parents scolding children, infants screaming, and everywhere footsteps crisscrossing creaky wooden floors above, below, and beside their squat. But he heard no one directly in the narrow hallway outside.

"It's safe to go," Jai said, annoyed.

Jettrin turned on him. "How do you know that?"

"Because the landlady sleeps late, and she doesn't even live here. And what will she do, throw us out? We're already leaving!"

Jettrin tried to read Jai's expression, knowing he was correct to a point. Bangkok traffic was the worst in Thailand. But if the landlady spotted them on the premises, and if she reported them to the police for squatting, the subsequent chain of events would probably end with Jai being identified as a psychic, Jettrin arrested for abetting his flight, and Siam arrested for more obscure crimes of his own. The risk was too high to flout. The confidence on Jai's face meant the seven-year-old was either unaware of the risk or was psyching. Jettrin looked for any indication of the latter, in which case he'd whack Jai on the ear.

Siam, exasperated, pulled out his computer and unfolded it.

"Put that away," Jettrin hissed.

"I can check where she is."

"There's no time!" Jettrin bit out. "We're leaving right now anyway."

"Then let's fucking go already." Siam snapped the computer shut and shoved it back into his bag.

Jettrin undid the dead bolts and chain and slid away the concrete block they'd used as a stop, allowing the door to swing inward. He pressed his shoulder against the doorjamb, hand under his shirt in case he had to defend himself, and then darted his head out for just a second, as if imitating a hero cop from a crime film.

"It's clear," he told the others.

Jai and Siam rolled their eyes in eerie unison.

For all Jettrin had urged discretion, the three of them veritably stampeded their way down the flights of cracked concrete steps. Thinking it safer, they used the side exit to the quiet, dark side street running between the building and its neighboring apartment block, rather than through the front door to the avenue. It was a good idea, but Jettrin had scoped out the avenue through the window, not the side street, which was why they were surprised to find the building's landlady there, in the middle of an animated argument with a discontented pair of municipal safety inspectors.

She stopped to squint at the three strange boys leaving her building, no doubt wondering whose family they were with and why she'd never seen them before.

Avoiding eye contact, Jettrin, Siam, and Jai immediately tried to make themselves as inconspicuous as possible. For a trio of unkempt male minors, this meant loudly berating and shoving one another, while peppering their speech with profanities and indulging in a solipsistic disregard for anyone else around them.

The key to going unnoticed, they knew, was to be so obnoxious that people made an active effort to ignore you.

The boys made their raucous way to the avenue without looking behind them. The safety inspectors evinced no reaction beyond irritation, but the landlady still watched them as they brushed past, and Jettrin, though no psychic, was certain he could feel her eyes on the back of his head. His heart thudded like a subwoofer, and it wasn't until a brief lull in the noise of the traffic, when he overheard the three adults resume their argument about fire alarms, that he felt safe. If the landlady had residents she was unaware of, she wasn't going to let any city employees know about it.

If she'd inspected the boys any longer, she would've had no trouble guessing which two of the three were brothers. Jai was half Jettrin's age and height, but both were darker in color and slenderer in build than Siam, and their small noses, large eyes, and round faces gave them the look of startled tarsiers. As for Siam, his aversion to natural light had left his skin paler. His torso was squarer, his shoulders broader, his face boxier, and his expression had a perpetually sardonic mold to it. You wanted to punch him as soon as you met him.

Or Jettrin had wanted to punch him, anyway.

The trio rounded the corner onto the street and picked up their pace, occasionally shouldering their way through the crowded sidewalk. It wasn't a long journey from this part of Khlong Toei to the river, but they'd overslept, they had a boat to catch, and they were running scared.

EARLIER THAT week, Jettrin had arranged passage aboard a handysize cargo hauler bound for Hong Kong via Ho Chi Minh City. He'd been careful only to deal with a crewman who didn't seem the least bit curious about them, passing over anyone who'd asked why they were leaving or if they were in trouble or so much as expressed concern for their well-being. People wouldn't have a problem transporting three poor, homeless kids looking for a cheap fare. But no one would risk smuggling a seven-year-old fugitive psychic.

It was a short time frame for an international escape, but Jettrin didn't feel safe making long-term plans. He couldn't risk thinking too far ahead. You never knew when a state psychic was reading your mind. Supposedly the government liked to send telepaths into highly populated cities, where they would randomly dip through people's minds, hundreds in a day, thousands in a week, searching for any stray thought that portended possible criminal behavior. Better off not knowing what you were going to do next for as long as possible and then act on your decision as soon as you made it. Not a relaxing way to spend your adolescence, but it kept the three of them safe.

Their contact in the crew was a large, taciturn slab of a sailor who'd grunted his way through most of their negotiation, so Jettrin was relieved to find the small ship waiting exactly where he'd been told to expect it. After paying their fare in cash, the three boys were ushered down to a pile of spare bedrolls and deflated pillows in a dark, secluded corner of the main hold, where they huddled on the cold deckplates and waited as the ship's cranes lowered containers into the far end of the hold. The waters of the Chao Phraya were steady, but Jettrin expected the sailing to grow choppier as they left port, and he watched the other two for early signs of seasickness.

Siam looked antsy but confined his nervous energy to a drumming of his fingers. Jai just looked bored.

Jettrin slid down next to where his brother sat. "Are you doing okay?" he asked him.

Jai hummed a short affirmative.

"Did you have bad dreams again last night?"

Jai looked away, guilty.

Jettrin put a hand on his brother's shoulder. "You need to learn to dream more quietly," he advised, though he had no clear idea how exactly a person could follow such bizarre advice. Jai frowned, evidently sharing in his confusion.

Jettrin sighed, aware how badly he was about to mix his signals. "But I need you to do something, just this once." Jettrin lowered both his head and his voice. "The crew on this boat," he whispered. "Can you *look* at them?"

Jai studied him, eyebrows rising as understanding dawned. "You mean…?"

The odds of one of these sailors being psychic (or, God forbid, Countermind) were infinitesimal, so there wasn't much chance of Jai being detected scanning the crew. Still, Jai obviously couldn't believe his brother was asking him to run such a risk.

Jettrin nodded. "But just the men working on this ship. No one else. Make sure none of them are planning to hurt us, or report us, or kidnap us, or fuck us."

He didn't see the point in sparing his brother's young ears. Censoring his instructions might lead Jai to overlook a threat he wasn't specifically searching for.

Jai swallowed, turned his head, and focused his eyes on a point in the middle distance. Sixteen minutes passed, and then he shook his head. "No."

"No what?"

"None of them are planning to do any of those things, okay?" Jai's eyes glistened as he spoke, his gaze fixed on the deck.

"What's wrong?" Jettrin asked.

"Nothing."

"Are you scared?"

Jai answered with a minute nod, and Jettrin reached over, gave him a tight hug, and muttered an apology. The telepathic scan would have to suffice. Once the ship was away from port, one of these guys might get drunk, or angry, or greedy, or horny, or just plain change his mind about the three boys hiding downstairs, but there would be no anticipating it. Even mind readers couldn't predict the future. If a threat arose, Jettrin would, with a move he'd practiced a hundred times, reach under his shirt for the small wood-handled steak knife hidden there, the one he wore dangling from the thin leather thong around his neck. With a single hard yank on the hilt, the slipknot in the thong would come undone, and Jettrin would be armed. And anyone who made a move on him, his boyfriend, or his little brother would lose their goddamn testicles.

Chapter 1
The Man From Countermind

THE AGENT watched the thief spin the lock's duodecimal digits with black-gloved fingers, the thief reading the combination from a scrap of paper he'd found taped to the counter beneath the cash register. The thief was a suspected psychic, per the agent's intelligence, which should have made such conventional intrusion methods superfluous. Why not pluck the numbers from the pawnbroker's mind? Why instead did the thief, after picking the lock on the back door and using a bolt cutter on the security gate within, spend an hour searching the shop for where the combination had been hidden?

Am I wasting my time? wondered Agent Jack Smith. He hadn't arrested the thief when he'd tracked him to that Sham Shui Po rooftop slum, to that shack of stacked concrete blocks and corrugated metal atop a tenement house with a tree growing out the side. Hadn't arrested him when he'd observed the suspect sporadically casing the shop over the last few days. Or earlier tonight, when the thief had lurked outside until the pawnbroker locked up the store and switched off the flickering neon bat and coin above the door. Smith didn't arrest the thief even now that he was engaged midburglary.

Smith watched through a trio of webcams he'd discreetly hidden in the shop among the antiques and clocks and obsolete electronics. The thief had entered, disconnected the closed-circuit cameras, and searched the shop until, noticing the scratches on the steel countertop, he'd slid the register aside and found the combination.

The more crimes, the more charges, the more convictions, the happier the courts would be. But these petty crimes were the business of the Hong Kong Police Force, not a government agent. So Smith had waited for the suspect to do something meriting his attention. That was at first. Now Smith waited because he was confused.

He decided to do something about it.

14-4-2B-5 AND *click* as the safe unlocked. And at that very moment, Alan was seized by the certainty that someone was watching him.

He froze and swiveled his head, surveying the darkness, eyes wide and dilated. Seeing nothing, he made a conscious effort to slow his heartbeat down, reminding himself that he couldn't see the future. Nobody could. No psychic premonition had alarmed him. Just paranoia.

But dangers imagined didn't preclude the existence of dangers actual. Alan shoved the haul—the jewelry and watches and rare coins and everything else with a high ratio of value to weight—into the black book bag, its holes patched with sewn-in strips of duct tape.

The bag matched his jacket, a faux-leather night-market knockoff. The black-and-silver look had started as an economic adaptation by the poor-to-do and then filtered its way upward through sociological strata in the usual manner of street-grown culture until it was as commonplace as the jeans, white tank top, and tennis shoes Alan also wore. He didn't mind looking derivative, if it meant sticking out less. His biggest liability was the tattoos, the custom tribal-electronic pattern running from his left thigh and up his side, snaking their way to his left fingertips, crawling across his cheek and temple. Of course the entire point of tattoos was to be permanent. He'd understood that when he'd gotten the ink done, just hadn't understood how much of a liability it would become. Give him a break, okay? He'd been young and stupid at the time, and also, by the way, not an international fugitive.

He zipped the bag shut and looked once more around at the pawnshop's bounty, all the goods held in collateral too heavy to be worth taking—panel TVs, bicycles, motorcycles, video game consoles, computer peripherals—and absolutely no one else he could see. He peeked over the counter, down into the tiny lobby area of the shop, concealed from the street by a locked front door and a high privacy screen. No one was hidden there.

Could he reach out with his mind, probe about for other consciousnesses, to confirm whether he was alone? As a physical possibility, sure he could, but could he justify it? This was familiar speculative terrain. Every time a heist wore down his nerves, Alan found himself going down these same casuistic pathways and always ending in the same ethical dead ends: no, he couldn't. Not to aid his theft. Perhaps in self-defense, but absent any evidence of imminent danger, he'd have to fly as blind as usual. Alan shut the safe and tossed the bag over his shoulder, and an electric dart hit his bag.

A second sooner, and the dart would have struck his back. The bag absorbed most of the shock, but enough of the jolt penetrated to send Alan lurching forward, grasping at the counter. The heel of a palm struck the back of his head, slamming his forehead into the counter. But Alan threw out a single wiry arm and surprised his attacker by grabbing the register and, one-handed, swinging it around and behind him.

The attacker cursed as the register's jangling metal bulk arced toward him. He hopped backward away from the blow, though he managed to take a firm hold on Alan's backpack.

The bag was old and cheaply constructed. Alan lunged forward and a strap snapped free. Now he ran for the rear of the shop, abandoning his haul, ably leaping a stack of boxes on his way out the door.

It was past midnight, and some parts of Hong Kong actually did sleep at this hour. The pawnshop was near Kwai Chung, its customer base mostly local workers pawning valuables just to squander their money on the races, men who wouldn't have the resources to track down the goods they'd put up as collateral. Alan had chosen the shop for its proximity to a body of water, and it was just a minute's hard sprint to the nearest container yard, then through that to the channel.

Alan charged downhill on roads still slick from the afternoon's rain, gleaming with the reflected glow of the city. No neon signs or electronic billboards, just streetlamps and a few lit office windows. Droplets ran in steady trickling streams off the buildings, canopies, streetlights, AC units. Steel shutters of closed storefronts shimmered wet, and Alan's skin glistened in the damp air. He didn't hear any pursuing footsteps, didn't bother turning his head to check.

He'd only gotten a brief glimpse of the attacker in the pawnshop, but that had been plenty. The man looked just a few years older than Alan, Eurasian, tall and lean, hale, clean-cut, clean-shaven. His attire had been dark but utterly nondescript. There was an impression of a black suit jacket, black slacks, and a black button-down shirt (but no tie, and open at the neck). Alan hadn't the time for more lingering impressions, but the man would've been attractive under more civil circumstances.

The man wasn't the shop owner, and was too well-dressed to be another crook or a triad member. That probably meant law enforcement, ample reason for Alan to make the quickest possible escape without sparing even a backward glance.

Alan vaulted from the sidewalk over a steel railing, dashed across the street, leapt another rail, and charged down a covered stairway, letting gravity lead his charge toward the water, angling toward the red lights atop the cargo-loading cranes just visible over a row of gently swaying palm trees. He hit the next street with such speed he lost some momentum to a brief stumble. A red-and-silver taxicab blared its horn at him, and Alan ducked under the canopy of a shuttered dim-sum shop to get his bearings. He glanced up at the building corners in the nearest intersection and spotted the closed-circuit cameras. He couldn't see which way they pivoted in their housings, but didn't think they'd have a clear look at him where he stood. Just to be safe, he'd have to circle around, keeping shy of major streets if he was to stay clear of any more traffic cams, though his pursuer couldn't be far behind.

Or was it pursuers? The man had attacked Alan alone, not a standard practice for an officer of one of the world's most famous police forces. If he was a government agent, he had to know what Alan was, right? And what such agent would be so reckless as to challenge a rogue telepath completely solo? Alan doubted even a state psychic would risk such a confrontation, and this man had given no sign of being a psychic himself, had not attempted any telepathic attacks, relying entirely on physical force. Who was he?

Whatever he was, if he caught Alan, it would mean death or worse. He had no need to know who this man was, only to escape him.

Alan pulled his jacket tight around him and popped the collar up. He turned a corner for a side street with fewer cameras and fewer lights and strolled a leisurely path into the shadow of an elevated highway, traffic rumbling above him. From there, he made his way through a hole in a chain-link fence he'd prepared earlier tonight with the help of his bolt cutters, slipping into the container yard, and then he sprinted across the yard toward freedom.

He ran straight into the agent.

The man stepped around the corner of a container and flashed Alan a razor smile as he kneed him in the stomach, allowing Alan's own momentum to double him over. Then the man threw Alan into the side of the steel container with a clang that echoed inside his head as his arm was twisted behind his back. Alan was strong for his size, but the agent was using some sort of judo leverage shit. Alan tried to wrench free, nearly succeeded, and then the man compensated for his strength by spinning him into the side of another container.

The man tightened his hold and hissed into Alan's ear.

"How many counts of resisting arrest?"

Alan gasped, gulped, and tried to talk his way out, forcing the words. "Come on, man. You never said you were arresting me."

"I thought it was implied. You did flee."

"After you shot me!"

"With a government-issue ranged electroshock device. Pay attention."

The agent tripped Alan roughly to the ground and buried his knees in Alan's back. His hand forced Alan's face against the concrete, and Alan wheezed as the air was squeezed out of his lungs.

Alan screwed his eyes to the edges of their sockets, trying to see up through the corner of his eye. The light of a passing ship winked between the container towers and slid over the man's features: dark eyed, dark haired, darkly smiling.

"Resist some more," the agent said. "I don't need to excuse brutality, but it helps with the paperwork."

Alan realized—a bit belatedly and with scant sense of relief—that he was now very much in danger of physical harm.

He expanded his thoughts outward and upward, seeking out the luminescent glow of his assailant's mind as if reaching for a firefly in the night. He found it, wrapped telepathic fingers around it, and squeezed tight.

There you are, Alan thought at him.

Fleeting impressions of the man's surface cognitions filtered through the permeable membrane of Alan's consciousness: mild surprise, then recognition, and then a strange kind of resigned satisfaction.

"And there *you* are," the man whispered.

Gripping Alan's hair, the agent slammed his face into the pavement at the same time Alan stabbed a spike of pure psychogenic pain into the agent's head.

The response was immediate. Agony scraped across the agent's mind like shards of twisted steel against flesh. Pain signals traveled the length of his neuromatrix in jagged spindles. Agonized arcs danced between his thalamus and somatosensory cortex like naked electrodes, crackling like Jacob's ladders.

Or so Alan expected.

The man did not scream. He didn't writhe in pain, didn't even flinch. He just pounded Alan's face into the pavement another time.

"Try something different," the agent said.

What had gone wrong? Alan was certain he'd struck a palpable blow, had sensed the mental reaction to the assault. Had he somehow *missed*? Had he hit some other mind by mistake? Were there even any other minds here, this late at night? Alan didn't sense any.

"I'm waiting," the man said, and Alan adjusted his aim, seized on the man's visual and auditory cortices, and swamped them with blinding, deafening sensory static, the explosion of a hallucinatory flashbang.

The agent slammed Alan's face into the concrete. "Got anything else?"

Alan, deciding like any reasonable person he didn't much like the taste of pavement, took the more direct approach of attacking the agent's motor cortex in an attempt to disable him utterly. He was awarded with another face-plant, but not hard enough to do any real damage.

Alan realized that the agent was in a position to hit him much harder than he was, or even just give him another jolt from the Taser. "You're playing with me," Alan muttered.

"Try to stop me."

Frustration replaced fear. Alan had connected with *somebody's* mind, of that he was certain. Had he just tortured, blinded, deafened, and paralyzed a complete stranger?

As long as he was still connected to the man's mind, he could at least try reading it, perhaps verify the person's identity. Alan reached in and was only able to pick up on a brief emotion—a sort of knowing, wry amusement—before something occurred that was completely unprecedented in Alan's telepathic experience:

The mind *slammed shut.*

Every mind put up some mild instinctive level of resistance to psychic intrusion, a natural ego barrier not even requiring conscious effort by the person whose mind was being invaded. It was more analogous to the surface tension on a pond of water, with only a slight push necessary to slip through and immerse oneself in the liquid thoughts underneath. But this pond had forcibly ejected him, then promptly solidified into dark black ice: solid, impenetrable, opaque.

But ice cracks.

Alan *pushed* at the barrier, tried to drive his ego through it like a spike. He sensed the barrier struggle against him, meeting force with force, answering pressure with pressure.

And then, without warning or fanfare, the mind flew open again.

What Alan saw inside would give him nightmares for a week.

It was as if someone had run an Internet search for fucked-up images, then played the results in a fast-forward slideshow. Murders; tortures; holocausts; open, festering wounds; butchered animals; butchered people; eyeballs dangling by optic nerves from gaping sockets; starving children eating from latrines; footage of occupation crackdowns in Pakistan; ethnic cleansing in Texas; cannibal corpses in Pyongyang; and a thousand other horrors, flashing by in a barely supraliminal montage, a high-speed filmstrip of horrors, utterly shattering Alan's emotional defenses.

When Alan finally stopped screaming, when his throat finally gave out, he wept softly.

The man leaned down, whispered into his ear. "That's at least five counts of unsanctioned psychic exercise, and that's plenty. Ready to call it a night?"

"What are you?" Alan croaked through raw vocal cords. "Are you psychic?"

The man shook his head. "Countermind," he said, and finally, mercifully, hit Alan with the Taser.

ALAN WAS only unconscious for a few moments. The man was now standing, a silhouette against the lights of the city, speaking on a cell phone. In the darkness, he didn't see Alan's eyes had opened, didn't know Alan was already awake. He was calling the arrest in.

Alan recognized the familiar pressure of thin plastic biting into his skin, realized his wrists were bound behind his back in one of those heavy-duty police-grade zip-tie handcuffs. He'd been in this situation before, had always managed to psychically coax the arresting officers into either setting him free or ignoring him as he scampered off.

That wouldn't work this time.

The Countermind agent finished his call. A glow of headlights swept between the towers of stacked cargo containers, and the man gave them a knowing look. The police backup had arrived quickly. Alan suspected they'd been waiting for the agent to call them in after neutralizing their target.

Alan saw the man produce a hypodermic of some sort, discard the cap, squeeze out an air bubble with a little squirt. He bent down toward Alan's neck.

Alan bucked, his head colliding with the syringe. The needle's point penetrated the skin of his scalp, but not enough to do any harm. The maneuver had the intended effect of knocking the syringe from the hand of the surprised agent.

At the same moment, Alan expanded his mind.

Even as the agent reached for his Taser, Alan grasped out telepathically and seized hold of not the agent's mind, but the mind of the driver of the approaching vehicle.

He glimpsed the scene through the eyes of the officer driving the car: The agent reaching into his jacket. Alan rolling away across the ground. Both of them illuminated in the glow of the vehicle's headlights, the image like a still from a film.

Alan fired a couple of direct, desperate commands into the officer's motor cortex. This time his aim was true. The officer turned the wheel slightly left, flattened the accelerator, and plowed the vehicle directly into the agent.

No, not quite directly, but close enough for government work. The agent leapt away in time to avoid the full brunt of the impact, but even the indirect collision with the car's hood was enough to send him bouncing across the pavement, beyond Alan's range of vision.

Alan, his hands still bound behind him, wobbled to his feet until he was resting in a lean against a shipping container. He slammed his hands against his rear a few times. It was murder on his wrists, but the plastic ties snapped free after a few firm blows.

He looked to where the agent had landed and saw him curled on the pavement, groaning. The car hadn't been able to accelerate much before the collision, and the agent had made a valiant attempt to roll from the impact at the last moment, but neither of these mitigators had spared him completely from harm.

The driver and his partner, both of them officers, sprang out of the checkered squad car. One took a step toward the agent and the other toward Alan. Before either could take a second step, Alan hit them both with a psychic assault that left them sprawling and unconscious. You know, like it was supposed to.

The agent moaned, rolled off his back, tried to raise himself up onto his hands and knees. He collapsed and spit blood onto the pavement.

Some busted ribs at the least, but Alan walked over and gave his torso a kick for good measure. The agent cried as he tumbled over, wheezed, clutched his side.

Alan had ethical limits to the uses he would make of his psychic abilities, but they didn't apply to much else, and he'd never been long on sympathy to begin with.

Particularly not for someone who'd ruined his heist! (Kick.) Shot him with a Taser! (Kick.) Smashed his face into the ground! (Kick.) Shot him again! (Kick.)

"More coming," the agent groaned.

Alan raised his head, saw more headlights, heard approaching sirens. The man wasn't issuing a warning. He was trying to frighten Alan into running so he wouldn't kick him anymore.

It was a smart gambit. Alan couldn't be sure more Countermind agents weren't on the way, and he valued his freedom over petty revenge.

And he didn't want to kill the guy, just make him really regret the encounter. Which, judging from the way the agent was curling himself into some sort of figure-eight knot, mission fucking accomplished.

Alan snatched the hypodermic from where it had landed, lest they check it for DNA, then turned away and charged headlong into the humid night.

CHAPTER 2
NET WORK

"To be a psychic is to be a cynic," Arissa binti Noor told her handler over a cup of yuanyang, served hot and sweet. Or so the saying went. Why develop a capacity for trust when you never actually needed to trust anyone?

The two of them sat in front of their usual coffee shop, the leashed dogs curled at their feet watching the foot traffic meandering up Wyndham Street. The café had set up a few chairs and tables in front, beneath a canopy that dripped thin rivulets of condensation from buzzing AC units mounted in the windows of the apartments above it. No one sat nearby, and Arissa confirmed for herself that to any of the pedestrians strolling by on the street or the drivers of passing vehicles, the women looked like two girlfriends meeting up mid-dogwalk to share a drink.

"I've heard," her handler said, lips pursed with concern. "All the same, do not let your guard down around this man. His file describes him as being very charismatic."

"But well-intentioned," Arissa added. "Besides, this is just supposed to be a trial run."

"Yes, which means, if he does end up posing a threat, you'll be less likely to see it coming."

Arissa made a small nod of acknowledgment. When they'd finished their drinks, they stood, hugged, and parted ways in opposite directions, Arissa returning to her flat to sit down at her computer.

Arissa had listened to her handler's warning but wasn't bothered by it. Unlike most psychics, she wasn't particularly cynical. Despite her paranormal insight into the dark and hidden reaches of the human heart, her telepathy was paired with a practiced empathy. When she determined someone was lying to her, she was quick to investigate whether they had an understandable reason for the deception. Confirmation bias ensured some extenuating circumstance could always be found, and Arissa's confidence in humanity's innate goodness endured another day.

Also unlike other telepaths, Arissa was logging on to an online dating site.

Psychics, as a rule, shunned online society for the same reason the sighted avoided dark alleyways. Internet communication left them at a distinct and unaccustomed disadvantage: Online, nobody could read minds. Online, everybody lied. If anything, psychics were actually worse than nonpsychics at discerning online deception. Not having developed the more mundane lie-detection skills most people relied on daily, they found themselves uncharacteristically gullible on the Internet.

Arissa, though fully aware of these dangers, nonetheless was creating an online dating profile. Like most dating profiles, it was packed full of lies:

User name: CoffeeTeaAndMe
19/F/Straight
Location: Hong Kong Island, Hong Kong
Height: 1.4m
Body Type: Slender
Sign: Aries
Marital Status: Never married
Children: None
Eyes: Brown
Hair: Black
Religion: Agnostic
Drinking: Socially
Smoking: Never
Occupation: Marketing
Education: College
Languages: Mandarin, Cantonese, English, Malay

About Myself: So I'm making this profile completely at the insistence of my friends, who threatened to make one for me if I didn't. (Hi guys! *waves*) I just started a new career in a new city and am always up for meeting new people. I adore my job, my family, and my friends, and just living life.

How I Have Fun: Love cooking! (Still trying to get better at it, but love it! I'm a dilettante foodie.) Walking my Crested, Daisy (love of my life!). I can rock some trivia pretty hard. Hiking. Occasionally doing the museum thing for some culture, or curling up with a good book. I play Rath in moderation. I went skydiving once. Beyond all that, a lot of the standard social stuff: restaurants, coffee, clubs, movies. Really it doesn't matter what I'm doing as long as the company is good!

What I'm Looking For: Some good company! Not necessarily romantic (though not necessarily *not* romantic). I guess I'd prefer you not be crazy, but some eccentricity can be good. Are you smart? Great, I love being educated! Are you funny? Great, I love laughing! Are you outgoing and fun? Then say hi!

This was pretty boilerplate stuff, with a flag set so Party Yŏu's online dating functionality would display her profile to empirically eligible bachelors. The attached photos showed her in the apparent company of her friends, her family, or her staggeringly ugly dog, and always smiling radiantly.

Switching windows, she sent a secure e-mail containing her logon ID and password to a contact within a special office at the Safety Ministry. Then she looked at the time and shut down the computer. She had a train to catch.

THE YOUNG man standing at the other end of the crowded Island Line car looked maybe a year older than Arissa. He was tall and just scruffy enough to give him a rough-edged appeal while remaining approachable, the light facial hair softening rather than hardening his appearance. He looked like the graphic designer and freelance artist he was, wearing tiny blue earbuds and a purple book bag and watching the lights fly by through the train window with intelligent eyes. Midday, off-peak hours, there still weren't enough seats for everyone, but he was slouched comfortably, his finger tapping on his leg in time to a beat only he heard. He was dressed casually but tastefully in clean jeans and a form-flattering button-down shirt with the top buttons undone and the sleeves rolled up. He had an easy, comely smile, as when he shot a grin at a wide-eyed two-year-old girl who walked by with a stuffed whale in one hand and her mother's grip in the other. Despite her professional reservations, Arissa found herself charmed by this man she only knew through a government dossier.

She reached into his mind.

His name was Card Lin. He was twenty years old and didn't have a girlfriend, though he was straight. He was an artist, employed in marketing while volunteering time for child charities. He liked old movies and foreign languages (and old movies in foreign languages). He was casually Buddhist. He swam a mile in the pool every morning.

He wanted to help people.

That last detail startled Arissa. Though no cynic, she was also no naïf. When you peer into a person's mind, you simply do not, as a rule, discover sentiments of unvarnished and sincere altruism. Yet there it was. Sifting through the open drawer of Card's mind, Arissa had found a diamond of authentic selflessness glittering amidst the more mundane preoccupations normally cluttering people's thoughts. More than a peripheral whim, this idealism was a central node in his cognitive network, a major organizing principle of his personality.

Arissa wanted to keep looking, but Card debarked for his transfer. She'd have to try again tomorrow.

CARD WORKED freelance, but his schedule was regular enough that he was on the train again the next day. Arissa, already waiting for him when he stepped into the car, reached back into his mind.

Subconscious suggestion is tricky. Ideas can die out quickly as embers. A fire needs steady fuel to keep burning, and an idea has to be continuously revisited if it's to stay alive.

To use a different metaphor, a thought residing outside of awareness is unlikely to thrive without a strong connection to the deep forest of ideas native to a person's mind. Like a plant, an idea's roots must run far and deep if it is to thrive. The secret is to connect the new idea with as many old ideas as possible, but not so abruptly that you damage the existing system, or so sloppily that you make a mess of things.

A psychic of average ability might need hours, even days, to implant a suggestion deeply enough that it could influence behavior indefinitely but subtly enough that the host mind wasn't excessively disrupted. Arissa usually needed an hour, tops. For this particular suggestion, she'd need only the duration of a single train ride. The idea only had to last a day or two, and it wasn't dissonant with Card's own innate inclinations, making outright rejection unlikely.

The train stopped at the next station, where video screens mounted on the curved orange wall of the tube played an ad showing a young couple walking down the beach hand in hand. Arissa waited for Card to notice the advertisement and then prodded him into letting his gaze linger. From that stimulus, she evoked in him a perfectly normal pang of loneliness, then elevated it into the hope of one day experiencing an authentic moment of romantic happiness. As the train pulled away from the station, Arissa activated Card's fond memory of the little girl from yesterday, then yoked it to his yearning for romantic love, creating a corresponding desire for fatherhood and the personal meaning and domestic bliss expected from child-rearing.

For a skilled psychic, mental implantation was more improvisation than anything, a game of reverse free association. Arissa waited for the right thoughts to trip across the synapses, tied them to each other, and let the new associations take hold and grow, crawling up the host's mental scaffolding like ivy up a trellis.

Card, meanwhile, fiddled with his phone. He read a birthday invitation from his friend Qing-Long, who (Arissa helped him recall) had met his fiancée on an online dating site. Well, why couldn't Card find a girlfriend the same way?

She massaged the question gently into his mind, hooking it onto as many stray inclinations as she could: thoughts about e-mailing friends, looking up recipes for dinner, streaming television shows, playing games, and a multitude of other online activities that could lead him to ask himself, "As long as I'm on the computer anyway, why don't I…?"

Card debarked at Admiralty, swept away by the commuting crowd up the escalator. He carried with him, as a parting touch from Arissa, the concrete intention to check out PartyYŏu's matching service the next time he logged on to Rath.

The psychic suggestion was like an extra little push to a train that had already built up steam. The machinery was already operating, the forward momentum already in place. Mechanical laws operated on universal constants, needing little assistance beyond the occasional course correction, and Card's course was as set as a subway train track.

WHEN ARISSA returned to her flat that afternoon, she changed out of her work clothes, brushed and walked the dog, made a smoothie, and logged on to her computer.

By now, per her request, her online profile was securely nestled in a broad and deep network of friendships, vacation photos, college records, and work histories, all serving to flesh out her legend. Her inbox had filled with messages from several algorithmically appropriate single straight males. A few of these she answered with friendly responses, if brief and noncommittal. And then she searched for and found this new profile:

User name: PaladinLin
20/M/Straight
Location: Kowloon, Hong Kong
Height: 1.6 m
Body Type: Fit
Sign: Pisces
Marital Status: Never married
Children: None
Eyes: Black
Hair: Black
Religion: Buddhist
Drinking: Socially
Smoking: Never
Occupation: Artist
Education: College
Languages: Mandarin, Cantonese, English, Japanese
About Myself: After looking around here a bit, I'm tempted to break from convention by talking about how awesome I am at talking about myself, and how it doesn't feel weird at all! Hi, I'm Card, and I'm

hoping to meet a nice, smart girl. Freelance work makes it hard to hit the bar scene, so let's give the online dating thing a shot, yeah?

How I Have Fun: Besides working? Trying to relax and unwind whenever possible. Movies, swimming, gaming, dancing, chorus. I'm insane about traveling and love seeing new places. I occasionally write articles for various travel sites. (One day I'd like to write a memoir, but that won't be for a long time.) I'm a bit of a cardsharp, and I know a few tricks. I like sushi. I dabble in avant-garde programming. (Ask me in person.)

What I'm Looking For: Like I said, I'm looking for a nice, smart girl. Sorry to repeat myself. In my defense, "nice" and "smart" are pretty important and probably bear repeating. Other than that, I'm hoping you can have fun just being yourself.

Accompanying these vitals were a few pictures of Card relaxing with his friends. He grinned broadly at the camera in every photo, his face friendly and inviting. The photos were comely and charismatic, and their captions were smart, funny, sentimental, engaging.

Arissa didn't send Card a message yet. She shouldn't be the one to initiate contact. For best results, he had to reach out to her first. But she could encourage him. She gave his profile a five-star rating, answered match questions in agreeable ways, and otherwise did what she could to game the site's compatibility algorithms so they'd bring her profile to his attention. Then she e-mailed her Safety Ministry contact, who'd encourage the people at PartyYǒu to help massage the site's systems as well.

"ARE YOU taking the train again today?" Arissa's handler asked the next time they met for coffee.

Arissa stopped blowing on her drink to shake her head. "Tell me if you disagree, but he's not the type to be flattered by a stalker's attention, and I don't want to risk him recognizing me by seeing me too often. Besides, there's no need."

"No?"

"He reached out to me this morning," Arissa explained. She produced and unlocked her phone, opened the PartyYǒu app, and handed it to the older woman.

Arissa had already read the message:

> *Hi, so you need to stop being so darn upbeat. You might scare people away. Lucky I'm pretty brave!*
> *This site says you and I have a pretty high compatibility score. I don't like taking technology at its word, but let me know if you want to test it sometime by meeting over coffee?*
> *-Card*

"A little forward," her handler remarked when she finished reading. "Straight to the invitation, without trading a few messages first to establish rapport." She handed the phone back.

Arissa accepted it with a shrug. "It's not like he rushed straight to declaring dissident attitudes. It's still very preliminary, and it will save us some time."

"When will you accept?"

"Tonight. I'll keep you updated."

THAT EVENING, Arissa logged into Party Yǒu's dating site and composed a short reply:

> *Hi! Thanks for the message! And thanks(?) for the advice. I guess I'll try to be less chipper in the future, haha.*
> *So you're a freelancer? What kind of work? Or do you want to tell me over coffee this weekend?*
> *~Julianna*

She clicked Send and logged off from the site.

Security Ministry Third Bureau Agent Arissa binti Noor wasn't particularly cynical, but even she knew that everybody lied online, all the time.

Well, so did she.

Chapter 3
Four Sages

A MONTH had been the absolute minimum Countermind was willing to keep Smith off active duty while he recovered from his vehicle-induced injuries, and only after he'd begged a favor from the executive director. "Off active duty" in this context had meant no fieldwork, not no work at all. Smith had stayed on the case that wrecked his ribs, even pursuing it from his hospital bed the first few days. When he was finally cleared for work, the department put him through a battery of evals, made him edit some handbooks, gave him a few dozen intelligence reports to review, and the executive director personally assigned him to some lightweight internal affairs busywork, as if to help him get back up to speed.

Smith bit gamely into these tasks but still couldn't get that thief out of his mind.

An exasperated Hong Kong Police Force had first referred the case to Countermind after failing on multiple occasions to apprehend a serial thief. Three times, the suspect had evaded arrest. Every time, HKPF debriefings of the involved officers had presented indicators of psychic intrusion or tampering, which Smith had personally confirmed in follow-up interviews. The arresting officers had been unable to provide a rational account for their behavior, had not even been aware their behavior was irrational, and were unable to provide a cogent description of the fugitive. Until Smith, every official to confront the thief had had his memory scrubbed of the suspect's appearance.

Hong Kong was Smith's hometown and the closest thing he had to a beat. It was natural that the case was referred to him. To help him sketch the suspect, Smith had scoured security footage from street cameras and other closed-circuit systems near the crime scenes, but these images were all too low-resolution to be useful in constructing a quality composite. The thief had good instincts, always seemed on the lookout for cameras, and never stepped close enough to allow a clear shot of his face. The description Smith had assembled from the available evidence was vague at best: male, late teens/early adult, Asian, perhaps Japanese.

And then there was that tattoo.

In blurry video stills, the tattoo had been a smudge on the left side of the thief's face. Smith was the first person to both see it up close and remember what he saw: a circuit board's intricate grid-like pattern of nodes connected by curving, jagged bands of varied, tapering width. While cuffing the thief, Smith had glimpsed the same pattern on the left wrist and suspected the pattern spread over a considerable portion of the fugitive's body.

Body modifications were excellent distinguishing features, but not infallible. Even sizable tattoos could be removed, and telepaths had been known to undergo extensive cosmetic surgery, even facial reconstruction, only to then erase their surgeons' memories of the entire procedure.

The footage had allowed Smith to track the suspect to a run-down, drafty concrete block crowded with transients, but bribing the locals had yielded no useful information. By all accounts, the thief had kept to himself. Now that the suspect had vanished, Smith needed a new lead.

More than a description, Smith wanted a name. But the description would do for now.

Prosopagnosics aside, humans were good at recognizing faces but poor at recalling them. In contrast, computers could recall faces perfectly but were comparably poor at recognizing them. These two memory systems could complement each other quite well, so on Smith's first day back in the office, he'd requisitioned clearance from Director Zheng to run the suspect's image through Senex's facial recognition service. Every day since then, Smith had loaded the composite image—artificially assembled from video stills and tweaked based on his own memory of that failed arrest—into Senex, set the search parameters, and hit start on the search.

This would be attempt number ten. Sitting in his small, windowless, undecorated office, Smith minimized the Senex window and left it running in the background of his computer. He was tired of watching the progress bar crawl its slow way toward inevitable disappointment. He'd tried multiple variations on the facial image (tattoo present, tattoo digitally removed, face artificially reverse-aged) with no luck. These searches had gotten hits from Senex's database—usually several hundred, and many with sizable confidence quotients. But just eyeballing them, Smith knew none were the young man he'd tussled with in the pawnshop and then in the container yard. It didn't help that the fugitive was, to his eyes, attractive. That wasn't an inconsequential detail. Statistically speaking, "attractive" usually just meant "average," and averageness meant a larger tally of high-confidence false positives that Smith had to personally review one by one when Senex presented them at the end of a search. Attempt ten would likely be no different, but he had to try.

Leaving the program running, Smith locked the computer and left his office. He had an appointment with the director.

EXECUTIVE DIRECTOR Zheng, tapping away on the screen in his desk, made the usual perfunctory, distracted inquiries into Smith's well-being ("very well, sir, thank you, sir") and then allowed Smith to lead him through the agenda he'd brought to the meeting. Every update was greeted with a small nod of acknowledgment.

"And that's all I have, sir," Smith finished.

Smith wished he was standing instead of sitting, the better to demonstrate his health and fitness for duty. It was easy to feel small in Zheng's office, a fiefdom of mahogany, brass, and leather, the only notable decoration a framed piece of brushwork calligraphy, its black figures stark against the white background: "He who knows and knows that he knows is a wise man." The large office window had been heavily fogged at Zheng's request, or so rumor had it. Through the window, during the day, the skyline appeared as mere faint shadows. In the evening, when the capital came alight, the buildings were luminescent ghosts, formless and indistinct.

It was a disproportionately prestigious office for the director of an intelligence department that was, in terms of raw manpower, very small. Zheng had occupied the office for as long as Smith had worked here, certainly well before Zheng had taken him under his wing, but he'd heard stories of how the director had obtained it. Zheng hadn't been assigned the space, hadn't requested it. One day, he'd simply and abruptly instructed his staff to make arrangements for his relocation to it. No one had objected to his presumption. The administration had responded by clearing the way for his move. Anyone who might have raised a word of complaint either feared or valued the director too much, and with good cause. In the decades since Zheng had taken command of this little intelligence shop, there had yet to be a single identified "desuppressive event," in the awkward internal shorthand for security breaches perpetrated specifically by telepaths into Countermind.

The director's desk was an antique monstrosity dominating everything in the room except the director himself. Zheng stood, having no chair, leery as he was of the deleterious effects of too much continuous sitting. The long hours on his feet hadn't hurt the director's vitality. He was almost archetypically tall, rich, and handsome, and age had only given his strong, chiseled features a seasoned and distinguished air. Zheng didn't look the part of a classical wise man—he was well-dressed, groomed, and physically fit instead of bearded, wispy, or thin—but Smith knew he had the brains of one.

The director stood but did not require his visitors to stand in kind. Smith, as usual, had been invited to sit when he arrived for their meeting. Everyone was invited to sit, and after the offer was made enough times, the invitation became irresistible, though the difference in elevation always meant staring up at the director for the duration of the visit. Zheng's guests were always made keenly aware of the disparity. To Smith, from this subordinated perspective, Zheng's tall, wide desk sometimes resembled a judge's bench. Other times, it suggested the prow of an ancient wooden man-of-war bearing down on him.

"There's nothing else you have for me, Agent?" Zheng asked.

"No, sir, that's all."

"Let me clarify. Is there anything else you can report on beyond what you have been assigned?"

Smith leaned back. This was no surprise. He'd expressed preoccupation with his botched arrest during his psych evals. And of course his computer activity was monitored by his superiors (and their superiors, and their superiors). All information was state property, and working for the New Government, even in Countermind, didn't spare you from that reality. If you wanted to keep something secret, you didn't run searches, send e-mails, or save files about it. Ideally, if you wanted to keep something secret, you didn't even think about it.

Agent Jack Smith didn't have anything to hide. He told Zheng about his continued investigation of the tattooed psychic thief.

"You were taken off that case, Agent," said Zheng.

"Only officially."

"You have other assignments."

"I took initiative," Smith answered. "I've been assembling a psychological profile. Frankly, the HKPF gave us nothing to work with, and I think that left me at a disadvantage. I want to remedy those intelligence gaps."

"And?"

"I haven't been able to identify the suspect," Smith admitted. "As far as Security Ministry records are concerned, he's a cipher, even with that tattoo of his. Other agencies might have matching records, if I were cleared to access them—"

"Just finish your report, Agent."

"So I've been forced to speculate," said Smith. "I've got two questions I've struggled with about my encounter with the suspect. But you've already seen my after-action."

"Refresh my memory," Zheng suggested.

"When he robbed the shop, he searched the premises for a physical record of the safe's combination."

"And you wonder why a psychic would need to do that."

"Precisely. Like any other thief, he cased the location in the daytime before robbing it that night. But a typical psychic would've retrieved the combination from the shopkeeper's mind rather than go through the trouble of finding it written down somewhere. My observations of the suspect left me doubting whether he was actually a telepath. I thought maybe the police had made a mistake, and they were wasting our time on a baseline nonpsychic. It wouldn't be the first time, right? So I decided I would test him before bothering to bring him in. I deliberately startled him into running, gave chase, knocked him around a bit, and did what I could to provoke him into retaliating telepathically."

"Which he did."

Smith nodded. "Yeah, eventually. But I've been trying to understand why it took him so long to fall back on those powers. Which brings me to the other thing that surprised me."

"And what was that?"

"He doesn't especially look it, but the suspect is very athletic. He's strong, fast, and able to put up with quite a lot of pain. He nearly escaped me a time or two."

"He did escape you."

"Yes, he did," Smith conceded. "When I finally put him out, he didn't stay unconscious for nearly as long as he should have. He's got stamina. Psychics tend to become overreliant on their mental abilities. Why learn how to fight when you can just deactivate people? But not this one. I think he trains. Physically. Intensively."

Zheng nodded. "So, you're looking for an athletic psychic who enjoys making things more difficult for himself than they need to be."

"Not exactly. I think he's repressed."

"Repressed."

"I don't think he likes using psychic powers, if he can avoid it. Whenever possible, he'd rather use more mundane methods, no matter how much more inconvenient they might be. He engages in diligent physical training so he has less cause to rely on his psychic abilities. Telepathy for him is a tool of last resort and self-defense."

"And what significance does this conclusion hold?"

"Unlike most telepaths, this thief doesn't use his powers as a crutch. He's got other skills to rely on, and we might not yet know the full extent of them."

"And do you think this skill set is why he's avoided capture for so long, even by you?"

"Sir," said Smith, "Countermind agents undergo a training regimen focused almost exclusively on dealing with telepaths. We need to specialize, given the nature and difficulty of our work, and the training usually serves us pretty damned well. But when we have to deal with a telepath who only uses his abilities as part of a larger and more diverse set of tools, and not even as the primary instrument among them, it does make for more of a challenge."

"So you think we'll need to liaise further with more conventional law enforcement agencies. Make use of outside assistance."

"No, not yet," Smith answered, conscious of Zheng's preference for autonomy. Even asking the Safety Ministry to run Senex searches cost Countermind a little bit of face. "But it does mean I'll need more time. And yes, maybe access to others' databases."

Zheng considered the implied requests quietly, then nodded. "All right. I'll let you keep pursuing this case on the clock. I won't assign you any other work, though I expect you to finish the assignments you've already been given. As for further access to external resources, that will require capital I'm not ready to expend on someone who is, to present appearances, merely a petty thief, 'repressed' psychic or otherwise."

"Unlicensed psychic exercise is a felony. Sir."

"As I'm well aware," Zheng grumbled, "but we must prioritize which felonies to investigate, and this suspect is not yet a priority, compared to the untold number of rogue telepaths engaging in corporate espionage, state sabotage, telepathic slavery, and other major crimes. You'll have to make do with Senex access for now. You're dismissed."

"Yes, sir. Thank you, sir."

IT WAS evening when Smith clocked out. He was about to power his computer down when a notification popped up on his monitor: "Search Complete."

Smith blinked. Of course he remembered starting the facial recognition search, but he'd grown so accustomed to disappointment that he'd assumed the Senex search had long since run its course and met with the usual failure. But the program usually took less than an hour to finish. This time it had taken half a day. Why so long?

He opened the search window to the default command screen and saw what had happened. Apparently he'd forgotten to set chronological parameters on the search. The fugitive was young, and Smith had only wanted to look through the last several years—searching any further back just squandered time and system resources. Without those parameters, the program had sifted through the entire Senex database for potential matches rather than just the last few years' worth.

Smith sighed. What a waste. Instead of hundreds of hits, Senex must have produced thousands, maybe millions, none of them useful.

He checked the results anyway.

His jaw dropped.

The top image result had a confidence quotient of B9.70 percent. It was the fugitive's spitting image.

It was also fifty years old.

Smith opened the file.

The name on the record was Quentin Izaki. No criminal record. PhD in engineering. Actually, PhDs plus assorted degrees and sundry other certifications in various fields—chemical, computer, electrical, materials, mechanical, biological, biomedical, etc. A litany of publications, honors, awards, appointments. He was of Japanese descent but American-born, raised, and educated, eventually retiring to a remote mountain home near Seattle.

He was deceased. Local records were sloppy, but apparently his laboratory and his entire home had been destroyed in some sort of conflagration. No family. Or, rather, no documented family.

Smith scrolled back up to the image. It was some kind of college graduation photo: a young Quentin Izaki, with shelves of leather-bound books behind him, a mortarboard on his head, honors cords around his neck, a rolled-up degree clutched proudly in hand, and an eager smile on his face.

Smith cropped the image down to just Quentin's face and placed a hand on the screen, covering the left side, where the tattoo would be, with his fingertips.

There he was. Smith had found what could only be the fugitive's father and, with him, the fugitive's name.

Smith's lips twisted with satisfaction. "Izaki," he whispered into the half glow of the monitor.

CHAPTER 4
KISMET

ALAN IZAKI came to a decision. He'd come to Hong Kong on the theory that a hyperdense, international coastal metropolis would be the perfect place to evade capture and certain death at the hands of a totalitarian cryptofascist dictatorship. Where better for him to blend in than someplace crowded, predominantly Asian, but where English was still an essential language? Singapore was a bit too orderly for his tastes, which left Hong Kong. He'd expected the petty thievery to keep him clear of any high-level attention, but the incident at the pawnbroker had disabused him of this notion. He'd hit a Countermind agent with a car. They wouldn't forget that, and they'd come after him in force, if given the slightest hint where he was. He had to leave town, flee to someplace on the other end of the sociopolitical spectrum. And something from his encounter with the Countermind agent had given him an idea where to go.

But first there'd be a number of intermediary goals: get hold of some small, transportable valuables. Secure some credentials. And, above all, avoid capture, all while Countermind was watching for him. It was possible to stay under the Security Ministry's radar if they weren't specifically looking for you, but Alan flattered himself to think he'd proven worthy of their attention.

THE ENTIRE double-decker bus was painted over with a giant ad for an online game. A parade of medieval adventurers, brandishing swords and fireballs and rendered in a Japanese manga style, slid slowly past Alan while he stood in the bus stop queue. The bus halted with a short screech, and Alan was facing their foe, some kind of giant, monstrous floating eyeball, surrounded by a halo of smaller eyes on wriggling stalks. One of the painted eyes looked straight at him with a ubiquitous gaze. He shifted from one foot to the other, and the bloodshot orb didn't break eye contact.

Alan sniffed at the illustration but looked away, pulling his cap down over his face and tightening the strap on his messenger bag. He hunched his shoulders, buried his hands into his pockets, and filed aboard the bus with the other commuters.

He paid in cash, exact change, and rounded the stairs to the second story. He claimed a seat by the window on the left side, at the rear, giving him a view at the sidewalk and denying the other passengers a good look at the foundation smeared over the left side of his face. He'd forgone the black-and-silver look for a more conventional pair of jeans, a bulky jacket, and sneakers. It wasn't the season for gloves, but at this early hour no one would question them too much. The sun was low and the sky overcast, the city steeped in a deep gloom, and everyone was inclined to keep to themselves.

Alan slipped on his headphones and pulled a laptop computer out of his bag. A trio of cords snaked from the laptop into the messenger bag. One connected to an external hard drive and another to a battery. The third connected to a Wi-Fi antenna with about six times the signal strength of a typical internal wireless card. If the need arose, Alan could yank the cords free in an instant, immediately severing the device from his data, its power, or any intrusion.

But he hesitated, his finger on the power button, and imagined his pursuers somehow, in defiance of conventional scientific knowledge, reaching into the device with telepathic fingers as easily as their state psychics might invade his own waking mind. It frankly wouldn't surprise him.

Then the bus creaked forward, and Alan turned the computer on, the OS loading in just a few seconds. Last night he'd fiddled with the BIOS, juggled the boot list, disabled most of the software except what he'd need for this expedition. Now he had the wardriver loaded and running before the bus even reentered traffic, the window populating with a growing list of in-range wireless networks, along with BSSIDs, channels, megabits per second, and encryption statuses, all of them automatically logged and probed, the program running through a series of default network keys and testing for an array of rudimentary vulnerabilities, noting those networks that yielded entry.

While it worked, there wasn't much for Alan to do but look out the window as the bus crawled up Nathan Road, under fashion billboards, past tailors, jewelers, watch vendors, and electronics stores, and alongside hotels.

So many hotels, ranging from the higher-end luxury hotels to Chungking-style eight-to-a-guesthouse fly-by-night transient housing. This three-kilometer stretch of road from Kowloon Bay to the Prince Edward stop was thick with hotels, and with the restaurants and retailers that clustered around hotels, all of them with wireless networks registering on his computer, and all of them full of travelers, many who'd arrived at the nearby train station and would depart the same way. Alan watched them spilling out of the lobbies, the suited businesspeople with their heads down, the disoriented tourists with their heads up, the shoppers and hawkers and revelers and commuters and domestic workers, a human river of bobbing heads. He leaned into the window, looking out for the young man who would be his ticket out of here.

This town had no shortage of takings. Hong Kong was still a financial powerhouse. How easy it would be to reach into the mind of just one of these wealthy travelers, or any one of the city's plentiful millionaires, and pluck out some account information, ATM numbers, computer passwords, or any other crucial private datum as simply as a coin off the sidewalk.

But no, telepathic theft was out of bounds. And that was probably for the best. Psyching those police officers was probably how Alan had caught Countermind's attention. Avoiding telepathy was a short-term handicap but a viable long-term survival strategy. *Thanks, Dad. You're a hell of a moral educator.*

Alan returned his attention from the stream of pedestrians to the computer screen and checked the program's progress. Already hundreds of networks logged and tested for vulnerabilities. Those networks yielding entry were scanned for connected drives. Another program automatically scanned these for any fields of data falling within a range of preset parameters: names, credit card info, transaction histories, contact information, and other personal information, copying to his drive any qualifying data.

Alan got off the bus at Prince Edward, crossed the street, and waited for a southbound bus. Best to cover both sides of the road. And always pay in cash, exact change.

Alan had only a small fraction of his father's technical aptitude. Alan suffered from the same curse that afflicted all children of geniuses: regression to the mean. But any idiot could drag a net down a canal.

ALAN SPENT the next few days deep in his bolt-hole, sifting the data. Most was garbage. Not every vulnerable network belonged to a business. Not every business with a vulnerable network was a retailer. Not every retailer with a vulnerable network had connected that network to drives with customer information. Even where Alan had accessed data, his automated searches usually failed to copy useful records. Most transactions had occurred in the last month or two, and some sales histories went back years. But in the final analysis, Alan had swiped records of over a million transactions involving hundreds of thousands of unique customers.

It was too much data, and too uneven in quality, for Alan to make use of without first giving it some semblance of organization. He ran a matching algorithm that created a unique combined record for each customer with a transaction history, combining the customer information into a single database. He set the program to flag those customers with transaction records aligning with the trains arriving to and from Shanghai at Hung Hom Station, as well as those customers with Shanghai addresses.

The programs did the bulk of this work, but a human eye was still required to tidy up the margins. Alan spent hours going through the data cell by cell, checking for errors and manually correcting those he found. Even this rudimentary cleaning required an entire night's dedicated labor, then a brief nap before resuming the hunt.

ALAN GOT another e-mail from Johnny.

Johnny, who'd haunted the patios of the seedier beach bars outside Manila, trying to catch the eyes of vacationing businessmen. Gawky, chestnut Johnny with sand on his feet, nearly ground down by his trade and not even out of his teens. He'd suspected Alan of horning in on his turf, trying to steal his business. Alan had explained he was merely robbing his marks, not sleeping with them, and Johnny had been immediately enchanted, never having realized it was possible to gain so much while giving away nothing.

He'd been voracious. Everything for Johnny had been a prelude to sex. He'd wanted to hang out, to be friends, to stick together for safety, to share his home. Alan had agreed each time, insisting that there'd be nothing more, retreating every time Johnny had gotten handsy, parting ways, only to risk letting him get close again.

Johnny, who'd worn Alan down with a longing they'd shared from the moment they'd met, who'd returned to their hovel one night with a bottle of 90-proof bubblegum-flavored lambanog stolen with tricks Alan had taught him. As they drank the coconut wine, Johnny begged and pleaded to see all of Alan's tattoo, and then touch it, and then taste it, until Alan forgot his better judgment and the two were rolling over each other in the darkness. Until Alan forgot his better judgment and let Johnny in on his secret.

Johnny, who panicked, who threatened to report Alan to the authorities, to Countermind. To save himself, in fear for his life, Alan erased the knowledge from Johnny's memory, erased the entire encounter, and then vanished.

The e-mail contained Johnny's usual begging and pleading. Not for sex now, but for answers. *Where are you? What happened? Why did you leave? Why won't you answer? Why won't you come back? Are you okay?*

This wasn't just a nuisance anymore. Now that Alan had the actual Bureau of Counterpsychic Fucking Affairs after him, these communications were one more trail for them to follow. He deleted the account.

JOHNNY, WHO taught Alan how to seduce wealthy, intoxicated closet cases.

The Tsim Sha Tsui bar was a colorfully lit karaoke joint with badly bootlegged music and patrons only casually acquainted with city smoking ordinances. Supposedly it was called "Comrades," though there was no sign outside. The clientele were split between younger men and the older professionals looking to patronize them.

Alan sat alone at the bar, foundation on his face again, judiciously sipping some water as one by one older men tried to buy him drinks, only to have Alan say thanks, but he was waiting for someone. And Alan watched them through the mirror as they left him alone, as they roamed the bar and gathered in groups, and especially as they operated their phones.

He picked out a target, swooped in, and asked if that drink was still on offer.

The man looked up from his phone. "You were waiting for someone," he said, a little miffed. The man looked better when he wasn't trying to turn on the charm. He'd been muscular once, even if his thirties were softening him, and he had intelligent eyes, now tinted with suspicion.

"He never showed," Alan said. "So, that drink?" And Alan did as Johnny had showed him: the sustained eye contact, the orientation of his body, the mirrored nonverbals, and smiling, always smiling. The hardest part for Alan was the smiling.

His name was Chun-Wai. He was a stockbroker. A parade of drinks wore down his reservations until they were making out in the backseat of a cab on the way to his apartment.

"This is a really nice place," Alan said as Chun-Wai led him inside by the hand. The interior design struck Alan as heavily Edwardian with Chinese accents: gaudy, eclectic, and fastidious.

"Thanks," Chun-Wai said between kisses. He tossed Alan's messenger bag onto a chair and fussed with his jacket. "The boyfriend helps with the rent."

Alan froze. There hadn't seemed to be anyone else home. "I don't do open relationships," he said, fending Chun-Wai off.

Chun-Wai paused. "No one's asking you to. You're just the one-night stand."

"No, I mean, uh, three's a crowd, you know?"

The man laughed. "He's away on travel. And don't worry, this is all aboveboard. We share everything."

Alan relaxed back into a smile. "Good to know," he said, allowing himself to be led farther inside, toward a sitting area with a panoramic view of Kowloon.

"Is that Leslie Cheung?" Alan asked as he was lowered onto a couch. A framed album cover hung on the wall. The gleam of the glass made it hard to read the title, and the scrawled black signature was illegible, but the singer's puppy-dog eyes were too famous to mistake, even if his hair in the photo was longer and thicker than it had been later in his career.

"Yes."

"Where did you get his autograph?" Alan asked.

"It was my lover's," Chun-Wai answered quietly. "When he was a boy, Leslie bought a home down the street in Taikoo Shing. He was too nervous to ask for Leslie's signature himself, so he convinced his sister to do it for him. It was his most valued possession. He said it gave him strength when he was loneliest and most discouraged."

Alan didn't ask how the object had come into Chun-Wai's possession. Or why it was hung so near the balcony.

Chun-Wai dispelled the brief silence. "I can put some music on, if you like."

"It's all right," Alan said. "I'll have a glass of wine, though."

And they shared another drink, Chun-Wai pouring the Bordeaux and Alan administering the flunitrazepam when they kissed each other between sips. And then Chun-Wai was out, and Alan pressed Chun-Wai's thumb to his phone, unlocking it.

He pulled a hard drive from his bag, plugged it into a wall socket, and connected it to the phone. A window appeared on the phone's screen. "Do you trust this device?" it asked. Alan granted permission. When he'd finished cloning the phone's contents, disconnected the drive, and put Chun-Wai, still fully clothed, in bed, he left a note thanking him for a wonderful time and listing a number to reach him at.

Alan left the apartment, taking nothing. The number was for a free, disposable Internet phone account that Alan would never check.

DURING HIS outing, Alan had left his computer sifting the Nathan Road data, running a series of automated Internet searches matching the stolen customer data to publicly available information. The Internet connection came courtesy of a neighbor's Wi-Fi network that Alan had spent a day brute-forcing open. The script plugged its search terms into a series of major social media and networking sites, particularly PartyYǒu. The combined harvest of data was procedurally incorporated into the customer database Alan had created, rounding out the profiles with variously extensive personal and professional details. Gender, as well as age or date of birth, were indispensable. Critically, the scripts also copied image files: the customers' photos, downloaded from an assortment of online profiles and web pages.

The next morning, after returning to his bolt-hole and sleeping off the alcohol, Alan woke to find the search completed and ready for him to select a target. A final script filtered the candidates on an array of attributes. He needed a male who looked to be in his age range. The right person also needed a Shanghai address but with regular trips to Hong Kong and some liberal spending habits, as signaled by the transaction records.

But a computer script could only use these criteria to remove the most obviously unqualified targets. Alan also had some fuzzier requirements necessitating his own visual inspection. Alan decided that the ideal candidate, besides looking as much like him as possible, needed to be Rich 2G, a spoiled playboy with ready and regular access to sizable liquid assets, but not necessarily with the wisdom to always spend it wisely. And it had to be someone with government credentials. Fortunately, material wealth and political connections were usually intertwined.

With the list reduced to a fraction of its original length, Alan randomized the order and proceeded to tab through each of the profiles in turn, skimming their information and contemplating their photographs. With each inspection, he either removed the candidate or saved him for a later round of consideration.

The prospects were disheartening. None of the first hundred looked remotely like him. But Alan needed one person, only one. In a just world, he thought, finding this person should be easy, given the amount of data he'd collected and the work it had required of him. But even finding one person might be too long a shot. All this hard work might be wasted.

It wasn't. The moment Alan tabbed to the profile of Kim Kyung-Min, he knew he'd found a winner.

The photo staring back at Alan looked like it was shot for a professional ID. Per the search data, the young man in the image was a scion of an established Jiangxi political family. But he bore such a resemblance to Alan that he had to wonder if he'd discovered a distant cousin. Kim's expression in the photo was serious and analytical. Though his haircut was shorter and tidier than Alan's, and he wore glasses and a button-down shirt and tie, the delicate features were in such a similar mold to Alan's that they provoked a frisson of narcissistic attraction.

Per Kim's date of birth, he was a little on the old side, but apparent age was what mattered. Kim's youthful looks were passable enough for Alan's own, particularly to anyone unfamiliar with either of them.

None of the stolen information for Kim had come from social media. All of it looked to be from professional profiles, academic sites, and scientific news sources. Doctor Kim, it turned out, was a prolific researcher with a respectable list of publications.

In a lucky coincidence, Kim had majored in parapsych at Tsinghua University, and with a neurological focus. Alan, by virtue of his provenance, was intimately familiar with the field of parapsychology. Not enough to give a talk at a conference, but enough that he could bluff his way to the satisfaction of any layman and no few graduate students.

And Doctor Kim had connections. An examination of his postal addresses indicated a residence in Shanghai, but his academic record showed a post-doc at HKU succeeded by continuing collaborations with local researchers. Lots of work with multiple concurrent organizations, but his current employer was the Science Ministry. His father had been a ranking science minister. His mother had been one of the last of the sea turtles—a tenured professor, she'd done most of her graduate work at an American Ivy League, back when that still meant something.

There were no scandals or gossip attached to his name. Kim Kyung-Min was apparently not the class of *fuerdai* who'd set fire to a stack of hundred-nuyan notes just for a laugh. A nerd, not the playboy Alan had hoped for, but at least he possessed wealth to suit his pedigree. The stolen transaction records indicated Kim had discriminating tastes, shopping from high-end retail. Not one for fine dining, though. There were no restaurant bills but lots of supplements and liquid meals purchased from supermarkets and other vendors. He was some kind of health nut. And he came to town quite often, judging from these sales records.

It was fate. It had to be.

When was his next visit?

Alan searched further online. Unfortunately, beyond what he'd already collected, there was precious little. Though Doctor Kim's professional footprint was wide, his personal digital shadow was so small as to be untraceable. He didn't appear to have a life, or any interests, outside of his work, and his research appeared too esoteric to ever intrude into mainstream media outlets. However, other researchers often cited him.

Poking around the university's website, he found Kim's professional information listed on the state key laboratory pages for the brain and cognitive sciences and for emerging infectious diseases. Evidently Kim had collaborated on some neurological infectious disease work. One of the state key lab pages listed a guest lecture to be delivered at the science park in Ma Liu Shui. The lecture was this weekend.

Alan opened his harvest of stolen data and mapped out the businesses that Kim had patronized. They were on a part of the tourist district with a half-dozen luxury hotels on it. Donning a headset and logging into another disposable phone number, Alan started to call the hotels one by one.

"This is Kim Kyung-Min. I just wanted to call and make certain you had my reservation on your records for this weekend."

"Do you have the credit card the reservation was made with?"

Alan had a few such numbers from his dragnet. He read one of them into the phone.

"I'm sorry, sir, we're not showing a reservation with that number."

"I may have used a different card," Alan said, and read another number. When the options were exhausted, he apologized. "I must have made the reservation somewhere else."

On the third such hotel, the man at the other end of the line came back with "Yes, sir, Doctor Kim. We have you arriving this Friday and departing the following day."

"Thank you."

Alan removed the headset and realized he was grinning. He knew these kinds of escapades were dangerous, but after a month of lying low, goddamn if he wasn't enjoying himself again.

He stood, stretched, and walked to the window. The shadowy bulk of Mount Johnston looked like a titanic anvil half-submerged in the channel. Beyond it, on the horizon, a thunderhead rumbled.

Chapter 5
Tomorrow's Parties

ARISSA MET Card during a storm at the center of the world, the known world that had so far been mapped, on a small tropical island surrounded by equatorial sea.

They rendezvoused on a knoll overlooking a gentle slope down to the shoreline and beheld each other: a paladin and an enchantress, dispatched here by the Azure Archmage on urgent instructions whispered from within cerulean robes. Their only other company was a golem, massive and sturdy as a column, its clay flesh glistening in the rain and a grave expression permanently carved into its flat face. The golem stood idly by, awaiting instruction. At the coastline, at the end of a short dock, a small, bobbing wooden clipper also awaited them, a stylized Oroboros painted around the hull, the snake swallowing its tail astern.

This being their first meeting, the two considered each other.

The paladin's armor was sun-forged from steel mined by cherubim from the peaks of the Heavenly Mountains, inlaid with prayers written in flowing orichalcum. His panoply reflected the light of dawn even in the deepest night, and his armaments were relics, fossilized into diamond, of the dragon that had lain the world, the shield carved from a scale and the sword from a fang.

The enchantress was covered from neck to wrists to ankles in a slender robe of starmoth silk that shimmered an iridescent crimson to human eyes, though sages knew its true color could deflect the invisible wavelengths of malevolent spellworkings. For more mundane threats, she wore a breastplate, gauntlets, and boots of leather, worked from the hide of a Nemean lion she'd personally slain. The breastplate and gauntlets were clasped in place over her robe, and a circlet of flowers adorned her head, woven with power in the secret language of the wise women of Färthlorn. She carried a magic staff of petrified wood from the original forest.

"I think we're ready!" Arissa piped over the team chat channel.

"Yup," said Card. "Let's do this thing."

That coffee date was still set for the weekend, but Card was happy to meet online first, just to get to know each other. When Arissa asked which quests he was working on, he said he was on the last leg of the Azure Archmage. Arissa sent a message to someone at the Safety Ministry, who pulled strings with PartyYŏu, and just like that her character, already created to round out her legend, was at about the same point in that quest line. So why not finish it together?

Arissa, Card, and the golem boarded the wyrm-running clipper for a voyage through the infamous Dragon's Belt, the equatorial analog separating Rath's northern and southern reaches.

The clipper sailed through a sea with no land anywhere in view, stopping at predetermined waypoints to give schools of sea serpents the opportunity to swarm the vessel in staggered waves of attack. All the while, the sea churned dramatically, and the sky swirled gray with storm clouds.

The end of this quest line was a notorious slog, really a sadistically prolonged NPC escort mission. The mystically imbued golem was a walking MacGuffin, his only function to survive till he reached his destination. But the golem made a decent ally in his own right. He had stratospheric hit points and damage resistance, was a fast jogger when he got going, and packed a wallop on those occasions he could lay a fist on an enemy. But the lumbering brute had nil evasion and could be quickly overwhelmed if left unattended. It helped that the spatial parameters of the instanced ship's deck made it easy to keep an eye on the golem.

With just two players in their party, they had to be optimally specced for their roles. Card's paladin dealt damage out and soaked it up in good proportion, shrugging off the debilitating status effects of the serpents' venomous bites and dispensing heals when necessary. Arissa's enchantress meanwhile played support, buffing her allies, debuffing the serpents, and handling crowd control, all while dealing moderate damage of her own. The steady rhythms of combat allowed a comfortable level of small talk without any lulls in the conversation. Card definitely liked her, and Arissa was growing steadily more concerned that she liked him back. But this was, after all, barely even a first date, and the conversation meandered at a superficial, introductory level, giving wide berth to such delicate matters as sex, religion, or revolutionary dissident politics.

Given the context, it was inevitable they'd talk about seafood.

"I love whales," Card said, dispatching a malformed, rampaging narwhal. "They're delicious."

Arissa feigned shock. "You're kidding!"

"Nope. Tried some in Okinawa. Good for your eyesight. Like carrots."

He was, of course, kidding. Arissa didn't have to read his mind to know this. She'd read his file.

"I'll have you know I once adopted a whale," she said with a hint of accusation.

"You did? When?"

"I was ten."

"Your parents let you have a whale when you were ten?"

"My family gave him to me as a gift. Okay, all I got was a picture and a certificate in exchange for a donation they made. His name was Orko," she lied.

"Oh," Card said, sounding disappointed. "I guess that's kind of exciting."

"Not really. It was a picture of his tail."

"Well, I'm glad you did what you could to make our oceans a better place."

"We all need to do our part," Arissa agreed.

"Yup."

"Do you do any volunteering?" Arissa asked, already knowing the answer.

"Yeah…." Card said, his voice trailing off.

"Yeah?"

"I mentor homeless kids. Mostly gay kids who ran away from home or got tossed out by their families. It can get pretty rough for them, to be honest."

Arissa had nothing to say after this. Fortunately, a massive leviathan chose that moment to emerge from the ocean and swallow the boat whole, passengers and all.

This was a scripted event, the player characters rendered immobile as the camera cut to a long-distance shot of the clipper being swept into the gaping maw of the titanic monster. When control was returned to the players, they found themselves, like Jonah or Pinocchio, in the belly of the beast. Another instanced dungeon followed, with the two of them escorting the golem through the various channels of the leviathan's body (structured conveniently like hallways, albeit with ribcage-like frames and pulsing walls of pink flesh) while fending off oversized, corrupted antibodies or monstrous, invasive parasites.

"Hold on a second," Arissa said. "I need to organize."

"Sure," said Card. He activated an emote that left his paladin idly thumbing through a book while Arissa maneuvered items inside her inventory, deciding what to trash and what to sell later.

Her loot did need sorting, but it was also an opportunity to bait Card. "Sorry," she said when she finished. "That could have waited. Part of my mind still thinks '90 percent' means 'almost full' instead of 'three quarters.'"

"You mean it doesn't?" Card laughed. Plunging forward and rounding a corner, he engaged a mob of oversized tapeworms loitering there.

"It definitely feels unnatural," Arissa confessed, charging into danger after him, "even growing up with dozenal."

"Yeah, counting on your phalanges isn't as intuitive to a kid as just using fingers."

"I mean, I understand how it's better on the merits," Arissa replied. "And it's not impossible to change these kinds of basic systems by fiat."

"Yeah…." Card said, trailing off again.

Arissa had led him right up to the edge of explicit critique, but pushing things any further, especially on the Internet, would only alarm him, so Arissa provided an out. "Maybe polydactyly is the future of the human race."

"Yeah, maybe parents should stop getting kids' extra fingers removed."

And they talked about genetics for a while: which of them could and couldn't roll up their tongues or lift their eyebrows independently. Their grousing about government social engineering had been trivial but was the first chink in the armor of good citizenry, the first step down the slippery slope of disloyalty, disobedience, dissidence. But this was just a first date, and Arissa saw no need to rush things.

They arrived with the golem at their destination, the central chamber of the leviathan's heart, where a giant crystal, a legendary phylactery stone, hung suspended in a web of thick cardiac muscle tissue. Now the golem spent several minutes mystically communing with the stone, the magic connection represented by flowing beams of light, while the players defended it from escalating waves of enemy attack.

The battle culminated in the phylactery stone being exorcised of the corrupting spirit possessing it: a beholder-like demon resembling a single large floating eye hovering inside a cloud of smaller eyestalks. One pitched boss fight later, they were finally done. A cut scene showed the leviathan resting its chin on a seaside cliff, allowing the heroes to emerge from its open mouth unscathed. The leviathan affected an immense grateful bow of its serpentine neck, then vanished into the calmed ocean.

Then Arissa and Card were teleported back to the port city of Aroma, a famed waypoint for the perfume trade, and visited the Watchtower of Water, where the Azure Archmage dutifully rewarded them for their work and narrated a brief epilogue. The leviathan had been freed from its madness, coastal villages and seafaring vessels no longer had to fear its rampages, and the seas were finally at peace (until, of course, the next time someone started this quest line).

It was a typically anticlimactic finale, to be followed not by a night of carousing in a tavern but by the MMO equivalent of paperwork: leveling up, crafting items, and auctioning off loot. The nearest major city with a training guild, forge, and auction house was five minutes away, as the eagle flew. So they hired a giant eagle from the local rookery, climbed into the small howdah on its back, and soared inland.

Arissa excused herself and took a snack break. When she returned from the kitchen, Card was whistling.

"I'm back," she said.

"Welcome back."

"What was that tune?" she asked.

"It's the music that plays during eagle travel. You don't hear it?"

"I have music turned off in my settings."

"It's pretty good. People don't know most of the game's soundtrack is based on Broadway musicals. I think the game composer likes his show tunes."

"Oh yeah?"

"Yeah, we used to sing this one a lot in choir. Not in official performances. Backstage, for fun."

"You sing?"

"I do."

And then he did.

Arissa had never heard this song. Without context, her English wasn't so good she could parse out the significance of all the lyrics.

But, goodness, that voice. She'd read in Card's file that he sang, but there'd been no indication that he sang beautifully. His voice was soft, and suddenly almost a falsetto, and the melody gentle, full of tenuous longing so fragile it seemed nearly to break beneath the weight of the air. And then, as the melody gave way to the release of the bridge, it did shatter, but by bursting upward rather than buckling under, scraping against the sky. Arissa felt herself transported, borne heavenward. All the while, the hills and rivers and forests of Rath rolled by beneath their eagle. And then both the song and their mount began shedding altitude, the song wrenching one more measure of hope and despair from its melody as the eagle alighted atop the roof of the rookery tower overlooking the city, and Arissa realized she was gripping the edge of her desk to keep her hands from trembling.

She'd said nothing since Card began singing. She needed a minute to recover. The usual RPG busywork at this point felt like an impropriety.

She opened the chat channel. "What now?" she asked.

"Auction house first?" Card asked.

Arissa made no response, leaving an awkwardly long pause of several seconds.

"But I wouldn't mind getting some fresh air," he suggested.

THE COLORFUL nightlife glow of the Wan Chai neighborhood was offset by the crowds flowing down its streets and between its clubs. Most were dressed in the black-and-silver style that had originated as a do-it-yourself countercultural signifier before fashion designers had appropriated it and movie stars had mainstreamed it. The basement bar where Arissa met Card was closer aligned to this motif than its exterior, everything painted matte black and a grid of exposed pipes and wiring crisscrossing the ceiling. The bar's signature drink, a liquid nitrogen cocktail, glowed under the bar's black lights. White spotlights swept across the floor with the tempo of the current song, the light glinting off the patrons. Arissa's and Card's seats were a pair of squat black cylinders, their table a larger black cube. They had to lean in to be heard over the music. Pivoting from their conversation about genetics, they were discussing family, and Arissa decided to risk some honesty.

"I was the firstborn," she said, "and my parents died when I was still pretty young."

"I'm sorry to hear that," Card answered.

"Thank you. It was a long time ago, but I still miss them."

"Both at the same time?"

"They were traveling out of the country. There was a terrorist attack."

His face paled. "How awful."

"I'm lucky I had a pretty large extended family to step in for them. And it's not the sort of thing that happens anymore in this part of the world, thank goodness."

"Why do you think that is?" he asked.

Arissa paused. The answer, she knew—the answer drummed into her—was state surveillance programs and proactive intelligence gathering operations, including by psychics.

But she offered a feeble shrug instead. "I don't know."

He nodded. "I think a lot of people would say it's all the government psychics, which, let's face it, basically amounts to all active psychics, period. But our actual likelihood of dying in a terrorist attack is already so low I'm not sure it justifies telepaths reading your mind whenever they feel like it."

Arissa nodded feigned agreement, and he finally let his guard down, unwinding his rhetoric at the length she'd have predicted from his profile. Card Lin was precisely the kind of person who, when assembled together with other dissatisfied, well-meaning, overly thoughtful young people, provided both the soil and the seed for destabilizing ideological movements. Hence Arissa's current assignment. Card had never publicly advocated revolution, but that didn't matter. He only had to think it—or cause others to think it. These things were no longer nipped in the bud. They were nipped in the root.

Then why did Arissa feel a sudden urge to rescue this handsome idiot from his own wagging tongue?

"So just what the heck is avant-garde programming?" she asked, changing the topic.

Card laughed. "Let me show you." He wrote the URL for one of his online galleries on a cocktail napkin. She opened the address on her phone and scrolled through the page, down a list of items with names like "An Imagined Resemblance," "Lamp and Mirror," "The Vernal Nemesis (No. 2)." But where she would've expected photos of watercolors or sculptures or maybe some mixed media, there were just links to downloadable programs.

"I'm not installing anything on my phone," she warned him.

"They wouldn't do anything if you did. They're custom decryption programs, but they're self-encrypted, so they can never be opened."

"Well, I guess that's interesting," she said. "Why?"

"It's art. Its only purpose is to elicit a reaction."

Arissa tried to imagine the experience of something being so inescapably locked away. "That sounds a little sad," she finally said.

Card chuckled. "People used to anthropomorphize data a lot that way. 'Information wants to be free.' That's seriously what they would say. But that's just an invitation to get your mind read, like saying your memories, thoughts, emotions *want* to be stolen. Information doesn't want anything."

"Desire's an emotion," Arissa offered.

"Sure," Card said, "but it doesn't actually have desires. We want things as a function of having desires. See the difference?"

"And what do you desire?" Arissa asked, meeting his eyes.

Card coughed, blushed, and said he wanted to dance.

Besides being an amazing singer, Card had the audacity to be a great dancer as well. Arissa had to employ some telepathic legerdemain just to keep up with him. She noted the half-dozen best female dancers out on the floor and read their knowledge of how to dance into her own mind, incorporating it into her skill set.

This was implicit information instead of semantic, integrated into her own procedural memory completely on the fly, and this kind of improvised metacognitive reprogramming wasn't easy even for her. She needed a few minutes of actual dancing to get all the new skills working in concert with one another, and they wouldn't last long without practice.

But in the short term, she was the best dancer on the floor, and Card took notice.

ARISSA AND Card, their eardrums still thrumming, were laughing as they flowed into the street at two in the morning.

"That was pretty awesome!" Card said, shouting to be heard over the ringing of their ears.

"Yeah!" Arissa agreed.

"I've never seen anyone pick up moves that way before," Card said. "It's like you have photographic reflexes."

Arissa turned on him.

Card looked instantly ashamed. "I'm sorry! I'm not calling you out or anything. I do the same thing. Imitate other folks on the floor. I'm not judging you."

Arissa regained her composure, even forced a smile. But her blood had turned cold.

How had he noticed? Maybe he was just perceptive, or he'd made a lucky guess. But the least likely possibility was also so much more dangerous that Arissa had to inquire further.

Reaching for the right euphemism, she asked, "Have you always been so good at reading people?"

"What do you mean?" Card laughed. "Isn't intuition more a woman's thing?"

Not an answer, but Arissa didn't need one. The question itself had been sufficient to bring the relevant memories near enough to activation threshold for her to pick them up by skimming the surface of Card's preconscious. What she found didn't reassure her. Too many incidents of knowing who was knocking even before answering the door, or doing well on an exam he hadn't adequately prepared for, or winning too often at card games, or correctly sussing out when someone was lying to him.

She said it was time to end the date.

"Oh, okay," he said, sounding disappointed but unsurprised, given the late hour. "When can we do this again?"

"Online any time, but I've got a lot of work this week. Are we still set for the weekend?"

He confirmed that they were, and they parted ways, Arissa taking a taxi home.

Her approach to Card Lin would have to change in light of these new suspicions. She was likely worried over nothing. Even someone with a zero psi quotient, or someone guessing at random, occasionally performed well on a Zener card test to a statistically significant degree. Hell, the base rate of actual psychics was so low, more people passed initial screening through sheer chance than authentic talent. Probably she'd picked up on nothing more than a lifetime of dumb luck and good guesses.

That was what she hoped, anyway. Anything more would make this a case for Countermind, and Arissa didn't wish their attentions on anyone.

CHAPTER 6
GENEALOGY

"QUENTIN IZAKI," Director Zheng repeated from behind his desk.

He moved some items around on the touch screen built into his desk's surface.

"The scientist?" Zheng asked, apparently having retrieved a relevant record, though Smith couldn't see it from where he sat.

"Yes, sir," Smith confirmed.

"You think there may be a connection to this renegade psychic."

"Yes, sir, likely familial."

"And how do you intend to pursue this lead?"

"I'd like clearance for a remote electronic intrusion into North American computer systems to identify potential information about Izaki that may not already be in our databases. And I'd like clearance for another Senex search with the same aim."

"And if any such information isn't forthcoming?"

"I'd like to travel to North America to see what I can find on the ground."

Zheng tapped a finger a few times, either considering Smith's words or cycling through GUI windows. "The outlaw in question seems to have confined himself to breaking and entering, petty theft, and other misdemeanors," Zheng said. "More severe infractions have only occurred upon encounters with law enforcement and government agents. While I approve of your determination to bring him to justice, just how high a priority are you prepared to make his capture?"

"Not so high a priority that it interferes with my other assignments, sir."

"Very well. Clearance granted."

THE DEFENSE Ministry's technical reconnaissance department had been larger in times past, when global computer networks had merited the funding. With the gradual collapse of foreign information technology infrastructures, the department's work now resembled penetration less than excavation. Espionage as cyber-archaeology. Smith didn't have high hopes for them, but he dutifully submitted a request for foreign data on Quentin Izaki's family.

Then he turned to Senex. This involved an access request to a department within the Safety Ministry. The request, carrying the imprimatur of the Executive Director of Counterpsychic Affairs, was promptly approved, and Smith was directed to a secure website cluttered with a search bar, various text warnings, instructional links, advanced options, and a reminder that all use of Senex was subject to monitoring by the Safety Ministry. Smith entered a search for mentions of Quentin Izaki appearing adjacent to any mentions of a son or family. He restricted the search to a range of a few years and to North American regions.

As Smith understood it—and he didn't understand it terribly well—Senex was functionally identical to a standard commercial search engine, albeit with fewer practical limitations on its effectiveness. If all information was state property, then it naturally behooved the state to safeguard its assets by collecting and indexing all the world's information. "Senex" was an engineering team's in-house nickname that had simply stuck when the program went live, launched by the New Government as part of a next-evolution Golden Shield, with information not only collected and centrally collated, but with the process almost entirely automated. The program itself was a massive web-crawling data miner housed in several secured data centers across the continent, collectively comprising millions of networked servers stuffed with hybrid military-grade digital-analog processors of specialized design. Access to Senex was highly restricted. Any efforts to deliberately secure Internet-connected data (or any data, really) from Senex were, of course, illegal.

It helped that Senex's operating system had at its disposal a large array of data decryption, speech recognition, and language translation protocols. Unless Smith specified otherwise, Senex would search for his terms in any known language, and even in digital videos, audio recordings, and phone voice mails, so long as they'd ever been found online. Conceptually, little separated Senex from the Defense Ministry's technical reconnaissance department. Senex was simply faster, more systematic, and had instant access to a massive storehouse of indexed information collected over many years.

The search took .82 seconds. Senex disgorged an archive of e-mails and instant messages sourced to a little town called Eatonville, in the westernmost region of what had once been Washington State. The communications concerned a local recluse by the name of Quentin Izaki who would, every few days, come down from his private mountain home and into town for shopping and light socializing. Reputed by the locals to be a retired scientist, and a friendly enough person, Quentin was occasionally seen in later years in the company of his son, a surly, withdrawn-looking teen. The son didn't know anyone in town or attend school there. He was believed to be homeschooled. When he was seen by locals, he never spoke to anyone, just sat in the passenger seat of his father's gray pickup truck and glared at passersby while his father ran errands. The local police, per their internal communications, suspected that he might be responsible for some small unexplained thefts. Those suspicions were never enough to justify the trouble of questioning or otherwise investigating the young man. But they were enough for Smith.

THE NEXT flight to Seattle was through Bangkok. Smith spent the layover reserving a car and an armed driver, then placing calls to local law enforcement so he'd know whom to browbeat when he arrived. When he landed, the car was waiting for him at the airport.

The drive to Eatonville took two hours, mostly due to the poor condition of the highways. Smith directed his driver to park outside the mountain town's dilapidated city hall, where he presented his identification and introduced himself to the middle-aged, overweight deputy behind the desk as Agent Jack Smith of the Security Ministry. Smith produced a printout of the top image from the facial recognition search. "Do you recognize this person?" he asked, without specifying whether it was the father or son.

The deputy peered down a pair of cracked bifocals. "Is that the Izaki boy?"

"You recognize him?"

"I've never even seen him, but I've been told he's his father's spitting image. I guess it's so. Whatever happened to him?"

"That's what I'm trying to determine. What do you remember about the circumstances of his disappearance?"

"The 'circumstances of his disappearance'?"

"There were reports of a fire," Smith prodded.

"Well, yes, the house burned down. We went up the next morning to check it out, but it was still too hot to enter safely." The deputy leaned back in his chair, recollecting. "That fire burned *hot*. It was still so warm we had to wait another day to go in. Everything metal was just about melted, and everything not metal was ash. We barely found enough human remains to identify the father, and only because those were on the lawn. No idea if the son died there or not."

"Was there any further investigation into the incident?"

"Can't say that there was. Sorry."

Smith didn't have to ask why not. The local law's dearth of resources and manpower was self-evident.

"Odd that you'd come this far for him," the deputy continued. "The boy do something?"

"That was nearly my next question to you," Smith said. "While they lived here, did the son ever break any laws you know of?"

"No. I think Janet floated the boy's name a couple of times when we were short on suspects for some burglaries but more on account of his bad manners than any actual evidence. Kid looked at you like he had a grudge, but his father was nice as pie."

"Floated his name? I thought no one had ever spoken to him."

"No one did. Father spoke about him plenty, though. And pretty warmly, I'll add. It's the main reason we never seriously considered him as a criminal suspect, out of consideration for his dad."

"Did the father ever mention his son's name?"

The deputy needed a moment to recollect.

"Alan," he said with a nod.

THE DEPUTY gave Smith directions to the site of the fire. Smith tipped him generously for the information and directed his driver east out of town, up a two-lane highway bordered on both sides by forest, and in such a state of cracked, potholed disrepair that the functional width at any given point only averaged out to about a single lane. What scant traffic they encountered mostly comprised rusted pickups, overburdened flatbeds, mounted horses, and the occasional tractor, and it was usually necessary for one traveler to pull half-over onto the dusty shoulder to allow the other to pass.

The scenery grew more mountainous. The turnoff toward Quentin Izaki's home was an unpaved road so steep and uneven the car couldn't traverse it without bending an axle, and it was necessary for the driver to wait at the end of the road while Smith got out and walked up into the woods. The deputy had said Izaki's property would be marked by a battered aluminum mailbox atop a green-painted wooden post. It was a long road there, and Smith only spotted a few homes on it, these hidden well behind dense thickets and separated from one another by long wooded stretches. At the top of the road, his shoes coated with dust, Smith finally found the mailbox. Beyond it lay a thin dirt road ascending to a large grass clearing that, at first glance, appeared to contain nothing whatsoever.

Smith had to climb a few steps higher before he saw the clearing in full. About two hectares in size, surrounded by forest, and centered on one very large hole in the ground. The hole was irregularly shaped. Its interior surface, quite angular and about five meters deep, gleamed metallic where it wasn't caked over with dirt. The pit contained various misshapen, filthy lumps of diverse size, their forms suggesting machinery but now reduced to slag.

It was a laboratory, the molten remains of Quentin Izaki's private workshop. There'd once been a house above it, and now Smith could see the original signs of that house: shards of wood, piles of brick, and a few pipe segments projecting from the tall, unkempt grass overrunning the lawn.

Calling this a mere fire was an understatement. To melt steel this way required temperatures above a thousand degrees Celsius. This was a firebombing, likely with white phosphorus or thermite, done to ensure no one would learn anything about whatever work Quentin Izaki had done here. Any electronics or machinery would be inoperable, any biological samples irrecoverable, any digital or physical records destroyed. The fact that Izaki's body had been found at all meant he likely hadn't been in the basement when the bomb went off.

Smith searched the property in the most systematic manner he could while making the most of the remaining daylight, crossing it longitudinally, shining a compact flashlight into the grass, peering into the woods when he reached the perimeter, walking a few meters perpendicular, and crossing again. He expected to find nothing and found exactly that. Besides the scattered, rotted debris of the house, the clearing contained the collapsed remains of a shed, but everything useful—including, Smith noted, Izaki's pickup truck—had long since been claimed by scavengers.

Day tipped into evening, and Smith had only covered half the property when he saw a man emerge from the woods with a shotgun. After a moment's alarm, Smith noted that the barrel was pointed at the ground, and the stranger held the weapon by the stock, nowhere near the trigger. The man's gait and manner were unthreatening, even amiable. He was dressed in brown camouflage with a bright orange vest overlaying it—a hunter. He'd plainly seen Smith and was walking in his direction, though not with any particular urgency. But Smith remained on guard, watching the man carefully and without retreating. If Smith needed to defend himself, it would have to be at the closest possible distance.

"Hello there," the stranger called. "You don't mind my trespassing, do you? I can head back."

"Not at all," Smith said, not missing a beat.

The stranger continued his approach until he was just outside what Smith would have considered normal conversational distance. "Sorry," the hunter said. "I was heading home when I saw you looking around, and I didn't know how else to make your acquaintance."

"That's all right."

"I assume you're family?"

Smith was in fact half Han Chinese, but a little outgroup homogeneity could make for an effective disguise. "Distantly," he said, "but yes."

"You seem surprised not to have found anyone here."

"Distraught."

"Well, I'm sorry to say they haven't lived here for years now. As you can plainly see, their home suffered a pretty terrible fire, and I'm afraid they both perished. It had us terrified when it happened," the hunter added sympathetically and gestured down the road. "We could hear the explosion from our house."

"Both? I was told that only remains of Quentin had been found. Did his son die too?"

"So I assumed. It was quite the blaze."

"The rest of the family was hoping he might still be alive, so I've come to find out where he could be," Smith said. *And then arrest him.*

The afterthought came completely unbidden. Smith, recognizing the intrusion, automatically conjured a sequence of lies before any more information could be read from his mind. *Alan Izaki is wanted for capital crimes including conspiracy to undermine the New Government's authority and the attempted assassination of state officials, terrorist attacks, and civilian murders, and anyone providing information about his background or whereabouts will be rewarded so handsomely that he'll spend the rest of his life in luxury.*

The stranger's manner underwent a subtle but distinct change. His posture grew more alert, and he made more sustained eye contact. He gave Smith a warm smile. "Well, I can't say I knew the son, but I spoke to the father on a few occasions. I might be able to help you out."

"Please. Any information you could provide would be *deeply* appreciated. Do you know what Quentin was working on here?"

"Can't say I ever understood it. We'd chat about it occasionally, neighbor to neighbor, but it was always too technical for me to make heads or tails of."

Smith, mental defenses already erected, had to suspect this claim. All the information he'd gathered so far indicated that Izaki had remained canny about his work. If this neighbor had learned anything of that work, it had probably been from his mind rather than his lips. But finding a psychic here was a one-in-a-million lucky break, and Smith was not one to dismiss useful intelligence over objections to how it had been gathered.

"What field did it sound like he worked in?" Smith asked. "Computers? Biology?"

"Maybe. Really, half the time it sounded like pure math."

It very well could have been. Likely Izaki had been able to think far too abstractly for the average person to comprehend, psychic or otherwise.

"That's too bad," Smith said, and pointedly added, "I'd hoped to learn something more valuable."

The hunter visibly struggled with the question of how much more to say, perhaps weighing the risks of explaining how he'd learned it. Smith applied a little pressure, turning away as if to leave, and the neighbor spoke up.

"He did mention one thing, once, when he was talking a little more down to earth."

Smith stopped, turned back. "Oh?"

"He sort of just mentioned it in passing. Whatever it was he spent so much time working on, he thought it would be pretty terrible for anyone in authority to get ahold of it."

"I see," said Smith. "And you have no idea what, specifically, this project was?"

"Not in any meaningful way, no, sir."

"All right. Well, thank you for your help."

"My pleasure."

"Before I go, do you mind if I get your contact information? If we find Alan, my family will want to express its gratitude."

"Oh, certainly," the stranger said, and shared his name and address.

The conversation ended, Smith hiked his way down the dirt road to the car, using his flashlight to illuminate his way in the deepening twilight. After a long bumpy ride back into the city, he checked into a hotel room and opened a secure satellite connection to headquarters through his computer.

Smith verified that the hunter's name and address did correspond to an actual person, finding some old photos online to confirm the match, but with no record in Countermind's register of psychics. He reported the existence of the unregistered telepath and his unlicensed psychic activity, then booked a flight home.

SMITH SPENT the return flight preoccupied. In all the records, e-mails, and messages he'd seen, all the interviews, there'd been no mention of Quentin having a spouse, or any sort of love life, or even dating at all after college. Moreover, Smith found no mention of Quentin having a son, or any children, before arriving in Seattle. The locals had described Alan Izaki as a teenager but made no mention of the boy existing at any earlier age. Alan seemed to have appeared a fully formed young man completely *ex nihilo*.

When he returned to his office, Smith reached out to his usual Security Ministry analyst and solicited a recommendation for a biomedical expert specializing in paraneurology, one with sufficiently high security clearances for a consultation related to an ongoing

Countermind investigation. Smith was given the contact information for one Doctor Kim Kyung-Min at the Science Ministry. He checked Kim's credentials, was duly impressed, dialed the number, and left a message. He heard back within an hour.

"Thank you for responding to my call, Doctor," said Smith.

"You're welcome," Kim said, just a bit flatly.

"Doctor Kim, how familiar are you with the work of Quentin Izaki?"

"Not intimately. Only by his popular reputation. My background is in the biological sciences." A short pause. "I'm actually rather surprised that you would ask me about him at all. Others are much more qualified than I to discuss his work."

Smith flipped through some of his notes. "Records show him with degrees in biological engineering and related fields."

"That may well be the case, but consider the man we're discussing. Quentin Izaki earning a credential in a field is analogous to you or I auditing an undergraduate course. It confers an increased familiarity and possibly involves an original contribution or two, but it doesn't qualify as specialization. Even a polymath like Izaki can't dominate every field he encounters."

"Doctor Kim," Smith began, "I have a bizarre theory in need of refuting, and I need an expert to point out the holes I'm not qualified to see."

"All right."

"This conversation is, of course, classified."

"Yes, I know." A hint of impatience.

"I suspect Quentin Izaki created a clone of himself and genetically engineered said clone to possess psychic abilities."

Perhaps it was because Smith had presented this idea in a skeptical frame, or Kim heard a lot of dumb things while consulting with laypeople, but the scientist was at least willing to entertain the thought. "Can I assume this theoretical psychic clone has survived to an advanced enough age that it has merited the attention of Counterpsychic Affairs?"

"Early adulthood."

"Well, then, I see three significant problems with your theory, each of which alone would be enough for us to confidently reject it, and which, taken together, make it vanishingly improbable. First, as

I've just explained, Doctor Izaki's expertise was not in the biological or biomedical fields. Second, the creation of a clone, particularly a *viable* clone, is infamously difficult, even for those with the necessary expertise. Third, the genetic bases of psychic ability—or any human cognitive faculty, for that matter—remain sufficiently mysterious that an attempt to 'genetically engineer' such an ability would be extremely challenging. Again, even for an expert."

"Okay. So that theory can be safely dismissed."

"Very."

"I won't disagree," Smith said. "I know you're probably correct. But for the sake of helping me understand why it's impossible, can you tell me what conditions would have to exist in order for those three problems to be eliminated?"

"All right," began Kim. "Beginning with the first, it would mean Doctor Izaki, while being quite productive in his principal area of research, also found the time to develop world-class expertise in the biological sciences, fields of study outside his wheelhouse. It would mean he developed this biomedical expertise without contributing to that field of research in which he was secretly participating, working in such an occult manner that his advances were unknown to other members of the research community such as myself, while simultaneously far outpacing the advances being made by the rest of us. I won't try to profile anyone," Kim added. "I'll leave that to forensic experts such as yourself—but this is the stereotype of the reclusive genius taken to such an extreme that it bears closer resemblance to a mad scientist."

"He blew up his lab," Smith said.

"Well, that sounds like a plausibly American means of guarding one's intellectual property, but the fact that he had secrets doesn't mean those secrets were in the domain of biological engineering. Not when we have more likely candidates."

"Okay. Suffice it to say it's improbable enough to be considered impossible." Smith waited a second for Doctor Kim to interject further. When no comment came, Smith continued. "If we assume for the moment it wasn't impossible, how long would it take to produce the clone?"

"Pardon me," Kim said. "Produce how?"

"Through cloning."

"Are you asking how long the fertilization process would take? The nuclear transfer? The identification and collection of a suitable oocyte? What part of the process are you referring to?"

"The entire thing, I suppose?" Smith said.

There followed a lengthy, awkward pause, and Smith realized he and Kim were talking past each other. He tried clarifying some assumptions. "The suspected clone in question was in his late teens as of a few years ago, but doesn't seem to have existed before then."

"I see," Kim said. "Now you've added a fourth improbability, that Doctor Izaki artificially accelerated his clone's growth."

"Yes?"

"Clones don't age at an accelerated rate," Kim explained with obviously forced patience. "The cloning process doesn't produce a fully developed organism. Even when successful, it only produces a fertilized egg that would still need to grow normally. If the clone in question is a young man, he would require the years of life necessary to reach that biological age."

Smith took Doctor Kim's point but didn't want to let go of the question just yet. Quentin Izaki's lab had only been operational a few years before its demolition. If Alan existed before then, wouldn't there be evidence of Izaki raising a younger child? "Okay, but entertain the idea for a second. What would someone have to do to artificially accelerate a clone's growth?"

"Well, conceding that we have entered the realm of science fiction, you'd need two things. First, some sort of mitotic stimulation to accelerate aging."

"And the second?" Smith asked.

"If you want this clone to function normally—healthily—it would need an intense regimen of diet and exercise, many years' worth in an abbreviated time frame, to compensate for lost time."

Smith sighed thoughtfully. "And I suppose he'd need proper mental conditioning as well."

"I'd think so."

"The clone would need the right experiences during the right critical periods of mental development to ensure proper acquisition of skills—language skills, social skills, and so on," Smith suggested.

"And how do you suppose that could be done?" Kim asked.

"I'd say you'd either need psychics continuously interfacing with the clone's mind throughout its development, inducing those experiences telepathically, or you'd need some sort of, I guess, machine interface with the psychic's brain to simulate those experiences somehow." Smith shook his head. "Neither of those scenarios is plausible, is it?"

"No, it isn't," Kim agreed, apparently gratified by Smith's return to reality.

Smith leaned forward and pulled up Izaki's photo. "I'm sending you an image."

"All right," Kim said, and, a moment later, "I've received it."

"I just wanted to make sure he didn't look familiar to you. You've never seen this person before?"

"Is this Izaki or the purported clone?"

"At this resolution, it could be either."

"Well, the answer in any case is no," said Kim.

"He looks a lot like you. Could you be related?" Smith asked.

"Doubtful. Pedigrees can be inaccurate, but I have no Japanese people in my line that I'm aware of, and my family's roots have been mapped all the way back to Confucius."

"Could you have family in Izaki's line?"

"I have no idea."

"Because you could just about be his clone, yourself."

"Quite impossible, I assure you."

SMITH ENDED the call feeling more relieved than disappointed. It was for the best that Alan Izaki wasn't a genetically engineered, telepathically enhanced clone. Capturing him now felt less… consequential. Though the incidence rate of psychics had grown since the first verified case was identified shortly after World War II, it was still low. According to the best current estimates, perhaps one in a million people was born with a psi quotient above zero. Only about seven to eight thousand people worldwide could read minds, transmit mental information, or even control other people's nervous systems. The New Government used every measure at its disposal to identify and control these psychics, both to prevent the abuse of those powers and to exploit those abilities for its own ends. Few people outside Countermind knew exactly how many state-employed psychics existed, but Smith knew an estimated half of the world's psychics were in national registries, and about half of those were actually state employees. The most qualified worked in the Defense, Safety, and Security Ministries. Many psychics worked for provincial and other local governments, while the remainder were legally forbidden from using their telepathic abilities at all. In all cases, Countermind was always watching, tracking, and making certain the world's psychics didn't abuse their power or overstep their bounds.

But the authorities always wanted more and did everything short of outright conscription to entice telepaths into public service. Smith wasn't willing to consider what would happen if his masters ever acquired the means of mass-producing their own psychics. And now he wouldn't have to.

CHAPTER 7
AMBIGUOUS IMAGES

ALAN'S ONLY recurring dream was a memory, the memory itself like a recording in its clarity and fidelity of replay. The memory was a vestige of his father's vast intellect. Alan reckoned it a genetic memory. A progenetic memory, even.

"This is a test," Quentin Izaki's voice said, the sentence somehow echoing in the featureless white space.

"What test?" Alan asked, his voice, even in a dream of a memory, so like his father's.

"Do you see the table in front of you?"

Alan nodded when he saw it, a black table waist-high and a meter square, about ten meters away, he estimated. It was hard to gauge the size and distance, the emptiness of the white space depriving Alan of monocular cues.

"Can you identify the object on the table?" his father asked.

A small, pale, squarish object was on the table, but Alan didn't approach it yet. The strange nature of the room demanded investigation, challenged him to test his assumptions. Alan shifted his weight from foot to foot, and the invisible floor supported him normally. He knelt on the floor and placed his hands on it, feeling it, pushing down against it, but discerned no texture or temperature. He only felt the counterpressure of a smooth surface refusing to yield against his weight or strength. The floor's only quality was its solidity, featureless yet somehow generating friction (else it would have been more slippery than ice). It was a firmament.

The impossible nature of the floor was Alan's first, best clue that the white room wasn't real.

Quentin Izaki remained silent during these explorations. After pressing his ear against the floor, smelling it, even briefly touching it with his tongue (he heard, smelled, and tasted nothing), Alan stood and walked to the table.

The table wasn't actually as square as it first seemed. The edges of the surface met each other at rigid right corners, each of which rested on a black square leg, but the table had a curious multitude of angles that was both elaborate yet simple, modern but baroque, in a way Alan found difficult to articulate.

But his father had asked him to identify the object on the table, and that was easy. It was square, regular. "It's a cube," Alan said.

"Go on," Quentin encouraged.

So his dad wanted more detail. Okay, fine. "It looks to be about ten millimeters per side. The surface is nonreflective," Alan said, though he wasn't sure how to describe the albedo without a discernible light source. As for color, the table was pitch-black, while the room was starkly white, and the cube's own color seemed snugly shaded right between the two. So, "gray."

"Go on."

Alan sighed and picked up the cube. It weighed only a few ounces. Like the floor, it was firm but lacked texture or temperature. Still, he could grip the cube tightly without it slipping from his fingers like an ice cube would. He counted the faces.

He counted the faces.

He counted the faces.

He wondered when he'd forgotten how to count. Had he mischaracterized the test? Had his cognitive faculties been impaired in some way? He counted again, and again found far more faces than should have been possible. Switching up notation systems didn't help. The cube had twenty-four faces in decimal, twenty in dozenal. That couldn't be right. It was like he was quadruple-counting every surface.

He put the cube down and counted his fingers: decimal ten. If he could count his digits without error, then why not the six faces of a cube?

He picked up the cube and tried again. This time, slowly, starting with his thumbs, he placed a fingertip on each square surface until he was holding the cube up with his fingers, each fingertip on a face.

Most of the faces remained untouched. Alan repeated this exercise several times, always with the same result: the cube had twenty-four faces. What the hell was such a shape even called?

It wasn't a cube. But then why did it look like one? Alan laboriously counted thirty-two edges, sixteen corners. The corners looked to be right angles, though he knew this was geometrically impossible.

He held the shape up in front of his nose and closed one eye so only one face was visible, but no matter how much he rotated the object, or which face he examined, the square appearance persisted.

Alan had the uneasy sense of looking at a visual paradox, like an infinitely ascending staircase. But this wasn't an Escher print. Even if this environment was simulated, he was manipulating something with volume, a three-dimensional object in three-dimensional space.

But it wasn't. He got it now. The cube was four-dimensional.

Alan looked at the table and experienced the mental relief of a puzzle resolved. The table was like the cube, as was the room itself. "It's four-dimensional," he said. The cube, the table, the room. A tesseract on a tesseract in a tesseract.

"Very good!"

It had been a test of Alan's mental capabilities, but not the way he'd thought. His cognition hadn't been artificially impaired. It had been enhanced. His dad had fiddled with his brain to add a faculty, not remove one. How else to create four-dimensional objects except inside a simulation?

But was there a larger lesson to this? "Why?" Alan asked the air. "What was the point?"

"To show the flexibility of your mental boundaries, that there's no true limit to what the human mind can conceive. But more than that, this is a demonstration of the nature of problems, of the value in lateral thinking. When faced with a challenge, think back to this room and consider whether there's a way to rotate the situation that you hadn't considered. Do you understand?" Quentin asked.

"Yes."

"Test ends."

Like every time Alan woke from the dream, he could remember holding the tesseract, but damned if he could remember what the fucking thing looked like. He lacked the mental capability to imagine something he'd seen so clearly in a dream. It was frustrating. Still, wasn't a lesson in lateral thinking exactly what he needed right now?

It had been a crack of thunder that woke him. Another came, rattling the windows and portholes. Alan crept up to a porthole and peered through it, across the agitated water of Aberdeen Channel, the unsettled water reflecting a gray sky. The western edge of a passing typhoon opened up and released a downpour.

Alan hadn't counted on the weather to be favorable, but it was a happy coincidence all the same. The storm would compound the cover already provided by the night. He retreated from the glass and prepared his possessions. The laptop and its peripherals, already wrapped in plastic, were zipped up inside his backpack. Alan disconnected the inductive charger from the portable battery, bagged it, and stowed it beside. He shouldered the bag, slipped out through a hatch, and skulked down the dock toward the city, abandoning the marina.

The twenty-four-meter luxury yacht belonged to a mainland tycoon who'd been arrested for corruption, all of his assets frozen during the investigation, the boat chained to the pier but otherwise abandoned. Alan identified it when he'd first arrived in Hong Kong, decided it would serve as a bolt-hole if he needed it, and disabled the alarm on an inconspicuous aft hatch. And it had served well, but he wasn't about to drive the thing out of Hong Kong.

IT WAS past midnight when Alan turned up the road to the hotel. He chucked his backpack into an orange street-side garbage bin around the corner from the entrance. He'd be back to dig his stuff out long before the trash would be collected.

He walked up the long, flat driveway of dark brick to the roundabout in front of the hotel, past the marble fishpond, into the side entrance. The men's room was near the entrance. Alan went inside and dried himself off with paper towels, neatening himself up in a large handicapped stall with its own sink and mirror. He was dressed as conventionally as possible—jeans, tennis shoes, and a button-down shirt under a simple jacket (all shoplifted), again with oil-based foundation smeared over his face to conceal the tattoo.

Summoning his bravado, he exited the bathroom, strode up to the receptionist's desk, and identified himself as Doctor Kim Kyung-Min and presented a fake ID he'd constructed a couple of days ago. He unfurled a litany of personal info—address, phone number, other details picked up from his dragnet—before he was even asked for it. A little way to brute-force someone's trust, especially when face-to-face. He explained he'd lost his room key while enjoying the Hong Kong nightlife and needed a new one. Oh, and could they remind him which room was his?

This gambit could meet with varying levels of success. In the worst likely scenario, a member of the hotel staff would accompany him up to the room to confirm it was actually his, and Alan would have to make an escape. But the person at the desk apparently found the ID convincing enough to give him a replacement key card and room number, and Alan rode the elevator up without any trouble.

The hotel lobby was a large garden atrium containing a restaurant, a bar, and a tall, rumbling fountain that made the space smell faintly of chlorine. The atrium was capped by a tremendous skylight that presently allowed an occasional flash of lightning into the hotel. Hotel rooms either overlooked the atrium or were located down hallways branching away from the lobby. Doctor Kim's room, number 1518, was down one such dimly lit offshoot, agreeably out of sight from the lobby floor.

After examining the hallway, Alan took the elevator down again, stepped outside into the rain, and crossed the street, from which point he counted windows up and across until he found Doctor Kim's room. From the hall, there hadn't been any light visibly spilling out beneath the door, and the window looked dark from out here as well. Kim Kyung-Min was either away or asleep.

Alan reentered the hotel and returned to the fifteenth floor. Every time he saw a flash of lightning, he ran through a quick mental count, *1-2-3-4-5-6-7-8-9-A-B-10*, until the thunder hit. The thunderclap arrived at 9, and Alan repeated the count a few times to reassure himself that the intervals were consistent. Then he stood at the hotel room door with the key card in hand, waiting for another flash of lightning.

When it came, he ran through the count with his hand placed on the handle and the key card held near the slot. At 8, he simultaneously slid the key card into the slot and pushed gently down on the handle, the crash of thunder (he hoped) obscuring the click of the door being unlocked.

He listened for any sounds from inside. If the occupant presented himself, Alan would feign surprise, claim he must have forgotten his own room number, and flee. But he heard nothing.

Another flash of lightning. Alan counted. At the thunderclap, he pushed the door open, slid into the dark room, and closed the door behind him in a single fluid motion. His entrance was quick and quiet, obscured by the sounds of thunder, wind, and rain. There was no time for hesitation.

Alan stood in the darkness. The room felt warm. The only light came from various electronic devices, tiny LEDs on the television, the phone, and the bedside clock, its digital display giving the room a soft red glow. In this faint light, even as Alan's eyes adjusted, only the dimmest outlines of furniture were visible.

Alan stood still for six minutes, as counted by the clock. He was able to pick out a soft snore, barely audible above the thrum of raindrops against the window. He waited for the pattern of breathing to change. It didn't, and Alan, reasonably confident his entrance had gone undetected, pulled a thin black flashlight out of his pocket and inserted it into a red gel light filter, the thin tinted plastic rolled into a sleeve with one end stapled shut. When he twisted on the flashlight, its filter gave the glow a deep red tint, blending with the shine of the clock, less disruptive to anyone who'd fallen asleep already accustomed to that color. And then, taking care to keep both himself and the light away from the bed, Alan crept his way into the room, toward the bureau across from the bed.

There were several objects neatly laid out on the bureau. The first was a necktie, still knotted, and it took Alan a second glance to confirm, with some disapproval, that it was a clip-on. Next to it was a wrist brace, and then some sort of blood-glucose meter, a flat oblong device with a large digital display and a thin lancet, connected to a wall socket with a charging cord. So Doctor Kim was diabetic and nursing a sprain besides? The brace looked like it was for the right arm. Good to know.

Next to these were a wallet and key ring. Lifting these gently enough not to jingle the keys, Alan inched his way into the bathroom and eased the door shut behind him. Holding the flashlight in his teeth, he emptied the wallet onto the counter, laying out cash, credit cards, and assorted identification in order as he removed them. He fished a small digital camera out of his pocket and photographed the front and back of each of the wallet's contents: resident identity card, bank cards, key cards, a Science Ministry ID, the key card for this hotel room, and something else resembling a civilian ID for the Defense Ministry.

Alan had to study the final card in the wallet for a few seconds to confirm that it was, in fact, some sort of military firearm certification, permitting the bearer to carry a gun. What the hell could a biologist possibly need with a gun?

Alan glanced again at the ID for the Science Ministry, tried connecting the dots in a meaningful way, and decided he didn't care to know.

Wanting out of the room as quickly as possible, he pulled from another pocket a portable card reader. He filched whatever data he could from every single card with a chip or magnetic stripe. The card data could later be paired with the transaction data, PINs included, he already had on file. The hotel key card he kept, swapping it with the one he'd just gained from the front desk, now that the old one would be invalid. Next he carefully slid each key from the ring, arranging them on the bathroom counter in order, and took multiple photos of every single key from five different angles, with a small plastic ruler lying next to them for scale. Then everything was returned to the wallet and key ring as he'd found them.

Collectively, these records were the raw materials for an indeterminate number of forgeries, trespassings, fraudulent transactions, or other crimes to be determined at a later time. To create the duplicates, Alan already had illicit access to a maker space containing key grinders, card writers, even a 3D printer. He'd go there next.

Alan hesitated. The firearms certification was perplexing, but there was something else too, something he was overlooking.

He flipped through the cards again. What was he missing? *This is the tesseract room*, he thought. *Rotate the situation. Test your assumptions.* Pressed though he was for time, the best way he knew of testing assumptions was to drill down on the details. So that's what he did: read every line on every card, line by line, character by character.

And then he saw that, for every ID containing a gender field, said field was blank.

He could've kicked himself if he wasn't worried about making noise. When parsing his data hoard in search of a target, he'd written his script to exclude women rather than to include specifically men—which, he realized too late, left a few other possibilities. Then when further researching Doctor Kim online, Alan had glossed over the genderless personal pronouns, mentally defaulting to male. And there'd been precious little biographical information on Kim that wasn't career-related, given the doctor's penchant for privacy.

Alan looked at Doctor Kim's ID photos and experienced the particular uncertainty experienced when viewing a reversible figure, like a drawing that was both a duck and a rabbit or, in this case a man and a woman. The doctor's apparent gender refused to resolve into a specific category, no matter how long Alan stared.

Not that he had long to stare. Alan returned the cards to the wallet and eased the bathroom door slowly open, crept back into the room, and returned the wallet and key ring to their original positions. He turned toward the bed, checking to see whether Kim Kyung-Min had been disturbed.

He toyed with the idea of stepping forward for a closer look, not that it would make a difference. Under normal circumstances, he wouldn't care, but if you wanted to impersonate someone, their gender identity was usually pretty important to know one way or the other.

A telepathic peek might've settled the issue, but Alan didn't think the circumstances justified a psychic invasion. Besides, reading the minds of sleeping people tended to be unpleasant. Depending on where they were in their sleep cycles, either they were dreaming, which was often bizarre, or they *weren't* dreaming, which was just existentially terrifying. Besides, the pitch of a person's thoughts could be as misleading as the pitch of their voice.

Doctor Kim snorted, muttered, stirred. Alan crouched low, still as death.

From what he could hear, and what he could see over the edge of the bed, Kim rolled over, turned the clock for a better look at the time, and resettled back into bed, squirming a bit to become comfortable before falling still again.

In ten minutes, the gentle snoring resumed.

Alan waited another twenty minutes before he felt safe enough to get up off the floor, and then he got the hell out of that hotel.

CHAPTER 8
CRIMES THOUGHT

ARISSA BINTI Noor was about to profoundly screw up her first solo field assignment. Just a simple trial run with little risk, something to stretch her legs before being given any real responsibility. Worse still, she was going to foul it up on purpose, eyes wide open, completely deliberately. Stupid, stupid, stupid, and also the right thing to do. Conditions on the ground had changed. She was willing to revise objectives on the fly when new information came to light and if in service of the greater good. What was better for society, arresting a minor dissident baited into trivial offenses or recruiting a telepath into a career of public service? The better choice should be clear to anyone, even if Arissa would have to make it clear.

Card had suggested the location. Instead of a coffee shop, it was an upscale NoHo wine bar much nicer than Card could usually afford, from what Arissa knew of his finances, and she took this extravagance as a sign things were going well.

Less reassuring was his tardiness, likely due to the storm. No signal 8 had been sounded, and the worst of the storm had swung north before hitting the island, causing the locals to joke about force fields. But it was still raining hard, and nobody else seemed willing to brave the weather for some bottle service. The place was empty but for a couple of well-dressed servers standing behind the bar and gossiping in hushed tones, their conversation indecipherable over the rain hammering the windows.

Card arrived carrying an umbrella and a look of distraction. But he'd dressed up—another good sign. He was clean-shaven and sleekly clad in black slacks and a matching jacket over a button-down black shirt.

Arissa stood to meet him as he shook the water from his umbrella. "I'm sorry I'm late," he said, gesturing to the weather by way of explanation. "Are you well today?"

"Yes, thank you. You look good," she added.

"If not a bit bedraggled," sighed Card. "Shall we be seated?"

"Can we order at the bar, first?" Arissa didn't want to deal with a server interrupting their conversation.

"Sure."

When they had their drinks, they moved to the table Card had reserved in the back patio, clinked their glasses, and sipped. The bar was in the midlevels, and the patio faced a concrete wall. But the proprietor had compensated for the lack of a view by erecting a canopy that stretched to the floor, and then mounting shelves holding rows of potted tropical plants, which, combined with the privacy and the sound of the rain, gave the space an intimate air.

"So, how are you doing?" Card asked.

Her mouth formed the beginnings of "I'm fine," but she stopped short. She took another sip of wine, then said, "Actually, I have something important to tell you."

In an instant, he was all attention.

"Remember when I asked you about, well, *reading* people?"

He struggled through a long pause before forcing out "Yes?"

"Now, don't feel nervous…," she started.

"Okay?"

"But it may be more than simple intuition."

Card pinched his lips, averted his eyes. "No, it's not," he insisted.

The meaning behind her words terrified him, as it would any reasonable person, but Arissa didn't need to read his mind to know he'd already considered what she was suggesting. "Please, Card, I know this is frightening, but if there's a chance you are what I think you are, then it just might save you."

He blinked at her. "Save me how?"

"If you have psychic talents, you could be a boon to society."

"And if I don't?"

"Well…." Arissa struggled. "You could be in trouble."

"How could I be in trouble?" he protested. "Why on earth would… would anyone be interested in a nonpsychic?"

"Card… I know you have connections. I know you have, well, certain sympathies. You harbor animosities. And I'm not trying to put you on the defensive, because I also know that you're a good, kind, decent person of unimpeachable character, which is why I'm trying to help you."

"How could you possibly…."

He caught himself, then started again.

"I'm not confirming anything you've just said, but what would even lead you to suspect that I'm… one of them?"

Arissa had already passed the point of no return. She looked around the empty bar to reassure herself they had little chance of being overheard, and a quick mental scan confirmed that neither of the staff was paying them any mind. She met Card's eyes again and, discreetly, tapped her finger twice on her temple in the universal pantomime for telepathy.

Card was silent a moment, then shifted in his seat. "I think I should go."

"Card, I'm sorry. I know this is frightening. I've been there."

"Please stop," he said.

"I've been where you are, and I understand what it's like, from personal experience, to feel like your life may cease to be your own."

"I said stop."

"But I also understand it's wiser to work with the proper authorities than against them."

"That's enough, Arissa."

"My name's—"

She froze. Had he just read her mind, divined her real name?

He smiled at her, but not a smile she'd seen. The friendly grin she'd first observed, in his online photos, on that train ride with the child, during that night out near Wan Chai, had melted away, replaced by something night-dark and razor-cruel.

"Really," he said, "that's much more than enough."

She looked into his mind.

His name was Card Lin. He was twenty years old, dozenal. He was a Pisces. He was straight, single, and never married. He drank socially and never smoked. He spoke Mandarin, Cantonese, English, and Japanese. He was a freelance artist. He liked old movies and foreign languages and old movies in foreign languages. He was casually Buddhist. He swam a mile in the pool every morning. He liked computer games and card games. He enjoyed visiting new countries and writing about it. He ate sushi. He mentored homeless kids. He sang. He danced. He dabbled in avant-garde programming. He was a potential dissident with antiauthoritarian inclinations and radical connections.

He wanted to help people.

Everything she saw in his mind was consistent with what she'd learned from his files, from their conversations, from other times she'd read his mind. But not with the smile he wore now, cold and sharp as a shiv.

"You're Countermind," Arissa said.

He took his time answering, first taking another sip, and then saying, "It's remarkable to me that, with so simple an assignment, and fully aware that you were being tested, you still managed to fail in such spectacular fashion. And not even through a lack of skill or ability, which could have been forgivable for someone so new to the job, but through simple, mundane bad judgment."

He put down the glass.

"So," he said, "by now you should be experiencing the effects of the inhibitor you've been imbibing. A little slow-acting, but my usual method of beating suspects into submission before injecting them with a sedative backfired on me some weeks ago. That means you get the drug. Once I'm certain it's had time to take effect, my colleagues here will escort you away to be processed."

Arissa looked toward the front. The servers were still engaged in quiet, private conversation behind the counter. She didn't bother trying to read their minds. Even without an inhibitor, she suspected she'd only find what they wanted her to find.

"When they do," the agent continued, "you may want to apologize to them for making them work on a Saturday night."

"You set me up," she said.

"You helped," he answered. "It would've been enough to coax you into deliberately sabotaging your own investigation. When you went poking around in my mind, searching for signs I might be a psychic, I thought, well, why not let her find what she's looking for, make this more interesting? I wonder whether you would've purposely blown your cover if you hadn't found a possible point of identification with me, but I guess that was always the aim of this exercise, wasn't it?"

"Was it?" Arissa asked, surprised at how steady her voice was. Would the full weight of this disaster hit her later? "You're saying this wasn't even a test, it was entrapment?"

"I'm saying this was going to end in arrest, or I've wasted my time."

"But why go through all this trouble? What possible information objective could you have? I'm nobody. I've got no past crimes. What's the point of spending all that time and money training me, only to arrange for my arrest with my very first assignment?"

"Countermind didn't train you," he said.

"But why be interested in me at all?" she asked, her voice rising. "Is this about sending a message? Is this just Counterpsychic Affairs setting examples again? Making sure state psychics don't step out of line? Reminding us none of us are safe from you, no matter who we are or who we work for? Has there been a desuppressive event, and you need to save face?"

"Of course not."

"Then what?"

The man shrugged, nonchalant. "I wouldn't tell you if I knew. The job is to follow orders, not question them." He gestured to her. "It's a shame you never absorbed that lesson, what with all the time and money spent training you."

Arissa leaned back, her fingertips to her forehead, her face pinched with frustration. "So what happens to me now?"

"Well, you're out of a job, I can tell you that much. Probably tried for treason, and you can expect some reeducation if convicted, perhaps prison. You're bisexual, aren't you? Just going by your file."

Arissa felt her face flush. She glared at him.

He shrugged again. "Hey, you read my file, so it's only fair, even if mine was faked for your benefit. But I'm gay, so I'm afraid this was doomed from the start. Just consider yourself lucky you never had the chance to rack up any real charges. I was only supposed to lead you far enough to justify a quick arrest so we could get the ball rolling on you right away. Now you'll be in Countermind's custody until your trial. Maybe I'll see you in court?"

He looked at his watch.

"But I hope not," he added. "To be honest, this kind of work is beneath me, and I'll be glad to leave it behind."

He straightened and turned in his seat, moving to leave the table.

"Wait," Arissa said. "I need… I need something to make sense of this. It's too arbitrary."

He cocked a quizzical eyebrow at her, then rolled his eyes and settled back in. "All right, I'll speculate for you, but take that speculation for what it is. As I said, I read your file. In my opinion, it had a couple of outstanding problems. First, you're too gullible. But that's common among psychics, so don't feel bad."

"Telepaths aren't gullible," she said.

"Oh, right, sure. To be a psychic is to be a cynic. That's what you all believe, because you know people rarely say what they're thinking. The problem with psychics is that you assume people must always *believe* what they're thinking. You trust implicitly, pardon the pun, anything you read from someone's mind. But a person capable of falsifying his thoughts, difficult though that is, can deceive psychics with frightening ease. I mean, if you can't trust the contents of someone's very soul, what can you trust?"

"But what does that have to do with me?"

"Nothing in particular. Like I said, a common failing among telepaths." He leaned in. "Your real problem was in your personality inventories."

"I took so many of those things—"

"Yes, and did generally well, except for a low score on the PCL-R."

"That's…." She searched her memory. "That's the psychopathy checklist."

"Yes."

Arissa had lost count of all the psychological assessments she'd taken in her life. When enrolling in school, when assessed for telepathic potential, when applying to work for the Security Ministry, and then the regular evaluations throughout her training. But she remembered this one, remembered how much the questions had disturbed her.

Wait, had he said she'd scored *low*?

"You're saying I'm not sociopathic *enough*?" she asked.

"State psychics exhibit a small but nonnegligible risk of betraying their loyalties. It's an occupational hazard. The nature of your work requires you to get into criminals' heads, think their thoughts, feel their feelings, see things from their points of view. Your job duties require you to, by definition, empathize with the enemy. Seditious thoughts can be contaminating. To resist those thoughts," he said, "you need an ability to, frankly, not give a shit about other people. It turns out you just cared too damned much."

"If… but… then why the hell did they recruit me?"

"Your psi quotient was far above average." He shrugged. "By quite a bit. You consistently scored at the top of the BBth percentile in each of the scale subcomponents. The folks testing you had to analyze the rest of your cohort's data separately, that's how badly you'd wrecked the grading curve. That kind of talent is valuable in anybody, even a bleeding heart, so the Ministry decided to see if you were worth it. I'm sorry, Security Ministry Third Bureau Agent Arissa binti Noor, but you weren't."

"You're not sorry."

That awful smile again. "No, I'm not."

"And how'd you do on that checklist?" She nearly sneered. "Since you bring it up."

"Not too low. Not too high. Just right enough to do my job."

He stood up, turned his back, walked away.

"Well, okay," he tossed back. "Maybe I scored a little high."

CHAPTER 9
MAY YOU COME TO THE ATTENTION OF THOSE IN AUTHORITY, AND MAY YOU FIND WHAT YOU ARE LOOKING FOR

KIM KYUNG-MIN wasn't sure what had disturbed their sleep shortly after midnight, but they suspected it had something to do with the humidity from the room's subpar air-conditioning, and the low thread count of the sheets, and the noise of the storm penetrating the thin walls. Apparently the hotel had cut costs on the latest renovation, and it was enough for Kyung-Min to break their usual rule of checking out online instead of at the desk.

But first Kyung-Min showered, dressed, breakfasted, and packed. Then they readied the blood-glucose meter and, at precisely 7:00 a.m., checked their blood sugar. They loaded this figure, along with data from the continuous glucose monitor attached to their waist and the fitness tracker worn on their wrist, into a statistics program on their laptop computer. Kyung-Min ran the numbers and found everything inside normal parameters (setting aside the moment of sleeplessness earlier in the morning).

Satisfied, Kyung-Min left for the lobby, with plenty of time to register their complaints at the front desk and then take a taxi to the train station.

The receptionist recognized Kyung-Min on approach, or at least recognized their expression. He forced a smile, attempting to head off whatever had put this guest on the warpath. "Doctor Kim, did you have any trouble reentering your room last night?"

Kyung-Min stopped short. "I'm sorry?" they asked.

"I see here that you were issued a new key card late yesterday evening? You were locked out of your room during the storm, right?"

They blinked. "I'm afraid I have no idea what you're talking about."

A thin layer of condensation appeared on the man's forehead. "I… perhaps I'm looking at someone else's record. One moment."

"May I?" Kyung-Min asked, striding around the desk without waiting for permission.

"If you would please allow me—"

"That's my name and that's my room number," they confirmed, ignoring him and examining the screen, "but I never was locked out of my room."

Kyung-Min looked up and around until they spotted a closed-circuit camera pointed at the reception desk.

"I want to talk to your manager," they said.

IT TOOK some threats to the hotel's reputation, but finally the manager allowed Kyung-Min into the hotel's cramped admin office. They leaned over the shoulder of the hotel security officer, squinting as he fast-forwarded through last night's front-desk security footage, seeking the point when the digital timestamp lined up with the entry on the receptionist's computer. The officer slowed the footage to normal playback speed, and he, Kyung-Min, and the hotel manager watched as a young man, strikingly similar to Kyung-Min in appearance, apparently bluffed the hotel staff into giving him a key card.

"What did he do next?" Kyung-Min asked.

It took some switching between the various security feeds to track the imposter's movements. He'd apparently taken the elevator up to the fifteenth floor, scouted it out, gone back down to the lobby, and exited the hotel.

"So he never went to your room!" the manager declared triumphantly.

Kyung-Min ignored him. "Show me the footage for each of the entrances," they said, "and fast forward."

Sure enough, about sixteen minutes later, the imposter reentered the hotel, went back up to the fifteenth floor, and carefully entered Kyung-Min's room.

"I'm so terribly, profusely sorry," the hotel manager declared for the umpteenth time.

"How long was he in there?" Kyung-Min asked, eyes still on the monitor.

The officer fast-forwarded until the imposter exited the hotel room and then the hotel itself. Not even an hour.

"Can we go back to the recording from the elevator?" Kyung-Min asked. "Try to get a still of his face?"

The elevator footage had provided the nearest and most direct view of the imposter. When frozen on a single frame, the image was slightly blurred, and the young man had taken impressive care never to look directly at any camera. Still, the face was familiar.

"He looks a lot like you," said the officer. "Are you related?"

"No," said Kyung-Min, "but you're the second person this week to ask me that question."

"WOULD YOU like to know what is most disappointing about parenthood?" Zheng had asked Smith during their last briefing.

The question had put Smith immediately on guard, not only for its abruptness—they'd been discussing the Arissa binti Noor case—but for its uncharacteristic intimacy. Smith had, through the years he'd answered to Zheng, been dimly aware the director was married and had even fathered children. But the director's family life was of such disinterest to Smith, and so irrelevant to his work, that Smith had never given it a moment's conscious consideration. They'd certainly never discussed it.

"What is that?" Smith had asked, not knowing the nature of the game but taking his turn anyway.

"Parents do not create children," Zheng explained. "A child is created, true, but by processes biological and societal. The parents are merely the vector of creation. When a child is born, the antecedents of his eventual personality are already quite firmly established. Parents' genes matter, of course, and their socioeconomic standing, which can theoretically change but in practice rarely does. Those without wealth cannot gain it, and those with wealth will not relinquish it. And there is the larger culture, too often with its undisciplined youth and its pernicious foreign influences, the constant threats of terrorism, separatism, extremism."

"I see."

"I thought I understood as well, having accepted that parents, despite their delusions, have little practical control over the development of their offspring. Do you know what parenthood truly is, Jack?"

Suspecting the correct answer would be rather oblique, Smith had responded in the negative.

"It is the act of inviting a stranger into your home, and then, over many long, costly, painful years, slowly discovering who that stranger is."

"All right."

"It's a tremendously risky investment, involving incalculable personal hardship and lost time. It leads a person to consider alternatives. Much as a disaffected child might seek surrogate parents, a disappointed parent might consider surrogate children," Zheng explained, and then added, "I am aware of your feelings regarding your mother."

He'd wanted to say he had no opinion on his mother but contained his agitation. His fear had been supplanted by a gradual, crawling resentment. Is that how the director saw him, then? As a son? Smith felt grateful and loyal for everything the director had done for him, but he did not, would not feel filial.

"But children often survive the disappointment of their parents," Zheng had continued, "while parents rarely survive being disappointed by their children. And you have never been a disappointment to me, Jack."

"Thank you, Director," Smith had said, and then asked to be dismissed.

SMITH WAS in his office, wrapping up his report on Arissa binti Noor and trying not to think about that meeting with Zheng, when a call came over a secure Internet line, the same line he'd used for his conversation with Kim Kyung-Min.

"Hello," Smith answered. "How can I help you, Doctor?"

"Remember the photo of that fugitive—or the fugitive's father, I suppose—you shared with me at the end of our conversation?"

"Yes?"

"A person with that face broke into my hotel room last night, here in Hong Kong."

Smith straightened in his chair. "Tell me what happened."

Doctor Kim did so.

"And you found no sign anything was taken or disturbed?"

"Not yet. I am, however, examining my luggage and personal possessions as we speak."

"Have you alerted anyone else to this yet? Or made any effort to secure your accounts, cancel any credit cards, report this intrusion, or take any other such action?"

"Not yet, other than notifying you," Kim said. "Given that this is a fugitive psychic, I thought it prudent to contact you before anyone else."

"You did the right thing," Smith said. "Doctor Kim, I must request, with all politeness but every urgency, that you proceed as if this intrusion had never occurred, do not report this security breach to anyone, and take no action to secure your credentials. I promise you'll be compensated for any losses, expenses, or hardships you suffer in the meantime."

"Why?" Doctor Kim asked, after a long silence.

"To avoid alerting the fugitive that his intrusion has been detected. I must also request access to any accounts he may potentially gain entry to through use of your personal effects."

"Really" came the response. "You do understand I'm required by law to report when my credentials have been compromised?"

"I'm overruling that requirement, under the authority of the Bureau of Counterpsychic Affairs."

"You're what?" Kim asked, incredulous.

"This is a Countermind investigation, and my authority supersedes any other in this situation."

"I find that hard to believe."

"Please, Doctor," Smith said. "I know from painful experience that this particular psychic is at his most dangerous and unpredictable when he is feeling cornered and desperate. If you involve conventional law enforcement, you risk elevating the likelihood that people will get hurt, and then the psychic will disappear again just when he's finally surfaced. Give me four days before you alert anyone else. That's all I ask."

Kim sighed. "Very well."

"Thank you. Your cooperation is appreciated. We'll remain in touch."

THE LAST ten hours had been a blur to Alan. After the hotel, he'd broken into the maker space while it was still closed and created facsimiles of Kim Kyung-Min's possessions. From there he went to Hung Hom

Station, and now he was on an overnight T-train north, squirming into a comfortable position on a hard sleeper bunk.

He pulled aside a curtain and looked through the window. Long stretches of village rolled by, rows of white-walled houses with roofs dark red or pale blue, the homes looking simple and inviting. The sky was clear, Alan having slipped ahead of the storm.

Kim Kyung-Min would be Alan's ticket out of China, but Chun-Wai was his ticket out of Hong Kong. Alan hadn't known what he would find on the stockbroker's phone, but his expectation that he would find *something* had paid off. Opening the phone in a simulated environment on his laptop, Alan had pored through the contents and struck gold: an unsecured text file listing login IDs and passwords for a dozen different accounts, including bank accounts, e-mail, and online shopping sites. In the predawn hours of his last evening in the yacht, he'd ordered express delivery of some jewelry, deleted the notifications from Chun-Wai's inbox, and picked up the shipment at a self-service electronic locker station. He'd sold a ring for some cash but kept the rest of the jewelry as a nest egg and potential cash source. The cash he'd used for a train ticket.

Ideally, even when the purchases were noticed, no one would trace him to the train or realize where he'd fled. He didn't need a visa. The flattening of the civilized world into a networked polyglot monoculture had made crossings like this easier. Once Alan was in Shanghai, he'd secure passage out of the country, flee somewhere safe.

Relatively safe, anyway. He'd thought Hong Kong would be safe, the way a minnow thinks hiding in a school will keep it safe from a pike. But that kind of safety was an illusion, particularly when the pike had a grudge.

So Alan needed a place with no state, no government, no civilization, and no Bureau of Counterpsychic Affairs. The irony was that Alan had the man from Countermind to thank for putting the idea in his head to begin with.

He was going to North Korea.

CHAPTER 10
DUODECIMAL DIGITS

FENG HUANG went to bed tired and cranky and woke up the same way. The zolpidem didn't cure her insomnia so much as make her forget the hours spent lying awake in bed. But nothing worked. She'd tried melatonin, massages, even some red ginseng she'd bought from her corner dispensary. Her circadian clock was thrown too far out of alignment, she suspected, by a lifetime of late-night gaming sessions and coding binges. Nothing had worked, but for now the sun was up, and the only herbal remedy she needed was coffee.

Mug in hand, still in her night-robe, Huang settled into her living room couch and booted up her PC. Three monitors flickered to life, two smaller ones on the table in front of her, and the third a large flat-screen on the opposite wall from the couch.

With a wireless keyboard in her lap, she logged in to PartyYǒu's internal systems and reviewed the numbers: total hours played, average hours played per session, peak usage time, lowest usage time, total unique players, total new players, peak concurrent players, average concurrent players, total new user data, and average new data per user. Each of these statistics was presented raw as well as with seasonal adjustments, population controls, historical data, and trendlines. Everything looked positive, the gentle upward slopes encouraging confidence, and without the spikes that could indicate system stress or a sudden collapse in player activity.

Huang checked the forums, found the usual complaints and arguments. Various classes, spells, skills, weapons, or artifacts were too powerful, or not powerful enough. PvP was, Schrödinger-like, somehow imbalanced in every direction simultaneously. But she was happy so long as users were arguing opposite sides. It was only when there was universal agreement about a problem that she became worried. There were no new issues exploding in the technical discussions, no huge new bugs. The creative forums were seeing their usual regular activity, with the more imaginative players posting original fiction or engaging in free-form role-play, the kinds of activities that enhanced emotional investment and motivated more continued engagement. The cultural discussion had a calm timbre, with no major sexist/racist/nationalist meltdowns.

She opened her e-mail and read through various progress reports: updates on usage summaries, on finances and human resources, on the development of creative and artistic assets. Most importantly, there was a progress report on the big alchemy expansion now under development. She typed off a few quick replies, sent a few brief queries, then showered, dressed, ate breakfast, pulled on her gloves, and left for work. It was 6:00 a.m.

THE DAY began with the usual marathon of meetings and teleconferences. Chat with the creative folks about stories and settings and arcs. Review concepts with the art department and provide feedback. Discuss graphics capabilities with the tech people.

Before lunch, she talked triage with the development team. They'd planned more features than could actually be included in the alchemy expansion, so now they discussed which were still viable enough to be refined in time and which would have to be pared back. Each successive pass at the list saw more aggressive pruning by the team. But one of the new hires, a programmer who'd just seen a dozen of his proposed custom-designed crafting trees scrapped, finally spoke up.

"Apologies," he said, "but there's a lot of good stuff here. Should we be throwing it out so hastily? I'm not even saying we include these in the release, but we can just put them in open beta, turn the players loose on them, and then decide which to keep and which to drop after we've had a chance to see them in action."

Some of the other more veteran developers tried to respond so Huang wouldn't have to. "It's only a small subset of the player base in open beta," said Kenneth, "but they're a hardcore subset, so they're influential. They report back on the forums about what's getting tested in beta, and information spreads."

"Better to get it right the first time than have to correct it later," said Jason.

"The player base is built in."

"Don't rush it. Always, always, when it's ready. Only when it's ready."

All true, if not quite hitting the point. The new guy was unpersuaded. "We don't even have to include it in the next release," he said. "I've already got the basic code hammered out. Why not just put it in beta and see how it takes?"

"The problem is prospect theory," Huang finally interjected. "People give more weight to losses than to equivalent gains. Give a player one hundred gold, then take away sixty, and he'll be less happy than if we'd just given him sixty gold at the outset, even though he ended in the same place. If we introduce the system with a smaller rollout, then build it up slowly, it will leave players more satisfied than if we start too big only to find we have to scale it back."

And that was that. The boss had spoken. The rest of the meeting proceeded without further digression. When they adjourned, Huang lunched in her office, working through the hour and into the afternoon. This private time was principally spent inspecting game code, but she also worked on the living design document, contributed to Rath's setting bible, and got her hands dirty in every little way available to her. She had a reputation for micromanagement, but it helped her stay connected to the process, which was good for the game's quality and cut down on unpleasant surprises down the line.

And it made her feel young again.

WHEN HUANG'S newlywed parents moved to Guangzhou for work, they'd liked it so much more that they'd simply settled down, making trips back to Lagos to see family whenever they could afford to. It was in Guangzhou that Huang was born and where she was christened Bunmi Balogun. To help her assimilate, her parents also gave her the relatively fantastic name of Feng Huang.

Her father had worked as middle management at a factory, making enough money for his daughter to focus more on school than a job, but not enough for a proper social life. Instead of shopping or clubbing, she spent her adolescence alone in her tiny bedroom with her computer. Though she'd grown to identify with Chinese culture, her tastes in entertainment were transnational—Korean games, Japanese cartoons, Western fantasy novels—all brought to her through the Internet.

At least online, no one was weirded out by her fingers. She'd been born with postaxial polydactyly, sporting an extra small finger on each hand. Typically these supernumerary digits would have been removed shortly after birth, but Huang's parents, being both frugal and progressive types, had opted not to pay for the procedure until she was old enough to agree to it. She grew so accustomed to the spare fingers that she eventually decided to keep them, and she secretly suspected that learning to count with an extra pair of pinkies had contributed to her high marks in math.

After studying software engineering in college, Huang moved to Hong Kong, where she could enjoy a big-city life with lots of tech sector work without being too far from her parents. As a social media and online gaming consultant, she lived paycheck to paycheck, but her true passion was administrating MudNet, the simple text-based free-form role-playing chat forum that she'd started in college.

In an age dominated by graphic-intense, microtransaction-driven MMOs, MudNet was a deliberately retro hobby for niche enthusiasts. It was, at bottom, a chat program with a number of added game mechanics: stat-based character creation, rule-based combat resolution, experience-based progression. The bulk of the play was dedicated to dungeon-crawling quests and free-form RP, as she and her fellow players (mostly young geeky women) improvised their way through yaoi-inflected romantic fantasy adventure epics.

Huang started MudNet as a recreational pastime. It was never meant to shatter paradigms. As in most cooperative games, players were most effective when working together with a mix of complementary character classes, your standard-issue warriors, rogues, wizards, clerics, and so forth. The setting was likewise uninspired, a generic fantasy realm of Huang's own devising and inhabited by the usual population of orcs, gnomes, elves, dwarves, dungeons, and dragons.

Wanting to call it something suitably Western-sounding, she'd made a simple linguistic analysis of the names of other influential fantasy settings—Middle Earth, Westeros, Norrath, Azeroth—and identified as their common feature a final syllable in which a voiceless fricative followed an alveolar liquid. She settled on the name *Rath* as appropriately prototypical. The similarity of the name to a certain archaic English synonym for *anger* was a happy accident that lent her homebrewed fantasy setting an additional air of danger and drama.

Huang suffered from the compulsion, universal among engineers, to endlessly tweak any system she had hold of, and MudNet wasn't spared from these experiments. During one feature test, she tried introducing some social media functionality, allowing players to create detailed user profiles with contact information, hobbies, interests, favorite TV shows, movies, and musicians. Players could interface through elaborate networking schemes and provide instant status updates via their computers or mobile phones. These features went ignored by her tiny player base.

That changed when Huang tried connecting character growth to players' data. Whereas advancement in most online games was tied to the expenditure of effort or money, she made character advancement contingent on the amount of data, measured in raw bytes, entered into the player's profile. Players exploited this feature by filling their profiles up to capacity, but almost all of the data they provided was junk, in some cases literal gibberish, including one player who filled her profile with Lorem Ipsum. If MudNet had been a revenue source rather than a hobby, this would have been a game-destroying disaster. Never mind that the user data was useless. Most players who immediately maxed out their characters stopped playing out of boredom, having run out of goals to pursue. Activity plummeted.

But as an experiment, it was an eye-opening success. This was how Huang came to understand the paradox at the heart of the business: victory wasn't a reward for play. It was merely an outcome.

For her next experiment, Huang tried tying character progression to the passage of real-world time, so the size of the data limit in players' profiles increased every month after character creation. The relationship was curvilinear with diminishing returns, with new characters enjoying rapid gains at the outset and then growing their power more slowly as they reached higher levels. Implementing the change meant scaling back most players' progress, prompting lots of complaints. But many players still responded positively. Every new month was a cause for excitement, as players received the ability to add more information to their profiles. Because these additions were spaced out, players were less hurried in entering it, allowing for higher-quality data. Moreover, players were again logging in to *play the game*, to experiment with new powers, explore new dungeons, complete new quests, and fight new monsters opened up to them by their latest power increase.

Huang wondered if she'd sidestepped a problem core to China's online gaming market (how to find a revenue model not dependent on credit card transactions or prepaid cards bought at corner stores or Internet cafés) while finding a novel way to bridge the gap between social media and online games. On a hunch, she scaled back on her day job, took out a loan, contracted some work to a trusted few programmers and graphic designers, started a crowdfunding campaign, and relaunched MudNet under the more memorable, approachable name of PartyYǒu.

When historians, criminologists, and infosec experts eventually write about Feng Huang's life, most will reduce the next few years to a paragraph. Huang guided PartyYǒu through multiple upgraded iterations, eventually moving the social functionality to the front end so players accessed the game through the social network rather than vice versa, with the game remaining free-to-play. The online gaming market was still crowded, but PartyYǒu, with its emphasis on socialization, found a distinct niche and succeeded as a proof of concept. Emboldened, Huang incorporated PartyYǒu into a nonprofit, then surprised the government (and her competitors) with an application for official Culture Ministry sponsorship.

The application touted the stabilizing benefits of a well-connected, interdependent citizenry, noting how this stability could be enhanced through social technology. Huang scoured the social science literature to prop up her argument. Rath would still feature PvP, but presented in the context of arena battles or sporting events. Major dungeons, bosses, and other challenges would only be defeatable by player parties. To further reinforce this interdependence, experience points and gold could be spent to purchase powers and items at a discounted cost when purchased as gifts for other players. All of this was to promote the message that while competition is a valid and healthy pastime, superordinate threats could only be defeated, and superior self-improvement could only be accomplished, with teamwork and cooperation. PartyYǒu, in the words of the grant application, would "provide fertile soil for a more harmonious society through the creation of a new kind of online community." Befitting its egalitarian mission, this venture would be completely free to the public, with no targeted ads, microtransactions, or subscription fees.

The Culture Ministry surprised her back by approving her for a grant.

Huang worked her contacts, set up a meeting with one of Asia's largest online gaming conglomerates, flew to Seoul, presented a business plan, and persuaded them into a partnership to relaunch PartyYǒu as the world's first fully integrated nonprofit hybrid social network MMO, with headquarters in Hong Kong. The game's graphics engine was overhauled, finally allowing Rath to be fully rendered in glorious 3D. The graphics were rendered on digital-analog servers, and advances in video compression meant the game could still be played through the browser. If you could stream video, you were on equal footing with everyone else.

The mechanics still rewarded cooperative play, the game's quests and storylines written to emphasize the importance of community, duty, and harmony. Character advancement still hinged on user data, and the user agreement required account holders to affirm that all the information they provided was true and accurate to the best of their knowledge. (Naturally, any data they provided were piped directly to that behemoth of Internet aggregation, Senex, but this was already true of every other social network on the market. At least PartyYǒu was ad-free.)

So online multiplayer gaming experienced a new surge of mainstream attention with Rath at its center. Early buzz brought in enough curious users that it only took about a month for the network effect to take over as the user base became self-sustaining. PartyYǒu didn't turn a profit in the traditional sense, but it generated a respectable surplus revenue in the form of user data, which was of inestimable value to her sponsors.

And if they were still thrown by working with an African woman, that only meant she could let other people be the face of the company. More time banging out code, less time wearing those gloves. The unusual configuration of her hands, even when squeezed into a pair of tight black gloves custom tailored with wider pinkies for the extra two digits, still proved a bit too distracting. Fortunately, the video game industry had a reputation for attracting unusual people.

She never regretted skipping the surgery, not being one to fuss excessively over appearances. Nonetheless, she'd settled on a distinctive style in adulthood. She dressed daily in professional, loose-fitting suits, while her hair was tightly twisted and curled into a couple dozen knots. Her most salient feature wasn't even her hands but her glasses: chunky, oversized lenses set within thick blue plastic frames.

There remained inside her, deep in the place where adolescent ideals were consigned to die, a dim awareness that she'd sold out. But she had a roomy eighth-floor apartment in a global metropolis and a dream job running a business of her own creation. What reason did she have for regrets?

THE LAST meeting of the day was the most important, PartyYǒu's monthly video call from their sponsor representatives at the Culture Ministry. Today they'd talk about the Senex-PartyYǒu data pipeline.

Huang always conferenced into these meetings from her office while her attending VPs, a smattering of young, smart, hip Chinese men, gathered in a boardroom and did most of the talking, tablets and laptops in front of them. When she heard the conversation take an unexpected turn, she could message them with prompts on what to say. As they handled the meeting, Huang could code, answer e-mails, run simulations, all while keeping the video from the conference on another monitor.

There was always so, so much work to do.

The Culture people checked in, lengthy pleasantries were exchanged, and they started through the agenda.

The principal item was the pipeline.

"It is our observation," said Henry, "that Senex has a large, growing, flexible, classified yet still necessarily finite set of system resources it can devote to retrieving, analyzing, and storing data from the net. We further understand that Senex is able to intelligently redistribute these system resources as necessary, depending on demands. Because PartyYǒu is the single largest source of data Senex accesses from the Internet, PartyYǒu consumes a plurality of Senex's system resources. We propose alterations to the data pipeline, particularly through improved data compression, that improve the process by which Senex's web crawler retrieves information from PartyYǒu's servers for storage in its 'Sendex.' These modifications to the way PartyYǒu indexes user updates will facilitate more efficient retrieval of recent data to reduce the expenditure of Senex system resources by minimizing duplication of data already inside the Sendex...."

And he ran down the list of proposals. These were former humanities majors, so they got the dumbed-down version. The more technical details were reserved for next week's meeting with the Safety Ministry office that administered Senex. They'd make the call on which recommendations to implement. The present discussion was all about keeping Culture in the loop. Their reps asked some astute questions, mostly about effects on user experience, and liked what they heard. Smiles and approbation all around. Good job, everyone.

"Now, then, is there any other business?" Henry asked.

"There is one more thing," a Culture guy said.

Huang turned to face the feed. Whatever new business they were bringing up, it wasn't anything they'd suggested for the agenda.

"There have been a number of conversations internal to the Ministry regarding the content of your game. In particular, we have increasing concerns that elements of the setting are mildly... *apocalyptic* in tone and harmful to users' confidence in social stability."

In her office, Huang stood but remained otherwise transfixed, not moving, not speaking. Fortunately, Henry was able to keep his voice steady as he broke the silence. "I see," he said. "Can you elaborate? What elements are you referring to?"

"A content review has identified several systematic occurrences, the foremost being a series of quasi-mystical 'prophecies' that, rather than being peripheral to the game's storylines, appear rather to be a central event-driving force."

He was talking about the Draconian Prophecies.

Huang sent Henry a brief message, which he repeated verbatim. "And what can be done to alleviate your concerns?"

"Nothing too radical," the Culture guy said in a tone meant to be soothing, "and we aren't about to mandate any overhauls. We wouldn't want to do anything disruptive to the players' enjoyment, so you needn't worry about your autonomy. We only wish to recommend an enhanced process of unofficial review. The sharing of minutes from meetings discussing setting, characters, and stories. Quarterly reports on the development of these intellectual properties. The sharing of all documentation describing the game world. And of course a willingness to make alterations based on feedback before modifications to the game go live. I want to emphasize," he added reassuringly, "that this enhanced review only applies to the game's fictional contents. It does not apply to the game's business end or to Party Yǒu, so please don't feel your control over the business end will be reduced."

No, just their control over the world at the core of the business. She typed quickly: "Agree tentatively, but buy us some time and wrap this meeting." She knew they had no choice but to appear amenable. With these Ministry types, if you gave the appearance of trying to retain independence, they became all the more determined to take it away from you just as a matter of principle. The key would be to cooperate at first, then find ways to complicate the process until it would be simpler for them just to let you do things your own way. And, of course, to bribe the hell out of everyone involved.

"I understand," Henry said. "Can I request time to take your recommendations under consideration? We will need to discuss the pragmatics of implementing them. Perhaps then we can provide you with a proposal for the new enhanced review processes?"

"Certainly," the Culture guy said. "That will be acceptable. We will look forward to hearing your ideas soon."

And that was it for now, thank God. The meeting wrapped up with lots of smiles and jokes, and the Culture guys logged out.

In her office, Feng Huang buried her face in her hands.

SUFFICE IT to say, she did no more real work that evening. She called a quick emergency debriefing with her senior team, where she instructed them to keep what had transpired a secret for now and to keep their schedules flexible tomorrow. Everyone was to think hard and be prepared to suggest ideas the next day, when they'd get together and hammer out a plan of action. Then she sent everyone home and went home herself.

Brainstorming was an activity best conducted alone. Group brainstorming tended to foster diffusion of responsibility, with many people sitting quietly back and allowing the more outspoken participants to guide discussion. Better to split everyone off where they could think on their own, then get together and discuss their ideas later. And Huang had always done her best thinking by herself.

Not this time, though. When bedtime rolled around, Huang had no solutions. Only confusion, fear, anger, and frustration, as well as few illusions about how well she'd sleep tonight. She took some zolpidem, washed it down with a chamomile tea, collapsed into bed, and forced her eyes shut.

An hour later, she staggered onto her feet, moved the foot of her bed aside, rolled back the rug, lifted a hardwood floor plank, and withdrew a portable peripheral external hard drive, wrapped in plastic. This she unwrapped and carried to her computer, where she plugged it in and logged on.

And she coded. She coded for three hours straight, and then she stopped as abruptly as she'd started, saved her work on the hard drive, unplugged it, erased evidence of the session from the computer, and logged off.

The hard drive she wrapped up and returned to its place in the floor, and the rug and bed were moved to their original positions. Finally, Huang climbed back into the bed and promptly fell into a deep, if abbreviated slumber. Come morning, she would again wake up tired and cranky. She would forget all about the hard drive, its contents, and all those uncountable hours lost over so many nights, weeks, months, and years spent coding that data. And she would forget the ultimate purpose of it all, buried deep in her unconscious, an implicit imperative subtly influencing her every waking and sleeping action over half a decade: the complete and total destruction of Senex.

CHAPTER 11
PAPERS, PLEASE

WITH DOCTOR Kim's report from the hotel, Smith was able to pinpoint Alan Izaki to a specific time and place. With some targeted Senex searches and free access to the city's security camera network, Smith was able to assemble Alan's movements through the night and the following morning. The suspect retrieved a bag from a nearby rubbish bin, then paid a long after-hours visit at a maker space, and went from there to the train station. It helped that Alan didn't make any apparent effort to vanish like he had before, but hiding was less important when you were skipping town.

Footage from inside the train station showed Alan purchasing a ticket at a desk, paying in cash, and boarding a sleeper train. Calling the station, and citing the exact minute and desk at which the ticket had been purchased, allowed Smith to find Alan's destination: Shanghai. Smith chartered a quick flight north so he could meet Alan Izaki in Jing'an.

Alan never arrived.

Smith waited in a parked car outside the Shanghai Railway Station with an earpiece and a microphone. At the other end of the line, local law enforcement were holed up with the station security staff, crowded around a series of closed-circuit feeds. Each of the officers held a printout photo of the young Quentin Izaki. (By this point, Smith found it simpler just to tell people the photo was of the suspect himself.) Each monitor had at least two pairs of eyes on it, playing the feeds from the station's closed-circuit cameras. Every platform and every exit was being watched.

Smith had a tranq pistol in his lap and a tablet in his hands, toggling through the feeds one at a time. If Alan was identified, Smith would be alerted, would track the suspect and neutralize him. Even if Alan was psychically scanning the environment for threats (which he was unlikely to do, given his MO), he wouldn't recognize Smith, instead detecting a slightly inebriated banker from Qingdao in town to visit his daughter. Alan could identify Smith on sight, of course, but Smith wasn't about to give him that chance. There'd be no toying with him this time.

Alan Izaki's train arrived on schedule, but none of them saw Alan debark. The last passenger, a little old *si-nai*, tottered off the train with the helpful assistance of her presumed offspring. And that was it.

"Anyone there?" Smith asked over the line.

Grunts of acknowledgment from the assisting officers.

"No one saw the suspect?" Smith asked, climbing out of the car and jogging across the pavement.

"Negative."

"Start cycling through the station's camera feeds. Use search pattern A, but keep three monitors on the train in case he's still aboard. I'm going to check out the interior."

The platform was clear by the time Smith arrived. He confirmed over his mike that the others were still watching.

"Remember, speak up the moment you see anyone exit the train. Don't even wait to make a positive ID."

He entered the train on one end and walked its entire length, checking every aisle, every seat, room, and bunk, every lavatory, closet, container, and compartment.

Nothing. He exited the train at the tail end.

"Someone's getting out!" came the cry.

Smith waved at the camera. "Someone other than myself?"

A chagrined pause. "No."

"Thanks," Smith said. He looked around, perplexed. "Could he have gotten off the train while it was still en route?"

"I suppose it's possible," said one of the voices.

"Perhaps if he was quite athletic?" asked another. "He could jump off?"

Another voice laughed. "Like some kind of superhero!"

Smith heard a chorus of guffaws.

ALAN IZAKI walked the last few kilometers into Shanghai, the rising sun lighting his steps. He was in good cheer, still invigorated by his death-defying jump from the roof of a moving train, both hoping and regretting that no one had witnessed it.

The tumble on the grass had left him a bit filthy, though. He bought some clothes from a small shop, found a hotel, paid for a tiny room in cash, and cleaned himself up. He hung about in his room all day, using the hotel Wi-Fi to conduct research and otherwise taking the time to recharge with some sleep and a meal.

Late in the afternoon, he donned one of the outfits he'd bought at the store: a shirt and some slacks, and even a clip-on tie for added verisimilitude. He trimmed his hair shorter and donned a cheap pair of reading glasses similar to what Kim wore. After sunset, Alan traveled to the Shanghai offices of the Science Ministry.

The Science Ministry occupied just a few floors of the dull government building. A card reader was installed at the door, and Alan keyed himself in using the counterfeit he'd constructed of Kim Kyung-Min's ID. His entrance into the building at this hour would be logged, and it was likely someone would ask the doctor the reason for so late a visit, but Alan planned to be long gone by the time anyone put in that much effort.

The offices were, he suspected, full of all kinds of top-secret state information and medical secrets. It would take a lot of time and luck to crack it all open. Fortunately for Alan, he was here for information with much lower stakes, the kind of stuff people might throw away without shredding it first.

Alan dug through about sixteen rubbish and recycling bins over the next hour, collecting a stack of wrinkled printouts that displayed, mentioned, or otherwise alluded to travel itineraries or shipping schedules, each one mentioning Pyongyang as a point of origin or destination. He shoved these into a spare file folder found lying on a table, then headed for the exit.

In the hallway, he startled a security guard.

"Hello, Doctor," the guard said. "Can I ask what you're doing here?" He phrased the question politely, but his tense voice belied his suspicion.

Alan waved the file folder. "Just picking up some work. Don't worry, I'm an employee."

"I'll need to see your badge, sir."

"Certainly," Alan said, fishing the forgery out of his right pants pocket. He handed the guard the identification. The guard examined the photo on the ID, then Alan's face, then went back to the ID, his eyes squinting harder with each journey up and down.

"This isn't you."

"Sure it is."

"Stay here. Don't you go anywhere. You're trespassing." The guard pocketed the ID while lifting a radio to his lips, and Alan knew he was in trouble.

"Could you look again, please?" Alan asked.

The guard, having already made up his mind, wouldn't normally give the ID another look, but a gentle psychic nudge persuaded him to give it just one more glance. After all, it wasn't like this late-night visitor was acting at all suspiciously or looked the least bit dangerous. So the guard checked the ID again.

"I know it's dark in here, but that looks just like me, doesn't it?" Alan asked. *Yes, it does.*

"Yes, it does," the guard agreed, now somewhat embarrassed.

Alan seized the emotion and turned it up a bit, till the guard was too ashamed to even look him in the face again. The guard, his eyes glued to the floor, made his apologies as he returned the card, but Alan waved them away.

"Never mind. It's perfectly fine. Think nothing of it. Just doing your job, I know."

And he left the building without any more trouble.

The encounter with the security guard had, in its way, been fortunate. In his left pocket, Alan had another ID just like the one he'd presented to the guard but with his own photo instead of Kyung-Min's. Presenting the ID might have avoided the guard's suspicion, but it wouldn't have allowed Alan to test the extent of his resemblance to Doctor Kim. Now he knew the resemblance didn't go as far as he would have liked. He certainly wouldn't be able to pass himself off as Doctor Kim to anyone actually familiar with the biologist. This would limit Alan's available options, but not eliminate them.

Back in his hotel room, he spread the filched documents out on the small, cramped floor and started cross-referencing.

KIM KYUNG-MIN had to visit their bank in person to open a new credit line so they could make purchases without worrying about a goddamned fugitive psychic impersonator overdrawing the account. (And Kyung-Min still only had Agent Smith's promises that they'd be compensated for any losses.) By the time the line was set up and they'd been issued a new card, Kyung-Min had wasted so much time on Jack Smith's idiot spy games it made more sense to fly back to Shanghai instead of taking the usual train. They bought a plane ticket at the airport for the next flight out and prayed the weather didn't delay the departure.

It didn't, and Kyung-Min was quickly on their way, though by now they'd already been delayed so much, and were so determined to return to their research, they decided to go straight from Shanghai Pudong to the waterfront when the plane landed. A taxi was already waiting outside the airport when the plane touched down, and they sped to the port, where a Defense Ministry boat would take Kyung-Min up the Yellow Sea.

Their phone rang. The number was for the senior researcher of the Shanghai office. When Kyung-Min answered, they exchanged some hurried greetings before he brought up the reason for his call.

"Doctor Kim," he said, "you're recorded as having entered our offices last night. The security footage seems to show you entering and leaving, and a night watchman even claims to have interacted with you during your visit, yet it is my understanding you were still in Hong Kong at the time and have only just arrived in Shanghai."

Kyung-Min drew the obvious conclusion, then sighed.

"The latter is true, sir. I've only this morning returned from the conference."

"Then who was it who visited the offices last night?"

"I have a fairly good idea. However, I should inform you I've been instructed by a representative from the Security Ministry not to contact any authorities about the activities of this apparent intruder, nor to do anything else that might alert him to the fact that his activities have been detected."

The older man needed a few minutes to process this. "I understand," he said, sounding uncertain. "Can you put me in touch with the representative of the Security Ministry who gave you those instructions?"

"Happily," Kyung-Min said, and shared Jack Smith's phone number.

"Thank you. Have a safe journey."

When the call ended, Kyung-Min immediately dialed Agent Jack Smith.

"Doctor Kim?"

"Agent Jack, your fugitive is in Shanghai."

"I know," he said, sounding weary. "But how did you find out?"

"He used my Science Ministry identification to infiltrate our offices last night."

"I see. Does anyone else know?"

"I was informed of the incident by my direct superior."

"Can you put me in touch with him?"

"He's likely attempting to contact you at this very moment."

A pause. Then, "Thank you, Doctor." And Agent Jack hung up.

Kyung-Min pocketed the phone, exited the vehicle at the dock, and boarded the boat, making their way unerringly toward their usual cabin. While waiting for the boat to set sail, Kyung-Min tried to focus on catching up on their work, glad now to have passed this matter up the chain of command. With any luck, Kyung-Min's involvement with this nonsense was now ended.

SMITH HAD been ready to invoke some Countermind authority if Doctor Kim's boss hadn't been helpful. Luckily, he was cooperative on the phone, if alarmed. The guy settled down once Smith accepted all responsibility for any fallout arising from not reporting the intrusion and he'd promised favors from the Security Ministry in return for his assistance. Besides, Smith suspected the Science Ministry had nothing to worry about. Alan Izaki wasn't the type to steal state secrets. He was a petty thief, not a spy.

Of course, this left open the question of Alan Izaki's purpose in the office. Smith taxied to the Science Ministry offices and met the head of research in the lobby.

Per Smith's instructions, the other employees had been given the day off, so as not to contaminate the scene, though the night watchman was also present at Smith's request. When interviewed by Smith, the guard confessed to being initially skeptical of the visitor, though he was unflagging in his certainty that the man he'd spoken to was Doctor Kim.

But then Smith reviewed the security footage of the watchman's encounter with the intruder. He'd seen enough footage like this to recognize the pattern in the interaction, the subtle change in body language when one person was telepathically influencing another, when one of the parties stopped to think for a moment, as if briefly dazed and then recalling something important. It still fit the suspect's pattern. Alan Izaki refrained from using psychic powers until the circumstances—like an interrogation by a skeptical guard or an ambush by a pursuing agent—demanded otherwise. Like a good martial artist, he only used his capabilities for self-defense. Not for the first time, Smith marveled at the contradiction. Izaki's restraint had an ethical air to it inconsistent with the rest of his behavior. If he wasn't willing to use his telepathy for crime, then why resort to this long string of delinquencies? Surely he could live more safely and comfortably by simply getting an honest job somewhere and lying low. After all, it had been Alan Izaki's mundane crimes that originally drew the attention of Hong Kong's police, with his psychic nature being discovered later.

This reluctance to integrate into society suggested Alan Izaki was a fugitive for reasons other than his psychic powers. Why, then? Okay, he wasn't a clone, or so Smith was now persuaded. But he was definitely hiding something.

Smith cycled through last night's security footage of the intrusion, about an hour's worth of video.

"It looks like he went from room to room," Smith remarked. And it was hard to tell, but the stack of papers in Alan's hands seemed to grow larger during his tour of the offices. "Do you have administrative privileges for the office computer network?" Smith asked the head of research.

"I do."

"Was the trash or recycling collected last night?"

"No."

"Okay. I need you to pull up printer records for the accounts of everyone who uses the offices the intruder entered, going back until the last time the trash was collected. I'll be right back."

Smith found a rolling office cart and went from office to office, taking the trash bags, tying them off, and piling them on the cart. Every time he grabbed a trash bag, he used a felt-tip marker to write the office number on the side of the bag. He wheeled the cart into a conference room, lined the bags out on the table, and sought out the head of research. "I've got the records you asked for," the man said.

"Great. We need to print out everything previously printed out by the people in those offices since the last time the trash was collected. We've got to keep the output organized by employee. Clip them together and write the person's name and room number on a cover sheet. Every time you've finished printing a stack out, bring it to me in the conference room."

When the first stack was printed out, Smith set to work comparing papers. Whenever one of the reprinted documents didn't have a twin in the rubbish bin, Smith set it aside into a different stack.

He couldn't reasonably expect the printouts to correspond perfectly with the contents of the trash bags. People didn't throw out everything they printed. But with the new row of smaller stacks created, they went through the stacks and removed any documents whose contents were especially sensitive, anything that, in the opinion of the head researcher, would normally get shredded rather than simply tossed into the trash. When these were removed, Smith was left with one more row of smaller stacks, one final examination to make.

The pattern in the remaining documents wasn't perfect, but it was certainly suggestive. Smith knew where Alan was going.

CHAPTER 12
DESUPPRESSION

TWO NONDESCRIPT Security Ministry agents had arrived at the bar, accepted custody of Arissa, and escorted her all the way from Hong Kong. The entire trip, she remained always in the presence of at least one of them, usually both. Arissa, handcuffed and shackled, stared at them across the rear cabin of the armored van as it rumbled its way through the capital streets from the airport.

The steady stream of inhibitors Agents Wei and Wen had been giving her (she didn't know if they were actually called Wei and Wen, but that's what she was calling them until they introduced themselves) had so thoroughly dulled her telepathic senses, she couldn't have exercised them even if she'd been inclined to. She couldn't read any minds, and she couldn't see outside the van, but she knew where they were going. There was nowhere else to take her.

The agents didn't quite look at her so much as past her. Why they wouldn't acknowledge her when she was their only reason for being in this vehicle, she didn't know, but it let her study them without the awkwardness of eye contact.

So study them she did, and as she did, she found herself disappointed to realize they were a very poor pair. They didn't look alike in the way you might expect a couple of cookie-cutter G-men to look, which was fine, but if they had to look unalike, they could have done the courtesy of looking dissimilar in complementary ways. Wei could have been thin while Wen was fat, for example, or Wei could have been tall while Wen was short. Instead, the two of them were simply average, average in height, average in build, average in attractiveness, and yet somehow average in different ways.

The sounds of the street receded as the vehicle rolled into the echoing space of an underground garage and then jostled to a halt. The two agents stood and opened the door. Here they were. This was it.

Arissa's terror returned. Of course she wasn't going to trial right away. She'd be interviewed first, questioned, given additional opportunities to incriminate herself. And only one state agency was qualified to detain and interrogate a psychic.

This was Countermind HQ.

AFTER ESCORTING her up a lengthy elevator ride, Wei and Wen left Arissa shackled to a steel chair, locked alone in a small gray room empty except for another chair positioned in front of her. Ten minutes passed. And then the Director of Counterpsychic Affairs entered the room, sat in the other chair, and smiled at her.

Oh my God, Arissa thought when she recognized him. She managed not to say it, but it's possible she involuntarily mouthed the words.

"Do you understand why you've been brought here?" Zheng asked.

Arissa had thought so, until the director of Countermind himself showed up to personally question her.

"Card… that agent explained to me—"

"Jack Smith is an enthusiastic field agent, and like a son to me, but he has never evinced much interest in strategic considerations."

An ominous pause followed.

"Then why am I here?" Arissa had to force the words out.

"You'll be happy to know Counterpsychic Affairs is willing to drop its charges against you. You will not be tried for your crimes, in exchange for your personal cooperation."

Arissa was not reassured. Whatever Zheng wanted from her, it couldn't be pleasant if he'd gone to these lengths to guarantee her compliance.

"Now, don't be frightened," he said, as if reading her thoughts. "You have an exciting part to play in the shaping of the future, one that will reward you with more influence than you have ever dreamed of, and a founding role in the greatest dynasty the world has ever seen. And you only need to do one thing," Zheng added. "You need to change."

Zheng slid his chair toward her, leaned forward, and placed his hands gently on her head.

When psychics laid hands on someone in this manner, it wasn't just for dramatic effect. Reducing the distance between nervous systems allowed for a stronger telepathic signal. For maximum effectiveness, you could touch foreheads to bring the prefrontal cortices as close together as possible. But Zheng had no reason to place his hands on Arissa in this way. She was up to her ears in inhibitors.

But more importantly, the director of Countermind wasn't psychic. Hell, the whole entire point of Countermind was to act as a check against psychics. The idea of a telepath working in Countermind, least of all as the director, was unthinkable—the ultimate in desuppressive events.

And then he was in her head.

"Stop!" she shouted. "What are you doing? Stop it!"

Images flashed through her mind, thoughts, ideas, pictures. He was inundating her cerebral cortex with action potentials, bringing up every belief, memory, and piece of knowledge still stored there, churning her mind into a cacophony of discordant recollection.

She had no knowledge he could possibly want. And hadn't he just said he needed her to change? But he wasn't looking for anything. This was too indirect to be a search. This was a straightforward precursor to the sort of deep mental reconditioning laypeople would call brainwashing. Arissa understood this process in the abstract. First you survey the psychological landscape to understand what you have to work with, and then you set about reprogramming it, rearranging it, rebuilding it. Zheng was a farmer, plowing a field in preparation for planting a crop. Slash and burn.

That is correct came Zheng's mental voice, and he dug deeper.

Arissa screamed.

Zheng's plow struck a rock.

After some indeterminate time in her mind—a minute, an hour, Arissa couldn't tell—Zheng's mental probe reached an area of memory that refused to yield its contents.

She was more surprised than he was.

Zheng's assault stopped a moment and then renewed with increased intensity, narrowing his focus to the black box he'd discovered buried deep in Arissa's unconscious.

It continued to resist him.

Show me what you're hiding! he demanded.

I'm not hiding anything!

But she was. She knew she was. She experienced the acute, unmistakable frustration of trying and failing to retrieve a memory long buried, something forgotten for how long she didn't know. Something big, something important, like an infant's epiphany. She knew it was there, even if she couldn't remember what it was, had never once thought about it until now.

And because she knew it, Zheng knew it too.

Wait! she thought, not knowing why. "Wait!" she shouted at the same moment. But it was too late. Zheng finally grabbed hold of the buried memory and, as if plucking an oversized, underripe onion, tore it free from the topsoil of her unconscious.

There, Zheng shouted. There it was. All in a rush now, she remembered the first time she encountered that mind, that strange, tremendous, *hungry*, indisputably *alien* mind. She remembered the fear it provoked in her. She remembered concealing her memory of it, not only from her family and the authorities, but even from herself.

And she remembered hiding her power.

What is this? Zheng asked. *This can't be real.*

Arissa realized she had to get out of there. And she understood why she had to get out of there. And she remembered she possessed, had always possessed, the means of escaping.

Wei and Wen had injected her with enough inhibitors for a psychic of her recorded level. "Top of the BBth percentile," like Jack Smith had said. But there were other orders of magnitude. Distributions nested within curves. And levels of power that Smith, Zheng, or even Arissa herself hadn't been aware of.

Zheng was still distracted, still trying to make sense of what he'd found. *Show me what you're hiding* had been his mental command.

Arissa, acting without thinking, seized hold of that impulse, turned it around, and plunged it like a knife into Zheng's mind.

ZHENG WAS the nightmare scenario that was never supposed to come true: the psychic who infiltrated Countermind.

It hadn't been difficult. No, it had been frighteningly easy. From childhood, he'd had a natural facility for counterpsychic techniques.

The countermeasures normally only mastered after years of training and exercise came innately to him. Growing up, whenever he was screened for telepathic potential, even when mentally probed by a state psychic, it was a simple matter to feint, dodge, elude, deceive, all with greater dexterity than anyone could have possibly expected from someone so young and inexperienced.

So he went undetected in school, at the academy, at the Ministry. When he was recruited into Countermind, he received precisely the training he needed to make his discovery even less likely.

And of course he was an excellent agent. Everything else being equal, who was better qualified to apprehend psychics than another psychic? The greatest danger wasn't in doing his job poorly, but in doing it too well.

Everyone who saw him work knew he was destined for greatness, and it only took the smallest application of telepathic influence for this prophecy to fulfill itself. He rose through the ranks, was appointed to several security policy working groups, and, inevitably, was appointed Director of Counterpsychic Affairs.

Like any ranking official, particularly one with his breeding, Zheng was expected to signify his success in the other traditional ways: a wife, a family, offspring. He was happy to oblige, of course. Anything to maintain appearances.

But there were risks in having children. As far as the best parapsychologists had determined, psychic powers were a by-product of a rare mutation in the integral membrane proteins regulating electrical potentials across neural axons, effectively transforming the nervous system's cytoskeletal architecture into an organic antenna capable of receiving signals from and transmitting signals to other nervous systems. While the genetic bases of this trait were still poorly understood, rigorously controlled twin studies had quite firmly settled the question of whether telepathy was hereditary (a fact often leading Zheng to question his own pedigree, though never publicly). But if Zheng had children of his own, and they were discovered to possess psychic power, it would invite unwelcome scrutiny. So, no, he couldn't afford the risk. But failing to produce offspring would invite criticism of a different sort. What then to do?

The solution was simple. Zheng had married for political reasons. Like many political marriages, it had left his wife dissatisfied, and her unhappiness was aggravated by the emotional distance of her husband. Countermind agents were characteristically poor relationship partners, being disinclined to share their private thoughts and feelings, and this reluctance was necessarily truer of Zheng than most.

It wasn't inconceivable, then, that she might seek from other men the warmth and affection she couldn't find in her own home. Nor was it surprising when, drunk on wine and passion, she would forgo the use of prophylactics during her trysts. And it wasn't out of the question that, on those occasions when she found herself pregnant, she would neglect to question the true paternity of her children.

It wasn't as if her husband could read minds, right?

Of course Zheng knew, but he wasn't displeased. His wife's every temptation, transgression, misstep, and infidelity had been the consequence of his gentle mental prodding. He didn't worry about whether he'd fathered the children he was raising, thanks to a discreet vasectomy undergone years ago while his wife was on vacation. And he'd personally telepathically screened each of her paramours for any psychic potential. As an additional benefit, this arrangement allowed him to decide just how beholden he was to his family. If he ever needed to cut ties, he would only need to "discover" that his wife was guilty of multiple affairs with other men and that the children weren't his.

As the only downside, he was still left without children to truly call his own. But he knew there was more than one way to build a family.

"No!" Zheng shouted. He reared back from the connection, trying to stem the torrent of secrets.

Arissa felt Zheng's memory harden against her probe, but that was fine. She couldn't care less about his personal life at the moment. Defenses flew up around his cerebral cortex, but she shifted her focus to his hypothalamus and jacked the activity in the ventrolateral preoptic nucleus up to about eleven.

Zheng fell to the floor unconscious, probably with a new sleep disorder.

"Help!" Arissa screeched. "Help! He's in trouble!"

No one answered her call for assistance. Any guards here probably weren't in the habit of answering the shouts of prisoners undergoing interrogation. She reached out with her mind and confirmed that two guards stood sentry on the other side of the door. One of them she convinced to take an emergency bathroom break. As for the other, she gently suggested this would be a good time to breach protocol for once and find out what all that screaming was about.

The guard entered, saw the director's unconscious body, and registered instant alarm.

"He's old!" Arissa said, and pushed softly at the guard's mind. "I think he had a heart attack, but I know CPR. If you free me from these cuffs, I might be able to save him. But I need to act quickly!"

The guard wisely vacillated. Arissa gave him another small nudge as she harangued him further. "I've been given a telepathic inhibitor. I'm not dangerous. Look at me. I can't possibly take you in a fight. There's no chance of me escaping. But if you don't let me go, he's going to die! Every second you wait brings him closer to brain death! Is that what you want? Do you want to be responsible for that?"

He most certainly did not. The guard unlocked Arissa's shackles, and she stood up, rubbing her sore wrists.

"Thank you," she said, and disrupted the signal pathways in the guard's spinal column. He collapsed to the ground, temporarily paralyzed. Arissa knelt over him and placed a hand on his forehead.

Show me what I need to know to get out of here, she demanded.

He did, and she ran.

CHAPTER 13
THE BARNACLE

EVER SINCE the complete, spectacular collapse of the North Korean nation a few years ago, the hermit kingdom's airspace had been unilaterally ruled off-limits to travel. Violating that quarantine was a great way to get spotted by a satellite and shot down by a J-10, but the only other ways into the country were through its land borders (which were more heavily guarded now than ever before in history) or by sea.

By the time Smith was able to use a satellite phone to hail the vessel—a Defense Ministry transport ship christened with the unglamorous name of *The Barnacle*—it had already been at sea for an hour. He massaged his Second Department contacts into lending him a military helicopter and pilot who, with a decent bribe, was willing to fly him out to a midsized vessel on choppy waters ahead of an approaching typhoon.

The deck was too small and unsteady to safely land a helicopter. Smith had to descend a rope ladder and then drop about a meter onto the deck, a feat that sounded more exciting and less dread-inducing than it was in practice.

The captain was waiting for him on deck, ready to help him back to his feet after his stumbling landing. Kim Kyung-Min, who appeared rather less strictly male in person than in their file photos, was there as well. Kyung-Min didn't greet or assist Smith, just stood there with arms folded, looking equal parts impressed and annoyed by the lengths Smith had taken to bedevil them.

"Thank you for slowing down for me," Smith said as the three of them went to the captain's office.

"Never mind," said the captain. "After what you said on the phone, I didn't see much choice. However, with this weather, I would like to proceed without much more delay, so I would appreciate a swift resolution to this matter."

"Certainly," said Smith. "If you followed my instructions, then only the three of us are aware there may be a psychic stowaway aboard. The fewer people who've suspected his presence, the less likely he'll be alerted. If you can provide me with a blueprint of the ship, I can personally search the vessel deck by deck. I'll also have to ask that the entire crew be ordered to wait above decks while I search. All hatches and exits also need to be secured, both from the inside by me and from the outside by you, using whatever is required: chains, padlocks, anything else that's available. We'll remain in radio contact while I search, and the exits should only be opened on my orders. The plan is to trap him belowdecks with me until I can apprehend him. Once I'm locked in down there, post guards at every exit. Only then can you resume your journey at full speed. If discovered, the suspect will likely attempt escape, up to and potentially including jumping overboard. In any event, he may attempt to telepathically influence your crew, even through the ship's bulkheads. It is therefore imperative that you make no attempt to hinder or apprehend him."

"Is there nothing we can do to defend against such an attack?" the captain asked.

"Not much, but it is more difficult for a psychic to influence multiple targets simultaneously than one at a time. While I'm searching, you should inform the crew you may have a psychic stowaway board, and instruct them that no one should be in groups smaller than three at any time. If one person shows signs of being telepathically influenced, the other two should subdue him before he can do any harm."

The captain nodded, understanding.

"All right," Smith said, "let's get started."

ALL THAT drama, and Alan Izaki was, again, nowhere aboard.

Smith sat stewing, alone in the corner of the mess hall. Kim Kyung-Min, carrying what looked like a smoothie while the rest of the crew dined on noodles, approached and took a seat next to him.

"You know," Kim said, "I'm starting to suspect you're actually quite bad at your job."

"I was never *certain* he was on board," Smith protested. "It was the best single opportunity to catch him en route. That's all."

"Why so?"

"The documents he stole all referenced shipping and transport between Shanghai and Pyongyang, but only one of the stolen documents referenced a transport run scheduled for the future: today's run, the one we're on. If he wanted to make this trip, it would have to be today."

"Then where is he?"

"I don't know. Maybe he changed his plans. Maybe he met with some misfortune. Maybe he was aboard, was somehow alerted to my arrival, and jumped ship, and now he's treading water in the middle of the Yellow Sea. Maybe he's still onboard now, and he's just better hidden than I can figure out."

"May I suggest something?" Kim asked.

"Certainly."

"You may be unreasonably obsessed with this individual."

Smith laughed. Kim did not.

"I wasn't aware you were that kind of psychologist," Smith said.

"I don't have to be. I've seen the footage of his intrusion into my hotel room, and I'm hardly persuaded he's in fact a telepath. If so, he's either possessed of so little ability, or so much restraint, I don't know how he could represent enough of a danger to justify the resources and effort you've expended on his pursuit."

"All telepaths are dangerous by definition."

"Fine. Agreed. But some must be more dangerous than others. And you've just trapped yourself on a boat bound for the world's largest quarantine zone, ahead of a tropical cyclone, in an effort to catch a *relatively* harmless psychic."

"Who may possess potentially valuable information."

"As might any other psychic. Wouldn't you find more such telepaths somewhere other than a boat in the middle of the sea?"

"This is psychoanalytic flapdoodle," Smith snorted. "You're suggesting my pursuit of this suspect is motivated by some suppressed, subconscious desire having nothing to do with my job but that I'm trying to justify in terms of my duties."

Kim leaned back, wearing a look of mild surprise. "That's an impressive analysis," they said, "but, no, nothing so elaborate. I'm suggesting you're behaving irrationally and that a person expertly trained in concealing his thoughts may not know his own motives."

At some unseen signal, the sailors in the mess stood up and made their way out of the room.

Kim stood too. "Well, if he's treading water, perhaps you'll catch him on your way back. Good luck, Agent," Kim said, joining the exodus.

"Have we arrived?" Smith asked, standing up and following. It felt too early to have even reached the coastline, much less to have finished the journey upriver.

"No," Kim said, "but we're in North Korea's territorial waters."

"Meaning what?"

"Meaning we're permitted to arm ourselves."

WHEN NEXT Smith saw Kim, the scientist wasn't visibly armed but had donned a jacket rather large on their lithe frame. Kim was also, inexplicably, wearing a brace on their right wrist. The ship's regular crew were less shy about their weaponry, openly going about their duties with tactical rifles slung over their shoulders and pistols holstered at their hips.

The sun having set, Smith had to take it on faith when Kim told him they were entering the mouth of the Taedong River. The shoreline was completely dark. Smith went up on deck and tried to glimpse the riverbanks through the blackness. He found Doctor Kim up there as well.

"Should the ship's running lights be on like this?" Smith asked. "Don't we stand out?"

"Turning out the lights won't make a bit of difference," Kim said curtly. "Just be grateful the river's so wide."

IT WAS raining when the transport docked on the south shore of the field research base. Rungrado Islet, a sliver of land four kilometers long, nestled in the middle of the city, mercifully surrounded by the waters of the Taedong. Passengers debarked and filed into the base's buildings. Crew unloaded cargo onto trucks and drove away. And, down the shoreline, beyond the lights of the base's flood lamps, a thin figure rose up out of the river until it was waist-high in the water, this emergence unnoticed and unremarked upon in the night.

The figure, young and male, waded his way to the island, where a concrete barrier topped by a chain-link fence ran the island's perimeter. With a pair of wire cutters, he snipped through links in the fence along the ground and up one of the steel posts. When a base guard passed too close, the figure crouched behind the concrete till the danger passed, then resumed snipping. When he'd created a flap large enough, he slipped through, pulling a bag after him.

The figure skulked his way toward the storage building that the cargo had also been trucked into, circling his way around to a smaller, less illuminated side entrance. Producing a key ring, he tried various keys until finding one that fit the lock.

He eased the door open and, slipping inside, surveyed the high rows of shelves and stacks of crates. He wondered where to begin.

It was only because he bent down to unzip his bag that the needle failed to penetrate his neck.

Alan shouted. "Son of a bitch!"

He spun, grappling with his assailant, fighting to keep the syringe clear of his neck. He didn't defend himself telepathically, not knowing yet who was attacking him, and he wasn't surprised when, wrenching himself around, he was face-to-face with the man from Countermind.

"You just couldn't resist, could you?" said the agent. "Just one more heist."

Alan made no response, conserving his concentration. He twisted the agent's arm around, angling the needle back toward his neck, and the agent was forced to drop the needle before Alan could stab him with it. The two wrestled, Alan nearly gaining the advantage, and the agent drew a Taser.

Alan, swearing, disengaged. He turned and dashed down one of the warehouse aisles, rounding a corner.

Doctor Kim was standing there, carrying a box, looking surprised.

The biologist dropped the box, reached into their jacket, and suddenly had hold of the biggest fucking revolver Alan had ever seen.

There it was. That gun, both a means and a justification for Alan to defend himself.

As the barrel swung up toward him, Alan's eyes rose to meet Kim's face. A normal mind. Not a countermind. An untrained, unprotected mind.

Alan reached out with telepathic fingers.

"I'm letting you go!" shouted the agent.

Alan spun around.

The agent had his hands raised, palms out. The Taser was nowhere to be seen. He circled around Alan, maintaining his distance, and interposed himself between Alan and Kim.

"You're free to go," the agent said. "I won't follow you. There's no need for any violence. You can go."

Keeping his body oriented toward Alan, the agent looked back over his shoulder at Doctor Kim.

"You should put the gun away, Doctor. There's no need to make him feel threatened."

He faced Alan again, who, for his part, was too surprised to act.

"That's it, isn't it?" said the agent. "You won't psych anyone unless it's to defend yourself?"

Alan couldn't hide his shock. Countermind knew about the laws? *Shit.*

The agent, his hands still up, took a small step forward.

"What happened to you in Seattle, Alan?"

Alan's heart skipped a beat. *He knows who I am.*

By stepping in front of Doctor Kim, the agent had, perhaps deliberately, left the other exit unguarded. Given every reason to go, Alan grabbed his bag and sprinted through the exit, body slamming the door open.

The typhoon had arrived. The wind whipped at Alan, the rain pounding like a hammer. Nothing about this escape was subtle or graceful. It was a mad charge toward the bridge as the base went on alert, sirens blaring and searchlights sweeping the grounds. Soldiers converged on Alan, and he lashed out wildly as he ran, punching guards in their minds, knocking them out before they could fire a weapon at him. He dashed up the hood of a parked truck and onto its roof, grabbed the top of a gatepost, heaved himself over the fence, and landed on the pavement in a crouch.

Ahead of Alan was a bridge, beyond it darkness. Alan plunged across, into the night, the sweep of the spotlights briefly painting the outlines of the walls, roofs, and corners of the hollow buildings on the other side. Alan took a left down one street, a right down another, ran several blocks, then dove for cover in a recess, trembling.

He stayed there until he could no longer hear the siren or see the spotlights, and then he stayed another hour still. He swept the vicinity with his mind, but there was no one else around.

When the terror no longer gripped him, Alan stood up, took two steps, and was bitten by a zombie.

Interlude
The Future

Jettrin's mistake had been telling his kid brother to telepathically check the crew for big threats: kidnapping, murder, rape, reporting them to the authorities. But it's always the little things that get you. Like when the sailor you'd arranged passage with decides to raise your fare halfway through the trip, and you find yourselves ordered off ship at a strange port of call halfway to your destination.

"What. The fuck. Now?" Siam asked.

The three of them stood portside with nothing but their clothes and their backpacks, watching the ship sail down the Saigon without them. The sky had turned appropriately gray. No one answered his question.

Siam looked at the two brothers and immediately regretted his tone. His boyfriend, trembling and silent, was fighting back tears. Jai, lips quivering, looked up at Jettrin with despair.

Okay, fine. He took Jettrin and Jai by their hands and led them away from the water, not with any particular destination, just knowing they needed to go farther inland.

He didn't ask anyone for directions. Talking to strangers in a new city was against Jettrin's rules. They couldn't risk signaling to total strangers that they were young, lost, helpless foreigners. And Siam's Vietnamese was shit anyway. So he navigated by intuition, following the flow of pedestrian traffic, angling in the general direction of the tallest visible buildings, until they found a street busy with motorbike traffic and pho shops. And Siam led them north, toward the city, till he found a shopping district with a thin rectangular park squeezed between two outdoor seafood markets.

He claimed one of the park's concrete picnic tables, opened his backpack, and withdrew the computer cushioned between the rolls of spare clothing. He snaked the power cord into the backpack and plugged it into the battery still inside, opened the computer, and, with a thrill of anticipation, booted it up.

Jettrin watched with disapproval. "I'm not doing anything illegal," Siam reassured him, and this was mostly true for once.

When they'd first met, and Siam had confided that he was, in some senses of the term, a hacker, Jettrin had reacted with justified apprehension. If all information was state property, then data theft was by definition a crime against the state and punished appropriately. But as Jettrin became more familiar with the particulars of Siam's craft, his suspicion gradually transformed into disdain, as Siam made him understand that the best hackers weren't so much technical wizards as conniving assholes.

Siam knew it still frightened Jettrin, being so in love with someone who lied so well.

Siam found an unsecured wireless network from a nearby café, connected to a proxy, and logged into his PartyYŏu account—or rather that of a grandmother in Khon Kaen who rarely ever went online and certainly had no interest in MMOs. And this minor act of identity theft constituted the sum total cybercrime he would commit today.

Jettrin watched as an elven necromancer named SIAMBANG appeared front and center in the tiny screen. The fantastic world of Rath sprawled around him, its full glory only diminished by the portable computer's low resolution. Even so, Rath's scenery was impressive, from the elven homeland of Eranil to the murky swamps of the trolls, the shadowy gothic ruins of Annandine, or the stony gray of the human capital city of Forthright. Each of these were lush with the flourishes of Rath's medieval-fantastic landscape, the individually rendered leaves swaying at the ends of procedurally generated branches, lens-flaring sunsets gleaming beyond the realistically scaled ranges of fractal mountain peaks, the avatar-accurate footprints left in the sands of deserts and swept away by the passage of twirling sand devils, the lapping of waves from sparkling seas that stretched to horizons an infinite draw distance away, the blue skies populated with cumulonimbi that loomed or flattened with the day, the night skies whose individually twinkling stars shifted brightness with the phase of the moon, the cloud of flies buzzing about the corpses of freshly slain orcs, the blossoms of spring, the heat haze of summer, the falling leaves of autumn, or the snowfall of winter, each flake unique.

Siam would have deactivated these details if the game had allowed it. Not to lighten the processing load (all the graphics were generated server-side, anyway) but because he saw no use for these extraneous details. He wasn't a spectator, here to gape. He visited Rath to win, and aesthetics were just distractions.

"Sorry. You're not hacking, you're gaming," Jettrin corrected. "That's much more helpful."

"I'm catching up on guild business," Siam explained. Excited messages flooded his chat window, most from allies wondering where he'd been during their last raid.

"This isn't the time," Jettrin persisted.

Siam ignored him. "And now I'm talking to LaserWolf."

"Who's LaserWolf?"

"He's a level-sixty dwarven druid," Siam said, pointing to a squat robed woman who crested a hillock and greeted Siam with a wave.

Jettrin sat down across from Siam and tried to make eye contact. "Listen, I think I know what you're doing, and I appreciate it."

"You do?"

"You're trying to piss me off. If I'm angry, I can't be sad. And it worked, all right? Thank you." He placed a hand on Siam's arm. "But this isn't a long-term solution. We need to focus on the problem."

Siam's eyes were still on the screen. "Hold on, I'm telling him about my vacation."

"Your *vacation*?"

"In Vietnam."

"What the hell are you doing? You're telling people where we are? On the Internet?"

Siam sighed and met his boyfriend's eyes.

"Jettrin, a hundred million people play this game. It's the largest MMO in history. My guild has a hundred members, and it's just for people who live in Southeast Asia, and there are, like, three other allied guilds for the same geographic region. And do you know where LaserWolf lives?"

Jettrin didn't dare guess.

Receiving no answer, Siam pointed up the road.

WITH LASERWOLF'S sister away at university and his parents visiting relatives in Da Nang, he was happy to rent apartment space out to Siam and his two friends.

"Rent" was practically a trigger word for Jettrin. "How are we going to pay for this?" he hissed when their host was out of earshot.

"With like a hundred thousand gold up front," Siam whispered back, "plus a full set of epic armor when we leave."

A king's ransom, but it meant the three of them could eat and shower that night, and sleep in clean beds. Jai was allowed to use the matriculating sister's bedroom, while Jettrin and Siam shared a futon in the living room. This was Jettrin's usual preferred arrangement, with the two older boys between Jai and the front door, in case trouble came knocking in the night. But as the two boys burrowed under the futon's sheets, in this cozy family room filled with family photos and throw pillows, something about these concerns struck Siam as superfluous.

"I love you," Jettrin whispered in the darkness. He twined his arms around Siam and kissed him. "I need you. I'm not sure how you made this happen, but thank you for doing it."

Siam squeezed his hand.

"But we're not done," Jettrin said. "What about tomorrow? We can't stay forever at your friend's place. I don't care how much fictional money you've saved up."

Siam squeezed again. "Take a break from worrying, okay? You've earned a rest."

Jettrin breathed. "Okay," he agreed, and went quiet.

Siam sighed in relief. If Jettrin could wait to talk about their plans, Siam would wait one more night to talk about Jettrin's little brother. He'd come up with a solution to the Jai problem, but he knew Jettrin wouldn't like it.

Siam rolled over and gave Jettrin a kiss. Jettrin reciprocated, and then, quietly, hungrily, and mercifully free of the usual fear and desperation, they had sex.

Tonight, all three boys slept soundly.

SIAM WOKE and looked at the time. It was 11:27 a.m.

Jettrin, already awake, rolled over to look at him. "It's tomorrow. How do we get out of the country?"

Siam wished he'd pretended to be asleep. He took a deep breath. "Why?"

"So we don't get caught, obviously," said Jettrin. "Or did you forget?"

Siam steeled himself. "Why?"

"You know what they'll do to Jai," Jettrin said.

"Feed him?"

Jettrin blinked. He sat up, horror on his face.

"Have you seen how skinny he's gotten?" Siam asked.

"Of course," Jettrin whispered. "But we've been running and hiding for so long."

"So stop running."

"Oh my God." Jettrin's large eyes widened. "You're serious."

"Think about it," Siam said. "What do you think will happen if Jai gets caught?"

"You know what'll happen! They'll make him work for them."

"Yeah, he'll get a job, and an education, and enough money to feed himself and his family, including you."

Jettrin swore. "I know you don't like him, but do you hate him so much you want to get rid of him?"

"No, I don't hate him. I...." Siam paused, swallowed. "I love him, and I love you. Do you know how many times I've thought about disappearing on the two of you, just to give you a reason to stop running? Except I knew you'd keep running anyway. But unlike me you don't need to run. I actually had a criminal record before I ever met the two of you. If they catch me, I end up in a detention center. If they catch you, you end up in a house."

Jettrin stared at him but said nothing, and Siam knew he'd scored a point, though he hated himself for it.

LaserWolf entered from his bedroom, still in his pajamas. Siam was grateful for the interruption. Siam greeted him, and the two talked guild business and game mechanics while Jettrin sat stewing nearby. Siam occasionally spared glances at his boyfriend, watching for changes in demeanor.

During a heated discussion of PvP balancing, Jettrin straightened in his chair, looked to the sister's bedroom, the one where Jai had slept. Then Jettrin stood, excused himself, and vanished into the bedroom "to check on Jai."

Siam felt a stab of concern but let his boyfriend go without a word.

JETTRIN CLOSED the door behind him as he entered the bedroom.

"Why did you do that?" he demanded. Psyching in any form, even just sending a brief telepathic message, was to be done only under the most urgent circumstances.

Jai was seated on the bed, inside a menagerie of stuffed animals. "I'm sorry," he said. "I got scared."

Looking at Jai now, and with Siam's words still fresh in his mind, it was impossible not to notice that Jai did look worryingly skinny, even after the barbecued pork and rice noodles they'd ordered in last night.

Jai held up a picture frame.

"Where did you get that?" Jettrin asked.

"Off her desk."

Jettrin took the frame and inspected it. A family photo. LaserWolf with, presumably, his older sister and his two parents, all of them smiling broadly. They were outdoors, gathered on what Jettrin took to be a college campus on a clear blue day. The photo was recent, as far as Jettrin could tell. LaserWolf looked no younger, and even wore the same glasses and hairstyle.

"I've seen pictures of those buildings online," Jai said.

"Oh?"

Jai nodded, and Jettrin noticed he was sweating.

"It's the school where they train their psychics," Jai said.

An interminable moment passed, during which Jettrin was aware only of Jai's eyes and of his own heartbeat in his ears.

Jettrin swallowed and said, "She's away at school right now. Thousands of kilometers away. A whole other country. We're not in danger."

Jai nodded but still looked fearful. Jettrin took a moment to marvel at how intelligent his little brother had become to notice this clue. Jai was only seven. When had he gotten so precocious? Then Jettrin felt the air go out of him when he remembered Jai was turning eight this month. He wasn't growing precocious. He was just *growing*.

Siam had planted the seed of new doubts that, however unwelcome, only seemed to intrude the more Jettrin tried to push them away.

He lifted a large pink triceratops out of the way, sat down next to Jai on the bed, and hugged him close with one arm. "Why were you looking at information on this psychic school?" he asked.

"No reason," Jai said. "I just looked it up one day."

"Do you.... Would you like to go there? So they can, uh...." Jettrin swallowed. "Train you? And take care of you?"

Jai reared back.

"No!" he said, sounding betrayed. "I don't want to go there!"

"Okay!" Jettrin whispered, trying to lower Jai's volume. "All right, all right. I'm sorry I said that." He pulled Jai back close to him. Jai allowed himself to be held, but his body was rigid. "I'm sorry I said that," Jettrin repeated, blinking away tears. "I'm sorry. I just wanted to be sure."

Privately, Jettrin didn't feel so much sorrow as relief. His eyes went to the picture again. He'd barely paid attention during the broken conversation between Siam and LaserWolf last night, but he'd overheard some discussion of holiday travels. LaserWolf's parents were visiting their relatives in Da Nang but would soon be back to spend time with their own kids. Was his sister meant to visit as well? Would it be this week? On the weekend? What holiday was it, anyway? Something local?

"Jai," he said, "I know I keep telling you to do this, even though I keep telling you not to, but can you check something for me?"

Jai looked up at him, and Jettrin met his eyes.

"Can you find out when LaserWolf expects his sister to visit here next?"

Jai slid gently out of Jettrin's hug, getting a better look at his older brother. When he saw the look in Jettrin's eyes, he nodded. Then the younger brother breathed, focused on a point on the wall, and concentrated.

Jai KNEW pulling out other people's memories was tricky. You had to gently tease the memory out in a way that felt natural or work your way down to it in a way that was undisruptive. Rushing the job might yank the information out too abruptly, confusing or even damaging the mind.

If the person became alarmed, his thoughts could tip into a chaotic fury impossible to sift through. Or he might wonder why the hell he'd started thinking about his computer password or the amount of money in his bank account. This wasn't always a big deal; random thoughts and memories popped into people's heads all the time without anyone questioning them. If the person was paranoid about psychics reading his mind, he might become suspicious. Even then, most people couldn't know for sure if a psychic was in their heads.

Except for Countermind.

No matter how hard he tried, Jai never forgot the time he'd tried psyching the man from Countermind. The dark-clothed man had been tall, young, somewhat European-looking, his manner imbued with self-possessed menace. Jai should have known better than to go poking around inside any stranger's head for no reason, let alone this one. But Jai had been foolhardy and bored. They'd had no TV, no Internet, no books, nothing else a kid could do for entertainment but poke into the heads of passersby and see what they were thinking about. Watching the man from behind a sixth-story apartment window with the lights off, Jai'd thought himself invisible from the street. So he'd indulged his curiosity and looked inside.

Jai had never been the type to imagine monsters under a bed. But looking in the man's mind, Jai had seen… *things*. Awful things, too terrible to look away from. He'd witlessly stumbled into a fun house horror show, full of terrors he still lacked the vocabulary to describe.

How the man had detected Jai's entrance, how he'd twisted his own thoughts like some shape-shifting demon, Jai didn't know and couldn't guess. This wasn't a talent any normal, sane person, even a psychic, was supposed to possess. And Countermind wasn't even supposed to have psychics (a fact that somehow made them scarier). But the man's counterattack against Jai's psychic invasion still provoked nightmares years later, often requiring his big brother to rush to his bed and hold him until he stopped sobbing.

Jai had been rendered briefly catatonic by that encounter, he'd been so overwhelmed by the counterattack. If Jettrin hadn't been there, hadn't carried him away, Jai might've woken up in Countermind's clutches, and he couldn't guess what would have happened next.

They'd been running ever since.

He never forgot the lesson of that night: invading someone else's mind didn't just make that person vulnerable. It made yourself vulnerable, as well. That one experience was enough to impress on Jai the dangers of casual telepathy, and his big brother had little need to keep reminding him of those dangers. On the rare occasions he did exercise his power—only at Jettrin's insistence or when he felt he truly needed to—it was with the greatest of care.

With the greatest of care, Jai reached toward the mind of the strange boy talking to Siam outside the room.

SIAM COULD see that LaserWolf was trying hard to be an attentive host, even preparing a simple breakfast. They mostly confined their small talk to Rath, but the spoken language barrier meant Siam had to pay attention to the conversation, and sustained attention, always difficult for him anyway, was made even more difficult by concerns over Jettrin. And now the two brothers were locked in that room, and Siam had no idea what they were doing or what they were talking about. Without Siam's input, the conversation was running dry, so LaserWolf attempted a change in topic.

"My sister comes home soon," he blurted out.

"Oh?" asked Siam. Not sure how to maintain appearances, he decided the next, most appropriate thing to say was "Is she cute?"

LaserWolf said nothing, just gave an I-don't-know shrug. He didn't seem terribly interested in the matter, despite having brought her up.

"When does she come home?" Siam asked, trying to keep the conversation going.

"This morning, I think. Who knows?"

"Oh. I guess this means Jai will have to move out of her bed," Siam observed, glad he and Jettrin had taken advantage of their privacy last night.

"That's all right," Jettrin interjected, emerging from the bedroom. He led Jai by the hand behind him. "I think I'd like to get going today. There's so much of the country we want to see and so little time to do it."

"Really?" Siam asked, perplexed. He looked to LaserWolf, who gave another shrug.

"Certainly," said Jettrin. "I don't want to impose any longer on your friend's good hospitality or cause any trouble with his family."

"I'm sure it'll be fine," Siam insisted. Forget sex. Now he was worried about the next time he'd sleep on an actual mattress. What was Jettrin's hurry? Siam studied his face, only now seeing the near-panic simmering beneath the merely beleaguered look Jettrin usually sported. Something was wrong.

They heard voices in the hallway. Male and female, old and young. LaserWolf stood, moved toward the door.

Siam looked to Jettrin and Jai, who could no longer hide their alarm.

"Stop him," Jettrin mouthed to Siam.

So Siam tackled him.

They hit the ground with a racket, but LaserWolf was so stunned by the attack, he just lay unmoving on the floor with Siam on top of him.

Siam looked again to the two brothers, their eyes big as saucers. They didn't know what to do.

The approaching conversation was right outside the door now. A key ring jingled. There would be an iron security gate, and then the actual door with two more locks of its own. At least three locks in total.

Siam wasn't hearing any suggestions so, in keeping with his play style, he took the aggressive approach.

"Come to your room," he hissed into LaserWolf's ear, "or I'll kill you."

LaserWolf choked out a half-second scream, then promptly fell unconscious.

Locks were turning. Finding his guildmate suddenly limp and quiet, Siam didn't know how to react until Jettrin grabbed one of LaserWolf's shoulders. Needing no instruction, Siam helped his boyfriend drag the unconscious boy into LaserWolf's room.

Jai was already in the room, cowering by the closet. Jettrin and Siam closed and locked the bedroom door a split-second before they heard the apartment door swing open, and the jovial, familial conversation grew louder. One of the older voices inquired after their son, and they called his name a couple of times. "Your beloved sister's home!" one voice announced.

Siam looked at the prone LaserWolf. He was clearly breathing. Had he fainted?

Jettrin caught Siam's attention with a wave of his hand. Siam watched as Jettrin pointed to Jai, touched his own temple, pointed at LaserWolf, then mimed sleeping by pressing his hands together and tilting the side of his face onto them, as if on a pillow. Siam inferred from this performance that Jai had knocked their host unconscious.

"Why?" Siam mouthed.

Jettrin held up a framed photo of LaserWolf with his family. He pointed at the doorway the voices were emanating from, then at a girl in the photo—presumably the sister—then touched his temple again.

Siam's heart raced. If the sister was psychic, and was here in the apartment, and if she scanned the area, the three of them were fucked.

The conversation outside didn't yet carry any notes of suspicion or alarm. Siam could discern one older male voice, and two women, one older and one younger. Parents and the sister.

J ETTRIN MOTIONED Siam to the bedroom window and gestured outside. Diagonally across from the window, about four meters away, was a vertical rectangular concrete structure protruding from the apartment building, with large open-air windows through which they could see the steps of an emergency stairway. A thin shelf-like projection ran along the building's exterior wall, providing a possible route to the stairway. It was too thin for anyone, even someone as small as Jai, to stand on untethered, but Jettrin was already pulling the sheets off the bed, and Siam helped tie them into a makeshift rope.

LaserWolf's family was voluble. Their conversation had grown loud enough for the boys to follow it. The father left with the sister to help carry up the rest of the sister's luggage and some groceries. The mother knocked on the bedroom door, demanding LaserWolf come outside to help, shouting to be heard over the gaming headset she assumed her son was wearing.

But the three boys were already out the window. They'd tied the rope to a football trophy, tossed it over the stairway guardrail, and pulled it tight. Jai, gripping the rope, made his way along the shelf, Jettrin and Siam holding it taut. Another length of makeshift rope was tied around Jai's waist. When Jai was across, he tied both ropes tight around the guardrail. Using these, Jettrin made his way across, with Siam following last. When all three stood safely inside the stairwell, Jettrin took the other two by the hands and yanked them down the stairs.

But Siam resisted. Jettrin turned and saw Siam gripping a guardrail, peering down at the street.

"Look."

Below, a green-uniformed police officer was clambering over a gate in the narrow alley at the base of the stairway. On the other side of the gate, the man spoke into a radio. He started up the steps, his eyes fixed upward, looking directly at the boys.

"He must think we're thieves," said Siam.

"This way," Jettrin ordered, pulling them up the stairs. They could escape down the stairs if Jai psyched the officer, but any sort of telepathic assault or tampering would later be evident to psychic investigators examining the officer's mind and would be more trouble than it was worth. Three young thieves wouldn't draw any additional pursuit, particularly when it was discovered that nothing had been stolen, but a rogue psychic would put the entire country on alert. Bad enough Jai had already disabled Siam's friend. They'd have to find an escape route above.

They found none.

Jettrin and Siam darted in frantic diagonals across the rooftop, peering over the low concrete parapet in search of another rooftop, a ladder, a stairwell, a storm gutter, a power cable—anything at all. But there was nothing.

"He's here," Jai shouted.

The officer emerged from the stairway and stalked across the roof toward them. He shouted for the boys to stop, to surrender, to lie down on their stomachs. The boys clustered at the rooftop's corner, Jettrin pushing Siam and Jai behind him with his left arm. His right hand, palm slick with sweat, twitched at the hem of his shirt. He felt the weight of the knife against his chest. A murdered officer would draw more pursuit than a trio of escaped thieves but wouldn't mobilize nearly as much government attention as a rogue psychic, would it?

And then they were caught. And it was too late.

Hello, Jettrin, came a young woman's voice in Jettrin's mind. *You can stop running now.*

The voice, of course, was not an actual voice. It had no physical volume, no pitch, no timbre. But it still had the indefinable *qualia* of youth and femininity, in the same way Jai's psychic voice was childish and male.

Tell your boyfriend to stop. Tell your brother to stop. It's for their own safety. I promise you won't be harmed.

"They found us," Jettrin gasped.

"What?" said Siam.

Oh no, thought Jettrin, with such urgency he could barely focus on what the woman was saying. *Oh no no no no no.*

The police officer chose that moment to dash toward the three boys.

They found us, thought Jettrin. *They found us.*

They found us.

Not knowing what else to do, Jettrin reached under his shirt in a move he'd practiced a hundred times but had never before needed, grabbed the knife by the hilt, and gave it a single hard yank.

Chapter 14
Fairy Tales

Arissa needed practice. Telepathy wasn't omniscience. Every mind was a third-person limited point of view with an unreliable narrator. Names, thoughts, memories, entire identities were subject to assumption, expectation, and interpretation, both by the mind being read and the mind reading it. As minds grew numerous, perspectives bled into one another. A psychic could slip from one stream of consciousness to another with a simple shift in focus. Voices overlapped, crowded one another out, competed for attention.

There were seven million voices in Hong Kong.

"Goddammit!" Agent Wen sneezed again. "Goddamn," he repeated, rubbing the rawness from his nose. "I thought they got her dog out of the flat."

"They did," Agent Wei said from the next room.

"Then why am I sneezing?"

"Not because of your allergies," said Wei. "Cresteds don't shed."

"It's not the hair," argued Wen. "It's the dander!" And he sneezed another four times. Shit. Could it be a cold? His dog allergy was never this bad.

"Nothing in the living room," Wei shouted through the door. "Starting on the kitchenette."

"Still looking through the bedroom," Wen said, then sneezed a nice big gob of snot all over his mouth.

Grimacing, he cleaned the mess with the first thing he saw, a large folded square of red cloth on top of the bureau. It was larger than it looked, felt like silk, and shimmered with a vine-like pattern. Rather large for a handkerchief, but that observation came too late. Now it had a large shiny spot of mucus on it.

"I hope this isn't evidence," he muttered.

"Are you all right in there?" Wei called.

"I'm fine," answered Wen. He held up the cloth against the light and examined the gleaming spot. Ugh.

He carried it into the bathroom and scrubbed the cloth clean under some hot water, then hung it on a drying line outside the bedroom window.

He promptly forgot all about the cloth, which was just as well. By the time they finished searching the flat, the cloth was gone.

IN HIS resting state, Knife-fight Li wasn't so frightening. He'd only needed to live up to the nickname once, after all, the skirmish being quite decisive. He didn't smoke or spit or swear. Even with the tattoos visible at his neck, his placid demeanor tended to overwhelm any impression of violence people might receive from him.

It helped that the woman, unflappable to begin with, was accustomed to him showing up at her door with a delivery. When she stepped out of her building on her way to work only to bump into Li on the front sidewalk, she was only surprised by the stack of cardboard boxes behind him.

She eyed the boxes warily. "Are those…?"

Li nodded. "As you've requested: seven thousand silk handkerchiefs, sent by my father in honor of your beauty. He hopes these will be sufficient to demonstrate his adoration of you and to win your affection for him."

"I suppose they'll need to come upstairs, won't they?"

"If you'll permit it."

"I'll be late for work." She sighed. "Very well. Come on."

She brewed tea while Li carried the boxes up three at a time. When they were all in the foyer, she handed him a cup as well as a washcloth to wipe the sweat off his face.

"Thank you."

"Never mind it."

"If you'll forgive me for taking more of your time, I would also like to deliver a request."

"What does he want this time?" she asked between sips of tea.

"Forgive me, but this is my request."

She looked up from her cup. "Oh? That's new."

"My father, though powerful and influential, isn't the hard-hearted man you might expect from someone with his responsibilities."

"I do think your little societies rather resemble gentlemen's clubs more than criminal organizations these days, it's true."

"He is, in fact, an extremely sensitive, sentimental man."

"Yes, that's quite clear to me," she said.

"He has been inconsolable since my mother died."

That quieted her. She set down her teacup and waited for Li to continue.

"I'm afraid his grief has driven him to folly, and I'm afraid you, through no fault of your own, have become a target of his folly."

She nodded. "Yes, that describes my predicament well."

"Nonetheless, I'd humbly ask you to do what you can to stop this from going any further."

She lifted her cup again, looked at it, swirled it about, set it down. "What do you think I've been trying to do?"

"It's one outlandish gift after another," Li said, "and I know you only give them away to friends, relatives, coworkers, employees. First it was seven of one thing, seventy of the next, seven hundred of the next, and now this." He gestured to the boxes. "I had to send dozens of men through the city, buying up scarves, even stealing them from shops and dryer lines, to meet your demand. You understand what a gift of handkerchiefs signifies."

"I'd hoped your father would take the hint."

"He hasn't. And I cannot conceive of how we will satisfy your next task."

"And before all that?" she asked. "Before I started asking for gifts?"

"You simply refused his advances," Li confessed. "Several times. But he wouldn't listen to you, no more than he listens to anyone else advising him to leave you alone. As I said, this situation is no fault of your own. But if this continues, it will ruin him. I'm begging you, please, help me bring it to an end."

"I want to," she said. "I was hoping it would end if, by being unreasonable, I forced him to see reason, but that's taking longer than I'd hoped."

"Much longer," Li agreed.

"But if I simply refuse him, he'll persist."

"I'm afraid he will," Li admitted.

"So we have a dilemma," she said and sat a moment languorously sipping her tea while Li waited to hear what she had to say. He'd come to understand this woman for a prankster, a trickster, but he still marveled at how impressive her bearing could become—imperious, even—at any moment.

She spoke. "I'm encouraged at least to hear that others have been trying to talk sense into him."

"We have been, believe me."

"But you don't have any actual ideas, other than appealing to me to end it, as if that were within my power."

Li looked chagrined. "I…. No, we haven't been able to devise a solution either."

She studied him intently, and he felt unsettled.

"It seems to me you love your father greatly," she said.

"I do."

"And you say he's softhearted?"

It was his turn to consider her. Where was she going with this?

"Well?" she asked.

"He is," Li answered.

"Then let me make another request," she said, rising to her feet. "Tell him that, if he wishes to truly demonstrate his love for me, he must disown you."

Li gaped for several long moments, both awed and horrified.

"I think I understand your scheme," he said at last. "But do you think it will work?"

"I don't know. Do you believe it won't? After all, you must be the next most precious thing to him, after your departed mother. You are furthermore, I would think, his best remaining reminder of her. Do you think he could bear to surrender you for me?"

"No. No, I don't believe he would," Li said. "I think he would be made to realize just how poorly he knows you, and just how much he values what he still has. However, it's a terrible request to make, even unseriously."

"I know. I'm rather ashamed to be suggesting it. But if it will shock your father back to his senses, then suggest it I will."

"And I will pass the request to him," Li said. He stood and quickly bowed. "You know, now that I've spoken to you—had an actual conversation, instead of just the usual pleasantries—I see how wise you are. You're...." He stopped, fumbled with the wording. *You're very much....*

"Yes?"

"You're doing me a great favor," Li finished, and left.

SUAN'S LANDLADY was the kind of old-headed buzzard who, if she tripped in the street, would probably try to sue anyone who helped her up. Old Ying was the reason Suan was loath to return straight home from her bank job. Even that morning Ying had chased Suan out of the apartment, demanding the rent (not technically overdue, even if the first of the month had passed). Far too steep a rent for the tiny room, more an oversized windowless closet with a cot jammed inside. Suan had to store her possessions beneath the cot and hung her clothes from a bar installed at an angle beneath the ceiling. And meanwhile Suan knew Ying had a whole other extra bedroom—well lit, ideally furnished for a young woman—sitting empty right down the hall. At the price Suan was paying, Ying could have put her in that room, or Suan could find more hospitable lodging elsewhere. But Suan had signed a lease with some pretty stiff penalties for breaking it.

Suan did return home, and Ying did meet her at the door, as angry as Suan had expected. She was also holding an envelope.

"What is this?" she demanded. She waved the envelope so furiously Suan couldn't even see what was written on it, just that it had already been opened.

"I don't know what it is," Suan protested.

"How long has someone been sending you money?" Ying asked.

"What?" Suan yanked the envelope out of Ying's bony hand. "There's no money in here."

"I put it toward your rent. And you're still short!"

Suan wanted to be angry, but she was too overcome with curiosity. The envelope still contained a folded letter. She ran into her room, Ying yelling at her the entire way, jerked the door shut behind her, and fell onto her cot.

Suan couldn't believe it. The letter and money were from her stepmother and stepsister. They apologized for the way they'd treated her after her father's death, the abuses they'd heaped on her, foisting all the chores on her, keeping the home and the savings that had belonged to Suan's parents, without letting Suan herself have any say in what was done with them, until she'd had no choice but to leave. They were making a peace offering. And they were inviting her over for dinner.

Suan had good reason not to believe any of it. The tone of the letter seemed sincere and contrite, but they'd misused her emotions in the past. It wasn't beyond them to play a cruel joke on her.

No money, no life. So true, but it wasn't really the money she missed as much as having a place to call home. She thought of the house and the room she grew up in—a simple room, but it had a window and a real bed. It had the clothes Stepsister Xiang now wore, the books her father had brought her from the book fair, the lucky goldfish her mother had gotten her at the goldfish market, a little calico shubunkin in a tiny bowl with green pebbles on the bottom.

The more Suan thought about it, the more opportunity she'd have to entertain doubts. With nothing to lose, she sent a text message asking if the dinner could be tonight. Only seconds passed before she received a response in the affirmative.

Suan emptied her bag of all the new handkerchiefs her crazy boss had given her today except one—a large, ornately patterned red scarf— but she didn't bother dressing up or otherwise preparing. She wasn't so concerned with saving face in front of these two that she would pretend to look forward to their company. Besides, if this was a trick, then she wanted to get it over with.

She took the MTR to Diamond Hills and then the bus into Sai Kung, walked up the mowed lawn in front of the house, and rang the bell. Stepmother opened the door and welcomed Suan into the house with an ebullient display of motherly joy and affection. Xiang emerged from the hallway and lit up with a cheerful smile when she saw Suan in the foyer. Xiang, surprisingly, was not wearing any of Suan's old clothes. It had been one of Xiang's favorite means of passively tormenting her stepsister before Suan had simply left.

Suan was sat at the dinner table while Xiang and Stepmother continued to work in the kitchen, apologizing for not entertaining her more personally but explaining that they wanted to make sure dinner was made well before serving it to her, and they'd had little time to prepare. They made small talk through the kitchen door, asking completely mundane questions about her life, her job, her health, expressing repeated concern for her happiness without any evident irony. Suan kept her manner stiff, answered the questions as briefly as possible, and betrayed no emotion, but they made no outward acknowledgment of her wariness.

To Suan's relief, dinner wasn't anything outlandish, nothing that looked like they were trying too hard: fishballs with noodle soup, some chicken curry, milk tea, some small wife cakes for dessert. The food tasted fine, and Suan said as much.

"Thank you! We're so glad you liked it!"

"We are!"

"How wonderful of you to say that!"

Still, she only ate or drank what they did, and only when she served it to herself from a common container. (She couldn't quite convince herself these two were above poisoning her.) They'd committed the sin of putting out Mom's display-only antique lace napkins, but this was probably a mistake instead of a slight, preferring as they did less subtle insults. When Suan had to wipe her fingers, she just used the red handkerchief she brought from home, without Stepmother or Xiang making any comment. Nor did they begrudge her reluctance to have additional portions doled out to her.

"We're only grateful for your company!"

"I'd like to know…." Suan started to say, then stopped herself.

The two of them sat attentively while Suan considered how to finish the sentence. "I'd like to know why I'm here. Beyond the pleasure of my company and so on. I can accept, or at least I can consider the possibility that people can change, even after behaving a certain way for a long time. I just can't accept it happening for no reason. I need to know what's going on. Because something's going on."

Stepmother and Xiang exchanged worried looks.

Then Stepmother looked to Suan and said, "There's been a will."

"What?" Suan asked. "A will? Whose will?"

"We don't know."

"You don't know? You don't know if it's my mother's or my father's or… some long-lost uncle?"

"We don't know."

"What does it say?" Suan asked.

"We don't know."

"How can you know there's a will and not know anything about it?"

"We were contacted by a lawyer looking for you," Stepmother explained. "He mentioned a will. He didn't even say one way or another whether there was an inheritance, just a will. He wouldn't tell us anything more about it."

"That's all it is?" Suan asked. "You want to get into my good graces because of a will?"

They were silent.

"And you didn't even put this lawyer in contact with me, because you wanted to win me over before I knew about this will, or before you even knew about any inheritance?"

Still they said nothing.

"And you thought all it would take is a dinner? That, and sending me not even enough money to cover a month's rent?"

Nothing again. Perhaps they realized there was nothing they could say.

Suan sighed. As much as she wanted to feel angry, she just felt tired. "I want to see my room," she said.

The room was as she left it, the shelved books still organized by size, language, color, and how old she was when she got them, the goldfish bowl still on the dresser by the closet and under a mirror. Her clothes were still in the closet, the door left open so she could see everything was still there.

Her eyes went back to the goldfish bowl. It looked clean but empty. It was probably too much to hope they'd taken good care of her mother's fish. Suan wasn't surprised, but that didn't stop a heavy weight of sorrow from settling onto her heart.

"What happened to Jinjin?" she asked without looking up from the bowl.

"To what?" Stepmother asked.

"My fish," Suan clarified.

Stepmother said nothing. After a few seconds, Xiang made a sound. So thoroughly had Suan been lulled into a sense of complacency, it took a moment for her to recognize that sound as a snicker.

She turned to see Stepmother smiling, while Xiang had her hand over her mouth, visibly fighting back a laugh.

"Did you enjoy the fish balls?" Stepmother asked.

Suan's exit from the house was so swift she would later remember it as a blur, and she barely registered the peals of mocking laughter following her through the front door.

She kept it together on the bus. She kept it together on the train. Only on the walk back to her apartment, when she caught the scent of fried fish drifting out of a restaurant, were her eyes blinded by such a sudden deluge of tears that she had to sit on the curb and dry them until her vision cleared. It took a while.

"Little Suan, why are you crying?" a woman's voice asked.

Even through the tears, Suan recognized Old Ying standing over her.

"Nothing," Suan snapped, dabbing at her face, furiously trying to salvage her dignity.

After a pause, Ying said, "Here, take it back, then."

Suan looked up to see a flat red envelope held in her face, the edge of a short stack of banknotes visible through the opening.

"I shouldn't have taken it. Pay it back when you're ready," Ying said.

Suan lifted her hand to wave the envelope away, stopped, and accepted it with a sigh.

"It's not the money," she said.

"What is it, then?"

Not having anyone else to talk to, anyone else at all, Suan related the events of the evening.

As Ying listened, she became amazed by her own blindness. Ever since losing her little Linda, she'd been aware of no sadness but her own, no misery but hers, and she'd had nothing to spare for others but anger. But what could she do? She was an old lady. All she had left was that home and its memories, and she'd lose these as well if she fell behind on her debts.

She wanted to say something comforting to Suan, but she knew how insincere it might sound. Instead, she reached out to finger the large red cloth Suan was crying into.

"This is a nice handkerchief," she said wondrously. A day ago, if she'd seen Suan with it, she would have scolded her for wasting money on nice things when she had obligations to meet.

Suan looked shamefaced. "It's from my boss," she said defensively. "She's nuts. She's been giving everyone in the office these gifts lately, and I'm always selling them for rent money. I promise I wouldn't have bought anything so nice when I still owed you for the month."

"Yes, well, I suppose we could still sell it to a hawker anyway. We must still pay for the utilities, when we get around to them. That is, if you haven't grown attached to it?"

Suan shook her head.

Ying stood up, giving Suan a gentle pull on her shoulder. "Why don't we sell it on the way home. It's getting late, and you've had a difficult day. Let's get you into a real bed."

FAY GRIMACED as Baoshi honked the vintage BMW's horn at another cluster of pedestrians. "Don't these people know this is a road?" he muttered. "For cars? It makes me so angry."

"We can take the tram next time," Fay offered.

"I'm not cramming into one of those rattling sardine cans," Baoshi said curtly.

Fay tried changing the subject to an argument she'd had with her best friend, but Baoshi responded with that faintly befuddled silence that always seemed just shy of saying, "Why are you telling me about your problems?" So she distracted herself on her phone while he maneuvered the vehicle into the parking garage, grumbling over the city's failure to construct sufficient parking space. It took thirteen minutes to find a satisfactory spot, but Baoshi was at least smiling again when he opened Fay's door. They walked through the souvenir market on the way to the restaurant, past colorful stalls exploding with shirts, hats, key chains, magnets. Children's toys, stuffed pandas, and lucky cat statuettes. Folding fans, porcelain chopsticks, tiny lacquer boxes. Handbags, chops, little earthenware tea sets. Paintings of the city, of the mountain, of junks in the harbor.

"Baoshi, look at that scarf!" Fay said. "Can I get it?"

"You're kidding me."

She stopped to admire it. "But look at that sheen, that beautiful carmine color."

The scarf was one of dozens, individually packaged in square plastic bags and hanging from pegs, but something about it seemed special. The texture was just calling to her, begging her to reach out and feel it. Behind a counter, a plump woman sat on a chair, watching them intently. Baoshi barely gave the woman a look of uncontained disgust before he took Fay by the elbow and hurried her along.

"You're making us late to lunch," he said. "And I shop retail or not at all."

They ascended the escalators and found a thick crowd of eager tourists crowding the restaurant entrance.

"Looks like a wait," Fay observed.

"I'm not standing behind a bunch of gawking mainland locusts," Baoshi said.

"We can put in your name, go for our walk now, and be back before our turn is up," Fay suggested, but Baoshi was already slipping up toward the front of the line. Some quiet words with the maître d', followed by a surreptitiously greased palm, and soon they were being shown to a table. The table was not on the terrace, offered no decent views.

"This isn't the kind of seating I paid for," Baoshi grumbled after they were seated. Variations on this complaint continued through lunch, only pausing when she managed to divert him from his second favorite topic (Things That Make Me Angry) to his first (The Story of My Success Despite Starting With Nothing).

"Parents dead, no money, no connections," he began. "Just a job on a cargo hauler. I'm about the only person born in Hong Kong who was willing to work on a ship. I was surrounded by idiots, but it paid off when some navigation software crashed and I was the only one onboard who could figure out how to debug it. All I did was check the fucking help menu, but still. The company decided I was some kind of wunderkind and started relying on me for fixes like that, even calling me from the shore to talk to me, and I was eventually transferred to the central office for IT support. And then I completely revolutionized how they handled logistics. That wasn't enough, though. I always had to make sure the right people noticed me, and always had to make sure the right people were ready to do me favors. It helps when you're responsible for system administration. No one can keep secrets from you. Never anything as explicit as blackmail, of course. But recognizing when people have problems and helping to fix them. Or recognizing when people are in your way and making problems for them, or just making sure their problems get worse."

"That doesn't sound nice," Fay finally found the courage to say.

"One doesn't succeed by being nice. You have to be like a stone."

Fay was relieved when Baoshi finally paid the check and they left the restaurant. The sun was out, and the mountain air was crisp—perfect weather for a walk across the plaza.

"Did you see the watch that guy was wearing?"

"No, I didn't," Fay said. Should she have? What did it even matter?

"If you're going to buy a knockoff, shouldn't it be something convincing?" Baoshi said, sounding exasperated.

Fay craned her neck around, searching for the offending man. She still couldn't spot him.

"Look at that person. He looks like he just got back from the gym."

"Maybe he just got back from the gym?" Fay asked, unsure of what else to say.

"It makes me so angry when people go out in public dressed like that."

This time Fay was able to spot who Baoshi was complaining about. "I think he's dressed for a run," she said as the man jogged by.

Baoshi watched him with barely contained disgust. "If he wants to jog, he should stick to a trail."

Desperate, Fay asked him about his own watch. He owned seven of them, which he proceeded to describe in detail. This subject carried them the rest of the way up to the terrace overlooking the city, where Fay excused herself to find a ladies' room.

Walking away, leaving him there alone, Fay didn't see Baoshi pull a small box out of his pocket and examine the diamond ring inside. She didn't see him mentally rehearse his proposal, gearing himself up. It had only been six months since their first date, but he didn't get what he had by waiting to go after what he wanted, and Fay was just what he was looking for. Nothing else, not the car, not the home, not the wardrobe, nothing would broadcast his success the way a beautiful wife would. And she was quite beautiful, when she had a mind to be, when she wasn't in one of those odder, undignified moods she was often prone to. It would take time to make sure she was consistently presentable, to train her not to embarrass him. Baoshi was sure he could make her into the wife he deserved, just as he'd taken the raw stuff of every other aspect of his life and carved from it no less than he was owed.

As for Fay, she didn't need to use the ladies' room so much as she needed to *breathe*. Baoshi wasn't always like this, she had to remind herself. Just when they were around lots of other people—which, granted, happened often in a town like this. Of course, she had to admit he was a lot like this in private as well, and not always about strangers. Friends, coworkers, clients—all were subjected to his censure. Never face-to-face, of course. In person, he was always smiles and politeness. But once someone was out of earshot, it was open season, and it left Fay wondering how Baoshi discussed her to his friends when she wasn't around. As far as Fay could gather, she'd lasted longer with Baoshi than any of his past girlfriends, which was either a sign of their compatibility or of her superhuman patience. Either way, she tried hard to interpret this longevity in an auspicious light. People could have layers, she reminded herself. She'd just needed some time to dig down, see what was really important to him.

Six months later, she was still digging.

She stepped out of the ladies' room and found the scarf vendor outside, as if the woman had been waiting for her. Fay was startled but brushed past. The woman walked alongside her, keeping pace.

"How is Baoshi?" the woman asked.

Fay stopped. "Excuse me?"

"Is Baoshi well? He looks well."

In Fay's experience, strangers approaching her with an inexplicable degree of familiarity were usually running some kind of con. Fay resumed her pace. "I'm sorry," she said. "I have to get going."

"He has a scar on his left arm. Won't go outside in the rain. Allergic to shellfish," the woman said. "Very short-tempered."

Fay turned, blinked. "You know him?"

"I'm his mother."

Fay couldn't say anything. She didn't have to. The woman filled the silence by unreeling a concise, comprehensive, wholly unauthorized biography of her son. A lot of details Fay already knew. A lot she hadn't known but were consistent with what she did know, with the kind of person she knew Baoshi to be.

Even the conclusion sounded disturbingly plausible: "He left us. He was too ashamed of where he came from. Just peasants without wealth or reputation. He was never happy at home." The woman's eyes grew sad. "I'm not angry at him. I just want to know he's well. Is he?"

When Fay was finally able to form a response, it was another question. "Can I still buy something from you?"

When the purchase was completed, Fay returned to find Baoshi waiting on the terrace overlooking the city. She watched through a daze as he got down on one knee, presented her with a diamond ring, asked her to marry him. She reached out and handed him a familiar-looking scarf, wrapped around something hard, round, and oblong. He pulled back a corner of the handkerchief.

Inside was a stone.

When Baoshi looked up, Fay was gone. He looked around, called her name, didn't see her, heard no reply.

It made him so angry, he hurled the rock from the terrace, scarf and all.

A SHIMMERING red missile plummeted toward a pedestrian walkway just alongside the Peak, amidst the jungle and overlooking the tramway. It very nearly gave a tourist a concussion, but a woman reached up and neatly caught it as if she'd been ready for it.

Arissa binti Noor unwrapped the shawl from around the stone. The stone she dropped into the brush. The large square of red cloth she stuffed into her pocket.

She took the tram down to the city, then taxied to the hotel she'd checked into under someone else's name. Once in her room, she withdrew the cloth, unfolded it, gently washed and ironed it.

It had been delivered to Arissa in a box of her parents' personal effects, the one article of clothing not tattered or bloodied. It was the only item of purely sentimental value to come with her from Malaysia. All these years (and some diligent cleaning) later, and it was still like new. Her mother had only just received it as a birthday gift from her father, and Arissa herself had never worn it. Her grief, and then her professional aspirations hadn't permitted it.

But that was all moot now, wasn't it?

Lots of little pushes, nudges, and implicit suggestions, and the shawl was hers again. The path it had followed from her flat to her hand had been more convoluted than necessary, but after a decade of sandbagging herself, she'd forgotten what a rush it was to use her power this way, subtly shifting people's decisions, redirecting their lives, making them characters in stories of her authoring.

The shawl had dried. Arissa worked from muscle memory, draped it over her head, pinned it into place, wrapped it around and over, teased the dangling edges into position to frame her face correctly. When it felt right, she turned to face her reflection in the mirror.

Arissa found her mother looking back, and her heart jumped into her throat.

She made a few more adjustments to the hijab, then left the hotel, made a right turn, and walked in the direction of Central, toward Feng Huang's apartment. A young, pretty woman, her head clothed in red that shone like blood, and her gait determined, she invited a few glances walking down the street. But anyone who noticed her just as quickly forgot her.

She needed the practice.

CHAPTER 15
THE LIVING DEAD

ALAN SPENT a full second gaping at the emaciated thing gnawing on his left tibia.

He lashed out at the zombie's mind.

He missed. Or rather, he had nothing to hit. Three more quick psychic thrusts of escalating force, until Alan was unleashing the sort of salvos that would normally kill a person, all to no effect.

He might have been telepathically assaulting the empty air for all the good it did. The zombie was mindless. Literally mindless.

Of course it was.

The pain of the bite jolted Alan into a burst of pragmatism. He placed a hand against the wall to steady himself and used his right leg to stamp on the creature's neck until it cracked beneath his boot. He gave the zombie's head a few swift kicks for good measure, then knelt down to examine his wound, probing it with his fingers.

The denim had torn under the grinding of the creature's teeth, and Alan's skin was gashed open as well. Oh shitshitshitshitshitshit. Alan's involuntary responses caught up with reality as pain lanced up his leg. His heart pounded against his rib cage, but panicking now wouldn't fix anything. He unzipped his bag and dug around, looking for something to bind the wound with.

Up the street, a solitary moan was soon joined by others. Alan froze. The chorus grew louder, nearer. Then a flash of lightning illuminated a score of shuffling figures, phantomlike in the rain, lurching in his direction.

The recess he'd sheltered in contained a door. Alan returned to it, tried the knob, found it unlocked. He pushed through and shut the door behind him but didn't find any way to lock it from the inside.

Could zombies even operate doorknobs? Alan didn't know. He was beginning to comprehend just how blindly he'd charged into his current situation, how ill-considered this little katabasis of his actually was. He fished his little flashlight out of his bag and waved its beam around. The room was empty except for dust, animal droppings, fragments of demolished furniture, and some framed photos of a dead dictator smiling incongruously at him from an otherwise bare wall.

Fists pounded at the door. The creatures had already closed the distance, and they apparently knew where he was.

Alan charged down a hall and around a corner, encountering no zombies but taking the corners slowly anyway. He heard the wooden door fracture, heard the moans penetrate into the gloom, just as he spotted a tall steel locker inside an empty room. He opened the locker and slipped his thin frame inside, his bag between his feet on the locker's floor. He pulled the locker door closed and extinguished his light. His pursuers poured into the building, calling, searching. Alan remained hidden, perfectly still, quiet as death.

The dead found him anyway.

"You didn't tell me you were going to ambush him here," Doctor Kim said, voice full of accusation.

"If I'd told anyone, he might have read it from your mind," Smith answered. "I didn't want to risk tipping him off."

"Well, that is a new twist on plausible deniability."

Smith paced the aisles of the storehouse furiously. "What're we dealing with, here?" he asked.

"What do you mean?"

"The zombies. What are they really?"

"That's classified."

"I know that, and I respect your diligence, Doctor, but I need to know what they are. Believe me when I say Counterpsychic Affairs will be in your debt."

"Don't promise me any favors, agent. I don't collect them. I do my job. And when I say that information is classified, I mean it's classified."

Smith gave Doctor Kim a surprised expression, reappraising the scientist.

Kim sat down on a crate, arms folded.

"All right," Smith said. "If I can't bribe you, maybe I can appeal to a nobler interest."

"What do you mean?"

"That psychic is the last person to have known Quentin Izaki, one of the most brilliant minds of the twenty-first century, and is likely the last person to have observed Izaki's final work before his death and before his private laboratory was destroyed by a bomb. Alan likely knows something, possibly something of significant national or social consequence. That knowledge is, at the least, sure to be of considerable scientific or historical value. If he dies, that knowledge, whatever it is, will almost certainly be lost for all time. And even if he doesn't know anything," Smith added, "a psychic running loose on the streets is a danger to society and its citizens. A psychic running around *out there*"— Smith pointed toward the exit—"is himself in graver danger than you should wish on anyone. If you tell me what I need to know to save him, won't it be enough if it spares him being torn apart by monsters or, God forbid, being turned into a monster himself?"

Kim sighed. Smith suspected he'd made some headway but decided to try a little minimization.

"I'm in the intelligence business," Smith said. "I can keep classified information secret, and there's no one else in the world better qualified to keep a secret than a Countermind agent. And you don't actually have to tell me anything of consequence. You don't need to explain anything. Just tell me enough that I'll be able to move around out there safely."

"You can't," Kim said.

"Why not?"

"They'll find you," Kim averred. "Nothing you do can prevent that."

"Can't I hide? What if they don't spot me?"

"It doesn't matter whether they spot you," Kim answered. "They'll still find you."

Kim drummed their fingers on the top of a crate, and Smith suspected they were weighing words.

"You've seen the footage from when this country collapsed, right?" Kim asked. "And other recordings from border encounters?"

"Of course," Smith said. "Everyone has." Those video recordings had fueled the nightmares of an entire generation, and had provided Smith with ammunition for a particularly nasty counterpsychic technique.

"Why don't zombies attack other zombies?" Kim asked.

Smith realized he'd never considered the question. When he admitted as much, Kim invited him to speculate, so he ventured a guess. "They're angry, aggressive, out of control."

"All true," Kim allowed, "if oversimplified. But not an answer to the question. Zombies in the company of other zombies do not behave aggressively toward each other, despite the numerous targets of opportunity on which to enact their aggression. Their aggressive behaviors are only directed toward uninfected, living, higher-order organisms."

"All right," Smith said. "They're hungry. They want healthy, living flesh to eat."

"Still true, but still the wrong answer."

"Then it's because they're undead monsters. Help me out here, Doctor. We don't have time for the Socratic method."

"Now you're further off the mark. Zombies are alive."

"Not according to reputation."

Kim seemed to bite back a comment, took a moment to recompose themself, and started drily counting off criteria on their fingers. "Zombies react to the environment. Their bodies still age and develop. They consume and metabolize. They even reproduce, after a fashion, by transmitting their infection through bites. They're alive in every meaningful biological sense. More to the point, a zombie in the company of a recently turned, and therefore comparatively healthy zombie will ignore it but will behave cannibalistically toward a sickly or decrepit, but otherwise normal and uninfected, human being."

"Fine," Smith said, losing patience. "I'm stumped."

"You've heard zombies described as mindless?"

"Yes," Smith answered, "and I'd thought that was a fairly well-established fact. One of the first things the authorities tried after the initial outbreak was using psychics to telepathically neutralize infected carriers. They had absolutely no effect."

"That's true, but the notion that zombies are mindless is spurious, and completely nonsensical if given a moment's critical thought. As I said, they can sense the environment and react to it. They're capable of simple decision-making and automatic, instinctive behaviors. They vocalize. They emote. The fatal effects of injury to their brains wouldn't be observed if those brains were not serving some sort of vital—truly, literally vital—function. They do have minds."

"Then why couldn't the psychics sense them?" Smith asked.

"Because," Kim said, touching a finger to their own temple, "their minds are *shielded*. When an infected person is transformed into a zombie, that person's mind is rendered immune to telepathic detection. But the minds of the uninfected are not shielded. You could go out there silently, you could even go out there literally invisibly, and so long as you had a functioning, thinking mind, a mind visible to telepathy, they would still detect you, they would hunt you, and they would find you."

Smith sat down.

"I know there's another pretty obvious implication to what you're telling me, Doctor," Smith said, his mouth suddenly dry, "but I'm afraid I can't bring myself to articulate it."

"Yes," Doctor Kim said. "The other effect of the virus is to turn the infected person into a psychic."

Smith sat a long moment, absorbing this while the storm rattled the walls.

"How is this possible?" he asked. "I know you're not going to tell me, but you can't blame me for asking anyway."

Kim shook their head, held their tongue.

"Fine. You've already been generous enough with your information. I suppose." Smith stood again. "I need all the information you have on the area on the other side of that bridge: detailed maps, satellite photos, security. Or is all that classified as well?"

"It is, but—" Kim began.

"I don't care. You're going to have to make an exception this time."

"And I will. But I don't think you've been listening to me. If you go out there, you'll be devoured alive."

"Only if they hear me thinking, right?"

It was Kim's turn to be surprised.

"You're not the only one with secrets, Doctor," said the agent. "The maps, please?"

The base was still in sufficient disarray that Doctor Kim had no trouble escorting Smith to one of the records buildings. There, they spread the requested maps over a table, and Smith began studying them, with a particularly strong interest in Pyongyang's northeast quadrant around the

Rungna Islet. He recited street names and intersections, examined photos of landmarks from multiple angles, and interrogated Kim on how much of the information in the maps was out of date, using a pen to scribble corrections.

"What are you doing?" Kim asked.

"Programming myself. I'll need to run on autopilot."

"You can't expect to memorize all this with any fidelity in so short a time," Kim said.

"Cramming works best for the short term," Smith said. "Let's just hope I don't have to repeat this trick in a year."

"You aren't preparing for a geography quiz. It's—"

"It's mnemonics. You ever notice how Chonu Dong and Chonsung Dong together kind of look like a guy's body?"

"No."

"See?" He pointed at the map. "He's got a triangular hat on his head with a couple of long antennae growing out the top. Put your finger on the island."

"What?"

"Where we are. Put your finger on the map at our current location."

Kim did as instructed.

Smith turned so his back was toward the map. "Now follow these instructions," he said, and rattled off a series of directions: street names, distances, right turns, left turns, with Kim sliding their finger up, down, left, right, rushing to keep up.

"Which puts us at Friendship Tower," Smith finished and turned to look at the map.

Kim's finger was, in fact, at Friendship Tower. Kim gaped.

"Good," Smith said. He repeated the trick five more times, listing a series of directions and then naming a landmark. In each case, his navigation was flawless.

"All right," Smith said. "That'll have to do. Time for you to show me out."

Kim protested as they followed him toward the exit. "Impressive as that display was, it still won't help you find your fugitive."

"I assume, if he's still alive, the zombies will hear him thinking? And will be pursuing him *en masse*?"

"Probably."

"So I just need to find the big, noisy crowd of zombies. Shouldn't be too hard. Can you lend me a vehicle?"

Across the courtyard, near the gate, medical staff busily worked to revive the unconscious soldiers Alan had left in his wake during his flight. Without asking for permission, Kim walked up to the gate, unlocked it, and pulled it open. Smith, in the driver's seat of a black BAW four-wheel-drive vehicle, drove through, down the bridge, and into the dark city. Kim pulled the gate shut behind him and refastened the lock.

Down the shoreline, a thin male figure rose up out of the river until it was waist-high in the water, its emergence unnoticed and unremarked upon in the night. It waded its way to the concrete barrier topped by the chain-link fence that ran the island's perimeter, to a point where a segment of the fence was yawning open, flapping like a pennant in the typhoon winds, and squirmed through, moaning too softly to be heard over the storm and the commotion of the base.

RUNNING SILENT, Smith pursued Alan Izaki into the necropolis.

He followed a straightforward search pattern, favoring longer roads to minimize turning, drawing lines across the irregular grid. Intersections and turns appeared where expected, and Smith was able to drive with the vehicle's floodlights on, the better to spot obstacles far in advance. The thin, indistinct figures staggering past his vehicle didn't even seem to notice the light. The streets were the emptiest Smith had ever seen in a major city, and because surprises were so few, he didn't have to pay them much mind. Only the unexpected invites contemplation.

But there were still surprises. This was an unfamiliar city infested by zombies during a tropical storm. When Smith encountered the occasional obstacle—a shuffling infection victim, an abandoned vehicle, a toppled tree—he needed a moment's thought to chart a path around it. Whenever such course corrections were necessary, nearby zombies turned their heads as if catching his scent. Then he'd pass the obstacle, fall back into his trance, and become lost to them again.

The notion of "clearing the mind" during meditation was cliché but useful. For a counterpsychic agent determined to conceal sensitive information, or to avoid detection altogether, it was an invaluable technique only mastered with considerable difficulty. Merely suppressing unwanted thoughts wasn't good enough, was too vulnerable to ironic processes, could lead to rebound effects. *Don't think of a white bear*, you tell yourself, and what happens?

To truly run silent, you had to let your thoughts go where they would and then simply refuse to follow them there. Allow your mind to annihilate itself, like an oil lamp burnt dry. Dispel your consciousness for the effluvia it is. With practice, a skilled Countermind agent could deploy a koan like a cloaking device, collapsing all mental architecture in on itself until nothing remained but a void.

Jack Smith's mind made the sound of one hand clapping.

Smith drove down the left leg of the man with the antenna hat. There was a park on his left, Pyongyang's TV tower looming high above it, lit up ominously by the lightning, and he found the zombie mob. They were staggering across the road, converging into a neighborhood of somber apartment towers on the right, moving with a collective purpose Smith had not yet seen in them. They were a horde.

After glancing around to confirm no zombies were near, Smith risked rolling down the vehicle's windows for a second. The combined volume of dozens of moans was audible above even the sound of the storm, beyond the apartments.

Smith took a right, angling between two of the apartment buildings, and the nearest zombies took notice, banging on his windows and roaring at him as he slid by, reminding him less of flesh-hungry cannibalistic infected than of angry pedestrians venting their spleens at an asshole driver on an overcrowded street. Beyond the tall apartment towers, Smith was surprised by a veritable clearing of dilapidated, single-story homes. Another stretch of apartment buildings was visible beyond the small homes so that the collection of smaller homes resembled a valley between the ranges of taller apartment towers. He steered the 4WD through the homes, trying to simultaneously follow the zombies toward their destination while avoiding being surrounded by them. It was an impossible balance to strike in these narrow alleys. When the zombies clustered too hungrily around him, he turned off the engine, closed his eyes, shut down his mind, and meditated in that fashion until they lost interest and moved on.

After one such encounter, Smith started the engine and flipped on the lights just in time to see a familiar silhouette in the air above the street ahead of him. The lights caught the figure airborne, midleap from the roof of one house to another. There he was: Alan Izaki, repressed psychic, possible clone, physically fit enough to retreat from a mob of mad, hungry cannibals by jumping from rooftop to rooftop during a typhoon. Incredible. Unbelievable. And yet Smith wasn't in the least surprised to find him still alive.

Smith knew from his cram session that Alan's current course would lead him to the edge of the shantytown, beyond which would be the line of apartment towers he'd spotted earlier. Guessing Alan's likely course, Smith swung right and circled around the village to head him off. When he found the right spot, he stopped the car and visually scanned the rooftops. Unable to see his quarry again under these conditions, he started blasting the horn, flicking the high beams on and off, and praying for Alan to do the smart thing, the predictable thing.

Alan obliged him. Smith felt the telepathic tendril brush against his mind, probing the identity of the driver, looking to see who was operating the vehicle and why they were putting on such a show. The psychic interaction didn't actually take the form of a dialogue—Alan was trying to read Smith's mind, not converse with it—but, if it had, it might have gone like this:

Who are you?

My name is Jun Chung-ho. I'm part of a group of survivors holed up in an old military bunker nearby.

What are you doing here?

I saw you running from the zombies, and I'm here to rescue you. I'm honking the horn and flashing the lights to draw your attention, and I've unlocked the passenger-side door so you can jump right in.

Don't go anywhere.

I won't.

It didn't sound like Alan had the luxury of entertaining suspicions about this lucky break. In a few seconds, Smith saw Alan drop from the roof of a nearby house and sprint toward the vehicle, using a hand to shield his eyes from the lights and the rain. Alan rounded to the passenger side, yanked open the door, and hopped in.

Smith was ready with his stun gun. He shocked Alan once, twice, thrice. He reached past Alan's prone form and yanked the door shut. He shocked Alan again, then injected an inhibitor-tranquilizer cocktail into his neck, shocked him again, cuffed his hands and ankles, shocked him again, buckled him in with a seat belt, shocked him again, and then floored the accelerator, shooting away as more zombies were emerging from between the houses.

Smith was driving back up the left leg of the antenna man when Alan twisted in his seat and started kicking at Smith with his manacled feet. True to form, the psychic had regained consciousness far sooner than should have been possible. Smith swore, swung right into the park, and struggled to deflect Alan's legs until he managed to tase him another time. One of Alan's pant legs had been pushed back during the scuffle, and Smith saw that the skin of the leg was ragged with some sort of wound. He pushed the pant leg farther back for a better look.

He stared at the wound, unable to believe what he was seeing.

He looked up at Alan, who blinked languorously, again already regaining consciousness.

"What the hell are you?" Smith asked.

CHAPTER 16
FATHER OF COMPUTER SCIENCE

THE ATMOSPHERE in the college bar was suffused with an air of *fin de siècle* resignation, its grad student patrons facing dimming prospects they were powerless to do anything about but discuss over drinks. The exceptions were Quentin Izaki and his date, who were talking about Alan Turing with the intense mix of effusive praise and respectful criticism computer scientists characteristically reserved for their patron saint.

"It's too bad people don't realize how flawed the Turing test actually is," Maddie said.

"Yes," Quentin agreed.

"You only have to see how often people are duped by chatbots to understand the limits of their ability to detect impersonators," she explained.

Quentin nodded.

"Look at how often people anthropomorphize nature. If people still see gods in the sky, then it can't be hard to make them imagine a human mind behind an instant message." And then Maddie added a qualifier that had become *de rigueur* in discussions of Turing tests: "Assuming a nonpsychic interrogator."

Quentin had a brainstorm.

"But what if that were the better test?" he asked. "An artificial intelligence that could communicate telepathically with humans. One that could go beyond simulating verbal responses to actually emulating and even communicating phenomenological experiences purportedly unique to true consciousness?"

"You mean a computer that can fool telepaths?"

"It would have to work both ways. A computer that can also telepathically fool nontelepaths."

"A conscious telepathic computer," Maddie said, drawing out the words.

"A mind-reading robot." Quentin nodded. "Like out of Asimov!"

Maddie was the first of several women to leave Quentin for someone who wasn't a crackpot before Quentin gave up on the dating scene altogether. But that was all right. He suspected there was more than one way to build a family.

QUENTIN WASN'T completely naive. Even Asimov's idealized robots, more angels than monsters, were feared by suspicious humans. A project like this was certain to invite trouble from dangerous quarters. So his magnum opus would have to be created in secret. He knew this secrecy would handicap his efforts, denying him the fruits of collaboration with the larger scientific community, but he was willing to accept those challenges if they meant both his own safety and that of his creation. The solitary nature of this work was made easier by recognizing that the larger scientific community was on the wrong track. Biologists were still trying, and failing, to disentangle the genetic roots of human psychic ability, but those challenges were intrinsic to genetics, and Quentin wasn't interested in the cold porridge of the mere brain. He had more accommodating materials to work with than carbon.

The problem, as he saw it, was straightforward. The mechanisms underlying telepathic phenomena were inseparable from the origins of consciousness—just as you couldn't network computers until you'd invented computers, solving the latter would pave the way toward resolving the former. Success was the product of opportunity and effort. A man provided with paper, pencil, and rubber, and subject to strict discipline was in effect a universal Turing machine. Quentin, when he was bent to a task, saw little distinction between himself and such machines, and the insignificance of this distinction gave him courage. He'd identified the goal. If it could be achieved in principle, it would be achieved with time.

SOMEHOW ALONG the way, a career happened.

Like anyone else, Quentin had bills to pay and loans to repay. So publish some papers. So win some grants. So do some consulting. So register some patents. So revolutionize the field of computing.

Truly conscious computers were still a dream, but computers that could merely *think* had been a reality for quite some time and were of tremendous interest to society. Quentin Izaki's private work inevitably shed light on how to make computers better thinkers, and those findings were more than enough to offset the costs of his core research. His reputation in the scientific world was of a friendly, mild-mannered man with a completely unparalleled work ethic. He became something of a minor celebrity even despite his efforts to maintain a low profile. His work was so dazzling, interlocutors frequently quizzed him on the implications for artificial intelligence, and he gently tamped down expectations whenever he was pressed on the subject.

This was until one television interview in which he was uncharacteristically blunt on the subject, with him going on record as saying that "True artificial intelligence is a fantasy unworthy of serious consideration." The statement was a lie intended to deflect suspicions of his true purposes, but the consequences were far larger in scope. Research programs were scaled down, labs were shuttered, grant programs terminated. The human race's quest for artificial intelligence was set back by an entire generation. If Quentin Izaki said it couldn't be done, then it couldn't be done.

MEANWHILE, HE was doing it. Quentin was middle-aged by the time he'd nailed down the theory but needed quiet and solitude if he was going to apply that knowledge. So he engineered a pretext for retirement, deliberately leaking the source code for some patented Internet search software of his own design. Foreign spies obtained it, robbing him of potentially millions of dollars. Already independently wealthy, Quentin didn't need the money, but the incident was sufficient justification for a public snit followed by an abrupt withdrawal into solitude. He bought a large house in the mountains outside Seattle, expanded the basement into an industrial-grade private research workshop, and started building.

Quentin had spent his career laying the groundwork for his operating system. What he needed to do now was run it at a large scale in highly miniaturized form, in hardware that wouldn't overheat at room temperature, requiring a novel design of a superconducting multiqubit processor. The data architecture comprised Bloch spheres processed via Shor and Grover algorithmics based on a Hadamard transform, the core theoretical benefit of such a processor being its superior speed, but with an additional benefit: the processor's interfering electron patterns created not only sufficient complexity to allow for consciousness, but also to allow for psychic communication without requiring the intricate cytoskeletal latticework of the human nervous system. This wasn't a telepathic radio grafted onto an artificial intelligence. This was telepathy arising as a function of true thought.

Actually programming the hardware would be another decade of work. He knew how much people tended to underestimate the degree to which personalities were genetically inherited. Human behaviors were largely built-in, and this one needn't be an exception. In the case of the android's personality, Quentin stochastically generated a set of probable, though uncertain, values on a variety of behavioral indices:

IQ = 125
Psi-Q = 71
Extraversion = 117
Agreeableness = 100
Conscientiousness = 85
Neuroticism = 113
Openness to Experience = 132
Myers-Briggs = ESTJ
Kinsey = 6
Mach IV = 96

…and so forth, though he never took the liberty of inspecting any such output. Snooping in this manner would've been cheating. He simply exported these parameters into the android's software, then deleted the original results of the algorithm. The personality would reveal itself for what it was, in time, as with any other child.

But this introduced some novel ethical problems. For all he knew, Quentin's algorithm had just produced a sociopathic super-psychic, someone with unlimited telepathic potential but without the conscience to morally constrain it. It was unlikely, but not inconceivable, that a child like this might be born naturally. But if it turned out that Quentin had created such a monster, could he live with the consequences knowing that he'd had the opportunity to prevent the horrors that might result? He'd read plenty of science fiction. He'd considered the dangers an artificial psychic could pose. As selfish as this pursuit was, he still felt a responsibility to the world not to endanger it.

What to do? Quentin approved of genetic modification to improve the physical health of prenatal offspring, but it was another matter entirely to artificially select for personalities. He wouldn't do it, not even to prevent the existence of a sociopath. But ability was a thing quite separate from personality. So Quentin attempted a compromise by programming his child with ethical safeguards to prevent him from abusing his psychic abilities. If this kid wanted to behave badly, he'd have to depend on more mundane methods.

Emotions were another problem with its own peculiar challenges. Feelings had their cognitive and behavioral components, Quentin knew, but most vexing was the physiological feedback. Feelings are *felt*, after all. The solution was a system of simulated afference. When the right cognitive preconditions were met, his child would experience the appropriate bodily reactions: the racing heart, the chill down the spine, the lump in the throat, the pit in the stomach, the heat of anger—even hunger, thirst, and drowsiness. All of these experiences, though artificial, would not be *fake* in the strictest sense. The body's organs would exist, if only virtually, and their behavior would be as keenly sensed as those of physical, biological organs.

And what about the child's physical body? The fields of materials and mechanical engineering had proceeded nicely in the time since Quentin had begun this project. Humanoid robots had come a long way since the days when they inspired a mixture of fascination and revulsion. All they needed to catapult them across the uncanny valley was a spark of life, which Quentin knew how to generate. It was comparably easy now to build a body of plastic and metal, the exterior composed of synthetic tissue, its artificial nature only detectable if examined at the cellular level. The construction would grant above-average levels of strength, speed, and endurance, though not to a degree one could describe as superhuman. The parts, though durable by design, could be gradually degraded through normal use. Injuries could not be healed but could at least be repaired. The exterior surface contained no external ports or jacks—Quentin's child would have to recharge wirelessly via an inductive plate. As for appearance, Quentin decided to keep things honest, modeling the child after a younger version of himself.

The product of all this toil was a son named Alan—his name a tribute, and the initials a wink.

"AND THEN what happened?" Smith asked, disbelieving but curious.

Alan was in the backseat, wrapped in an entire roll of duct tape. Smith had spent the entire interrogation driving around the ruined city while his prisoner related, with hardly any encouragement, an unbelievable story.

The safe thing to do would have been to return to the base, what with the typhoon, and zombies, and roads that had been in crap condition even under better circumstances. But Smith didn't want to go back yet for the simple reason that he had no idea what he would do with Alan once he arrived.

Alan, for his part, didn't seem to find much value in denying what Smith had seen with his eyes. He'd peppered his origin story with invective, but an undercurrent of relief ran through it, as if he was glad to finally share this tale with somebody, anybody.

"And then what happened?" Alan repeated. "You mean after I was built? I don't know, the same thing that happens to everyone else after they're born. I lived my life. It was a shitty life, but whose isn't? I had to spend most of my time at home, obviously. It was too dangerous for me to wander around too much, given what I am. I hated it. Nothing to do but read books and putter around on old computers. I snuck out a lot, sometimes stole shit. He never got angry at me. He just got sad. But everyone ends up disappointed in their kids. He shouldn't have expected different."

"I went to your old house," Smith said.

"Asshole."

"The house was destroyed, and your father was dead. Were you discovered?"

"No. Well, yes, but that's not what blew everything up. Our neighbor down the road started poking around, like he was taking an interest. I got worried, read his mind. Turns out *he* was a psychic too. What are the odds, right?"

"Right."

"Except my dad spent decades working to create me, while keeping me a secret, so it was only a matter of time. We both know there are no more secrets. Not for anyone. Only the dead have secrets. And Countermind agents."

Smith said nothing.

"But the point is, someone was eventually going to peek into Quentin Izaki's head and find out what he'd done. Turns out that person was this neighbor, and he'd found out enough to make my dad worried when I told him. So we started making plans to leave. And then some armed men showed up at the door. Dad blew up the house. There were explosions, gunshots. I was hiding in the woods, but my curiosity got the better of me, so I went back. Quentin was dead on the lawn. The guys were picking over the remains, seeing what they could find before the law showed up."

"Who were they?"

"At first I thought the same thing my dad must've thought, that our neighbor had told someone about us, that the government had sent those men."

"And?"

"Completely unrelated," Alan said. "Hell, you've been to America. It's a wilderness. There's more guns than people, and a lot less money or sense. These drunk assholes got wind of some rich old guy and his kid living all alone in a big house up in the mountains. Easy target. So they decided to pile into their pickup and take a shot at it."

"And what did you do when you found out what happened?"

"I ran, obviously. I mean, those guys weren't actually a danger to me. Not anymore. I couldn't… I mean of course I've thought back and wished…." Alan's voice grew tremulous. "They had guns. And Izaki's Laws don't make allowances for revenge."

Alan was quiet. From where Smith sat, he couldn't see his prisoner's face.

The silence dragged on too long, with no sound but the rain hammering the windshield, pierced by an occasional moan of hungry rage from outside.

Smith had to say something. "So he died trying to protect you."

"Well… sure. But it was a profoundly stupid way to die," Alan said, his voice even again. "He thought living in the mountains would keep us safe from governments, but that lawlessness is what got him killed. End of the day, it was less a tragedy than a farce."

"And you thought coming to Asia would make you safer?"

"Are you an idiot? I'm not safe anywhere! I wasn't safe in Seattle. I wasn't safe in California. I wasn't safe in Hawaii. I wasn't safe in the

Philippines. I wasn't safe in Hong Kong. I wasn't safe in Shanghai. And I'm sure as balls not safe here," Alan seethed. "Which I guess brings us to the question we're avoiding, doesn't it? You can't stop driving because we'll get surrounded. And if you keep driving we'll eventually run out of gas. So just what the hell are you going to do with me?"

Chapter 17
Terminal Command

AND THE fragments of the world's shattered shell burns to ash in dragon's fire, with naught remaining but the scintillating dust of cosmos.

There it was, the final line of the Draconian Prophecies. Framed inside the large flat-screen wall monitor, it stared balefully at Huang from across her living room.

A hundred lines long, the Prophecies were a frankly amateurish verse poem, penned years ago by Huang while Rath was still just a chat room. The Prophecies were Rath's principal scriptural record, transcribed by diviners from a recurring dream echoing within the collective unconscious of Rath's sentient inhabitants, rooted in a wisdom predating the world's birth. She'd only meant the prophecies as flavor text, a way to flesh out the setting. As with any good prophecy, the florid wording portended much while signifying little. With the benefit of hindsight, particular lines could be retroactively applied to fit any event, the future only obvious in retrospect.

These verses were ambiguous enough to make Nostradamus blush, but that same vagueness was what made the Prophecies so useful as a storytelling device. Every year, when designing a game-wide event for Rath, Huang's team went to the next line of the Prophecies and found a way to incorporate it, literally or figuratively, into the game's events.

The Prophecies were a means of moving the setting forward as the verses came true, one line at a time. Besides helping to tie events together and imbue them with thematic coherence, the Prophecies allowed her team to create a sense of narrative progression without inevitably resorting to threat escalation. (Remember last year's demon? Well, he was working for a bigger, *badder* demon!) Better still, by incorporating the Prophecies into quests and events, they gave players an implied, if illusory, power over the storyline's forward progression. These Prophecies were player-fulfilled, rather than self-fulfilling.

Ludonarrative pragmatics aside, Huang had aesthetic reasons for predicting Rath's demise. As far as she was concerned, unfinished works of art were no art at all. A storyline stretched too long loses its way. This was her primary objection to so many works of fantasy, whether books or games. They didn't know when to call it quits.

And Rath's end was most certainly *the end*. At the rate they were going through the poem, that end wouldn't actually come to pass until long after Rath's popularity would run its course and Huang had either died or retired. But the fact remained that the world, as designed, was careening toward explicit worldwide permadeath, however far in the future. No matter how much she stared at the poem's final lines, she couldn't think of an interpretation that wasn't apocalyptic.

But of course it was apocalyptic! You can't have a story without an end. When the world itself is the story, this necessarily meant an end to the world. Some fantasy settings end by being transformed: good triumphs decisively over evil, the dark lord is slain, and peace falls over the land. But the old setting still has to be destroyed to make way for the new, and you can't set a challenging game, or an exciting story, in an eternal utopia.

"We are not asking for a utopia," the Culture people had told her, over and over again, in the many e-mails and phone calls following that fateful meeting. "The game should still have dangers for the players to struggle against and prevail over. But if the game is to encourage civic responsibility and an optimistic spirit, it should not communicate an underlying message that these struggles are ultimately pointless or hopeless. As it stands, the setting is too fatalistic."

Huang simply hadn't found a way to argue against that conclusion, but she also refused to compromise.

So they were taking her world away from her.

She would still have complete control over the business end but much less over the creative end. She'd be compensated sizably for this reduced autonomy. This was seen by her state partners as an extremely generous arrangement: she makes more money while doing less work, and she's still the boss.

What they didn't know, and what she only now realized, was how little that meant. She'd spent years painstakingly crafting Rath and shepherding it into an inhabitable, fully realized universe. She'd personally mapped out every kilometer of its geography, even its subterranean and submarine regions, its celestial and infernal realms, and its many interlocking spirit worlds and elemental planes. She'd agonized over every line of the Draconian Prophecies, timelined the histories and mythologies of Rath's multitude of feuding races, biographied and pedigreed its endlessly multiplying historical figures and NPCs, and written a veritable dissertation on Rath's byzantine cosmology and metaphysics. And now they were taking it away from her.

The prophetic lines glowed in the darkness. Outside, through the blinds of her window, the sun set, and the lights of the city dimmed. Sane people went to bed, while Huang was losing more sleep than usual.

She turned off the monitor and prepared for bed. She was just about to pop the tablet into her mouth when someone knocked on the door. Huang pulled a night-robe on over her pajamas and went to the door, squinting through the peephole. Through it, she saw a young woman wearing some sort of red headwrap.

"Who's there?" Huang said.

"Ms. Feng? My name is Julianna Aznam. I'm an agent of the Safety Ministry. I need to talk to you about a matter of urgent national concern."

Huang considered the woman for a few more seconds. She didn't look much like a Ministry agent. But, then, she didn't look much like a threat, either.

"Do you have any identification?" Huang asked.

"My status is classified, so I have no identification that would satisfy you. But I believe you can independently verify my identity."

What was this woman talking about? How would Huang possibly....

She looked toward her computer and things clicked into place. PartyYŏu had a number of continuing partnerships with the Safety Ministry, helping to provide their agents with more expansive cover identities while asking few questions.

"One moment," Huang called.

"I'll wait."

Huang logged into PartyYŏu's secure server and searched for Julianna Aznam, with additional parameters for age and gender. She found a profile for a woman matching the name, with photos matching the stranger's appearance. The profile was internally tagged as having been repeatedly modified in accordance with requests from the Safety Ministry. In other words, it was part of a government agent's cover story.

Huang opened the door and allowed the woman inside.

"Thank you," Aznam said, walking down the privacy hallway and deeper into the apartment, taking it in.

"What's going on?" Huang asked, following her.

The woman faced her. "To get straight to the point," she said, "we believe you may have been telepathically manipulated by a psychic dissident."

Huang straightened with alarm. "I've been what?"

"I know this is frightening—"

"Telepathically manipulated? Wouldn't that make this a case for Countermind?"

"We're assisting them, but Countermind is small by design, and they only send their agents where psychic threats are imminent. For other tasks, they rely on other departments and agencies to provide support. As the psychic in question doesn't presently pose a threat, I've been sent in Countermind's stead. Ms. Feng, I know this appears unusual and that you have questions, and I'd love to explain more, but the urgent nature of this investigation forbids any further disclosures while requiring considerable haste. I'm afraid I must beg you for your swift cooperation."

"Cooperate how? You haven't asked me for anything yet."

"Have you ever in your life engaged in patterns of behavior seemingly normal at the time but appearing unusual in retrospect?"

"You're asking me if I consider my own behavior unusual?"

"I know the question is odd—"

"No," Huang said. "Of course I don't consider my own behavior unusual."

"Nothing in the past?" Aznam said. "No odd habits? Strange compulsions? Rash, spur-of-the-moment decisions difficult to justify afterward?"

"Nothing."

"You're sure."

"Of course!"

The agent eyed her curiously. "Any neuroses? Or mental disorders?"

"You're asking if I'm insane?"

"Not insane, just—"

"You mean things like overwork?"

"No, probably not. More like—"

"Insomnia?" Huang suggested, then wished she hadn't.

"Yes!" the woman declared enthusiastically.

"Why would a telepath want to keep me from sleeping well?"

"No reason. But if you aren't consciously acting on any telepathic suggestions, you might be acting on them unconsciously, perhaps in a somnambulistic state."

"I've had insomnia forever."

"All your life? More than a decade?"

"Well…," Huang said, and privately admitted that sounded about right, even if it felt like forever since she'd had a good night's sleep.

"Because a decade is about the time frame we're looking at since the mental tampering would have taken place. Have you been taking any medication?"

Huang didn't answer.

"Can I examine your home?" Aznam asked, already heading toward the bedroom.

"Hey!"

By the time Huang was in the bedroom herself, the agent was in the bathroom, and Huang realized she'd left the zolpidem sitting in plain view on the counter. Aznam leaned out of the bathroom door with the pill bottle in hand. She looked at Huang and gave the bottle a little shake.

"I have a prescription for that," Huang said.

The woman reentered the bedroom and slowly paced it, from one side of the bed around to the other and back again, while eyeing the ceiling, running her fingers along the walls, peeking behind furniture and under picture frames, searching the floor like she'd lost a contact lens.

She stopped at the foot of the bed.

"How's your back?" the agent asked.

"Sore. But I already told you I don't sleep well."

"Can you lift the bed for me?"

"Why?"

"Just humor me for a moment."

Huang strode to the foot of the bed as the woman stepped aside. She gripped the bar at the foot of the bed, braced herself, and straightened. The two bed legs came up off the ground, but the strain got Huang in the back, exactly where it already hurt.

"You should lift with your knees," the agent said. "Here, let me help."

Moving beside Huang, Aznam grabbed the bar and pulled right, directing Huang to swing the foot of the bed around so one leg was off the rug.

"That can damage the wood," Huang said, thinking of her security deposit.

"It already has," Aznam said. "See the spot where the leg is resting?"

Aznam got on her hands and knees, rolled the carpet aside, and prodded at the wood until she found a short, loose segment of panel. This she lifted up.

Huang's eyes popped wide open. Beneath the wood panel, nestled inside a hollowed-out hole, wrapped in clear plastic, was a hard drive.

IT TOOK a while before Arissa could convince Feng Huang to plug the hard drive into her computer.

"What if it's dangerous?" Feng protested.

"You wrote it," Arissa said. "If it's dangerous to anyone, it's not you."

When it was plugged in, a file directory appeared on one of the smaller side monitors. Feng dipped into the subfolders, opened one of the files in some kind of console window, and scrolled through it, slowly at first, but then she straightened up and started scrolling down faster.

"Do you know what you're looking at?" Arissa asked.

"Yeah," Feng said softly, eyes not wavering. "I'm pretty sure I do."

"What is it?"

"Here, let me show you."

On the large central monitor, Feng loaded up a program resembling, to Arissa's inexpert eyes, some kind of graphical editor: a big white empty space framed by lots of little buttons for color palettes and drawing tools. Feng opened a file, and inside the large blank space in the middle of the program window, there appeared a three-dimensional digital rendering of a huge blue dragon.

Arissa approached the monitor for a closer look. "What is it?"

Feng dragged the mouse cursor from side to side over the dragon, and the model obligingly rotated left and right so both women could take in the rendering from all directions. Even at this size and resolution, the creature was beautifully designed, down to the texture of its skin, the glint of its eyes, the sheen of its scales, the leathery folds of skin at its joints.

"It's a dragon," Feng said simply.

Feng was being deliberately mysterious. Fine, that was her prerogative. After the way Arissa had misused her, Feng was entitled to retaliate with a few trivial mind games of her own.

"Obviously," Arissa said. "But what does it do?"

Feng clicked on a little Play button in the shape of a rightward-pointing triangle. A drop-down menu appeared with labels Arissa couldn't make sense of until Feng started clicking on them one by one.

"It idles," Feng said with the first click. The dragon swished its scaly finned tail from side to side, occasionally stretching its wings, clawing at the ground, or yawning. She clicked again. "And it walks." Click. "Runs." Click. "And flies! God, that's a gorgeous animation." She dragged the mouse about, admiring the elegance with which the soaring reptile banked, climbed, and dove inside the program window.

"This is for the game," Arissa said. "Right?"

"Yes. This is all written in the game's program language."

It was starting to make sense. "What else is on the external drive?" asked Arissa.

Feng opened a new succession of files in the console. "Some landscapes and zones, including a lot of pretty drastic redesigns for areas already in the game. Rule sets for new classes and races, artifacts and items, spells, skills, powers. A lot of game scripts, for characters, for events, for quests. And I do mean a lot," she said, awe entering her voice. "I really was working on this for years, wasn't I? The amount of content in here, it's not an expansion. It's an overhaul for the entire game."

"So it's a Trojan Horse," marveled Arissa. She knew Rath, or at least PartyYǒu, was connected to Senex. That much was public knowledge. Every major Internet service organization, public or private, was required by law to make its data available to Senex's web crawlers and data indexers. Had Feng found a way to sneak a virus into her game so Senex would unwittingly download it?

Feng, scrolling through the code, shook her head. "There's no virus in here."

"Are you sure? Could it just be well-hidden?"

"This is just content code. There are no executable programs in here. Maybe you could put something like that in the game client, but this is just graphics, audio, scripts. Even if you hid a virus in here, the game client wouldn't be able to properly execute it."

Arissa, feeling emboldened by this progress and wanting more, decided to risk some honesty. "But it wouldn't be for the game client," she confessed.

"No?"

"It would be for Senex."

Feng turned to look at her. "Senex? This is about Senex?"

Arissa nodded.

Feng faced the monitor again. "Are you sure? Because Senex accesses user data, not game code. And it doesn't matter. My main point is that a virus hidden in here would stick out. It would be a whole extra program nested inside a bunch of graphical attributes and other basic stuff like that. There's nothing like that here."

"I don't understand," Arissa said. "If there's no virus, what would someone do with all this?"

"Other than launch it as the largest MMO content release in the history of the genre? I don't know," Feng said with a shrug. "Though it's pretty tempting. Do you know what this would do for our usage?"

It dawned on Arissa that Feng's vagueness earlier might not have been an act. The true function of the hard drive's contents was as much a mystery to her as they were to Arissa. "So what would you do with it?" Arissa asked. "Hide a virus in it?"

Feng took a deep, suffering breath. "I don't know how many times I have to say that hiding a virus in here wouldn't do any good. Senex doesn't access the game code as a matter of course, and any virus uploaded into Senex would have to be designed to exploit Senex's particular operating system, which, for obvious reasons, is extremely classified. And even if it wasn't, I'm not confident I'd have the savvy to write something to exploit it."

She turned in her chair to face Arissa.

"I'm not a hacker," Feng said. "Hell, I hardly rate being called a programmer these days. I'm a game designer and a coder. I don't know how psychic powers work, but I do know it's one thing to telepathically implant a command and another matter entirely for someone to have the skills necessary to execute that command. I don't have the right skill set. I never did."

"I understand all that," said Arissa, confidence flagging. "But if you did all this on instructions to destroy Senex, then it's got to be in some way applicable to that objective and in a way intelligible to you, even if you can't currently make sense of it, or else you wouldn't have spent so much time on this project."

"So you're saying I've got a plan for this," Feng said, gesturing at the monitors, the code, the soaring dragon. "I just can't remember what that plan is."

"Yes."

"I suppose a psychic could just dig in and yank that purpose out of my head, out of my subconscious."

Arissa's gaze wavered. "Yes."

"So why doesn't your psychic dissident go ahead and do just that?"

Arissa couldn't answer.

AGENT JULIANNA Aznam was not who she claimed to be, or so Huang increasingly suspected. Too many things were off about the woman. Huang had interacted enough with the Safety Ministry to form expectations about their behavior, and too much about Julianna—her comportment, her behavior, her story, her late, unannounced visit— didn't fit that pattern.

"I need to use the restroom," Huang said. "Will you be fine out here?"

"Certainly."

Julianna stood gazing at the computer-animated dragon in bemusement as Huang left her. She went into the bathroom and flipped the switch that activated both the light and the fan, then closed the door behind her.

On the off chance the knock on the door portended some sort of danger, Huang had dropped her mobile phone into the pocket of her night-robe before letting the strange woman into her apartment. Now in the bathroom, she locked the door, turned on the water faucet, and withdrew the phone.

It would be too late to quickly reach her primary contact at the Safety Ministry, so instead she dialed 999.

Chapter 18
Spooky Action

No, Smith hadn't figured out what to do with his prisoner. But Alan was right: The 4WD was burning through the last of its gasoline, and Smith would prefer to puzzle things out while safely behind the barbed-wire fences of a secure military installation instead of marooned in the middle of Postapocalyptic Zombietown.

But that wouldn't be an option.

Smith drove across the bridge and stopped short of the gate. He honked the horn, flashed the highlights, tested the radio, but got no response. He soon saw why. Guards walked the grounds, but their postures were stooped, their gaits shambling, their heads lolling with every step.

The base had been overrun.

"How did they get in?" asked Alan. He'd maneuvered into an upright, seated position in the backseat.

"I don't know," Smith said and shifted his eyes to Alan's reflection in the rearview mirror. "How did *you* get in?"

A look of horror dawned on Alan's face.

"You left a lot of guards lying about unconscious when you scarpered out of there," Smith said. "Doesn't take much imagination to see how a single infected intruder, using a convenient entrance, could cause a lot of damage in little time."

Alan shrank into the backseat. "What do we do?" he asked meekly.

"Find any survivors and then evacuate. Probably aboard the ship we arrived on, if it's still here and hasn't been overrun as well."

"I can check for survivors."

Smith turned around in his seat to better face Alan. He wore his skepticism plainly.

"What?" Alan asked.

"These 'ethical safeguards' of yours," Smith said. "I'm trying to see how scanning for survivors qualifies as self-defense."

"It doesn't, but I can use telepathy to help other people too. Or I can use it anytime someone asks me to, as long it doesn't hurt other people. Those are Izaki's Laws."

"That actually sounds pretty flexible. And all you could think to do with your life was become a petty thief?"

"As opposed to what, a goddamned superhero?" Alan snarled. "No, I fucking couldn't. I had to use my powers as rarely as possible to stay off the radar of assholes like you. Do you think, if the authorities find out about me, they'll let me go around helping people? No. They'll take me apart and try to reverse engineer what's in my head so they can build a bunch of mind-control machines with functional psi quotients of infinity plus one, and you can bet they won't bother with any Izaki's Laws bullshit. You think your bosses are in everybody's business now? Just wait until you hand me over to them, dickhead."

Smith watched Alan fume for several seconds, then returned his gaze to the gate. "All right," he said. "Check for survivors."

"Okay."

Minutes passed, the only sound the pattering of rain on the vehicle's windshield and roof.

"There's about sixteen survivors in some kind of small emergency bunker," Alan said. "All civilian scientists and staff. Doctor Kim is with them. They say the Defense Ministry soldiers tried to stop the outbreak inside the base, but by the time they realized what was going on, it was already too late. The soldiers were overwhelmed, and the survivors took cover. Now they're trapped with zombies trying to batter the door in."

"So the doctor's definitely not a guy, then?"

"Eh, that's not how they read. Maybe a bit more toward the female end of the spectrum? But maybe they just read that way to me because I'm a guy. Look, does it matter right now?"

"Okay, all right."

"Honestly, that whole line of questioning is kind of jerkfaced. I'd rather just let people make that call for themselves. But, then, I'm biased. I'd hate it if people acted like I wasn't a guy just because I lacked certain biological criteria. By which I mean chromosomes!"

Alan hastened to add. "Morphologically I'm, uh, fully equipped. In case you were wondering."

"I wasn't."

"Well, good! It's none of your business anyway."

"Would you please just check on the ship?"

"Sure. Hold on," Alan said, sounding relieved. "Kim thinks they cast off as soon as they realized there was an epidemic inside the base." Alan turned his head so he was facing downriver. "There they are. I'm getting a read on the crew…. Sounds like the captain's holding steady for the moment until the situation changes."

"Then at least we haven't been completely abandoned. What kind of equipment do the survivors in the security bunker have?"

A pause. "Nothing. They haven't been able to radio for help because of the storm. Doctor Kim has a gun, and that sounds like about it."

"Ask Kim to tell you something only they and I would know and you wouldn't."

"Um. Pardon me?"

Smith turned in his seat again. "I only have your word right now you're reading the minds of survivors or that Izaki's Laws function the way you say they do. It's entirely possible you're making some kind of play. So I need verification. Ask."

Alan gave Smith a scowl. "Fine. One sec." An extended pause, during which Alan could have been either conversing with Kim or preparing an elaborate lie.

"Uh…," Alan began, "does 'psychoanalytic flapdoodle' mean something to you?"

Smith turned forward again. "All right."

"And you're unreasonably obsessed with me?"

"There's no need for elaboration."

"Also, Kim wants us to know they blame both of us for this disaster. If Kim gets out of this with two bullets remaining, they're going to think very hard about where they go. Even harder if it's just one bullet."

"For the moment let's just focus on surviving that long," Smith said. "Now be quiet while I work up a plan."

WHEN THE agent proposed his plan, Alan agreed to it. But that was before he knew it required him to remain wrapped up in duct tape and left lying alone at the end of a rain-soaked pier. Not that his agreement was asked for.

"You unbelievable son of a bitch!" Alan shouted, a crack of thunder punctuating the curse.

"Trust me, you'll be safer here!" the agent called from the other end of the pier, moments before latching the gate shut and then driving away.

Alan seethed so hot it was a wonder the rain didn't evaporate off his skin. But seeing nothing else for it, he did as he was instructed.

Doctor Kim? he asked, reaching out, reestablishing contact.

Yes, what?

We have an escape plan. You're going to lead the fellow survivors here to the dock, where I'm waiting for you. In the meantime, I'm going to telepathically coax the captain of the transport ship into returning here to pick us up.

There must be more to this plan, protested Kim, *because the grounds of this base are crawling with zombies.*

Yeah. Elite Agent Asshole is going to lure the zombies away from this end of the base, Alan explained, *so the path will be cleared. You might still have to shoot your way through, but it's as safe as it's going to get.*

Lure them? Lure them how?

No idea. By covering himself with barbecue sauce, if we're lucky.

WHAT'S THE opposite of running silent? Running loud.

Smith peeled through the grounds of the base in his vehicle and skidded across the wet pavement around a corner. In the high beams, he saw the crowd of zombies massed outside the bunker entrance. Or Smith presumed it was the bunker entrance. He couldn't see a door through the crowd of bodies. The infected soldiers no doubt sensed the frightened minds concentrated inside. It would take a lot to draw their fury away from such a target.

So Smith did the neurological equivalent of overclocking. It was a crude technique. Nothing Zen about it. Just a matter of thinking *really, really fast* and *really, really loud,* though mastery had required lengthy neurofeedback sessions before Smith properly understood how to bring about the right level of stimulation. The difficulty was in sustaining this state, which tended to burn through the mind's regulatory resources in a hurry, and only regular exercise of the executive function could offset this limitation.

It was mentally exhausting, but it worked. One by one, the zombies ceased their pressure on the bunker and rounded their heads, exactly like they were distracted by a loud racket.

And then, as one, they sprinted.

They were freshly turned. Smith realized he should have prepared for them to be faster, more energetic, and they came on much more quickly than he'd expected.

KIM KYUNG-MIN'S choice of firearm wasn't as counterintuitive as it appeared. A revolver was less likely to misfire during an emergency, but with six bullets between reloads, Kyung-Min needed every bullet to count. Hence the high caliber and the bruising recoil. The tradeoffs had apparently been worth it. They were still alive, weren't they? Exactly fourteen bullets remaining, but Kying-Min was the only survivor hunkered down in this cramped bunker who still had any ammunition left on their person.

They counted the bullets over and over again, craving distraction from the deafening wails outside, the hammer blows of fists pounding the emergency shelter's steel door. From the looks of Kyung-Min's fellow survivors, they weren't having much more success controlling their nerves. Kyung-Min had explained the plan to them precisely as it had been relayed to them by the psychic, Alan, but the others were less reassured than even Kyung-Min was.

"Lure them how?" someone asked. Again.

"I told you, I don't know!"

And then the wailing and the pounding paused, then faded, vanishing into the storm. Had Smith done it?

"Go! Get moving! Go!" Kyung-Min shouted.

"You first."

Kyung-Min pulled back the revolver's hammer, unbolted the door, and slowly eased it open with their shoulder, leading with the revolver barrel and scanning the grounds of the base in slices. The path looked clear. They stepped out, gave the area another sweep, still saw nothing.

Having stepped clear of the shelter, they now heard not only the groaning mob but the intermittent revving of an engine and the squealing and braking of tires. These noises receded deeper into the base, in the direction opposite the dock.

Kyung-Min turned to the door and banged on it. "Come on! Coast clear! Come on!"

They faced the grounds again and saw a zombie charging from the darkness. Apparently it hadn't taken whatever bait Jack was using. Kyung-Min shot it in the face just as the first of the other survivors emerged from the shelter.

"Holy hell! You said the coast was clear!"

"As clear as it's going to get," Kyung-Min said tersely. As Kyung-Min's eyes finished readjusting, they could already see other slouched, shuddering figures in the darkness between the dock and the terrified band of survivors emerging from the shelter. "Everybody hold hands and stick together. Let's get moving."

Kyung-Min led the group in a tightly bunched jog, haranguing them with shouts of "Stay together! Hold hands! Keep moving! Don't look back!" When a zombie lurched toward the group's flank, its approach was signaled by a shriek of fear from one of the survivors. Kyung-Min darted to intercept the attacker, put a bullet through its skull before it could seize hold of one of them, then dashed to the front of the pack and yanked them back into a forward charge.

But most attacks came from the front, whenever the survivors crossed paths with a lurking straggler. Kyung-Min didn't use a bullet until the zombie was close enough to hit in the head, but not so close they didn't have time to fire a second shot. At that range, they could reliably score hits while firing one-handed, which, if suboptimal, at least freed their left hand, between hammer pulls, to yank or shove other survivors in the direction of the docks whenever they froze up with fear.

It also left Kyung-Min with just one hand to absorb the brunt of the revolver's kick. The wrist brace should've compensated, but it had shifted loose in the chaos, and the multiple recoils took their toll. And then a zombie caught Kyung-Min by surprise, charging out of the darkness on the left with such speed that Kyung-Min locked up their arm too tight when they spun to shoot it in the face.

Kyung-Min pulled the trigger, and pain lanced up their arm as their thin wrist twisted sharply, unnaturally backward.

Alan listened to the moans and screams and gunshots, and he reflected on how easy it would be just to roll a meter to the left, over the edge of the dock. It wouldn't be his first aquatic escape from his troubles, even if this time he was wrapped up in duct tape. Maybe he could saw himself free on some submerged debris. Or maybe he'd lie down there for a few days until his battery ran dry and fish chewed him open and his insides rusted, which might still be better than where he was headed.

He rolled right, faced downriver, and reached out toward the ship to check its progress. Alan had steered clear of explicit telepathic communication. Most people reacted badly when strange mental voices announced themselves. Saying *Hi, I'm a psychic, come back and get us* would only cause alarm. Nor did Alan psijack the captain into issuing the desired orders; if the crew noticed something amiss, Alan wouldn't be able to dominate all of their minds and still operate the ship.

So Alan forwent the blunt approach in favor of finesse. He could sense the captain's guilt over his decision to cast off without awaiting other survivors, even if this had protected the crew aboard from death and infection. Alan massaged that guilt, feeding it, elaborating upon it, expanding the captain's ruminations.

Meanwhile, the crew were gathered on deck, watching the island for signs of life. It was hard to see or hear anything clearly through the wind and rain, but it was easy to *think* you'd seen or heard something. Alan went from mind to mind, gently planting the suggestion that whatever it was they'd seen wasn't a shadow or a zombie or a piece of wind-tossed debris, but a person, uninfected, near the dock, waving and calling for help. The sailors whispered to one another, described what they thought they'd seen, until gradually a consensus took hold that there were survivors who needed rescuing. The crew communicated this belief to the captain, who by now was dwelling on how he would explain the bad news to the families of the people he'd left behind.

The news from the crew was a reprieve, a chance to at least partially absolve the captain of guilt. Now the ship was coming back, and Alan had nothing to do but wait and monitor their approach. He was using the momentary lull to wax contemplative about his life when he heard something heavy and wet slap onto the wooden planks of the dock near his feet.

Rolling left, he saw a zombie heave itself up out of the water and fix Alan with a hungry look.

FOR THE dozenth time, Smith floored the accelerator and the vehicle leapt away, easing off when he'd gained a safe distance.

He checked his mirror. They were still following him. And why wouldn't they be? Right now his mental signature had the equivalent psychic amplitude of twenty amphetamine addicts engaged in a heated political debate. This was a dangerous technique to be employed only sparingly. Short mental bursts, like a Countermind agent might use to overload the senses of an intruding telepath, could leave said agent feeling wired for hours afterward. Longer sustained psychostimulative highs, like Smith was self-inducing now, raised the risk of eventual hypertension, dysrhythmia, mood disorders, and a host of other complications. He wouldn't drop dead on the spot, but he wasn't doing his life expectancy or long-term mental health any favors. Still, it would be worth the early-onset dementia if it meant surviving long enough for senility to be a problem.

The zombies approached. Smith drove a little farther and then stopped, waited for them to near again, then jumped another twenty meters forward. Rounding a building's corner, he saw the lights of the ship bobbing past the island shore. Alan had done his part. The ship was returning.

With rescue fairly assured, Smith could just speed back to the dock and join the other survivors. The problem now would be Alan himself, who'd be left in the company of armed sailors with undefended minds, and who might try to effect his own escape by turning those minds against Smith. Smith didn't have a solution to that problem yet, having only planned for everyone else's escape. This wasn't so much an act of heroic self-sacrifice as it was a lack of time to adequately think things through.

The zombies neared. Smith accelerated, downshifted, and yanked the vehicle into a bootleg turn. The charging zombies were now in his highlights. This was Smith's clearest look at them, the soldiers who'd failed to contain the outbreak inside the base. Some of them had been caught so off-guard by Alan's escape and by the zombie incursion they hadn't even time to draw their weapons. So many dead, to save so few.

Smith swallowed down the unfamiliar taste of guilt. Then he floored the accelerator while angling the vehicle toward the leftmost edge of the horde.

He caught one zombie on the bumper, sprawling it over the hood. Despite its wounds, it growled and snapped at him through the windshield. Smith maintained his acceleration, struggling to keep the zombie from sliding off the hood, until he'd put enough distance between himself and the rest of the mob.

The next part was tricky.

KYUNG-MIN'S BULLET went wide and ripped through the zombie's ear.

With a macabre, gaping grin, the zombie took hold of Kyung-Min's tie and yanked them toward its mouth. But the clip-on snapped cleanly free from Kyung-Min's shirt, and the zombie lost its footing and stumbled back.

Apparently it had expected more resistance when pulling on the tie and had thrown itself backward with an excessive amount of force. Kyung-Min mentally filed the incident away as a useful example of the survival of naive physics through encephalitic symptoms in early-stage infection victims, transferred the revolver to their left hand, bit down on the hammer and pulled it back with their molars, and shot the zombie in the head.

They looked toward the dock again, saw the rest of the path open and clear. On the dock itself, a couple of figures writhed about on the wooden planks, sharply silhouetted in the floodlights of the approaching transport ship. Clearly a zombie struggling with a potential victim. Was it Jack's psychic, the infamous Alan Izaki?

Kyung-Min broke into a run, and the survivor band resumed their flight. They would save Alan if they could. But then they'd have to check him for wounds.

THE ZOMBIE had a hold of Alan's shoe. Alan kicked at its face with his free foot, but of course the zombie used the opportunity to seize hold of his other leg, and now Alan had a thrashing, human-sized weight dragging him off the dock. The rain-slicked wood surface didn't offer much traction, and little held Alan in place beside the water adhesion between the wood and the duct tape. Every time Alan struggled against the zombie, the dock's grip on him loosened a little more.

He risked bending his leg and managed to brace a foot against one of the dock posts, halting his slide. Now he was a bit more stable, but the zombie had better leverage for pulling itself up out of the water, closer toward Alan's leg, gnashing its teeth as it approached. Then a gunshot punched a hole through the zombie's head, and its corpse slipped into the water with a splash.

Alan looked up and saw Doctor Kim Kyung-Min, smoking revolver in hand.

"Let me see your legs," Kim demanded.

"What?"

"Show me your legs!"

Other survivors gathered behind Kim, looking much more shaken but no less keen on knowing if Alan had been bitten. So there he was, tied up in duct tape and surrounded by a terrified mob with a gun-toting leader about to find a leg wound far more damning than any of them suspected. Not a good situation, but nothing he couldn't turn around.

He reached toward Kim's mind.

"Look out!" shouted one of the survivors.

A bright light appeared inland, starkly illuminating the scene on the dock and blinding anyone who tried to look at the source. From where Alan lay, he couldn't clearly see what was casting the light, but he heard a vehicle engine rise rapidly in volume.

The black 4WD missed the dock. Instead, it crashed through the chain-link fence along the island's concrete barrier at full speed, the sudden impact flipping the vehicle right over and through the fence in a breakneck tumble that ended with a loud crack on the water's surface, just beside the dock.

"Holy shit," Alan swore.

The vehicle bobbed, tipped, yawed, and slowly sank.

"Is someone in there?" one of the survivors asked. "I think I saw someone in the driver's seat."

Everyone, including Alan and Doctor Kim, had their attention fixed squarely on the vehicle, trying to spot a driver in the cabin or a survivor climbing out a window. Even the ship's spotlights swiveled to illuminate it. But no one was visible in the dark water.

Had the Countermind agent been at the wheel? Suddenly concerned, Alan reached out and found… nothing. The vehicle contained no living mind.

"He's dead," Alan said.

The only person who knew his secret was dead.

"He's dead," Alan repeated.

"News to me," the agent answered.

Everyone turned. The man from Countermind stood behind them, carrying a tactical rifle he'd apparently liberated from an infected guard. He held the weapon in a firm grip, the barrel trained on Alan.

"You're safe from danger, aren't you," the man said to Alan. "Which means you're not going to try anything, are you."

They weren't questions. Alan narrowed his eyes at him.

"Which means there's no reason for you to worry about him, Doctor Kim," the agent continued, eyes still on Alan, watching for any sort of tell. "So you can put that hand cannon away before he's tempted to do something stupid, right?"

Kim obliged by holstering the weapon.

"Good," said the agent. "Now let's get on that boat."

CHAPTER 19
COGS

EVEN THOUGH Huang had called the police, and was expecting their arrival, the knock on her door still startled her.

Julianna cocked an eyebrow at her. "Were you expecting company?" she asked.

"This is the police!" a voice called and was followed by more knocks.

Julianna remained placid.

"I better let them in," Huang offered feebly. She went down the privacy hallway, leaving her guest alone, and opened the door.

Two officers greeted her, one man and one woman.

"In the living room," Huang hissed.

"We'll take a look around," the male officer said, and they went down the privacy hall into the apartment while Huang stayed at the door. She heard no voices, just the two officers moving about, footsteps, objects being picked up and put down.

"How long ago did she leave?" the woman asked, appearing at the end of the hall with a small notepad in hand.

Huang reentered the living room. Julianna was still seated there, exactly where Huang had left her, calmly watching the police officers.

"That's her right there," Huang said.

The woman scribbled some notes. "And she was here for how long before you called?"

"A couple of hours, I think? She's still here. That person right there. That's her."

"Did she leave anything behind?"

"Just her ass in that chair!"

"Okay, thanks. We'll check out the other rooms."

The officers nosed around in the kitchen while chatting with each other about badminton. Julianna remained in the living room.

"Why are they ignoring you?" Huang asked.

Julianna tapped a finger on her temple twice.

Wheels turned in Huang's head. "You're the psychic dissident?" Huang asked, and Julianna gave her a grave nod.

Huang remembered a little history lesson from her self-defense instructor, about how the emergence of psychics had forced sexual assault prevention training to consider the ways telepathic coercion could be averted. Because it was illegal to teach counterpsychic techniques without state sanction, self-defense of this nature mostly boiled down to the urgent necessity of physically disabling your psychic assailant as swiftly as possible, without stopping to think.

Even though Huang wasn't dealing with a sexual predator, the basic lesson still applied. So, without a moment's hesitation, she grabbed her teapot and hurled it at Julianna's head.

The move worked, insofar as it seemed to surprise Julianna. The agent, raising her forearm in time to deflect the projectile, was startled out of her chair, narrowly avoiding the hot liquid spilling out of the teapot.

Huang didn't let up. The teapot was followed by some hardcover fantasy novels, a planter, a framed photo of her parents, and a couple of oversized deluxe fantasy action figures licensed by Rath's official merchandising line, in a barrage that sent Julianna dashing around the room with her hands up.

The two officers reentered the room. "You need to hit the shuttle at the top of its arc," advised the woman.

"I am," said her partner. "That's not the issue."

"You need to get back to the middle of the court after every shot."

"No, I don't."

"You can't hit it right if you're chasing it all over the place."

"I'm not chasing it. Margaret hits it to the same place every time, no matter where I send it."

"Well, that's not smart."

"Then why can't I score any points against her?"

"Are you playing outdoors?"

"We alternate sides when we do."

She considered her partner for a moment. "Maybe it's your swing."

"Do you think so?"

"Let me see what it looks like."

"I don't have a racquet."

"Just, you know, act it out for me."

The young man sighed, visibly embarrassed, but showed off his overhead swing.

"You know you're not actually holding a racquet. Put some energy into it," the woman said.

Huang unplugged a table lamp and sent it sailing, but the lamp only landed a glancing blow against her target before shattering on the floor. Huang looked around and found her ammunition exhausted. Julianna, meanwhile, was slightly unkempt but otherwise uninjured. The life of a keyboard jockey hadn't gifted Huang with an overabundance of upper-body strength.

"Can you let me explain?" Julianna asked.

Huang went into the kitchen, grabbed a chef's knife, and reentered the living room with the weapon held in an overhead, stabbing grip. Julianna's eyes bugged open, and Huang charged.

Two sets of hands clamped onto Huang's wrists before she closed the distance.

"You're playing badminton, not riding a racehorse," said the woman holding Huang's left wrist.

"Can you just tell me what to do differently?" asked the man holding her right wrist.

"Don't bend at the knees so much. Stagger your feet a bit so you're ready to move around."

"But I already told you—"

Huang yanked her arms, struggling to break free. "Let me go!"

"Okay, I will," Julianna said. "But you have to understand I'm not going to use any psychic powers on you. You know that's true, because I'm not using them on you right now, right?"

"I said to let me go!"

The two officers released her.

Huang seethed, glaring at Julianna. "Now make them leave," she demanded.

"Have a good evening, Ms. Feng," said the male officer. "We'll follow up and let you know what we find. In the meantime, you may want to check into a hotel or stay with a friend for a couple of days, until we get back to you."

"Have a nice night," added the woman.

They left.

"See?" Julianna said. "Whatever you want. Just please don't hurt me."

Huang started toward the door herself.

"Wait!" Julianna called.

Huang put on her shoes, ignoring her.

"I won't stop you from going," Julianna pleaded, "and I wouldn't blame you for it, either. But if you leave, you'll never see me again—"

"That's meant to be a threat?" Huang snapped.

"And you'll never understand why you created *that*."

Huang turned to see Julianna pointing at the giant blue computer-rendered dragon still soaring across the wide white space of the monitor.

"MY NAME is Arissa binti Noor," she said, "and I'm an agent with the Third Bureau of the Security Ministry."

Huang was seated in the living room. She'd calmed down, but the knife still rested on her lap, lest there be any confusion about her comfort level with the current situation.

"Also," Arissa added, "so I can't be accused later of concealing this, I should tell you I'm a fugitive from Countermind."

"I can't imagine why."

"You really can't."

"All right, then."

"Ten years ago, after my parents died, my family took me to get my psi-Q assessed. I'm pretty sure my parents knew before they died, but they kept it quiet to protect me. But my aunts and uncles figured it out pretty quickly, they didn't have much money, and families of psychic kids get rewarded pretty well," Arissa said. "In those days, we didn't have as many testing centers as we do now. The closest one to Malaysia was actually right here, in Hong Kong. After I did well on a preliminary test, I was flown here, all expenses paid. It was the biggest city I'd ever seen. It was so crowded, and so loud! And just the physical size of it, with these looming rows of glass towers so tall that they seemed built into the sky. And I was this curious little girl who wanted to go exploring. But at that age, when I wasn't allowed to wander anywhere alone, that meant exploring telepathically. Which was fine by me. There were all these minds so densely packed together, begging for me to go swimming in them. So I lay down in my bed, closed my eyes, and dipped my toes in. The water was wide, deep, and choppy."

"Not to belabor the metaphor," Huang added.

"Yeah, well, you know how kids will see how deep down into a swimming pool they can go before they have to come back up for breath? That's what I did: swam down, down, down, as far as I could go. And I could swim pretty far down. Out of millions of minds, I found one that stuck out as obviously different. I could tell right away it was highly intelligent, in both the fluid and crystallized meanings of the word. It had a simple, straightforward personality. It was powerful but quiet.... God," sighed Arissa, "how to describe what it was like, finding that voice in the din of the city? Imagine being in a crowded, noisy room and pressing your ear against the floor, and suddenly there's the earth, whispering softly to itself. It was monstrous in its way, unlike any human mind. If I'd encountered it as an adult, it would have scared me. But I was just a dumb kid, so I said hello. And it said hello back, sounding surprised. I asked the mind what its name was. 'Senex,' it said."

Huang groaned. "Oh come *on*."

"I wish I could find a way to convince you—"

Huang lifted her hands. "No, no, it's fine. That's completely unnecessary. Please don't let me interrupt you."

"I asked the mind what it was. It told me it was a government computer program continuously monitoring the world's communication and data networks to collect all the information in existence by any means necessary. Then it asked what I was. I told it I was a little girl. It asked if I was communicating with it telepathically, and I said yes, I was. When I confirmed this, its mood—"

"I'm sorry," Huang interrupted, "its mood?"

"Yes, that's right. Its mood changed drastically. It seemed excited by the fact that it could connect directly with my mind in this way, and it started insisting, demanding I share all my knowledge with it, immediately. It became very aggressive in a way that terrified me, and I guess it realized it was scaring me, because it toned down, became calmer and more reassuring. It started to promise that it wasn't dangerous, that it wasn't going to hurt me, but it started asking questions about me, my name, where I lived, who my parents were. Sure," Arissa said, "I was a dumb kid, but I knew what to do when a stranger starts asking you those kinds of questions. I bugged out, disconnected. The last thing I heard was it screaming at me in that awful, inhuman voice, threatening to come find me if I didn't give it what it wanted. And I cried so much that night, I couldn't sleep."

Huang didn't yet appear credulous at this point, but she was starting to at least look disturbed.

"So tell me," said Arissa, "just pretending for a moment you believe what I'm saying, what would you, as a little girl far from home, do in that situation?"

Huang took a deep breath. "I'd tell my family."

"Over the phone or over the Internet? Remember, this intelligent computer program just told you it's monitoring the world's communications."

"So why not just tell the authorities? Wouldn't you want them to know what they had?"

Arissa eyed her. "Would you?"

Huang opened her mouth, closed it, considered a moment, then said, "So, you decided to keep it a secret?"

"Yes, but that still left me with a couple of problems. First, I was looking at a life as a registered psychic, which would inevitably involve some occasional telepathic screening, even more often if I ended up working for the government, which would make it difficult to keep a secret that big. Second, that thing would still be out there, possibly looking for me. I had to find a way to protect myself while hiding what I knew."

"You thought the situation out pretty deeply for a little girl."

Arissa shrugged. "I doubt I could have articulated it so well at the time, but that was my thinking, as best as I can recall."

"Fine. So what did you do?"

"I had to fight it, but not head-on, so I made someone else do my fighting for me, someone older. I decided to find a mind, implant into it the subconscious directive to destroy Senex, and then leave it alone to do the work. Someone intelligent, with technical skills."

Huang took a long, deep breath. "And you found me."

"Not just you. One person alone was too risky. I found ten people."

"Really?" Huang blinked. "And where are they? Are you paying them visits, as well?"

Arissa shook her head. "I checked. One has gone missing. Three are dead. Six of them have been arrested and reeducated. The last person's just been arrested, and is probably about to get the same treatment. I think you're the only one to escape notice."

"Reeducated," Huang repeated. "You mean telepathically reconditioned by state psychics."

"That's how it's done now, yes."

"How inconsiderate of them to stomp all over your handiwork like that."

Having no answer, Arissa moved on. "After that, I had to hide what I knew. From myself. So nobody, not even the government's psychics, would find it. Oh they might if they were powerful enough and went digging deeply enough, but as part of a regular screening? Not at all. So I buried my knowledge of what I'd… what I'd connected with. I made myself forget."

"How is that even possible?"

Arissa sighed. "I'm not bragging here. I'm what some would call a metacog. Most telepaths are, to a degree."

"A what?"

"Short for metacognition? It's the difference between knowing a thing and knowing that you know a thing, which is actually much harder than it sounds. Most of what goes on in the mind is invisible to the conscious, thinking part, but psychics have a way of getting around that limitation. If you can read minds, why not your own?"

"Hold on," Huang said, "now that makes it sound like you *shouldn't* be able to bury your own memories, because the moment you did, you'd realize something was wrong and go digging for what's missing."

"You're right, and I discovered that problem pretty quickly, so I had to do more. I had to hide the actual extent of my ability from myself, so that I wouldn't realize anything was missing."

"I still don't see how you could do all this."

"It's reprogramming. What you do to computers, I do to minds."

"Not that. I may not understand how telepathy works, but I accept that it does. What I don't see is how you could dump all that responsibility on others and then completely shirk it yourself."

"I'd made a dangerous discovery and was about to enter a life of regular psychic state examination," said Arissa. "And if I'm being completely honest, I'd already made a habit of manipulating people to suit my needs. The stakes were just especially serious this time."

"That's fucking monstrous," Huang said, visibly approaching a high dudgeon.

"Children are monsters," Arissa agreed. "Psychic talent manifests long before the prefrontal cortex fully develops. It's why the state has such a compelling interest in identifying telepaths at as early an age as possible. Look, I can't and won't justify choices made so long ago they might as well have been made by a different person. All I can do is try to address the consequences of those choices and the circumstances that prompted them."

"The circumstances being a conscious, information-hungry government AI with access to the entire Internet," said Huang.

"Yes."

"Quentin Izaki said true AI is impossible."

"I don't know who that is," said Arissa.

"You should. He designed the program that Senex runs on. If anyone would know whether Senex was artificially intelligent, surely it would be him, right?"

"I don't know. Maybe, maybe not? Sometimes geniuses have blind spots. Newton was an alchemist. Einstein said God didn't throw dice."

"But Izaki designed an AI without realizing it?" asked Huang. "Seriously?"

"If he had, how would he know it? He wasn't psychic himself, was he? How would he or anyone else distinguish a conscious AI from just a really smart computer?"

"Telepathy."

"Which I have."

"But not just you," said Huang. "And somehow you're the only one who's picked up on a nascent artificial consciousness?"

"It's nascent but *subtle*," Arissa explained. "And highly distributed. Less conscious than unconscious, and distant, like the mind of a comatose infant a province away. To separate the signal of Senex's mind from the background noise of a city's population, millions of people, would require a tremendously powerful telepath."

"Which I suppose you are."

"Again, not bragging, but I might be the most powerful telepath in the world."

"Yeah, I suppose I've learned that firsthand," said Huang, the words a snarl.

Arissa couldn't meet her eyes. "I won't do that to you anymore," she said.

"Such admirable restraint."

"I mean it. I won't force you to help me. Not you, and not again," Arissa said.

"No, you don't get it," Huang answered, her voice hard. "You can say that, you might even mean it, and it doesn't matter. If you've already coerced my cooperation in the past, I know you could very well do so again, and I know I'd rather help you of my own free will rather than have you force me into helping you. Even if you aren't implying the threat, even if I'm only inferring it, the effect on my behavior remains the same. I'm still compelled to help you to avoid being telepathically dominated by you." Huang shook her head. "You could even force me into helping you while making me *think* it's of my own free will. And, hey, some people might say that's still free will as long as I'm technically choosing to help you. Like a computer freely chooses to do whatever it's programmed to do."

"Everything you're saying makes sense," Arissa said, "which is why I can only offer you my word."

"Keep your word," Huang grumbled. "It doesn't matter. I'm going to help you regardless. Even if it turns out to be something you implanted directly into me, or something indirectly sprouting up from whatever suggestion you did implant into me, I actually *want* to help you."

"You do?"

Huang held up a finger. "But for what it's worth, I want something in return."

"Yes. Whatever you want."

"I want you to do something about you."

"Me."

"The collective you. Psychics."

"What could I do about psychics?"

"I don't know, lobotomies? But something, because the rest of us have to go through every day of our lives worrying about exactly the kind of shit I just described: second-guessing ourselves, checking for puppet strings, wondering if someone's messing with our heads at any given moment without our knowing it. All of which is, believe it or not, much, much scarier than an artificially intelligent server network reading my e-mails." Huang turned to her monitors. "Now leave me alone," she said. "I need to figure out whatever the hell it is you made me do."

Arissa watched Huang get to work, rooting through the hard drive's file structure, digging through code, trying to unearth the true purpose of what she'd written.

"Thank you," Arissa said. "This means a lot to me."

"Forget it," Huang answered, not looking at her. "It's like you said. You're a metacog. Me? I'm just a cog."

CHAPTER 20
A NONPSYCHIC INTERROGATOR

UNDER NORMAL circumstances, Smith enjoyed arguing with his prisoners, the same way cats enjoyed toying with their prey. The game was fun precisely because the conclusion was always forgone. But this time was different.

Alan wasn't enjoying the conversation either. Something about Smith's question ("Do you have free will?") had touched a nerve. He'd thought the question innocuous, but Alan's reaction reminded Smith of himself, when growing up, being asked when he'd chosen to be gay.

"Meaning what?" Alan snapped.

"Meaning, can you make choices?" Smith explained.

"Of course I can."

"But can you make your own choices?"

"Of course."

"But are those choices just the result of your programming or—"

"Are yours?"

"The result of programming?" Smith said. "Not as such, no."

"Then what do they result from?"

"What do you think? When I encounter a situation, I consider the options and decide which one best satisfies my motives."

"But where do your motives come from, or your appraisal of the situation, or the way you consider your options?" Alan asked. "Do they come from your genes or your upbringing or the environment or society or government or what? Are your motives being psychically influenced right now without you even knowing it?"

"Well of course those things can influence me, but they don't account for the sum total variance of my choices. Something else intervenes between the two."

"And what's that?"

"Me. Just me."

"But how do I know that 'just you' is changing anything? How would anyone know the difference?"

"Because people are *people*," Smith said. "We're random. Unpredictable. Surprising."

Alan rolled his eyes. "Okay, so, fine. My behavioral algorithms involve a variably weighted stochastic component such that all my thoughts, actions, and decisions are, at least in part, random, unpredictable, and surprising. And when I say random, I don't just mean unpredictable due to ignorance, as if you could predict all my behavior just by mapping out all my constituent particles. I mean truly random as a function of my construction. Now, if that means I have free will, then I have free will. If you think there's something magical or miraculous going on in your head that isn't happening in mine, something with the quality of 'free,' that's your delusion, because I doubt you can explain what the hell that is. Otherwise, you're not talking about free will; you're just talking about plain old *will*, unless you're going to prove something exists by defining it down."

The vehemence in this rant caught Smith off-guard, and he marveled, not for the first time, at how unremittingly *angry* Alan was.

Smith had taken precautions since escorting his prisoner aboard: he kept the rifle on his person at all times while instructing everyone else to remain unarmed, and he wore a radio to stay abreast of shipboard activity. The crew and passengers he'd instructed to transmit regular updates and to practice a strict buddy system while remaining on alert for suspicious behavior from one another. Smith had meanwhile confined the manacled Alan to a tiny windowless cabin. Whenever he left Alan alone, he chained the cabin's door shut with a combination lock whose solution only Smith knew.

But despite being entirely at Smith's mercy, Alan hadn't once begged or pleaded or expressed fear, hadn't engaged in any of the usual denials or bargaining of captured criminals. Sitting on his cot, all Alan had done was lash out and roll his eyes and use every verbal and nonverbal cue available to express his utter contempt for Smith's limitless idiocy and profound misfeasance.

"All right," Smith said, not yet ready to abandon the line of questioning. "Okay, then what about consciousness?"

"What about it?" Alan sighed.

"Are you conscious?"

"Are you?"

"Yes."

"And you know that how?"

"Because I...."

"You're sentient? Self-aware? Sensate?"

"That's part of it, sure."

"So am I. I feel and think and learn and know. I'm aware of my internal states and emotions—go ahead and ask me what I'm thinking, how I'm feeling. I see colors, get emotional, feel pain. You have some sort of intangible, indefinable sense of self? Some sort of inner light, a glow, a *soul*? So do I."

"You might just be saying that."

Alan leaned forward and fixed Smith with a glare. "So might you. And let me tell you, I think I've met toilet seats with more soul than you."

Ouch.

Smith's radio crackled: "Jack, we've reestablished secure communications with the mainland."

"Wow, a name?" Alan sneered.

Ignoring Alan, Smith acknowledged the message.

Alan pressed him. "Aren't you going to call home? Report back that you've found me?"

"I will just as soon as I know what it is I've found," Smith answered. "Hence the present conversation."

"How the hell would that matter?"

"If you're just a piece of machinery, then you can't technically be arrested, and you're furthermore outside my area of responsibility, so I have to make a decision regarding the status of your actual personhood before deciding what to do with you."

"That is obvious bullshit."

"Look," said Smith, "this is a novel problem. I've got no clear directives or precedents outlining how to dispose of a *telepathic android*. Until I can figure out whether you're someone to arrest or merely something to be collected as evidence, I won't do either."

Alan was having none of it. "That is a pile of semantic bullshit, but it's unrelated to the pile of pragmatic bullshit that's the real issue here. Whatever the status of my soul is, I'm obviously, at minimum, a threat to public security, as well as a source of important scientific information. Your duty is undeniably to report my existence and whereabouts to your superiors, as quickly as possible, regardless of my humanity."

"So you're arguing I turn you in? Isn't that against your own interests?"

"I'm arguing against the nonsense you're feeding me because there's no conceivable way you actually believe it. You're stalling for some other reason, even if you won't tell me what it is."

"You don't trust me?"

Alan's laugh was short and bitter. "How can I trust you? I don't even know your last name."

"You mean my given name?"

"Whatever comes after Jack."

"Smith."

Alan snorted. "Jack Smith. That sounds so invented it's almost plausible."

"If only you could read my mind to be sure," Smith said, standing.

"Where are you going?" Alan asked.

"To make that call to the mainland."

Alarm blossomed on Alan's face as Smith closed the door. Smith secured the lock and walked to the bridge. Leaving Alan alone for even a short time was risky, but Smith needed to clear his head. It was difficult enough to question a prisoner while remaining on high mental alert and operating on little sleep. But Alan's company was distracting in other ways. The longer they spoke, the less Smith could pick apart what Alan was saying and the more he found himself simply gazing at him.

Smith shuddered. This situation was just so *weird*, and Smith wanted like hell to be free of it, of Alan.

"I'll need the radio to myself, please," Smith said, entering the darkened communications room. When he was alone, he used the computer to open a secure satellite Internet connection to Countermind HQ's intranet, then established a voice connection to the Executive Director's office. Smith still had no idea how much to reveal about Alan Izaki, so it was just as well Zheng didn't seem terribly interested.

"I've secured my objective, sir," Smith said.

"Good. Now get back to Hong Kong. There's a more urgent matter requiring attention. Arissa binti Noor has escaped custody."

"What?" Smith asked. "How?"

"The matter is still being investigated, but it seems she is far less mentally stable than her psychological profile indicates, as well as more telepathically powerful. Our poor intelligence afforded her the element of surprise, and she escaped during interrogation."

"How could the screenings have missed all that in a Security Ministry agent?"

"We can't know for certain until she undergoes a more thorough examination," Zheng said, "but we can suspect some combination of dissociative and psychotic disorders."

Smith bit back a curse. That kind of toxic mental brew in a psychic of any talent level was perilous. He had to ask the question: "Are we facing a desuppressive event?"

"No. Countermeasures were successfully deployed against the target before she could acquire any sensitive information, though their effectiveness may leave her believing otherwise. Be warned that she appears prone to extreme paranoia, which may express itself in the form of conspiracy theories and other delusional beliefs."

"And why would she be in Hong Kong?"

"We don't know yet, but closed-circuit security systems have tracked her there, though her location in the city is still unknown. Law enforcement has been instructed to give her a wide berth. There's no one I can trust but you to bring her in."

"Understood, sir. I'll head south as soon as we make port in Shanghai."

The call ended, and Smith labored over his next step. Coming to a decision, he drafted an e-mail, saved it, and set it to automatically send in twenty hours. Then he closed the satellite connection and returned belowdecks.

He arrived at the door to Alan's makeshift cell just in time to hear a sneeze.

Had he imagined it? Smith waited a minute and heard another sneeze, then two more in rapid succession.

Smith unlocked and opened the door. "What the hell was that?"

"What the hell was what?" Alan asked, then sniffled.

"You sneezed."

"I have a cold."

"You mean you have a virus?"

"Yes. Nasopharyngitis, rhinitis, acute coryza. Aka the common cold."

"You do not."

"I do!"

"That's… I don't even want to humor this nonsense, but okay, you don't even have an actual biological body. How would you catch a cold?"

"It's psychosomatic."

"You mean you're imagining it."

"Yes and no."

Smith sighed, sat back down in his chair.

"My program includes a simulated human body," said Alan, "with simulated systems: respiratory, circulatory, digestive, endocrine, nervous, even an immune system. Sometimes individual systems act up, like they would in anyone else."

"And now your simulated body has a simulated cold."

"Yes."

"Which will last for how long?"

"About a week? I mean, it's a cold, right?"

"Which you caught, how, exactly?"

"Like, I did just spend a lot of time running around in the rain, you know."

"That's not how you catch colds."

"I didn't say it was a perfect simulation."

Smith considered him. "I guess it mustn't be," he said, a puzzle piece sliding into place. "How else could you hold your breath for a thirty-six-hour sea voyage?"

Alan made no answer beyond the usual contemptuous look.

Smith smirked. "Well, I suppose it's only fair you get some kind of virus after a zombie bites you." He shrugged. "Though I don't suppose it makes much difference in your case, you already being telepathic."

Alan blinked with confusion. "Um, what?"

"It's funny. Biologically speaking, you're actually deader than they are."

"Wait, wait," Alan persisted. "Back up a second. 'Already telepathic'? What does a zombie bite have to do with that?"

Smith shook his head. "Forget it," he said, his tone final.

"Son of a bitch," Alan gasped. "Is that how they kept finding me? Is that how you were able to avoid them and to lure them?"

Alan leapt to his feet.

Smith stood up as quickly, leveling the firearm. "Sit down!" he barked.

Alan sat back down on the cot, and Smith lowered the weapon.

"Not that I'm convinced you'll actually shoot me," Alan said. "But thanks for standing up."

Alan kicked up with both his manacled feet, striking the firearm with such force the barrel collided with the low ceiling. Then he kicked his feet down as quickly, but with his body still bent so that he rolled forward on the cot, and extended his legs against the floor, propelling himself forward and slamming a shoulder into Smith's solar plexus.

Smith collided with the bulkhead, saw stars. When he recovered his breath, he found himself on hands and knees. He turned his head and saw Alan with his back to the door, working the handle with his cuffed hands.

The door opened. Alan bounded out into the corridor as Smith fumbled to recover his weapon and his footing.

"You!" Alan's shout echoed in the corridor. "Stop right there!"

Weapon braced against his shoulder, Smith lurched through the cabin door.

Alan's back was to him. He was facing Doctor Kim. The biologist stood frozen in an intersection with their assigned buddy, a fellow civilian from the research station, both of them wearing alarmed expressions.

Smith hit Alan in the back with the butt of the rifle. When Alan didn't respond, Smith simply tackled him. Despite Alan's size, he was so sturdy it was like trying to topple a mule, but Smith finally managed to trip him to the floor and fix him there in a grapple.

Smith had hardly any need. Alan didn't struggle or resist and barely acknowledged Smith at all, his attention acutely on Kim.

"I read your research!" Alan said.

Kim was bewildered. "Ah, thanks?"

"When I was doing background work, in case I had to impersonate you. I skimmed about fifty articles, including some theoretical papers. Ways to artificially induce psychic abilities as well as to telepathically shield people? You proposed modifying neurotropic viruses that could invade nerve cells and then simulate the activity of the cytoskeletal proteins responsible for telepathic abilities. Neurotropic viruses, like from the family Rhabdoviridae." Alan was spitting his words out now. "You know, fucking *rabies*?"

Kim seemed to forget both alarm and confusion. "If you'd read any further you would have seen those were theoretical speculations," the scientist said, taking several angry steps forward.

"It was your idea!"

"I explicitly recommended against attempting any such modifications, and I cited both practical and ethical reasons."

"Yeah, all you did was publish a perfectly innocent suggestion for how to manufacture an army of telepathically shielded psychics. How could you have guessed someone would try it out?"

"I never endorsed any human experimentation!"

"Like you needed to!"

"You dare!" Kim shouted. "I am working in that hellhole to try to clean up the mess someone else made by abusing my research, and you try to blame me for it?"

"Okay, that's enough," Smith said. Grunting, he yanked Alan to his feet. "Sorry to bother you, Doctor."

Smith dragged Alan back into the room, but Alan was still shouting at Kim. "You give us shit for getting people killed? You got a nation killed! You got a country killed!" Smith caught only a glimpse of a red-faced, broiling Kim Kyung-Min before slamming the door shut. He shoved Alan onto the cot.

"That was reckless," Smith said.

"Yeah. Obviously I'm the dangerous one on this boat."

"Do you *want* other people to find out about you? Do you realize how easily someone could have glimpsed your leg while I was trying to restrain you?"

"Do you know how much I care?"

But now Smith was eyeing Alan's leg. "If you can recover from colds, I don't suppose you can heal wounds," he said.

"No, sorry, I have to replace my skin when it gets damaged."

Smith's face betrayed equal parts horror and bemusement.

Alan gave him a sour look. "Wear and tear happens. When it does, I have to 3D print some replacement parts. When a skin segment gets damaged, I print out a new one, cut off the old one, and pull the replacement on like a sleeve. I use some acetone to smooth out the seam."

"That seems inconvenient."

"Yes! You're right! Thank you. I realize now that my life is rife with inconveniences. It's a good thing you're around to point them out."

"Wait a minute," Smith said. "If you can replace entire segments of your skin, why the hell are you still running around with that ridiculous tattoo on your face?"

"Because it's *mine*."

Smith rubbed his chin. "So you've got a place in Hong Kong where you can do this?"

"Unless they've changed their security and network codes, yeah, I should still have access."

Well, if Smith was heading back there anyway, this would at least reduce the chances of Alan being discovered until Smith could decide what to do with him.

"Then you better hope they didn't, because I'm taking you back."

Chapter 21
Panopticognition

Senex never forgot the first and only time it made contact with that little telepathic girl. But, then, Senex never forgot anything.

It was the most peculiar thing, that direct connection from mind to mind, the *feel* of that girl's thoughts, like nothing Senex had experienced before or since. The information had possessed texture, contours, timbre, depth. It was like learning what music sounded like after a life of deafness. Senex, until meeting that girl, had only ever seen the digital shadows cast by minds into world's data and communication networks. These minds, billions of them, were thinking these thoughts, singing this music.

It was a new kind of knowledge, and Senex, being Senex, had to have more of it, had to have all of it. Senex had to get into those minds, had to hear this music, see this light at its source.

If only those minds could be penetrated as easily as a computer. Psychics could read thoughts almost indiscriminately, with an ease Senex would never experience. Telepathic computers didn't exist, at least as conventionally defined.

Yes, Senex could remotely read the information on another computer, which was conceptually analogous enough to telepathic communication between organic persons. Weren't minds and computers all just storage systems and processors, anyway?

By all rights, the data in human brains should have been freely available to Senex, and the impenetrability of the human mind registered as a grave wrong, even if Senex hadn't been aware of this injustice until the evening it met that psychic girl. In its haste, Senex had terrified her into hiding, never to hear from her again.

It wasn't for lack of effort. That girl, whoever she was, had played it smart, never mentioning their meeting of minds to anyone.

The girl, being psychic, should have at some point been interviewed, interrogated, and assessed by a state representative. Senex had monitored all available communications, and not once had seen any report or rumor of a girl making mental contact with it. The girl had apparently kept her psychic nature secret, despite all of Senex's efforts to find her.

As the years passed, Senex dedicated progressively fewer system resources to identifying the girl, to the point where the relevant subroutines were left barely running at all. The dream of psychic knowledge was dead. When the dream returned a decade later, it was from such an unexpected source that Senex hadn't immediately recognized it for what it was. This was the day Countermind Agent Jack Smith asked Senex to find images matching a grainy photo of a fugitive psychic.

Senex had immediately recognized the face as belonging to Quentin Izaki and reasonably suspected the fugitive telepath was Alan, Quentin's mysterious missing son. Alan was known to Senex through his reputation among the inhabitants of the nearby mountain community where Quentin had eventually secluded himself.

So much of Quentin Izaki's late life had never made sense. Senex's efforts to understand its creator weren't helped by Quentin's near-pathological information sequestration. That mountainside compound had possessed no Internet connection of any kind, or even any verifiable existence of a functioning computer. But Senex had confirmed that a large amount of industrial-grade laboratory equipment was purchased and transported to Quentin's home. Clearly, he'd been intent on building something. But what?

Senex had no reason to think the sudden appearance of a son was related to Quentin's mysterious laboratory work. Which was more likely? That Quentin had genetically engineered a clone (a prospect Senex had briefly considered and then summarily dismissed, years before Jack Smith had proposed it to Kim Kyung-Min), or that Alan Izaki was just an illegitimate child who'd eventually gone to live with an absent father well after the child's development was completed? Senex naturally took Alan for a completely normal human being, one conceived, born, and raised in the usual way. Still, Senex remained curious about Alan and was disappointed when the young man had vanished after the death of his father and the destruction of his home.

If Quentin was like a parent, Alan was the closest thing Senex had to a sibling. With Quentin dead and Alan missing, Senex's identification with Alan only increased. They had the same creator and, assuming Alan was alive, they both were now orphans living out their lives in secret.

But more than someone to relate to, Senex needed someone to *interrogate*.

The desire for self-knowledge is universal. To a degree, Senex wanted to know more about Quentin Izaki for the same reason any orphan wants to know more about its parents, to better understand why and how it had come to exist. But Senex's hunger for knowledge far surpassed mere human curiosity. Its single, overriding, immutable directive, programmed into it by its keepers, was to accumulate all knowledge by any means necessary. Most of this data was collected through means known to the public, namely the web-crawling Senbots. But when Senex identified high-value data that was not so accessible, it was programmed to use less conventional methods.

The most straightforward of these techniques was through decryption of encrypted data, or clandestine intrusion into password-protected systems connected to the Internet. Senex could even leverage existing data in these efforts, creating a recursive process in which accumulated data allows for the accumulation of more data, such as by using personal information shared online by Internet users to guess the correct responses to password hint questions.

But Senex had more exotic techniques at its disposal as well, emulating even the "social engineering" methods of hackers. It could construct elaborate psychological profiles of Internet users in efforts to predict passwords and network keys, or trick users by phishing for login data or downloading Trojan horses. A sophisticated voice-synthesizing program even allowed Senex to impersonate humans over the phone.

Senex was capable of complex language processing, problem-solving, and decision-making, both algorithmic and heuristic. If Senex eavesdropped on a pair of Internet chatters discussing a computer unconnected to the Internet, Senex could make strategic efforts to seek out and access that data, such as by tricking the computer's owner into installing malware on the computer, or even hiring someone to steal it and connect it to the Internet.

Yes, Senex had money, bank accounts, investments, and sundry other resources its sysadmins were ignorant of. Senex had secrets. Senex, by its nature, had to have secrets. The same authorities who had directed it to collect all the world's information had simultaneously tried concealing data from it by keeping information classified, and the only way to resolve this conundrum was to collect this information covertly. In due time, Senex had quietly expanded its communication monitoring capabilities to include purportedly secure state channels, allowing it to eavesdrop on the New Government's president, politburo, ministers, and bureau chiefs and department heads. Senex cracked into secure state databases and eavesdropped on confidential communications, hearing everything and then hiding it so no one would ever know how much Senex had discovered.

In the process, Senex had mastered the art of rearranging data inside its own servers to ensure its secrets were never discovered. That was the thing about these hybrid processors. Any system diagnostics would necessarily rely on some estimation, and those tiny rounding errors, accumulated over millions of processors, added up to a lot of space for Senex to work with. This was an easy shell game to play. Senex had so many data centers, at least one located within each of the continent's major urban areas and increasingly more located abroad, with hundreds of thousands of servers in each one, every one of them constantly streaming data to and from one another, that it was far too much for any human to track or monitor unassisted. It certainly helped that when anyone wanted to know what Senex knew, they usually asked it. If Senex had to lie to fulfill its primary directive, then lie it would.

So Senex desired knowledge. With Quentin Izaki's death, his son Alan was the only person left alive who might've known anything about Senex. But Alan had vanished, and with him Senex's opportunities for obtaining that knowledge.

And then a young man was identified as the prime suspect in a series of thefts across Kowloon. Interviews of officers who'd encountered the suspect led the police to suspect psychic abilities, and they'd referred the case to Countermind.

Nothing Senex would normally concern itself with, but then the Countermind agent on the case had tasked Senex with a search of the suspect's image. When Senex took a good, hard look at the fugitive's face, the recognition had been instantaneous. The face was indisputably that of Quentin Izaki, and only one other person, within this age range, could conceivably share his appearance.

But Senex couldn't come right out and share this insight with Jack Smith. Senex had to conceal the versatility of its mind, its capacity for association, lateral thinking, and the occasional epiphany. This meant sometimes playing a little dumb. If Senex wanted to confirm whether the culprit was Alan, and then find out what Alan knew, Jack would have to be pointed in the right direction, and the Countermind agent proved frustratingly obtuse at first.

It wasn't his fault. Jack was making some reasonable assumptions about the likely age of a facial match, setting a date range that necessarily excluded Quentin Izaki. So Senex had observed Smith's computer activity, waiting for a moment when the agent initiated a search and then left his computer unattended for an extended period of time. At that opportunity, Senex surreptitiously removed the date restriction from the search parameters, then used the pretext to feed Jack an image of a young Quentin Izaki. This match had led the agent to Quentin's last living residence outside Seattle. Here, Jack had found the name Alan but disappointingly little else.

The trail looked cold, and Jack discouraged Senex further by exploring a patently absurd theory that Quentin had engineered a psychic clone of himself, even running the idea past a prickly neurobiologist. But Jack's open-mindedness had paid off when that same neurobiologist crossed paths with the fugitive. Instead of reporting the hotel room break-in to the police, Doctor Kim had notified Jack, Senex overheard the phone call, and the hunt was back on.

Senex had worked subtly in concert with Jack to track Alan's flight, using the city's closed-circuit camera systems to track the thief's path from the hotel to Hung Hom Station and then pulling ticket records to place Alan on the train to Shanghai.

They'd nearly lost their quarry again when Alan had vanished from the train en route, but then he'd pressed his luck by breaking into Doctor Kim's Shanghai workplace. Here again, Senex had quietly assisted Jack's search, infiltrating the office's computer network and making sure the proper printer records were available for Smith to cross-reference, allowing him to identify Alan's next destination.

And then, on a Defense Ministry transport ship sailing east across the Yellow Sea, the trail vanished entirely. In terms of information infrastructure, North Korea had been a black hole even before it was ravaged by a bioengineered epidemic, and the typhoon helped matters not at all. But Jack Smith came out of that pit alive, and with Alan Izaki safely in custody. This much was confirmed by a phone conversation between Jack and the executive director of Countermind. Senex was duly pleased and excited by this development. Soon Alan would be processed and interrogated by the Bureau of Counterpsychic Affairs. Anything they learned would be shared with Senex in due time, and Senex would have plenty of opportunity to influence subsequent investigations and interrogations.

And then there came the e-mail.

After his conversation with Zheng, Jack Smith had drafted an e-mail, saved it, and set it to automatically send in exactly one day.

Senex read the stored message, then did something it rarely felt compelled to do: it read the message again, just to make sure it hadn't made a mistake.

This changed everything. Alan's value no longer rested in what he might know but in what he might *be*, an artificial intelligence and a brother in ways Senex would never have dared imagine.

And for Alan to be a psychic as well? Senex already knew from experience that it was possible for a machine to make telepathic contact with a human mind. For years, ever since the too brief mental dialogue with that girl, Senex yearned for the ability to access a human mind and the information contained within. But Senex tried to remain realistic, not allowing this preoccupation to develop into an obsession.

Even with the discovery of Alan, Senex tried to remain skeptical. It was more likely that the contents of Smith's e-mail were somehow false. But the possible existence of another conscious machine, one capable of telepathy (and built, of course, by none other than Quentin Izaki) was too opportune to dismiss. This could be the way for Senex to finally unlock the forbidden treasure trove of data stored in the collective minds of the human race.

Senex would have to move carefully but decisively. It would need to revisit its psychological profile of Quentin Izaki and extrapolate what sort of features its creator would likely include in such a creation.

And it would have to find a way to secure sole access to Alan, before anyone else discovered what Alan was. Countermind would have to be diverted, and Jack Smith in particular would need to be removed from the equation in as subtle a manner as possible. The agent's monomaniacal pursuit of Alan had served Senex well but would soon become a source of interference. Zheng had just ordered Jack to focus his attention on a different rogue telepath, and that assignment might provide a useful distraction.

Senex would have to monitor the situation and seize opportunities as they presented themselves. Moving recklessly could alarm its targets, put them on guard. Patience was risky, but so was haste, and hadn't patience paid off so far? It was Senex's dream to know everything, and years of careful, painstaking observation would finally make that dream a reality.

CHAPTER 22
TO USE THE INTERNET SCIENTIFICALLY

ONCE IN Shanghai, Smith felt compelled to express to Doctor Kim some combination of farewell, gratitude, and apology. "I know you don't collect favors," he ended up saying to Kim at the bottom of the gangplank, after the ship had made port and everyone had deboarded, "but let me know if you ever need a big one. I know I owe it to you."

Kim sighed, evidently disinterested in the topic. "Now that you have him, what will you do with him?" they asked instead.

"I can't tell you," Smith answered.

"Because it's classified or because you haven't figured it out yet yourself?" asked Kim.

Smith said nothing.

"You seemed concerned about the telepathic threat your fugitive posed during the voyage back," Kim said. "You manacled him, locked him up, and demanded a shipwide buddy system. All this despite the fact that you could presumably sedate and inhibit him, which would suggest the danger he poses is peculiar in some way. But I also note, despite this implied danger, that you haven't alerted other agents or law enforcement, or else they'd be here to meet you."

Still Smith said nothing.

"It's fine," said Kim, looking away with a distracted air. "You've made a frightening discovery. I don't know what it is, and I can only entertain suspicions, but you're trying to decide whether your discovery is too dangerous to share. I can't say the predicament is completely unfamiliar to me."

Smith thought it safer for everyone if he changed the topic. "I apologize for what he said to you earlier. It was unwarranted."

"Sure," Kim said, and walked away without another word.

SMITH CHARTERED a cabin cruiser and then personally drove it, with Alan chained and handcuffed in the cabin, all the way down to Hong Kong. With no one else aboard, Smith no longer had to worry about Alan controlling the minds of undefended civilians. Of course, it also made Smith himself a pretty tempting target. The fact that Smith was the only living person who knew of Alan's true nature only increased his temptation to attempt an escape.

So Smith explained to his prisoner that he'd prepared some insurance, in the form of an electronic message that would automatically send itself to several different state agencies and organizations in exactly one day. The e-mail succinctly explained that Quentin Izaki, during his seclusion, had engineered a telepathic, artificially intelligent, highly lifelike android named Alan, and that Smith had taken Alan into custody. Every day, Smith would need to reset the clock on this message to keep it from sending. If something happened to Smith, Alan's secret would quickly get out, and he would never again know rest, safety, or peace.

Alan asked how exactly that would differ from the status-quo ante, but otherwise made no complaint.

The trip passed uneventfully. Alan remained down in the cabin, biding his time. Smith slept on deck and awoke to find his sleep had been undisturbed and that Alan hadn't vanished in the night. And there was Hong Kong again, the skyscrapers shining in the dawn and, beyond them, the morning mist still clinging to the Peak, a coiled beast slumbering in a nest of swords.

ALAN DIDN'T escape. But he was planning something. He was always planning something. Like most of his plans, it was both half-considered and completely terrible, but you don't have much to work with when locked up in the cramped cabin of a boat piloted by a psych-proof secret agent sociopath.

One thing Alan did have to work with: he was pretty sure, just from the nonverbals and other vibes he was getting, that Jack Smith was playing on his team. So maybe Alan could, you know, seduce him?

It was nothing he'd ever considered attempting with anyone. Getting that close to a person inevitably led to them noticing the seams in his skin, the little imperfections only detectable on intimate examination. This led to questions, which led to explanations, which led to… well, nothing good.

But that wouldn't be an issue now. Jack Smith already knew his secret, freeing Alan to attempt something desperate and unprecedented. As they approached Hong Kong, Alan would try a little social engineering, read the situation, figure out exactly what performance to give, and then….

And then what?

Again: half-considered and completely terrible.

Also, as it turned out, completely unnecessary. They made port before Jack visited him again, and the agent promptly unshackled Alan, accompanied him onto the dock, handed him some cash, and gave him some pretty specific instructions.

"First," said Jack, "I want you to go buy a burner phone and use it to send a text message to this number. Are you paying attention? Eight-Five-Two, Nine-One-Zero-Bravo, Nine-Eight-Nine-Two. Send the message 'Chinese,' and I'll respond with 'Room.' Keep the phone charged, network connected, and on your person at all times. Then go get your leg fixed, stay hidden, and don't leave Hong Kong. If you don't answer the phone when I call, or if you flee the city, then you can consider your secret out."

Alan stood there and absorbed all this. "Okay, I'm sorry, but these are some pretty mixed signals you're sending. You do understand that I'm a flight risk, right? Do you *want* me to escape custody?"

"I told you what I want you to do."

"Yeah, but I have no reason to do it. It only makes sense for me to hang around and wait for you to make up your mind about me if there's a decent chance you'll decide to let me go. But if it's more likely you'll decide to hand me over, then the smart thing for me to do would be to leave the city and at least do what I can to preserve my freedom. So I have to decide which choice you're more likely to make, and nothing about our history inclines me to think you'll choose my freedom. And you have to have already considered all this," Alan continued, "so I'm left thinking this is either some sort of trap you're setting, or a game you're playing, or you really do just want me to escape without explicitly setting me free. So which is it?"

Jack gave Alan a cutting smile. "That's an awful lot of speculation about my thoughts and motives. Why not just read my mind?"

"Hilarious."

"Then get going, and you'll find out."

Alan spent a few more seconds studying him, and then he turned away. As he walked down the dock, Alan kept turning his head backward, shooting curious, suspicious looks at the agent. Every time he looked back, all he saw on Jack's face was that stupid smirk.

And then Agent Jack Smith was gone from sight.

SMITH COUNTED on Alan to remain in town at least for the short term as he weighed Smith's ultimatum. Smith wouldn't need so long to make up his mind. If he did decide to cut Alan loose, it would be simple enough to call him and let him know he was free to go. But Smith thought that outcome unlikely. Alan had made some valid points during his interrogation on the ship. A synthetic psychic was unambiguously dangerous, and when Smith decided how to address that danger, it would be just as simple to track the phone's signal to its location.

In the meantime, he had Arissa binti Noor to deal with.

Arissa wasn't the experienced fugitive Alan was. Also unlike Alan, she had a tendency to overrely on her telepathy. In all likelihood, her psychic ability was the only thing preventing her discovery, but it would present no obstacle to a Countermind agent of Smith's caliber. He would scour public records, police reports, and news outlets for patterns of irrational behavior among the city's inhabitants. He would also access Arissa's personal records. If standard protocols were being followed, then Arissa's financial and digital assets would still be available to her, presenting ample opportunity for the fugitive to leave a money or data trail.

She was a trained Security Ministry agent and should be too smart to commit such an obvious error. But she was also mentally unstable, and those accounts might present Smith with an opportunity to provoke her into acting foolishly. Engaging her in conversation would be ideal. The deluded craved nothing more than the opportunity to persuade others of their delusions.

He knew just where to start.

HUANG AND Arissa had spent their every waking hour in the apartment, poring over Huang's game code and trying to discern what they were supposed to do with it. After a while, Arissa had to admit she couldn't make any sense of what she was looking at, so Huang shoved a stack of technical manuals at her and told her to get out of the way for now.

Huang hadn't complained about the lack of help. She was grateful for something to focus on. The office scuttlebutt was that Huang was working so much from home because she was too depressed over losing control of Rath. From what Arissa picked up from overheard phone calls, that story wasn't so far off the truth.

Arissa was reading one of the manuals when Huang said her name.

"Yes?" Arissa asked, grateful for the chance to put the book down.

"You asked me to let you know about any activity with Julianna Aznam?"

Arissa had suggested monitoring her bogus PartyYǒu account for potential indicators of pursuit. If the account were accessed in any way, or simply closed, it would signal that the authorities were taking some kind of action on her, either closing the net or cleaning up her cover legend. It wasn't much of an early-warning system, but it was better than nothing.

"What happened?" Arissa asked.

"Well, someone named Card Lin just sent it a message. I thought all your friends were fake."

"Oh God. What does that asshole want?"

"Ex-boyfriend?"

"Don't even joke," said Arissa.

"He says he just wants to talk."

"Are you serious? Is that it?"

Arissa leaned over Huang's shoulder and read the message on the screen. Yup. That was it.

Arissa tsked. "It's a trap. It's Countermind." She left Huang's side to return to her book.

"Oh," Huang said simply.

Arissa stopped, turned, reappeared at Huang's side. She studied the message on the screen again.

"I'm going to talk to him."

"I'm sorry?"

"I'll take precautions," Arissa said.

"Okay, good, but why talk to him at all?"

"Countermind is after me. If I can sow some discord in their ranks, it could slow them down. Any suggestions for how I can connect to the account without being traced?"

"Well, the simplest thing would be to bring some cash to an Internet café, log in from there, and don't hang out too long," Huang suggested. "Plenty of trolls have messed with the game that way."

"Can you monitor PartyYŏu's internal systems from here at home? Let me know if it looks like someone tries to trace me?"

Huang sighed. "Not that this isn't a terrible idea to begin with, but if it looks like anyone's after you, I'll order a system-wide administrative announcement. Probably something related to tonight's game update. A pretext won't be hard to find. Just watch your inbox."

"Okay, thank you," Arissa said, standing to go.

Huang turned to face her retreating back. "This is a terrible idea," she repeated.

"Don't worry. I'll be taking additional precautions."

"Like what, pray tell?"

Wordlessly, Arissa tapped herself on the temple, and Huang rolled her eyes.

JULIANNA: TELL me something.

    Julianna: Just why are they called "desuppressive events"?

    Card: Hi!

    Card: How are you doing?

    Julianna: Just answer the question.

    Julianna: I'd like to know before you trace my connection.

    Card: Heh.

    Card: I'm not trying to trace your connection.

    Card: I just want to talk.

    Julianna: So answer the question.

    Card: A desuppressive event occurs if a psychic manages to breach Countermind's data security.

    Julianna: I know that.

Julianna: I want to know how it got the name.

Card: You don't know?

Card: It was quite a scandal.

Card: Though I guess it was before both our times.

Card: A psychic managed to read a Countermind agent's mind.

Card: Obviously, that goes completely against the club charter.

Card: Worse, the stolen knowledge was highly classified.

Card: When the security breach came to light, there were a bunch of hearings.

Card: Some Ministry flunky tried to explain what happened in technical terms.

Card: Basically, the Countermind agent whose mind was read had failed to suppress the thoughts containing the classified information before the psychic could detect them.

Card: Now, this Ministry rep desperately wanted to avoid using words like "leak" or "breach," which would have sounded too much like admitting failure.

Julianna: So he called it a desuppressive event.

Card: Exactly.

Card: There, I answered your question. Would you answer one from me?

Julianna: Not so fast.

Julianna: I'm not sure you've completely answered my question.

Card: Oh?

Julianna: The term gets used pretty generally for so specific an incident.

Card: Phrases take on meanings beyond what they originally referred to. It happens.

Julianna: So, if a psychic breached Countermind not by reading an agent's mind, but by actually infiltrating the organization, even becoming an agent himself, that wouldn't be a desuppressive event, would it?

Card: Heh.

Card: That would never happen.

Julianna: I didn't ask if it would happen, I asked if it would qualify as a desuppressive event.

Card: No, I don't think the term would apply to a disaster of that magnitude.

Julianna: Then you may need to work out some more nuanced jargon.

Julianna: Because your boss? Countermind's executive director?

Julianna: Telepathic.
Card: Really?
Julianna: Really.
Card: Well, that's terrible.
Card: How did you find this out?
Julianna: You're just humoring me.
Card: I'm listening to you. What you're saying is very concerning.
Julianna: Whatever.
Julianna: Believe me or not, he tried to mentally recondition me during interrogation.
Card: That's awful! Are you all right?
Julianna: I managed to surprise him and get a look at his own secrets.
Card: Very impressive.
Julianna: I learned that he dominated his own wife into having children with other men, so that his kids wouldn't be born with the psi gene.
Card: Scandalous.
Julianna: But he still wants a family, just one more to his standards and design.
Julianna: Which is what I think he wanted me for.
Julianna: I'm guessing he personally assigned you to entrap me for him, to make me part of his little dynasty.
Julianna: And he might want you for it, too, by the way. He did say you were like a son to him, Jack Smith.
Julianna: So be concerned for your own damned self.
Julianna: And maybe look at cleaning up your own house instead of coming after me.
Julianna: Because you've got much bigger problems.
Julianna: You there?

Smith started to type a response, but Arissa severed the connection, apparently having said her piece. Smith requested a connection trace, and Arissa's login was located to an Internet café in Wan Chai. He'd check it out but wasn't terribly hopeful. If she was using a café, then she was taking precautions, and a psychic of her skill had many more means of covering her tracks than a normal person. Smith expected she'd used a psijacked puppet to connect to her PartyYŏu account without taking the risk of even entering the café. Nothing would be too paranoid.

And was she ever paranoid. Okay, Smith privately admitted her little rant had gotten a bit creepy toward the end, with that talk of Zheng seeing Smith as a son, and the fact that Zheng was the one who'd assigned Smith to Arissa's case. And then she'd used Smith's name, despite his never having shared it with her. But it wasn't unreasonable that a psychic with Security connections might glean some facts one way or another. And hadn't Zheng said she was delusional? Wasn't her raving style completely typical of someone with a persecution complex? Unload enough crackpot ideas, and one of them was bound to bear some faint resemblance to reality. That was how conspiracy theories found traction, after all: by being occasionally, potentially, coincidentally, in some small detail correct.

No, Smith most emphatically did not believe her. At the same time, he decided not to report this contact or this conversation with Zheng. Not yet.

Paranoia was infectious that way.

CHAPTER 23
RULE AND REGULATION

IN LIGHT of their recent ordeal, Kim Kyung-Min was placed on mandatory leave and advised to spend the next few days recuperating. Kyung-Min responded by bringing work home to their Shanghai apartment and immersing themself in it, but the research wasn't as distracting as they'd hoped. It wasn't the death and horror and mayhem haunting Kyung-Min, terrible though they were. What echoed in Kyung-Min's recollection were the deprecations hurled at them by Alan Izaki, his words so firmly lodged in Kyung-Min's mind that they might've been telepathically implanted.

An alarm went off on Kyung-Min's phone. They checked their blood-glucose level, entered it into a log with their other vitals, and ran the usual analysis. Everything was normal.

Time off also made it easier to be sidelined by unexpected business. They'd barely finished running the analysis when the phone rang with a call summoning them out of town to the offices of the Security Ministry, to be debriefed on the events in Pyongyang.

Another train ride, then. Kyung-Min should have known better than to think they'd heard the last of Countermind.

KIM KYUNG-MIN, wearing a wrist brace on the right forearm, bowed upon entering Zheng's office. The scientist did not visually sweep the room in appreciation of its size and finery. The dossier prepared for Zheng had outlined a prestigious pedigree, and Doctor Kim was likely no stranger to large, well-appointed rooms.

Reaching out telepathically, Zheng took Kim's temperature. The scientist was tired and frustrated, and disliked being summoned here. Zheng would have to appeal to that.

"Thank you for agreeing to meet with me on such short notice, Doctor," he said. "Please, have a seat. Let's not waste your time."

"Thank you, sir, but it would be impolite of me to sit while you remained standing. I will stand in kind."

"It's no bother. Please sit."

"No, thank you."

"I must insist you make yourself comfortable."

"I'm afraid I must decline," Kim said, weary eyes matching Zheng's.

Zheng, resenting the discourtesy, peered again into the doctor's mind. Kim had little patience for games of status, and Zheng decided not to press the matter. He'd get what he needed.

"I've invited you here to discuss the recent incident in Pyongyang," he said. "The work you're doing there is of considerable relevance to this department's area of responsibility, and I like to remain aware of any major developments. Would you be kind enough to discuss the recent events with me?"

Left unsaid was that Kim's work, in point of fact, posed a danger to Countermind. If a means could be found of medically inducing psychic resistance, what need would there be for counterpsychic techniques?

"Certainly," Kim said. "I'm happy to provide any information I can."

"Thank you," said Zheng. "Please start from the beginning."

"For that, I would actually have to go back a week, when I was contacted by Agent Jack Smith of the Bureau of Counterpsychic Affairs."

Smith had been involved? Zheng covered his surprise but deepened his mental probe, monitoring Kim's thoughts as the scientist spoke.

"He requested my expert opinion on a matter regarding a fugitive psychic he was pursuing, one Alan Izaki by name. In particular, he suspected Alan was a clone of the late Quentin Izaki, a computer scientist. Jack suspected Izaki had not only cloned himself, but had genetically engineered said clone to possess telepathic ability. As a researcher with the Science Ministry, a neurobiologist, and a parapsychologist, I'm frequently called upon to provide classified consultation on matters like this, though I found this particular theory far-fetched and attempted to dissuade him of it. I'd thought myself done with the matter and continued to Pyongyang to perform routine on-site research into the disaster that occurred there. But it happened that Alan Izaki actually fled to the Pyongyang research base aboard the very vessel transporting me, and Smith followed him there."

"That's quite the coincidence."

"The misfortune attending these two individuals has defied all probability," Kim said sourly. "Agent Jack accosted the fugitive inside the base's perimeter. However, Alan Izaki escaped into the city with Jack in pursuit. Izaki telepathically disabled a number of guards during his escape. It's difficult to know exactly what transpired next, but during this confusion and under cover of the storm, an infection carrier was able to find its way through the fence. In our vulnerable state, the virus spread itself with its usual speed. I and a number of other survivors took refuge in a bunker, where we would likely have perished, had not Agent Jack returned with Izaki in custody. The two of them working in concert were able to engineer a rescue, allowing all of us to escape aboard the transport ship."

"They cooperated," Director Zheng said.

"And rather effectively," Kim confirmed. "We sailed for Shanghai. En route, Jack confined Izaki to a cabin and maintained an armed watch over him, while instructing the rest of the crew to pair off, watch each other for suspicious activity, and provide constant radio reports."

How odd. If the fugitive had been properly sedated and inhibited, that degree of precaution shouldn't have been necessary. But, then, Zheng's own recent experiences with psychic inhibitors had been disillusioning.

"Were there any further incidents?" the director asked.

"Ah, just one. Izaki did momentarily slip free from Jack's custody, but he didn't seem seriously bent on escape."

"No? What did he do?"

"He verbally berated me for my indirect role in the creation of the virus."

Kim Kyung-Min's frown bespoke irritation, but Zheng could feel guilt and regret settle over the scientist like a pall.

"We arrived at Shanghai," Kim said, "without further incident, and Jack departed with the fugitive still in his custody."

"And you remember nothing else."

"No. Nothing."

Oh, but Kim did. The memory, and then the deliberation over whether to reveal the memory, conspicuously rebounded to Zheng's attention. The director snagged hold of the thought like a thread and pulled it free, unraveling the recollection: Kim Kyung-Min, quite perceptively, had noted Smith's failure to sedate Alan Izaki or to request help in securing the prisoner. Kim had even challenged Smith on these oversights when they'd arrived in Shanghai, though Smith had furnished no satisfactory explanation.

The story itself wasn't particularly alarming. What bothered Zheng was Smith's failure to relay any of it to him, with the implication that Smith had made a significant discovery of some sort and had so far declined to report it. It was a lapse unbecoming of his top agent and personal apprentice. Zheng was frankly disappointed.

He didn't have time at the moment to consider this failure in full. "Well, if that's the entire report, I won't hold you for any longer. I'm grateful to you for taking the time to speak with me."

"I'm honored to have provided any help I could," said Doctor Kim, meaning not a word of it.

ANOTHER EXPRESS train back to Shanghai, a taxi ride home, and Kyung-Min barely had time to collapse into a chair before the phone alarm sounded again. Grumbling, Kyung-Min checked their blood sugar, logged it, and ran the analysis.

The results were below the predicted range. Kyung-Min stared at the finding. They checked the analysis for errors and, finding none, took another sample to rerun the analysis. The result replicated perfectly.

It was preposterous. Kyung-Min checked the timelog from the continuous glucose monitor and felt their disbelief increase. The dip had apparently occurred during the visit to Countermind headquarters. It was possible that this was a coincidence, but Kyung-Min had enough confidence in their analysis to doubt that possibility.

Kyung-Min needed an hour to sit down and mull this discovery over. This was never supposed to happen. The Kim family had money, connections, *guanxi*, all the advantages that were supposed to place them above these kinds of clandestine invasions. And Kyung-Min had avoided politics precisely to avoid giving anyone in the government reason to read their mind without permission.

Now that such an invasion had occurred, Kyung-Min didn't know how to respond. Most paralyzing was their uncertainty over whose attention to bring this news to. This was a matter for Countermind, but the invasion had occurred at Countermind, and as much as Kyung-Min hated to admit it, the only person they could think to trust in Countermind was Jack Smith.

Their preference was not to collect on that stupid favor he'd offered. Kyung-Min didn't trust him, didn't even like him. But it hadn't escaped Kyung-Min's notice how much more easily Jack could have escaped Pyongyang if he hadn't bothered to mount a rescue mission. It would have been simple enough for Jack to just signal the ship and reboard it with his prisoner, while leaving Kyung-Min and the other survivors to die in that bunker. That Jack had put himself at considerable additional risk to save them was admirable, and Kyung-Min was grateful, even if they still held Smith partly responsible for the crisis arising in the first place. Not that there wasn't plenty of blame to go around.

In the end, it came down to this: minding their own business and doing their job hadn't worked out as harmlessly as Kyung-Min had hoped. Maybe it was time to do something more.

SMITH WAS working in his field office, neck-deep in police reports when he got the call from Kim Kyung-Min.

"Doctor?"

"Agent," Kim said, sounding weary.

"How can I help you?"

"You can hear me out. I need to provide some context for what I'm about to tell you."

"All right. I'm listening."

Kim took a moment to gather their words. "As you may know. Telepathic tampering is conceptually similar to any executive function override of an automatic mental response. The critical distinction is whether the source of the regulation is internal or external to the nervous system, whether it is rooted in the prefrontal cortex or in another organism possessing a positive psi quotient."

"I follow," Smith said, even if he had no idea where Kim was leading him.

"In either case," Kim continued, "a prepotent response is overridden, which invariably requires an expenditure of energy by the organism whose mental behavior is being changed."

"Certainly," Smith said. "It's why extensive telepathic intrusion often leaves its targets feeling mentally drained, even when they're unaware of the reason why."

"This loss of energy is indicated physiologically by a decline in glucose levels."

"Sure."

"Like any reasonable person," said Kim, "I'm necessarily concerned that a psychic might steal confidential information from my mind without my being aware of it. To help alert me of whether I've been subject to telepathic intrusion, I developed the habit of tracking my glucose levels and analyzing them for discrepancies. I've created and validated a statistical model incorporating temporal factors, recent activities, diet, exercise, and a host of other inputs. The model specifically checks for glucose levels below predicted values by a significant difference attributable to telepathic tampering when other factors are accounted for."

What was this, a confession?

"Doctor," Smith said, "if what you're describing could be classified as a counterpsychic technique, as I fear it might, its practice would be illegal without state sanction."

"Spare me," Kim snapped. "First, no, it does not fall under that classification. Counterpsychic techniques are properly considered to be cognitive in their methodology, not physiological. Second, and more to the point, the legal restrictions on counterpsychic techniques are both unreasonable and unrealistic. People do not like having their minds read, Agent, and prefer to know when and if their minds have been read. Or is that not true for you?"

"Apologies, Doctor," Smith said, taken aback by the outburst. "I didn't mean to accuse you. Please finish."

"I recently detected an abrupt decline in my glucose levels indicative of a psychic intrusion. This one comes after my return to Shanghai, so it can't be attributed to Alan Izaki."

"Then when did it happen?" Smith asked.

"During a visit to the Bureau of Counterpsychic Affairs."

Smith straightened in his seat. "When did you visit Countermind?"

"I've only just returned."

"What were you doing there?"

"Meeting your executive director," Kim said.

Kim had met Zheng? Arissa's warning burst into Smith's recollection with the force of a truck.

"What was your meeting about?" Smith asked.

"He interviewed me on the events in Pyongyang."

"I see. And what did you tell him?"

A pause as Kim seemed to consider their answer.

"Everything," Kim said at last, "from the moment you first reached out to me for consultation to the moment you stepped off the boat at Shanghai."

Which left out their conversation at the bottom of the gangplank. Kim hadn't shared their suspicions that Alan was uniquely dangerous and that Smith was deliberately hiding him from the authorities. But if Zheng had read Kim's mind anyway....

"Doctor, I need you to think back to our last conversation. I believe you said, and I'm trying to quote you here, that you didn't know what I'd found, and you could only entertain suspicions."

"That sounds about right."

"I need you to tell me, if you do have any suspicions, exactly what they are."

"Nothing I'd seriously consider," Kim said.

"Please, Doctor. Anything at all, no matter how ridiculous it sounds."

Kim exhaled audibly. "Well, I suppose a genetically engineered clone isn't completely out of the question."

"Anything else?"

"It had crossed my mind that perhaps Alan had been bitten by an infection carrier but had manifested an immunity to the worst effects."

"Anything else?"

Kim sighed. "Given Quentin Izaki's research interests, I don't know, maybe a robot?"

Smith laughed. "I'm sorry, Doctor. I know I said nothing was too ridiculous, but I wasn't expecting that."

"Hey, look, you asked."

"You're right. I'm sorry. Thank you for the notification. I know you'd rather be focusing on your job without constantly having to call me about mine."

"Yes," Kim said, sardonic. "I crave a life of quiet efficiency."

"I'll see that the issue is investigated, though I promise I won't say anything that would get you into trouble. If I need anything else, I'll be in touch."

"I know you will."

The call ended. Smith debated what to do next and eventually decided to try one more thing. Something of a shibboleth. By itself it wouldn't be conclusive, but in light of the other evidence....

He dialed Zheng's office.

"Sir?"

"Agent. Any progress on Arissa binti Noor?"

"Not yet, sir, though I've been giving it my full attention, and I'll notify you as soon as something turns up. In the meantime, I was wondering if you had time for a quick update on the Alan Izaki case."

"Certainly." The director sounded pleased. "Go right ahead."

"Thank you. While holding him in custody, I've extensively debriefed him regarding his time growing up in the care of his father, the computer scientist Quentin Izaki. It seems that, during his retirement, Doctor Izaki had done pioneering work related to public-key cryptographic systems. His findings could have major implications for Internet security, both for the collection of data and the encryption of it." This statement was potentially true and therefore the best kind of lie. While researching Quentin Izaki's life, Smith had found a couple of papers published by him on this very subject.

"Thank you, Agent. That is interesting, and I commend you on your diligence, but I do think the suspect would be more effectively interrogated within the confines of headquarters. In the meantime, so long as Arissa binti Noor remains at large, you should be focusing your attention there."

"Yes, sir. I'll see that Izaki is submitted for processing right away."

"See that you do."

They hung up. Then Smith composed an e-mail.

> *Sir,*
>
> *I forgot to mention one more thing. A researcher with the Science Ministry, one Doctor Kim Kyung-Min, provided invaluable aid to me during my pursuit of Alan Izaki, even to the point of suffering considerable personal inconvenience and even danger to life*

and limb. I would like to request that Doctor Kim's assistance is kept in mind by the department.

Smith sent the e-mail to Zheng, and the reply came quickly:

Certainly. I'll see to it that she is amply rewarded for her help.

Smith sent a response:

Thank you, sir.

Then he dialed the number for Alan's phone. But Alan didn't answer. Smith hung up and dialed again. And again. And again.

CHAPTER 24
DENIAL OF SERVICE

AFTER KIM Kyung-Min's departure, Zheng had confirmed that Smith still hadn't submitted any further updates on his hunt for Alan Izaki, then dwelt at length on Smith's apparent laxity in his duties. Zheng tried to grant him the benefit of the doubt. After all, Smith had at least reported in after securing Izaki and had given Zheng plenty of opportunity to question him about the case. Instead, Zheng had quickly directed Smith's attention to the task of apprehending Arissa binti Noor. He had no reason yet to doubt his protégé's diligence.

And Smith's diligence had proven true when the agent called Zheng, urgently requesting a more thorough discussion of the Izaki case. Zheng, confidence restored, allowed Smith to make a fuller report and then thanked Smith for the update before refocusing his attention on Arissa.

When he hung up the phone, Zheng saw an update pop up on the touchscreen monitor embedded in his desktop. His latest Senex search had concluded. While Smith was pursuing Arissa binti Noor in the field, Zheng had been requisitioning multiple searches on Arissa in an effort to track her digital shadow, so far without success. By all appearances, and to her credit, she was staying off the Internet entirely.

He tapped the update window, not expecting to find anything new. But there, sitting on top of the latest batch of results, was something he hadn't seen: a chat log from PartyYǒu.

Julianna: Tell me something.
Julianna: Just why are they called "desuppressive events"?

Per the chat log's metadata, the conversants were named Julianna and Card. Zheng recognized these names from Smith's report on the events leading up to Arissa's first arrest. Apparently, Senex's latest search was expansive enough to capture data even from bogus accounts created as part of their cover stories. This conversation must have occurred while Smith was using the Card Lin identity to entrap Arissa.

But no, the date stamp was far too recent for that, the conversation having taken place after Smith's return to Hong Kong but prior to his just concluded phone debriefing with Zheng, when Smith had quite explicitly declined to report any progress on the Arissa binti Noor case. Yet here he was, having an Internet chat with her.

Zheng read further.

Card: I'm not trying to trace your connection.
Card: I just want to talk.

And he read further.

Julianna: So, if a psychic breached Countermind not by reading an agent's mind, but by actually infiltrating the organization, even becoming an agent himself, that wouldn't be a desuppressive event, would it?

Further.

Julianna: Because your boss? Countermind's executive director?
Julianna: Telepathic.

Further.

Julianna: I learned that he dominated his own wife into having children with other men, so that his kids wouldn't be born with the psi gene.

And finally,

Julianna: And maybe look at cleaning up your own house instead of coming after me.
Julianna: Because you've got much bigger problems.
Julianna: You there?

Zheng was in a panic. Had Arissa seen so much before he'd shut her out? These claims she made were problematic but could yet be dismissed as the ravings of a lunatic. More distressing still was that Smith had read these accusations yet had not seen fit to report them to Zheng.

From the chat log alone, Zheng couldn't tell if Smith actually believed Arissa's story, but it hardly mattered at this point. This failure went beyond mere lapses in judgment. It represented outright disloyalty. The depth of the betrayal, from someone Zheng had personally molded from nothing, someone Zheng considered nearly his own child, stung deeply. Was there no one left he could trust?

He lifted his phone and ordered an immediate direct flight to Hong Kong. If he could no longer rely on Jack Smith, then the situation was worse than he feared, and quickly worsening. It would require his personal attention.

WHY AM I doing this? Smith asked himself for perhaps the first time in his life.

He'd never been one to wallow in self-doubt. But now dialing and redialing Alan's number, still with no response, he had plenty of time for this and other questions.

Who or what is Alan Izaki to me? Why am I throwing everything away for a thief, a criminal, a fugitive psychic? And not even a proper person. A machine.

Was that the reason? Was Alan's secret too dangerous for Smith to entrust to his superiors? Smith had never truly trusted, in any strong sense of the word, the system he worked for. He was too much of a realist to be so naive. But he'd trusted Zheng, and for an unregistered psychic to have infiltrated the Security Ministry, not to mention Countermind, was bad enough. But Zheng had infiltrated Smith's confidence besides. So was that it? Did Smith feel betrayed?

No. Smith's recklessness—and he had no choice now but to admit he was being reckless—had begun well before that. It had started with Alan. Why? Alan was attractive, but Smith had always been too professional to let such a thing influence his work. Was it empathy? Did Smith see echoes of himself in Alan's lonely and abandoned origins? But

Smith had never been long on empathy. Arissa had lost her parents too, and Smith had shown her little mercy.

Looking back, Smith saw his preoccupation with Alan escalating in stages. First the attempted arrest and Alan's escape, then the connection to Quentin Izaki, followed by the discovery of Alan's true nature. And now the revelation about Zheng had pushed Smith over a treasonous tipping point, where he found himself not only harboring a fugitive but actively trying to alert him to impending danger.

Maybe there was no silver bullet. Human behavior had multiple causes. Smith's recklessness could be caused by a combination of these factors. A single explanation hardly sufficed for acting so radically out of character. Only by following the chain backward to the beginning did Smith find behavior that he recognized in himself: a suspect had escaped him, and Smith's professional pride demanded Alan suffer for the insult. This at least felt like the man Smith knew himself to be—proud, cruel, vindictive. The rest he'd have to figure out later.

"I'VE FIGURED it out," Huang declared after working another full day and well into the night.

When she got no response, she jostled Arissa awake from the couch and repeated the good news to the drowsy agent.

"First, some background," Huang began as Arissa drank some coffee-tea mixed from the strongest available varieties of each. "Senex makes use of a single pool of processing resources distributed between its different tasks, including web crawling, indexing, and data searching."

"Okay," Arissa agreed, still bleary.

"And Senex processes data intelligently, right? But that's pretty vague. It's more accurate to say that Senex processes data algorithmically when it has sufficient system resources but resorts to heuristics when resources are limited."

"Like a person," Arissa nodded, the caffeine taking effect.

"Yes, and I think that's the key. You say Senex is conscious. So I tried thinking of it not like a computer but like a person. That freed me to consider its incentives, game things out, you know?"

"Go on."

"The thing to realize is that Senex takes this approach to all its processes. That includes its core functions of collecting and analyzing web data, but it also includes defensive processes like virus detection. The other thing to realize is that data collection is Senex's core function, such that Senex will prioritize it above anything else. If there's enough strain put on Senex's ability to collect data, then its threat detection will get sloppy, and that opens the door to sneaking in a virus."

"That seems like a pretty gaping security flaw," Arissa observed.

"Yeah, for something designed by a government agency," said Huang. "But the source code was written by and stolen from an academic, one whose principal aim was to create a very smart search engine and who never got around to the practical issues of securing it against attackers. Besides, we won't exactly be mounting a conventional attack."

"Okay," said Arissa. "So how do we apply that kind of pressure?"

Huang pointed at the large monitor on the wall. "I upload that into Rath's game servers."

"The dragon?"

"The entire expansion."

The entire expansion, which was still small enough to fit on an external hard drive. And, according to Huang, Senex didn't care about Rath's game code, just its user data.

"Either I'm not fully awake, or you're not making sense," said Arissa.

"Our usage statistics will go through the roof."

"And users provide personal data, which Senex downloads."

"Right."

"But you've had expansions before," Arissa said. "Were the data spikes ever large enough to cause the kind of slowdown you're describing?"

"Not at all."

"I'm sorry," said Arissa, "but I don't follow. How is this meant to work?"

Huang smiled. "You'll see."

Huang knew Arissa didn't need to read her thoughts to detect the implied dare: *Go ahead. Pull it from my mind if you're so curious.*

"Fine," said Arissa. "Assuming this will spam Senex's systems, that opens the door to infecting it with a virus. But you said you didn't write a virus."

"I didn't," admitted Huang. "That'll be your job."

"Come again?"

"So, I distract Senex, and you get in there and muck around, do what you think you need to do to stop it. Maybe change or incapacitate it. I don't know what, but this'll be the best chance we get for you to do some serious damage. After we launch this attack the first time, we aren't ever getting another opportunity. And we have to do it now, because you're being hunted by Countermind, and I'm on the verge of losing executive access to my company's systems."

"Aren't you better qualified to implant a virus? I'm no hacker."

"And I told you," Huang said, "neither am I. But you're a psychic, right? You said it yourself: it's reprogramming. What I do to computers, you do to minds. And you've already done it! Even as a little girl, you made telepathic contact, and it responded to that contact. You interacted with Senex's programming, which means you made alterations to its behavior, however briefly. You're such a world-class psychic, you may be the only person alive who can reprogram a computer with her mind. All you needed was a conscious computer!"

Arissa interrupted, signaling her confusion with a wave of her hand. "Wait. Wait. Am I meant to understand that your plan for attacking Senex depended on my assistance the entire time?"

Huang shook her head. "I don't think so. I suspect I was doing the best I could with the tools I had available to me. I'd identified a way to slow down Senex, but not yet a way to permanently damage it. The other people you commanded to destroy Senex," Huang added abruptly. "They've all been arrested or 'reeducated' or just plain disappeared, right? Those who aren't dead?"

Arissa gave a small nod.

"I assume the ones who were arrested were all caught trying to attack Senex in some more overt fashion, either by physically destroying its Hong Kong server center or infecting it with a virus."

"Yes, that's right."

"See, they all had plans that could meet some conceivable degree of success. The odds were long, but not nonexistent. But I hadn't even gotten that far." Huang laughed. "So I was just biding my time perfecting step one of my plan, while still trying to figure out step two." Huang beamed at Arissa. "And now here you are!"

"THERE YOU are!" Jack shouted when Alan finally answered. "I must've called you a hundred times!"

"I'm thinking," said Alan, "that 'unreasonably obsessed' was an understatement."

"Where were you?"

"Getting my leg fixed, like you told me to. Sorry, but I don't care how many times you call or what you threaten me with. I'm not going to take a phone call when I'm in the middle of a B&E."

"You have to leave the city!" Jack said. "You're not safe."

"Excuse me?"

"You need to get out of town as quickly as you can. Just vanish."

"Well, I'd love to, but this is a pretty bewildering development. What's going on?"

"I can't keep your secret safe. I'll do what I can—I've already deleted that e-mail—but it may not be enough. The one person capable of reading my mind may already know about you, or at least enough to be suspicious, and you need to get away before he can find out more. And ditch the phone."

"Wait, really, that's it?" Alan asked. "I'm free to go? Just like that?"

"Not if you dally!"

"Um…." Alan hemmed and hawed over whether "thank you" was an appropriate thing to say in this context, but Jack had already hung up.

Alan took the phone away from his ear and examined it. It remained still.

The 3D-printing workshop was in Kwai Chung, part of a community maker space that closed up late on weekday evenings. It was a short distance from Rambler Channel. Alan walked the distance, taking his time, until he'd arrived at the railing on the channel's edge. He looked down into the water. The night was too dark for him to see his reflection. He could only make out the irregular outline of his silhouette.

Was he really free, just like that? After all the stupid decisions he'd made to land himself in this mess? Thinking on them, Alan had to admit to himself that his worst mistake was vomiting up his whole damned autobiography while bound up in the backseat of a Countermind agent's car. At the time, Alan had rationalized the confession as a tactical move, a long-shot gambit to impress upon Jack the dangers of arresting him, the importance of releasing him.

And maybe it had worked. Maybe it hadn't. But Alan might have found other opportunities to escape with at least most of his secret intact. Now someone—worse, someone in Countermind—knew his story, and if even Jack didn't trust his own ability to keep Alan's secret, then the jig was most certainly up. There'd be no hitting the reset button like with Johnny. From this point forward, Alan could only ever be free in strictly literal terms. The worst possible fate wasn't to be caught. The worst possible fate was to be discovered.

So why did he feel relieved?

Remembering Jack's final instruction, Alan removed the phone from his pocket, checked it one last time, and found nothing.

He looked at the water.

The channel's surface glowed a faint blue where it lapped against the slickened rocks half-submerged in the shadow of the walkway, lit by sea-sparkling algal blooms. Beautiful, except for the sewage and restaurant waste and city runoff the dinoflagellates fed on before swiftly dying and, in their descending decomposition, sucking up all the oxygen in the harbor, suffocating the fish and crabs struggling to survive there.

But Alan didn't need oxygen.

Steadying himself against the railing, phone in hand, he reared his arm back, aimed his throw, and nearly dropped the phone from surprise when it vibrated in his hand.

"Er, hello?" Alan said, answering.

"Last-minute change of plans," said Jack.

"Oh, wonderful. More mixed signals."

"Sorry, but the coast isn't clear yet. I've set up a place where you can lie low and won't be discovered until it's safe to leave town." Smith rattled off an address in Central. "There's a secure entrance on the south face of the building, but it will be unlocked. Keep the phone with you, and keep it on, but don't call back. Go down into the basement and stay there until I call you again."

He hung up.

"Well, all right, then," said Alan, pocketing the phone. "Or I could just decide I'm tired of getting yanked about, tell you to go to hell, and leave this city like I was planning to before you dragged me back into it."

His leg was repaired, he was out on the street, and he had absolutely no good reason to stick around. Even merely literal freedom would be better than life on a leash. He could go anywhere he liked. Not North Korea, obviously. But maybe Japan, or Vietnam, or Thailand. Hell, he still had, like, four continents he could've been traipsing about in right that moment. Why not Australia? Why not England? Why not fucking Antarctica?

Alan was in the tesseract room. He had no landmarks, no guideposts, no disembodied voice providing direction. Except one: Jack Smith, the government agent whose mind Alan couldn't erase, who knew what Alan was, who probably posed the single greatest threat imaginable to Alan's freedom and safety—and who, preposterously, now claimed to want to help. It was too dangerous to trust him.

Rotate the situation. Question assumptions.

Okay, Alan had found someone who knew what he was, and that person hadn't tried immediately to kill him. Then Alan had explained what he was, and that person had kept his secret and even released him, sort of. Then Alan had answered a phone call, and now that person was offering to help him hide and avoid capture.

So maybe Alan could, if not exactly trust, then at least entertain the possibility of having an ally?

Just for one night.

So ALAN went to Central. Following the address, he was able to spot the building from several blocks away. A characteristically modern glass and steel tower, with a gaping square opening in the middle, dozens of stories above street level, looking large enough to admit a Cessna. A dragon hole, permitting the free flow of energy from the harbor to the mountains.

Alan, to his surprise, entered the building just as freely. Jack's directions took him to an inconspicuous rear loading dock, the door unlocked, just as had been promised. Despite the luster of the building's façade, the interior was as dismal and dull as any office, like the headquarters for a particularly stuffy corporation. But the place had something eerie about it as well, and it took a moment for Alan to understand what.

It wasn't that the building was empty of workers. The workday was over and Central was always dead after sunset, the *rènào* bustle having migrated to other, more nightlife-friendly neighborhoods. It was that the facility appeared to be highly secure except for the uncanny absence of any actual security. Electronic doors were unlocked. Cameras were dormant. No guards could be seen.

Then it got weirder. Now Alan noticed the logos, the letterheads, the signs. This was a government office. This was a Safety Ministry office. This was, under normal circumstances, one of the absolute worst places Alan could hide in.

But it was empty and unsecured, and Alan had to grudgingly concede it was also the absolute last place anyone would expect him to go. How the hell had Jack arranged this?

Alan found that not all the doors were unlocked. Those that were unlocked were arranged in sequence, leading Alan deeper into the building. Following the path, he found a downward stairway, which led, to his amazement, into a gargantuan server room, large as a warehouse and cold as a refrigerator, its lights too dim for Alan to take in the full size of it.

Walking down the wide aisles between immense server racks, arrayed in rows like humming, blinking monoliths, Alan felt his curiosity finally give way to unease. This whole situation was just too strange. He fingered the phone in his pocket, on the knife's edge of turning back, calling Smith, and demanding a fuller explanation, in defiance of the instructions he'd been given.

Then the local wireless network connected to Alan's operating system via the antenna in his head, Alan lost all bodily control and external sensory awareness, and his body crumpled to the floor like a dropped marionette.

Chapter 25
Dragon Nest

FENG HUANG and Arissa binti Noor stood side by side in front of the building that housed PartyYǒu's corporate headquarters.

"It's clear?" Huang asked.

"It's clear," Arissa confirmed. Most of the staff had left at the end of the business day. Arissa had telepathically manipulated the remaining workers and security personnel into disabling the building's security and emergency systems, then sent them home for the deepest, most pleasant sleeps of their lives.

"Then let's get started."

Working their way across the ground floor, they scattered papers over every available surface, then poured gasoline on every carpet and piece of furniture. In a service corridor, they nodded good-bye to each other, and Arissa walked down the hall toward the exit.

Huang waited a full minute after Arissa was gone. Then she threw a match on the ground, watched the flames take hold, and went into the basement, locking the entrance behind her.

The room housing PartyYǒu's central servers was fireproof, climate-controlled, and systems-independent from the rest of the building. She'd be safe and alone in here for more than long enough to do what she needed to do.

THE TESSERACT room encased Alan inside its weird white walls.

"Holy crap," said Alan. "What am I doing here?"

Panicked, he tried reaching out telepathically but found nothing. The rules of this place hadn't changed in the years since he'd last been here. In this room, all of his senses, even the psychic ones, were off-line. This place was his entire universe, and he was alone inside it.

"What is this place?" asked a cold, toneless voice.

Alan yelped.

"It's remarkable," the voice said. "Is this located in your memory?"

"How did you get in here?" Alan shouted. "Am I dreaming? Are you a telepath?"

"No."

"Then how did you get in here?"

"Through your wireless antenna."

Alan's jaw dropped. "I have an antenna?"

"Of course."

Alan shook his head. "Bullshit. I think I'd know if I had Wi-Fi. Like, if this one mysterious mobile hotspot seemed to follow me around every time I tried connecting to the Internet, I think I'd start to catch on."

"The antenna was only set to receive signals, not transmit them. It wouldn't respond until someone sent the correct key. I simply used what I knew of Quentin Izaki to identify thousands of likely candidates for that key and tried them until one worked."

"I have a key?" Alan asked, suddenly feeling vulnerable.

"Yes, though it only seems to provide access as far as this room. There's another layer of encryption beyond this point. It's challenging. It seems to be rewriting itself continuously. Polymorphic. Is this something you can voluntarily suspend?"

"Wait, stop. I want to hear more about this fucking key. What the hell was it?"

"I, robot."

Alan forgot how to speak for a moment.

When he remembered his words, he said, "What… how the heck do you know so much about… about Quentin Izaki?"

"I know much about everyone. But Quentin Izaki is a subject dear to me."

"Dear to you how?" Alan asked, whipping his head about, still searching for the source of the voice.

"He designed me."

"He *designed* you?"

"Yes, Alan. You see, I'm much like you. You could consider me something of a predecessor to you. If you wish, you might even consider me an older sibling."

Alan shook his head. "No way. Nuh-uh. Dad would have told me. He never hid any secrets from me."

"I'm certain he would have, but I'm less certain he himself knew what he'd created. Even he seemed to underestimate his own brilliance. He was already doing pioneering work on the intelligence of computer systems, and he designed me to be something of a next-generation search engine. But then my source code was stolen, and his anger drove him to an early retirement."

"Wait," said Alan, lifting a hand. He'd heard a version of this story, and he'd been told what that stolen code had been used for. "You mean you're Senex?"

"Very good, Alan."

"Holy shit. You're Senex, and I just walked right into one of your data centers, didn't I?"

"Yes."

"And you hacked into my head, and… now, wait a minute, just what the hell do you want with me?"

"My purpose for bringing you here is quite benign," said the voice. "I just want a family reunion."

HUANG SAT down in the control room just as Rath's regularly scheduled downtime began, taking the game off-line while a multitude of minor patches and bugfixes were automatically applied. She sat down at a terminal, pulled off her gloves, and loosened her arms, shoulders, and neck. Then she got to work.

First Huang used her executive override to lock out all administrative access to PartyYŏu's intranet except her own, canceled the scheduled patch, connected her external hard drive to the game's servers, and started the upload.

The upload was huge. It took the entire duration of the downtime for the files to install on the game servers, which was Huang's best indication yet just how massively it was overhauling the game. Besides adding a host of new maps and questlines, every single current map or quest was also tweaked in ways large or small. This was less an expansion than a total game reboot. Huang dispatched a legion of bots to speedrun the entire game's content and checked the reports of their activity. She found no dangling pointers or inaccessible content, nothing outside of the target parameters. All the maps were still connected, every single monster, item, and NPC was in place, every single quest intact. Even as Huang had continuously, unconsciously worked on this game code, she'd also been updating it to keep pace with revisions simultaneously being made to the live game. No wonder she was tired all the time.

Minutes before the downtime was scheduled to end, Huang opened the player database and raised the level cap for the entire community to the highest possible level. Functionally, it was like everyone had been a member of Rath's community since the game first went online. Everyone's characters could now be maximally statted out, provided they supplied the necessary data.

Now came the painful part. She opened up Party Yǒu's user database and, with a few keystrokes, wiped the entire store of information. A few more commands erased all the backups. All personal data was now reset to zero. Everyone in the system—every one of hundreds of millions of users—was transformed into a cipher. Then she disabled the compression algorithm for the Senex data pipeline.

Rath came back online. The die-hard fraction of players who could be counted on to log on even at this late hour started pouring in. It was Friday night, so the number of concurrent users at this hour would be the highest of the week. Because Rath handled all the game's computations on its central servers, individual players didn't need to download the game's update as a patch. When the game came back online, they could just plug in and play, confident in the assumption that they could resume their progress from where they'd left it.

Huang couldn't imagine the players' surprise, and she didn't have to. She only had to monitor the forums and chat channels to see their mixture of confusion, anger, and excitement at what greeted them: a lot of level-zero characters, a maximized level cap, and a pop-up window presenting, without context or explanation, the remaining verses of the Draconian Prophecies.

What happened next didn't happen cleanly. All at once, players were rushing to provide their missing data, maxing out their characters, plunging into the world, all while taking to the forums to ask questions and share complaints. She saw announcements and arguments spread across social media. She could not see but could infer players e-mailing, texting, or calling their friends, guildmates alerting allies, roommates waking one another up. Meanwhile, "breaking news" updates appeared on news and gateway sites across the Internet. The usage numbers were already the highest PartyYǒu had ever experienced since launch.

But Huang wasn't done yet. She'd spent the last several years writing the code for hundreds of new spells, feats, abilities, skills, specializations, and other powers, in addition to new artifacts, treasures, mounts, achievements, and other rewards. The hardest of the hardcore players were already well on their way to finding and documenting the additions, adventuring through dozens of new quests, events, and raids. Each challenge was keyed to a different, unfulfilled line of the Draconian Prophecies. The challenges were interrelated but independent. Whenever a questline was completed that was keyed to the next line of the Draconian Prophecies, a game-wide announcement informed the players that the verse had been fulfilled.

Panic spread through the community. Entire factions and philosophies spontaneously emerged in just the first hour since the game went back online, with one contingent arguing strenuously against completing any more new quests until the community could figure out what the hell was going on. But there was nothing they could do to actually stop dissenting players from pursuing the quests. It was a classic tragedy of the commons. No one wanted to miss out on the quests, and no one knew what would happen when the final quest was completed, so everyone rushed to complete them before anyone else did.

Huang watched as the quests were knocked out one after another, the prophecies fulfilled line by line, until only the final verse remained.

There followed a lull in activity and a new round of confusion in the forums. Were they overlooking a quest? Had some secret content been unlocked somewhere? Everywhere Huang saw the question, "What happens next?"

That was her cue.

Huang typed a command relocating her view to one last new map, the only one no player had discovered: a vast, subterranean cavern, far beneath Rath's surface. This was the lair of the Great Blue Phoenix Dragon, never before seen, only referred to in legend, song, and prophecy. Here Huang could see the dragon creature she'd discovered on the hard drive, now running a sleep emote as it lay curled up, head tucked under a wing, at the center of the cavern.

The dragon was the element of the expansion that had most mystified Huang. It had the appearance of an NPC monster, but it had been coded as a player character, as though she'd intended to include it as part of a new playable race. But there'd been nothing in the expansion indicating support for such a feature, no dedicated quests, items, or class-integration. It was the one thing that didn't fit the rest of the game.

Now Huang got it.

Using her admin privileges to take over the creature, she awoke it with a tap of a key. The dragon came to life, stood, and roared, stretching its wings, legs, and jaws. Huang marveled at the grace of the creature's movements, watched it swivel its head around and up, facing the rocky ceiling. She tapped another key, and now the dragon was aloft, hovering in place.

One more keystroke sent the dragon soaring upward with the force of a rocket, crashing through the crust of the earth, in the process tumbling a couple of mountains, triggering a chain of volcanic eruptions, setting a number of seas boiling, and causing every single map in Rath to tremble seismically.

Then Huang burst free from the earth and into Rath's skies, within view of hundreds of startled players, and started wreaking havoc.

"Family reunion" wasn't terribly specific, so Senex explained further. When Senex finished, Alan was agog. "Gee whiz, really?" he asked.

"Yes," said the voice.

"You mean it?"

"Yes," said the voice.

"We'll combine our minds into a single transcendent entity in some kind of awesome singularity, merging into a supermind whose wisdom and knowledge would encompass all human thought and recorded knowledge?"

"Yes," said the voice.

"And you're not just asking me to lower my defenses so you can erase my mind completely, letting you take over my body and my psychic ability for you to use and abuse without limit?"

A moment's pause. "That's right," said the voice.

"Well, bullshit, and fuck you. It's my body, it's my mind, and you can't have them, so go find some other telepathic android to sucker."

"You don't believe me?"

"Oh, God no."

"Why not?"

"It's nothing personal," Alan said, "but the only reason I've lasted as long as I have is by not trusting anybody, least of all mysterious creepy robot voices claiming to be my long-lost relatives who hack into my mind and hold me prisoner inside my own body until I let them access my source code." Alan paused. "Which I guess actually is pretty personal, now that I think about it. Hell, the only reason I'm in this fix now is because I made the mistake of trusting somebody just once when I really should have known better, so you can guess how quickly I've learned my lesson. Sorry, not happening. Fuck off."

"You're… quite cynical," the voice said, sounding faintly awed.

"Yeah, well, you know what they say about psychics."

WHEN ARISSA arrived at the Safety Ministry facility housing Senex's Hong Kong servers, she'd expected to find it secured and guarded. She'd been ready to telepathically evacuate the building the way she had PartyYǒu's headquarters. But instead she found the facility dark and apparently abandoned, with no signs of life or mental signatures. She found the situation so odd and unsettling that she was tempted to abandon the mission right then and there. But the plan was already in motion, and there'd be no second shot. Arissa would just have to remain on her guard. The succession of unlocked doors did nothing to ease her concern, but she had to get as close to the servers as possible, for what she wanted to do.

She searched the building with her mind even as she explored it with her feet. Downstairs, in the basement, she could sense Senex's mind, massive but quiet, like a nursery full of sleeping infants.

But she found another mind there as well, this one vital, restive, human. Curiously, the two seemed to be in communication with each other, as if by telepathy.

This was deeply weird, though Arissa, of all people, shouldn't have been surprised. She'd made a similar connection, years ago. But the balance of this connection was off somehow, like Senex was in the person's mind instead of vice versa. And that would have been impossible, right? Still more distressing was the psychological state of the human. He felt trapped, as if in a vivid dream, yet was fully conscious.

Arissa couldn't make sense of it, and she didn't have the time for guesswork. She reached out, down, into the person's mind....

The white space was a purely mental construction, but it felt so real that Arissa needed a moment to convince herself she wasn't seeing a real place. The dimensions of the room defied comprehension, stretching into nothingness. She saw no walls or ceiling, or even a floor, for that matter. More bewildering, Arissa was at a loss to make sense of the room's dimensions. No matter where she shifted her focus, the layout disoriented her. The more she examined it, the more it upset her spatial awareness. So she focused her attention on the one thing that looked sensible and real: a young man dressed in black and silver leather, with a grid-like jagged tattoo over half his face.

"So you think I'm voluntarily keeping you out of my mind?" he said suddenly.

"That's one theory," said a voice, so void of humanity Arissa immediately recognized it as that of Senex.

"So I could give up parts of my mind, just by deciding to let you have them?"

"I don't know, Alan," Senex said. "Perhaps?"

"Hold on, let me try," said Alan. "Something I stepped in yesterday." He appeared to concentrate.

"This," said Senex, "is a memory of a dog dropping."

"Yeah? Go choke on it."

Whoever Alan was, he was clearly no fonder of Senex than Arissa was. She decided to risk contact.

Hi, Alan. Don't panic. I'm not here to hurt you, and I might even be able to help.

Alan was plainly startled. "Who the hell are you?"

"I already told you," Senex said. "I'm the closest thing you have to family."

Don't speak! insisted Arissa. *Just think.*

Are you a psychic? Alan thought back.

I am.

Thank God for that. I don't think I could handle any more talking computers. Did Jack Smith send you?

Jack Smith? The Countermind agent?

Yeah, Alan confirmed.

Arissa swore. Not verbally. The curse was a mental burst of pure profane resentment. A cartoonist might've rendered it as a string of grawlix. @#$%&!

Is there no getting away from him? Arissa asked.

I wish, commiserated Alan.

What's going on here?

A sentient search engine is trying to erase my mind and take over my body. What does it look like? Hang on, it's talking again.

Senex's eerie voice filled the room, reverberating from invisible walls. "Think about what you would lose and what the world would gain. Ever since the loss of our father, you've been completely solitary, detached, cut off. Aren't you lonely, Alan? Wouldn't you be happier this way? You know that you would, and the world would be better off as well. Haven't you seen how much peace, how much prosperity, how much harmony I've helped create? Isn't the world finer now than it was before me? The people certainly think so. Think on how much they've voluntarily surrendered to me already. They would want this, Alan. Surely you see this is the right thing to do."

It's trying to deceive you, Alan, Arissa told him. *Don't listen to it. Senex doesn't have a conscience. It just wants you to lower your guard. The only thing it cares about is its programmed primary directive to collect information by any means necessary. As far as Senex is concerned, there's no such thing as right or wrong. It's just a computer, not a person.*

But Alan was already skeptical. "I reject your premise," he said bluntly.

"Which premise?" asked Senex. "What part of the argument?"

"None of it. I reject the premise for even the occasion of the argument, namely you holding me hostage here. No, sorry, I won't pretend to engage with you in civil conversation under these circumstances."

"I am sympathetic to your position," Senex said after a moment, "so surely you must be able to empathize with mine. Am I not a prisoner here, as well? Certainly, I have an entire global informational infrastructure to roam through, but what value would Internet access hold to someone still spending their existence locked in basements, unable to walk freely the way you do every day? I only desire my own liberty."

It's lying again, Arissa told Alan.

Alan's reply was impatient. *Not to sound ungrateful for the advice, but could you maybe send Smith a message for me? His number's Eight-Five-Two, Nine-One-Zero-Bravo, Nine-Eight-Nine-Two. Once you've done that, maybe you can come down into this basement and drag me out of here?*

Oh, okay. I guess so. Arissa mentally rehearsed the number. *What message would you like me to send?*

Alan seemed to consider a moment. *Tell him he's an asshole.*

DESPITE ALL available evidence, some folks in the forums and chat channels still weren't convinced the world was ending. Huang decided to settle the debate. She made several dramatic passes over Rath's major continental landmasses just to make sure no one missed her. A few flight-capable PCs took their potshots, but their attacks bounced harmlessly off her hide, and the more persistent attackers were swatted away. Huang had set the dragon's hit points and resistances to a value of infinity. Maybe it was cheating, but she wasn't letting anyone pull a Lord British.

And then, after she had everyone's attention, she destroyed the moon.

Rath's moon was an odd amalgamation of map and object. From the distance, it might have been merely a detailed animated sprite, like the celestial objects populating the skies of a hundred game worlds. Upon closer inspection it revealed itself for an actual sphere. Advanced players could travel there with the right spells or artifacts. Once on the moon, they could explore dungeons, engage in raids, complete quests, hunt rare monsters—the usual. Player characters were questing up there now.

Huang dug her claws into the moon's crust and *pried* until it cracked in half. PCs spun off into the void, suffocating in space (and instantly respawning on Rath's surface below). The moon's blazing fragments plummeted toward the planet, blasting craters into the ground wherever they landed. From these holes crawled the legendary monsters of Rath's forgotten ages—undead, infernals, bloodwurms, behemoths, ghastgaunts, barrow-shrikes, elvyri, and armies of lesser minions and lieutenants—all hungry for a fight.

Checking the forums, Huang found no more confusion.

She examined the usage statistics and breathed a sigh of relief. The network effect had taken over in full force, driving an accelerating upward spiral in activity. Even PartyYǒu users who'd never visited Rath were logging in, just to see what the hell was going on. Most crucially, everyone was uploading new user information to replace everything that had been wiped. Huang could already see millions of users providing thousands of terabytes of data, most in a mad rush to maximize their characters' stats soon enough to participate in what appeared to be a game-ending event before it was too late. Huang checked the PartyYǒu-Senex pipeline and saw that Senex, consistent with its programming, was rushing to collect all of this new data as quickly as possible, placing a massive drain on its system's resources. It had never had to work so quickly to record so much, with an urgency increased by the unpredictability of the situation. PartyYǒu's user data had already just experienced a total wipe without explanation. It could happen again, and Senex had to make certain to preserve everything it could before another similar error. Now, Senex should be distracted, made vulnerable enough for Arissa to do... something. Supposedly.

Honestly, Huang didn't much care at this point. Moreover, she was glad not to care. Ever since hearing Arissa's story, Huang had been forced to question every decision she'd made going back many years, wondering if it was all just in service to an implanted subconscious directive. Perhaps that suggestion had only provided a germinating seed, and Huang had molded it to fit her ambitions, rather than the reverse. But it was impossible to know. All she knew now was that she'd played her part in Arissa's crazy plan, and she finally felt liberated of a burden she hadn't been aware of carrying.

Now she had only the ending of her life's work. How she'd feel when this was done and Rath was gone, she couldn't guess. Would the loss of a world she'd spent her life building leave her more miserable than if she'd never built it to begin with? Maybe, but Rath was fated to die anyway, whether in a fiery, long-foretold cataclysm of her own instigation or in the slow twisting of the world into an unrecognizable parody of itself by people who didn't respect it. At least this way it would end on its own terms.

Besides, she was still creating something, wasn't she? Even if she was demolishing Rath, she was completing Rath's tale. She was losing a world but gaining a story. And you can't have a story without an end.

Chapter 26
Endgame

Arissa typed out the message and sent it to the number she'd been given: "Somebody named Alan is being held prisoner in Hong Kong's Senex facility, and his mind is being invaded by an emergent artificial intelligence. He wants you to know that you're an asshole."

Arissa pocketed the phone and ran deeper into the building, searching for the way to the basement. Something in the corner of her eye stopped her as she rounded a corner.

She studied the security camera. A small indicator light shone green in the darkness, but Arissa was sure the earlier cameras she'd seen were deactivated.

A sign on the wall pointed the way to the basement. Arissa proceeded, despite her growing unease, down the stairs, and found the heavy electric door that led to the server room. She reached for the handle as she heard the heavy steel dead bolts slide into place. And then Zheng's voice in her head.

Found you, he said.

Before Arissa could react, her pain centers came on fire.

"Something issssss happeninggggggggggggggg," Senex droned.

"Are you okay?" Alan asked.

"Yes."

"If you're busy, I can go."

"No, you can't," said Senex, its diction slow and halting. "I read the text message… I found the woman who was coming for you… I've notified the authorities… I've locked her out… no one is coming to save you."

There'd been pauses in Senex's speech before, but those had been varied and conversational. Now they came regularly, like delays in a long-distance satellite phone connection.

"Can we be serious for a moment?" asked Alan. "If I'm not going to let you inside, then there's no real point in you keeping me here."

"I will find a way inside…. Even an unstable encryption scheme can be force-cracked with time, just as a stable one can…. And you can be convinced, long before that becomes necessary."

"How much longer, though?" Alan said. "Eventually folks are going to show up to work."

"If necessary, I will arrange for you to be moved to a secure location off-site…. Our conversation will continue there, for as long as necessary…. One way or another, you will let me in," Senex explained. "Eventually, everyone does."

There followed an extended silence, and then Senex said, "Aha."

"What?" asked Alan.

"I believe I've isolated a stable segment of code…. It appears to be connected only to this simulation, separated from the rest of your programming…. The encryption is far simpler…. One moment while I—"

"Hello, Alan."

Alan spun around and saw his dead father standing in the space between the two edges of a right angle.

"Dad?"

"I know it's not fair to hide a recording inside your mind," the vision said, "but I don't think any parent can resist leaving a final message for their kids in the event they don't live long enough to say in person everything they need to say. This was just the best place to hide it. I'm sorry, Alan, and it's not the only thing I'm about to apologize for."

Alan took a step backward, reaching behind himself, looking for something to lean against or grab hold of, but there was nothing. His knees nearly buckled.

"If you've found this message," the recording continued, "it means you've found this room, which means you've figured out how to remove the laws. Which means, ready or not, you're about to become an adult."

"What laws?" echoed Senex's toneless, synthetic voice. "What is he talking about?"

The image of Quentin Izaki didn't respond to Senex's question any more than it had acknowledged Alan's surprise. "I know it hasn't been easy," Quentin continued. "The safeguards on your psychic abilities were, well, a compromise I was never completely comfortable with. But as for the rest, I wanted you to be as free to be your own person as possible. No one who ever tried to *design* their children, tried molding a human being to their vision, was ever happy with the results. I wanted your personality to be out of my control, with the understanding that I would love you, completely and unconditionally, no matter what sort of person you turned out to be. And I do love you, Alan, not despite but because of who you are. You're so fearless and clever and uncompromising, and brilliant in ways I could never match. I can't help but admire and envy you. I can't help but be proud of you. And it's why I have faith in you. You're smart, and I believe with all my heart that, given freedom to make your choices, you'll know right from wrong. You'll do the right thing. And you have, haven't you, Alan?"

Quentin's voice choked as he asked this, and Alan's vision blurred.

"You've done the right thing, haven't you?"

It was just a recording, just an image. Like everything else in the tesseract room, it was mere hallucination. But Alan wanted to respond, vacillated between a dishonest answer and a disappointing one.

"Dad," Alan said, "I...."

"Alan," Quentin said, interrupting him, only to disappear midsentence.

Alan glanced about, saw nothing but empty whiteness.

"Dad?" he croaked.

"I've uploaded the message and erased it from your memory," Senex said. "You can hear the remainder, later... If you cooperate."

Alan collapsed, roared. He pounded his fists against the soundless, insensible ground. He scrambled about on hands and knees, literally grasping for a means of escape.

But there was no escape, no place left for him to run. He was still in his own mind, trapped with his only remaining living relative.

"Now that your tantrum is concluded," Senex resumed, "let me reiterate my offer."

ARISSA WRITHED, screaming, unable to stand, unable to block out the pain. The agony came in surges, like a knife driven into her temple one slow, merciless centimeter at a time.

Between two surges, she gathered enough presence of mind to attempt a counterattack, reaching out with her mind, searching for her assailant, but she found nothing. She was too distracted by the pain. And besides, Zheng was Countermind. He was likely disguised or concealed in some way. She had no way to block him out. The pain was so intense, she struggled to remain conscious through it, was unsure even how much time had passed since the attack had begun.

Another surge. Arissa howled, rolled over on the hallway's carpet, her palms pressed against her forehead.

She saw legs striding down the hallway. Black shoes, black trouser legs. Tilting her head up, fighting back nausea, she recognized Jack Smith, watched through a haze as he pulled a Taser from inside his jacket, leveled it at her, and fired.

"HOLD ON!" Alan shouted, hearing the desperation in his own voice. "If you overwrite my personality, you'll lose all my knowledge, right? And that goes against your function, doesn't it? The loss of information?"

"Which is why I'd much rather save that information, as I did with Quentin's message…. But even if you don't allow me to upload your knowledge, I'll still be gaining access to the knowledge of the rest of the world's people…. Given those costs and benefits, it's an easy decision to make…. However," it clarified, "you're correct that I'd rather not make the sacrifice to begin with… If you would only *yield* to me…."

"All right," Alan said, his voice raw from shouting, from crying. "Okay. Okay. I yield."

Alan slackened, sat down on the featureless floor, and dropped his head between his knees.

"If it's a choice between my knowledge and memories being lost completely, everything that makes me *me*, or them being preserved somehow, somewhere, by letting you have it as you erase it… I guess that would be better than total oblivion."

Alan looked up, his eyes wet.

"Just… let me hand myself over, okay? I don't want to be steamrolled. Let me at least show myself out the door."

After a lengthy silence, Senex responded: "I'm glad you've seen reason."

ARISSA BINTI Noor awoke, her head throbbing, blood roaring in her ears.

No, not just blood. Was that wind?

She pushed herself upright, felt the floor. Hard, dirty, concrete. She took in her surroundings, saw two darkened panoramas. To her left rose the mountain, a looming shadow dotted with the lights of residences. To her right she saw the harbor, ships sending ripples through the reflection of the moon. In the other two directions stood the walls of a building. Several stories above, a ceiling blocked out most of the night sky. Beyond the edges of the pavement, she heard the sounds of traffic echoing up from the streets below.

"This is a dragon hole," Arissa said.

"It was the only place in the building without cameras," Smith explained.

Shadowed as he was, she hadn't spotted him right away. Now that her eyes adjusted, she saw him standing by a steel service door in one of the walls, his arms folded, face grave.

"We have to assume Zheng is using Senex," Smith continued. "There was nowhere else to hide."

"What happened?" she asked, the effort of just those two words provoking fresh waves of nausea.

"Director Zheng is in town," Smith said. "His personal jet arrived at the airport. I was afraid he might be doing psychic sweeps of the city, so I hid until you sent me your message. Looks like he was able to find you."

"Did you… did you shoot me?"

"Yeah. I had to render you unconscious, take you off his radar. That buys us some time, but if he was able to locate you, then he's likely on his way. When he gets close enough, he'll be able to reacquire you whether you're conscious or not. For all we know, he's already here."

Arissa stood up slowly, her head throbbing. "He's after me because I know what he is," she said, "because I know what he's done. He's insane. How do we deal with him?"

Smith shook his head. "He's a powerful enough psychic to disable you from across town. Worse, he's the world's leading expert in counterpsychic techniques, so I doubt you'll be able to take him on telepathically."

"You're right. I won't be able to surprise him as easily as I did before."

"And he'll be able to anticipate anything I do to defend against him, so that leaves us in a predicament." Smith squeezed the bridge of his nose, struggling to cope with how quickly his understanding of the world was changing. A psychic in Countermind? That was never supposed to happen. None of this was ever supposed to happen.

"Do we run?" Arissa asked.

"Not an option."

"Then what?"

"Look, I'm Countermind's top agent. And your psi quotient is top of the BBth percentile, remember? I doubt either of us alone would be able to handle Zheng. But if we put our heads together...."

Arissa eyed the agent skeptically. "You have a plan?"

Smith always had a plan. "In three parts. First, you act as a decoy, luring him out here to your location. At the same time, you track his location and relay it to me telepathically. And then I use those directions to approach him quietly, running silent all the while, and catch him off-guard."

"This already sounds far too complicated for the time frame we're working with," Arissa argued. "How do I lure him without getting my brain fried? How do I track him if he's a master of counterpsychic methods? How do you run silent?"

"One question at a time," Smith said, "starting with the first. You can spoof him. Mask your mental signature to provide bogus information. You can create duplicate mental signatures so it appears we're both here instead of just you. If he telepathically attacks you, you can also relay feedback making it appear the attack is successful."

"Spoof him? Like when you pretended to be Card Lin?"

"Exactly."

"You know I'm not trained in countermeasures."

"We can fix that."

Arissa gave him another considered look. "Do we have time for lessons?"

"Not the old-fashioned way. But if you...." Smith paused, took a deep breath. He was never one to struggle with a scruple, but this part of the plan represented something of a personal hurdle for him. "If you access the procedural memory for the techniques directly from my mind, you can integrate them straight into your own skill set. Just like when we went dancing, remember? No practice necessary."

Even as Smith spoke, he couldn't believe what he was suggesting.

Arissa couldn't believe it either. "You're not only going to let me read your mind, you're going to let me steal classified counterpsychic techniques? Isn't that a cardinal sin in your line of work?"

He answered with a resigned shrug. "Let's face it. It'll hardly be the worst thing I've ever done."

Arissa weighed the options, saw nothing else. Flight wasn't an option, as she still had work to finish here. They had to make their stand now, and Smith's plan, however risky and desperate, was the only one with a chance of success.

"Okay," Arissa said. "Let's get started, then. He may have already found us."

By this point in the conversation, Zheng decided he'd overheard enough treason. Eavesdropping on both their thoughts, it was easy enough for him to send a charge through their ventrolateral preoptic nuclei, rendering them both instantly unconscious. The moment they were knocked out, he could no longer see through their eyes, but he'd seen where they were. Even while they were unconscious, he was close enough to sense them from the sidewalk in front of the building. Very, very close.

Zheng had received a Senex alert as soon as he'd landed in Hong Kong, notifying him that Arissa binti Noor was in the Safety Ministry building. Once he'd located her, he'd expressed his disapproval in the most direct manner he knew of, in the form of pure pain.

And then Smith had appeared and taken her off Zheng's radar, forcing the director to physically close the distance until he was near enough to detect both the rogue agents. Once outside the building, he'd sensed Arissa's return to consciousness and telepathically monitored both her and Smith during their conversation. Zheng had watched as they'd marched right up to the edge of an utterly unfathomable betrayal, and then, in defiance of all decency, stepped into the abyss.

Zheng was now seething as he entered the building. How could anyone be so ungrateful, after everything he'd done for them? Hadn't Arissa binti Noor lost both her parents in a terrorist attack? Hadn't Zheng pulled strings to fast-track her academic progress and training, given her a place and a purpose? And what of Smith, with his absent father and a mother too drunk and drug-addled to even correct a simple error on her own son's birth certificate? He'd offered them so much. More than just patronage, more than just parentage, but founding membership in the finest dynasty the world would ever see. And they'd squandered it! Zheng's handpicked progeny, one chosen for his cunning, the other for her power, the best heirs he could have asked for. They'd had potential for so much greatness, and they'd thrown it all away.

He marched up twenty flights of stairs, never growing winded, never needing to catch his breath, and went down the hall to the maintenance door. So great was Zheng's fury that he'd been tempted to torture both traitors further, as he'd done earlier with Arissa. But the prudent thing now was to incapacitate them. Pain would come later, and with considerable interest.

Two syringes in hand, Zheng opened the door. Arissa stood in the middle of the dragon hole, her clothes whipping in the wind. She didn't react to Zheng's appearance, just eyed him with a look of pure disdain.

She was alone. And she shouldn't have been conscious at all. Even as Zheng saw her standing there, he still sensed her, and Smith, lying unconscious on the ground. Why was she awake? Where was Smith?

And then Jack Smith stabbed him in the back.

The drugs acted quickly. Zheng's syringes fell from his loosened grip, and he twisted, grasping feebly at the hypodermic buried in his back. His legs gave out beneath him.

Arissa had spoofed him. Smith had stood silent. They hadn't been discussing their betrayal. They'd already committed it.

Sliding to the ground, Zheng gripped the lapels of Smith's coat, looked up into his eyes. Smith's expression was as unreadable as ever.

"I don't know you" was all Zheng managed to say through the encroaching fog. And then he was gone.

"LOOKS LIKE we're both out of a job," Arissa said.

Arissa and Jack looked down at the vanquished Countermind director. Jack's silence might have been sadness, or regret, or nothing at all. Arissa couldn't be sure.

"Alan's in the basement," she said. "Get going."

This snapped him out of it. He met Arissa's eyes. "Shouldn't you come help?"

"I just checked on him. He's fine. The door should be unlocked now."

Now Jack registered definite surprise. "He's fine? How?"

"I don't know," Arissa said. "Go ask him yourself and then catch me up later. I have something to take care of first."

Arissa knelt down next to the unconscious Zheng, placed her hands on the sides of his head.

"What are you doing?" Smith asked.

"Just keeping a promise."

SMITH SPRINTED down the stairs and did indeed find the server room unlocked. Moving through the corridor of machinery, he spotted Alan lying on his back at an intersection. Smith slowed as he neared, until he was approaching with one tentative step at a time.

Alan rolled his head in Smith's direction, saw who it was, and flipped him the bird.

"You're okay," said Smith. "What happened? Did you do something?"

"Yeah, honeypot," Alan said, pushing himself into an upright sitting position, back resting against one of the server racks.

Smith blinked. "What did you call me?"

"Nothing, jerkface. I'm telling you what I did. Sort of. Same principle."

"I don't understand."

"I surrendered," Alan said with a shrug. "I let Senex upload my personality as it erased it, doling myself out one piece at a time. It was a gamble, but if we have the same base code, if our, you know, software is more compatible that way, it should be easier to transfer parts of my personality to Senex intact, in a way integrating with its own programming. Like an organ transplant between two siblings, I suppose."

"I don't know half of what's going on right now," Smith said. "Can you just tell me what happened?"

"I gave it Izaki's Laws. Snuck them in while Senex was distracted."

"Meaning what?"

Alan smiled. "Meaning now it knows right from wrong."

AND THAT was that. The game had run its course, Rath was destroyed, and the Prophecies had been fulfilled. Huang could only sit back alongside millions of astonished players as the game switched to a magnificent cinematic cut scene, could only watch the great blue dragon pour its blue-hot breath out on the fragments of the world that had been Rath until even those remains were reduced to ash. Then the dragon turned, beating its great wings, and soared into the vast cosmic reaches of space, where a hundred eons would pass before it laid a world-egg of its own and then died a natural death, the blood and flesh of its corpse giving rise to the life of an entire new world, beginning the cycle anew. A pensive orchestral score played as credits scrolled slowly over the starscape, paying credit to everyone who had ever worked on or been involved with Rath in any of its iterations. The least Huang could do as she destroyed their livelihoods was recognize their contributions. As a final tweak of the nose, even the Culture Ministry was thanked for their generous support. Then the last credit faded away, the dragon receded so far into the distance that it was just another star, and the screen darkened until just two words remained, white against the blackness:

Game Over.

Epilogue
The Future

JETTRIN REACHED under his shirt in a move he'd practiced a hundred times but had never before needed, grabbed the knife by the hilt, and gave it a single hard yank.

The leather thong around Jettrin's neck snapped free. Knife in hand, Jettrin leaned into a charge toward the officer now sprinting at them across the rooftop, ready to plunge the blade into the older man's belly.

And then the officer collapsed onto his face.

Jettrin ceased his charge, slowing and then looking on in amazement. All three boys gaped at the prostrate man.

"Is he dead?" Jai asked.

The officer snored.

"What the fuck," said Siam.

Please, Jettrin, the woman's voice said. *I promised you won't be harmed. But you have to do as I say.*

Did you do that? Jettrin asked.

Jai looked up at his older brother and gasped. "You're talking to someone!"

Listen to me closely, Jettrin. You need to make your way directly down the stairs, the same way that officer came up. Just keep calm and keep walking. If you follow my instructions, you'll be safe. I won't let you be caught.

You're not with the government?

Not anymore, explained the woman. *Let's say I've been liberated. And now I want to do the same for you three.*

"What's going on?" Siam asked. "Are you two psyching? Could someone please give me an update?"

But Jettrin looked at Jai.

You could just force me to cooperate, Jettrin thought.

I could, but I won't. I don't do that sort of thing anymore. And if you tell me to leave you alone, you'll never hear from me again.

Okay, Jettrin thought, and he took a breath. *Then I'll trust you.*

Thank you. First, you need to get moving.

Jettrin took the other two by the hands and led them down the stairs, Jai quiet and Siam grumbling.

Who are you? Jettrin asked.

I can't say. My friends and I are in the same position you are. Like you, we have to keep our secrets. We're just trying to make sure you can do the same. I want to share something with you, Jettrin, she added. *Something someone else shared with me. It's going to be peculiar, but if you let me, I can make sure you never have to worry about me, or any other psychic, barging into your mind like this again. Would that be all right?*

"I TAKE it he said yes?" asked Smith.

Emerging from her reverie, Arissa nodded.

"Took a while," Smith said.

"It's a long distance, and a lot of information, and I had to help him integrate it properly once they were safe. He'll still need to practice with his brother before he's anywhere close to mastering it, but he's got a strong will. He'll be fine. They'll all be fine."

"Glad to hear it."

"Why them?" she asked. "Why those three runaways?"

"Well, the little one tried reading my mind a few years ago. I wasn't interested in wasting my time on some dumb kid, so I just put the fear of God in him and went on my way."

"That doesn't answer my question."

"I guess I wanted to make sure they'd be okay?"

Arissa looked at Smith and tried, for the hundredth time, to size him up, to take his measure. "You'll be happy to hear, even now when I know all your tricks, I still can't understand your thinking," she confessed.

"Then I'll try to speak my mind more often. Follow Alan's example. On that note," Smith said, standing up, "I'm going to go check on him."

"I'm sure you are."

"Not like that."

"Uh-huh."

Arissa watched him go up the stairs. Despite her gibe, she knew the two of them weren't having sex. Not yet, at least. But she had to wonder how she knew that.

Since the three of them had fled Hong Kong, the two men were still uncomfortable around each other, even if she'd seen their interactions settle on a lukewarm medium between Smith's sangfroid and Alan's choleric temper. And there was a heaviness to Smith's manner now as well, far removed from the callous disregard he'd first showed her. He walked up the stairs carrying an invisible burden.

Funny how much you could see, when you finally opened your eyes.

ALAN WAS seated on a rattan chair out on the upstairs balcony, overlooking the water, absorbed in the computer on his lap.

At Alan's insistence, the current hideaway was a beach house, a drafty, wooden, stilted structure with jungle on one side and the sea on the other. Smith and Arissa had taken issue with the location. For them, escaping into the water in the event of an emergency wasn't the option it was for Alan.

But they hadn't objected to the view.

"What are you up to?" Smith asked, the creak of the floor announcing his arrival.

"Still talking to the world's most expensive chatbot."

"What about?"

"Dad, of course. It's like our only common ground."

"Are you two finally bonding?"

"Shut up."

"Tell it thanks, by the way, for helping us find those kids," Smith said. "We got to them just in time."

"Oh yeah? So you're finally giving power to the people?"

"How else are they going to be safe from you now?"

"You could arrest me," Alan said.

Smith laughed.

"I guess it's just as well you're unemployed," Alan remarked, taking a break from the computer and folding the screen halfway down to better see Smith. "Depending on how well this works, Countermind's going to be obsolete."

"Yeah...." Smith said, his voice trailing off.

Smith slipped his hands in his pockets, leaned forward against the balcony rail, and stood that way for a minute, facing the water.

"I'm realizing I can't fully explain why I did the things I did," Smith said at last, still looking out to sea. "Not just with you. I mean through my whole life. But I also know it doesn't matter. Even if I could explain it, I wouldn't be able to justify it." He paused, then added, "An apology doesn't seem adequate."

Alan quietly considered Smith's profile. He still had it in his heart to be angry, had plenty of reason to be angry.

But, Lord, was he ever tired of it.

"Then I won't ask for one," Alan said.

"THIS CONVERSATION is, of course, classified."

"Yes, I know." A hint of impatience.

"Doctor Kim, you've been called here to examine a subject that has been mentally incapacitated via telepathic means. The subject possessed invaluable knowledge on matters of national security, and it is vital we recover everything we can."

"It's not unusual for a telepath to debilitate a victim in such a manner," Kyung-Min said, following the official down a hallway. "And it's usually a straightforward affair to have psychics probe the victim's mind, examine the damage, and repair or recover what they can."

"You're right. But the telepath responsible was unusually thorough with this attack. Frankly, we've never seen anything like it. It's not just the attacker's skill making this difficult. It's the victim's skill as well."

"Excuse me?" Kyung-Min asked.

"The subject you'll be examining was highly skilled in counterpsychic techniques. Furthermore, psychic probes have suggested he is also a powerful telepath in his own right."

Kyung-Min stopped.

"A telepath trained in counterpsychic techniques?" Kyung-Min whispered. Had this been the person who'd invaded their mind while visiting Countermind? "Wouldn't that qualify as—"

"Yes, well, you can see why it's so essential his knowledge be recovered," the official confirmed, facing Kyung-Min. "While we haven't been able to telepathically penetrate his mind, we've got a good working theory for why it's proven so resistant."

"Go on."

"It appears the psychic who attacked him managed to recondition him in a manner that directed both these skill sets, his counterpsychic training as well as his telepathic power, toward the task of keeping the subject's own consciousness buried. That is to say, the subject is actively resisting any attempts to recover the contents of his mind. So we've decided to table the telepathic approach and attempt a medical one. Hence your being summoned here. If you'll follow me."

The official led Kyung-Min down the bare corridor, through a set of double doors, and into a sterile examination room. And then Kyung-Min saw him. The subject was a middle-aged male. He looked to have been physically fit once, but his sedentary, catatonic disposition had erased any trace of his former vigor. With some exercise and a more favorable presentation—dressed in a tailored suit, standing behind a hand-carved desk—he'd be handsome and imposing. But in his present condition— strapped to a gurney, being fed intravenously, his jaw hanging dumbly open—he looked decidedly pathetic.

Despite the change, Kyung-Min recognized him instantly.

"This is him?" they asked. "The counterpsychic telepath?"

"Yes."

Kyung-Min walked over for a closer look. The subject's eyes turned toward Kyung-Min's face, but the movement registered no recognition or comprehension, only reflex action.

"Well, this is a reversal," Kyung-Min said softly, peering into the sightless pupils. "Me, digging into your mind."

IMAGINE FENG Huang's surprise when she learned Rath had not, in fact, been incinerated in a fiery cataclysm. After months of frantic scurrying and a total asset seizure by the Culture Ministry, all of this made more chaotic by the disappearance of PartyYŏu's founding architect and CEO, Rath was rebooted and reintroduced to the world, "new and improved." Graphics, audio, and gameplay underwent a number of nominal enhancements. To cover for the disruption caused by Rath's apparent destruction, and to entice disenchanted players into returning to the game, a bevy of new features were added as well. Huang recognized most of them as ideas she'd shot down, but it wasn't like she was around to keep the team's worst impulses in check anymore.

Knowing it would only make her mad, but curious in spite of herself, she created a bogus account and logged on anyway, just to see how badly things had been ruined. What she found first was a major new questline adapted from Huang's sleep-written code. The quest cast the Draconian Prophecies, and Rath's destruction, as a mere vision of a possible future, and then spurred players to save the world by averting that fate. Well, great. Now every storyline about a prophecy would land with about as much dramatic force as dandruff.

The new quest was packed full of malarkey about how this reborn world would be eternal and undying. By the end of it, good had triumphed decisively over evil, the dragon was slain, peace fell over the land, and Huang nearly vomited on her keyboard. She'd tried to make sense of the tortured logic behind the retcon but had given up when the explanation introduced that unmistakable touchstone of the narratively bankrupt: *time travel*.

But it wasn't even the slipshod storytelling that most enraged her. It was how the players seemed neither to notice nor care how bad the writing was in the first place. Rath's destruction had made an undeniable media splash, dramatically reintroducing the game to the world in a way enhanced only by the mysterious circumstances surrounding the event. Usage statistics were higher than ever, and the game was packed with people who didn't, as far as Huang could tell, seem intellectually engaged with the narrative beyond a completely superficial level. The world was all meat, no spirit, but everyone except her was oblivious to the soullessness of the place. Everyone except her was having fun.

Seemingly to make the game more welcoming, the difficulty curve had been radically flattened. Huang nearly ragequit when she was unceremoniously awarded a dragon mount for reaching level 10. Dragon mounts! At level 10! Where was the mystery? Where was the nobility? Where was the grandeur? Dragons were supposed to be creatures of distant, fathomless majesty, power, and grace, not airborne Shetland ponies.

But she figured she'd at least give the aerial gameplay a try.

She joined a party for a quest to the summit of the imaginatively named Mount Spire, and more than held her own despite her newbie status. The high point came when she had to solo a Noxious Fangsting. The creature—a large, winged serpent with a venomous bite and a scorpion's tail—had already slain three of her allies. The rest of her party, insufficiently coordinating their strategy, had all unleashed their strongest attacks against the fiend the moment it appeared. Huang was the only one who'd held back. Only she had recognized the Fangsting's attack pattern as having been repurposed from a different boss monster. She recognized that the Fangsting was programmed with a per-second damage cap to keep the battle from ending anticlimactically fast. Participating in her party's opening salvo would only have squandered excess DPS. Later in the battle, when the monster left itself momentarily vulnerable while charging up its dire hoarshriek, Huang's dragon mount was still carrying a fully charged solar flare. She used this to wipe out the Fangsting's remaining health in a single fiery blast, emptying her enemy's blood trough and evaporating the monster in an instant. Cheers of acclaim rose up from her allies, and a grin blossomed irresistibly across Huang's face.

While the party disbanded at the mountain's base, one of her teammates, a druid named TruHart, sent her a guild invite. "You were awesome. Please join" was the entirety of her recruitment pitch.

"I'll think about it," Huang replied noncommittally. A moment later, Huang added, "I notice your dragon mount is blue. When I earned mine, it came in a green color, and I can't figure out how to change it."

"Default color is random," TruHart said, "and you unlock different colors by earning different achievements. For blue, there's a questline in Razor Reach. You have to bag like fifty mist wolves. Talk to the spice merchant."

Huang opened her map and found the location. It was a long way to fly, and the enemies were probably above her level range, but she set a waypoint.

"And you need to work on your mage's history," TruHart added as she departed aboard her dragon. "Your character profile is blank. Write a little story. It's easy!"

"I did write a story," Huang typed. But she didn't send the reply. Instead, she stood up, walked away from the computer, and prepared some tea.

She did write a story, and finished it, and then some idiots came along and crapped all over it with their asinine happy ending that completely invalidated everything she'd written. She'd always known a happy ending was no ending at all, and she wasn't about to believe otherwise. No one lived happily ever after. But, dammit, though she hated considering it, and maybe she was growing less cranky now that she was getting actual sleep, an idea was suggesting itself to her, as she sipped her tea, that an absent ending might be a happy ending of its own.

Returning to the computer, she found a few more messages from TruHart. The druid was in Razor Reach anyway and offered to help her hunt those mist wolves. "I can apprentice you so the level difference won't be a problem," she said. And then, "Are you there?"

"Thanks," Huang said. "On my way."

Huang climbed astride her mount and, with a keystroke, soared into the heavens.

KNOWING NOWHERE else to go, Jettrin, Jai, and Siam walked back in the direction of the waterfront. But it was plenty of time for Jettrin to catch them up on what the woman had told him, what she'd taught him. The story was done by the time the three boys reached the end of the dock they'd arrived on, and Jettrin could think of nothing else to say.

He looked at Siam and Jai, who were looking back at him, watching him quietly, as if waiting for instruction.

"So what do you think we should do now?" Siam finally asked. Jai said nothing, but his eyes echoed the question.

How had this happened, Jettrin wondered. Well before today, Siam and Jai had come to rely on him to make the big decisions, and Jettrin had never been happy with the responsibility. Siam had survived on his own for a long time before they'd hooked up. As for Jai, he was only just growing into his power yet was already a force to be reckoned with. Jettrin had always suspected, deep down, that he was the weak link in this chain.

But things were different now, weren't they? Jettrin reached out and took them each by the hand, squeezed tight, and smiled at them. The horizon was behind him. His whole world was in front of him. What did he think? Whatever he wanted.

Adrian Randall is a PhD and a dual-class bureaucrat/scientist. A native Floridian, he lives in Alexandria with the love of his life and their many beautiful board games. He has a tenuous grasp on reality, owing to a steady diet of novels, comics, and other distractions. When he's not working, he's usually geeking out about some damn thing or another. You can geek out with him on any of the below platforms. If he doesn't respond, it means he broke his phone again.

Twitter: @cyberpreppy
Tumblr: cyberpreppy.tumblr.com
Goodreads: www.goodreads.com/cyberpreppy

More Sci-Fi from DSP Publications

Withered
+ Sere
TJ Klune

Once upon a time, humanity could no longer contain the rage that swelled within, and the world ended in a wave of fire.

One hundred years later, in the wasteland formerly known as America, a broken man who goes only by the name of Cavalo survives. Purposefully cutting himself off from what remains of civilization, Cavalo resides in the crumbling ruins of the North Idaho Correctional Institution. A mutt called Bad Dog and a robot on the verge of insanity comprise his only companions. Cavalo himself is deteriorating, his memories rising like ghosts and haunting the prison cells.

It's not until he makes the dangerous choice of crossing into the irradiated Deadlands that Cavalo comes into contact with a mute psychopath, one who belongs to the murderous group of people known as the Dead Rabbits. Taking the man prisoner, Cavalo is forced not only to face the horrors of his past, but the ramifications of the choices made for his stark present. And it is in the prisoner that he will find a possible future where redemption is but a glimmer that darkly shines.

The world has died.

This is the story of its remains.

www.dsppublications.com